# They Met
## *in a*
## Tavern

# They Met *in a* Tavern

MYCOLOGY ✳ VOLUME 2

## SIR NIL

Podium

Published in 2023 by Podium Publishing, ULC
www.podiumaudio.com

# They Met
## *in a*
## Tavern

# 1.00

<hr>



—A Yoloist's Guide to Adventuring

There were several requirements one needed to fulfill before they could start a mercenary guild.

First and most obvious, mercenaries, adventurers—whatever the hell you wanted to name them. To form a guild, you needed combat-capable people. The very minimum needed was ten people, one of whom needed to be silver plated or above, who'd become the guild master.

Secondly, one needed a guild hall. The definition of such a place is actually pretty broad—all it needs is a location where guild members can meet up and have quests posted. There were a myriad of ways we could procure such a location.

The third requirement would be the completion of a major quest. Most people default to fighting off Wayshard Rifts, but that is mostly because they are pretty regular and most other campaign-level quests require you to be of a famous guild or silver plated, otherwise the quest giver won't even consider you. Essentially it was the "you need job experience to get job experience" conundrum. There were also contingency contracts, emergency quests issued by the Protectorate for problems that needed rapid response.

The requirements are easy to fulfill in principle, but in actuality, there were several things we needed to consider.

For one, Noam and I had already filled twenty percent of the first requirement. We have rather synergistic builds that can be easily leveraged with some degree of teamwork, but unfortunately, both of us shine best when dealing with huge groups of enemies and large amounts of setup. Such strengths would be invaluable when completing the requirement quest if we planned on going the Rift route, but until then, we were only average in other areas. To better round us out, a single-target-damage front and back liner would be best. Along with some kind of battlefield healer. The question, however, was whether we planned on working with non-Travelers.

I needed to ask Noam for his opinion, but it would be a mistake not to. NPCs should greatly outnumber Travelers at this current time, and that represents a great wealth of possibility. I can't ensure everyone we pick up would be as good as someone like Naukoth, but to completely rule out the possibility would be foolish. At the very least we should form connections with talented noncombatants like crafters. If we were to work with NPC combatants, then there were two people that I currently had my eye on.

The second requirement was slightly more difficult. There were two ways I could think of to gain a guild hall. First and simplest, we purchase one, though prices would definitely vary. Anywhere from a thousand to millions of gold coins, all depending on location and place. The second option was available only because this is still a medieval setting—we claim unclaimed land and build a location ourselves. That option is simpler because we wouldn't have to deal with bureaucracy, however, we would still need to deal with construction costs, along with the fact that we would be tasked with defending ourselves. Most unclaimed land would be at the edge of civilization, which forces us to be frontiersmen. It was a risk, but a manageable one.

Regardless, it would be a high-cost investment.

"We could theoretically set up in a random hole in the middle of nowhere," Declan proposed.

That would technically fulfill the requirements, but it would be rather lackluster, wouldn't it?

At minimum, I think we need somewhere in the ballpark of thirty thousand gold to have a respectable base. The good news is that we didn't need to use Traveler gold for that; normal money would suffice just as well, though it was largely more difficult to get. Mostly because we were still unestablished murderhobos. As people we have little to bring to the table other than combat ability. In some ways being a mercenary wasn't a choice—it was the simplest path we could take.

Which brings me to another tangent: Where to bring my build?

"There are multiple paths currently."

First I had to accept I can't be a tank. I'm a tanky mage, but not a *tank mage*. It was proven well enough that though I can take a lot of hits, I can't effectively hold my ground. A tank was about disruption via damage absorption and redirecting, forcing enemies to waste damage on nonkey targets. While I could fill the role of an attack disrupter, it would not be in the form of damage absorption, but in CC and area denial.

At best I am a midliner, though at the current moment I could be said to specialize in area denial and information gathering. However, I was also not fully utilizing my power.

**<u>Available Spell Slots:</u>**
**T0: 2**
**T1: 1**
**T2: 2**

As a mage with so many open spell slots, I was not even utilizing half—no, seventy-five percent of my current potential. There was only one way I knew for certain that would get me spells, and that was questing back in Gaia. However, looking at Noam's feats gave me some ideas.

**<u>Available Feats</u>**
**Player Killer (3 SP): Once per day, you may choose one source of damage you possess to be empowered against Travelers.**

**Coup de Grâce (3 SP): Once per day, you may choose one source of damage you possess to be empowered against downed or noncombatant opponents.**

**Brawler (3 SP): You gain +1 to STR or CON. You gain proficiency and knowledge with unarmed strikes or improvised weaponry. (Note, as you already have proficiency in unarmed strikes, your current proficiency will increase.)**

**Backpfeifengesicht (9 SP): You gain +2 to CHA. All magical taunting effects now have their potency doubled. All magic-based charm effects now automatically fail. Once per day you may choose to emit an aura that forces all creatures with visual sight of you to make a Wisdom save against your Charisma or be taunted into attacking you. This will last a minute, and the affected may continue to make Wisdom saves to break out your taunt effect.**

**Jack of All Trades (6 SP): You gain proficiency and knowledge with all weapons you wield. If you already have proficiency, the level of proficiency does not increase.**

**Weapon Master (9 SP): You gain +2 to any Body stat of your choice or two +1s to any Body stat of your choice. You gain proficiency and knowledge with five weapons of your choice. If you already have proficiency with your chosen weapon, the level of proficiency increases. This increase can be applied multiple times on a single weapon.**

What he decided to pick from this feat list was up to him, however, these feats told me a crucial thing: "Our actual skills matter and have a mechanical effect."

Noam's Brawler feat and my own Strategist feat both mentioned that we already had proficiencies that were not listed on our character sheets. Not only that, but the main draw of a proficiency was not the actual in-game effect.

It was the fact that our real-world selves would gain that same proficiency.

Noam learned beatboxing in a night because of his class skill, and I had little doubt that if I took up my cooking feat, then my real-world self would learn cooking, and if Noam took up Weapon Master, he would actually master a weapon.

Such mental enhancements, while not illegal, were certainly treading a gray area. Mostly because it would render one of the few industries that still needed humans obsolete. While I wouldn't mind never going to school again, many people still maintained that a school education was imperative for social behavior. They were the reasons why a person had to complete at minimum a year-twelve education before they could start receiving a universal basic income.

But that was not the important part here. These skills go both ways; there is a good chance we can have our proficiency increased by both our own improvements and the system's assistance.

So, we broaden this theory. Would it be possible for me to learn magic naturally? And if so, would it take up one of my spell slots?

For the first, the evidence points toward yes. Though the hard rules of magic are rather wibbly-wobbly, people do learn from different schools here, and there are many schools of thought on how magic works. If it is possible for me to learn, say, cooking, by practicing it here, then the system should count it as a new proficiency, given by the patterns from Noam's unarmed combatant and my martial proficiencies.

As to the second, I had a lot less evidence for this theory, but I was leaning in the direction that it would not consume any spell slots. Currently, I have two character sheets, the one I got from the system and the one from Analyze. The system does not seem to count anything not gained from it on its character sheet. Hence why my Analyze and Observe Paths along with our own learned proficiencies don't appear on it.

As such, it should be possible for me to learn magic naturally, if not in the short term, then as a long-term goal.

Which led me back to my spell slots.

If I could learn spells not limited by the amount of spell slots I had, then what I did with my spell slots mattered a lot less; *however*, until I have definitely proven that a Traveler was capable of learning spells, I should still spec as if I was limited by my spell slots.

Which meant I had a few calls to make.

With a lack of a global Traveler chat or at least forum board, I had to directly contact people to procure what I wanted rather than leaving posts and waiting for offers to come to me. Currently, I believe . . . Ah, Valhorn and his group were still inside Gaia, and so was the potato man whose name was apparently Murphy. Peps moved inside Indiri, likely somewhere nearby, though I wouldn't be able to track him.

So for now, I sent messages to the people still in Gaia, a list of spell crystals and categories I was willing to purchase from them should they encounter it.

But until then . . .

In the distance, Noam helped Utoqa to his feet. The lizard's eyes glowed slightly blue in the dark, and he was silent as he pulled out my corpse from behind himself. At the edge of Noam's vision, I could see my knife holstered on one of Utoqa's many belts.

I returned to my view, seeing the well-lit waiting room we were given. On the other side was the elven swordswoman staring at her bronze plate with a mixture of awe and disbelief. Celine had left long ago, and the gnome whose name can fuck off was busy making sure her other friend had survived.

Standing up, I drew a glance from the elf, but there was something I needed to confirm, so I paid her no heed.

I left the room, meeting the two outside as Utoqa stared at Naukoth's corpse.

He noticed me, head jerking toward me in an unnatural manner. As if he was unused to the gesture.

He was . . . surprised? No, something very close to it. Strange—his face showed no expression, yet I could still feel it dimly.

"I guess I was right," I started, gesturing to the empty spot where the knife was. Traveler bodies can remain under certain conditions. Unfortunately, I can't dupe items.

"Perhaps use our new capital to dupe bodies for magical materials," Declan suggested with a chuckle.

That was one option. Though I do have to wonder if the experience loss was worth it.

Utoqa still stared at me, his face . . . unsettling yet familiar. Like an old friend I had forgotten.

We stood there, in a strange silence Noam must've perceived as awkward, because he swiftly tried to speak of another subject. "Well, it's great that you survived."

"Indeed," the lizardfolk answered.

Something was strange about him now as he stared at Naukoth's corpse. No, he didn't change—I was the one who did. Somehow, I could see him slightly better than before. And in him, I saw two bundles of power, two ideas.

Noam put a hand on Utoqa's shoulder. "I'm . . . really sorry about your friend."

"It is a loss"—he turned to me—"I was taught that those who help me should be rewarded. Else they won't help me again."

From one of his pouches, he pulled out a finger. My finger, actually, wrapped carefully in the string mycelium.

I took it and felt a familiarity. A familiar but dim thrum of power, and with it I realized something.

"Hey, Utoqa."

He stared at me, unmoving.

"What is a 'friend' to you?"

"Something that helps you."

"And what is that?" I asked, pointing at Naukoth's corpse.

"A pile of meat," he answered frankly.

A slight chuckle escaped my lips, as Noam reached the same conclusion I did and began to frown.

I stared at the severed finger in my hand with renewed understanding of the nature of Utoqa's first Path.

Scavenge.

To take from a kill and create something with its former power. Always lesser, always scraps, but always *something*.

He looked at Naukoth's body not because of grief, but because he was assessing what he could take out of that corpse.

"God, he's like a worse version of you, innit?" Noam muttered with an eyebrow raised.

A true sociopath. Loyal only because it was beneficial. No goal and never seeking greatness, only survival. A scavenger content to live on the scraps of others, even if it meant desecrating a former friend.

Yes . . . I could see it now. I'd learned the first Path and now I glimpsed the second.

Paths you gained yourself were intrinsically based on you. I understood that better now. I was one who observed and analyzed everything. He was a scavenger who took scraps, but he was also one with endless tenacity. A creature with no qualms about what to do in order to Survive.

"What do you plan to do now?" I asked.

"Get food and rest."

"And after that?"

"I do not know," he answered honestly, not because he was *honest*, but because he saw no benefit in deception. "Naukoth helped me learn many things. Without him it is difficult."

A small smile formed on my lips. "Then, how 'bout you join us?"

If he were me, he would've shrugged, but he did not have that human gesture, so instead he simply said yes.

# 1.01

——

*"If you can't get yer hands dirty, then why the fock are you even in this profession? This is focking life 'n' death righ' 'ere."*

—*Simon the God Noodler*

Now that that was handled came the fun part.

"I have a question." I signaled a random passing member of the Ivory Tower. "What do you do with the corpses of the deceased?"

"Hmm? We give them all proper burials at the local graveyard. Priests hallow the ground and do all the ceremonies and whatnot."

"Can someone like a family member claim a body for their own rites?" I followed up.

"Why, of course!" he replied. "I know many people prefer their own funeral rites, even though Light can do pretty comprehensive rites."

"Great, then may I claim one of the bodies?"

"Sure . . .? I'm not sure which one of them you are related to—"

I pointed at my corpse. "I am a Traveler, and that is my corpse. That should satisfy the requirements, correct?"

The man paused, and I could practically see the neurons misfiring in his brain.

"Just need it for one thing; you guys can do all your rites on it later on," I offered.

Strangely, he seemed more confused. "You—that—what?"

"It's all right." Another voice pinched in, and the helpful camp mage from before lightly slapped the other man on his shoulder. "You can take it, though what do you plan on doing with it?"

"Oh, just some things." I shrugged, gesturing to Utoqa. "By the way, do you have a room I could borrow that you wouldn't mind getting dirty?"

"What do you need it for?"

I shrugged again. "Oh, you know. *Science.*"

All of it was their fault, Writz thought as he stalked his way along the night town's street.

It was all their fault. None of the blame fell on Writz, who was the utmost paragon—a noble, after all. The incompetence of his servants who didn't die for him when he was swarmed by monsters. Frankly, it was also that cursed deviling chimerist's fault. He didn't just roll over and die as was his place when Writz Ger Diation entered his blasted cavern. It was also the Ivory *peasants'* fault for not escorting him back to his manor.

They were the reason his house had to use their insurance. But Writz was wise; he knew this was a momentary setback, and his father would get the peasants to earn all the money back. They knew their place. Though it hurt Writz's heart that his beloved father would have to work so hard to regain their wealth.

Everything was their fault.

Maybe that was the peasants' fault as well. They didn't earn as much money as he desired, and it was all because they wasted time on *rest* and *sleep* instead of doing what was proper for them.

If only there were more people as competent as he. Then it would be easy, but unfortunately, he was cursed with idiocy at every turn. No one could ever even be half as smart as he was. Even the idiot vice guild master who wouldn't let him bring all his guards into the battle, forcing him to settle for the inexperienced child. Writz smiled; he would love to see that fool keep her job later.

He slammed his fist into an alley wall. "Goddamn knaves, the very least they could've done was die for me—"

"Goddamn, you made this easy," a voice said behind him.

Writz began to turn, just as the sound of tearing paper came from behind.

"Who—"

Noam rushed him, his arm outstretched and slamming into Writz's neck before he could even get his second word out. His knees gave out as another force pushed them in, and Writz lost balance, falling to the ground. In a smooth, practiced movement, Noam had a knee on Writz's back, his right arm pinning his shoulder and neck while his left leg pinned Writz's outstretched arm by the wrist.

"Argh! What—" It happened too quickly. One moment he was standing, and the next he was pinned to the ground by an unknown assailant.

"What—" he choked as Noam increased the pressure on his neck slightly, forcing his voice out of him.

"Goddamn, you are stupid," Noam chided, almost disappointed. "You walked into a random dark alleyway at night. I thought I'd have to wait fer hours before I could jump you."

The words snapped Writz back. "You—you're that cursed deviling who spat on me earlier! I swear I can still smell the peasantry—"

He choked again as Noam pressed down on his neck once more. "And you didn't even bother to check your possessions." One of his pockets moved, and though Writz couldn't see what moved out, Greenie fist-bumped Yellow as it crawled onto Noam's shoulder.

"Don't bother calling for help—I used a scroll of silence. No sound will leave or enter this location for a while.

"Oh," he added as almost an afterthought, "but do try anyway. I'm trying to decide between your screams and words I would prefer to hear, but I haven't heard you scream yet, so—"

"AAAAAAAAAAAAAAAAAAAAAAAAAAAAAAAAAAAAAAAAAAAAA AAAAAAAAAAAAAAHHHH! SOMEONE HELP ME! GUARDS! PEASANTS! ANYONE—*gurrafff.*"

"Huh," Noam said as he blocked his mouth. "It seems I liked neither."

It was only a few moments before the noble was unconscious.

"I thought Dustin said murder wasn't worth it?" Yellow curiously asked.

"He's a rather literal ass," Noam answered. "He said a murder *charge* wasn't worth it. If I get away with this with no consequences, then it isn't a 'net negative,'" he said, mimicking his friend's voice, fingers raised in air quotes.

"Plus, I haven't decided if I wanted to kill him yet."

"Are you going to?"

Noam sat on the unconscious man, scratching his chin in a thinking pose. "On one hand, he's an ass, but is he a *big* enough ass to deserve death?"

The wisps mimicked his posture as they sat on his shoulder. Yellow spoke first. "He could call the guards later and you would get a murder charge anyways."

"Not how that works, but still one in favor of killing him then," Noam said, raising one finger on his right.

"He did also seem like a focker."

Noam gasped, "Who taught you that language, Greenie?!"

"You did!" it cheerfully replied.

Noam wiped away a fake tear. "I know, I am such a good role model. Anyways"—he raised another finger on his right—"that's two in favor."

He glanced at his left hand. "Hmm . . . On the other *hand*. . ." Noam glanced around, seeing only a confused Greenie and Yellow giving him a pity clap. "Pfft, you're right, it's weak. But on the other side of the argument, I really wished he put up more of a fight. Killing him while he's unconscious is just assholish." He raised a finger on his left.

He glanced at the two wisps on both his shoulders, who in turn shook their heads. "Hmm . . . that's it, huh? Well, it looks like we're killing him—"

The noble coughed as his eyes flickered open.

Immediately, Noam's left hand was pinning his neck and his other controlled the man's dominant hand, stretching it away from the weapon handle on his hip.

Writz, barely conscious, stared at him, eyes full of hate. "I swear! You deviling! You will rue the day you went against House Diation! Let me go and beg on your knees and I may have mercy on you and make sure your—"

There was a loud crack. Writz screamed in pain as Noam broke his arm.

"Should've stayed down," Noam said. "Would've been easier for you."

Tears streamed down the distraught man's face; snot fell freely and mixed with the tears in a puddle underneath him.

"Man, don't make this harder on me," Noam said. His hand was no longer needed to pin a broken arm, so it went to draw a single dagger.

"Go to your happy place or sumthin'," he muttered before Noam realized that the man's lips were moving.

" . . . "

"What was that?" he asked as drew in closer.

". . . wasn't my fault . . . It wasn't my fault . . . It wasn't my fault . . ."

Noam sighed. "God you feel too pathetic to kill now—"

"It wasn't my fault!" he yelled, desperate. "It wasn't mine! It was theirs! It was all their **Fault**!"

The word thrummed with a nascent power as Writz's broken arm slammed into itself, resetting and no longer broken. Noam's reaction was instant; he stabbed the man's neck from behind, biting through bone and cutting his spinal cord.

His body fell limp, and his mouth moved lifelessly for a few final moments, but no words came as his eyes turned glassy and dead.

Noam tsked as he stared at his bloodied hand. "Goddamn bad habits."

"Is he dead?" Yellow asked in genuine childlike curiosity.

"Probably, but I guess I need to make sure he's dead now. Dec's gonna have a shitfest if I only paralyzed him from the neck down," he muttered, annoyed, as he turned over the corpse. He stabbed the noble a few more times before rising and kicking him a few times more.

Several kicks later, he said, "Yup, feels sufficiently dead. Now the problem is to get rid of the body . . ."

"Perhaps I can help."

Noam jumped, both his swords drawn in an instant. *I took too long*, he thought. *Silence ran out.*

He stared deeper into the alleyway, and his eyes caught on a glowing red light. A dagger stabbed into the ground, a bloody red eye with a cross-like pupil staring back at him.

"Greetings," the dagger said, voice deep and thrumming with power. "I am Celigarn, the Blood Drinker. I am one of the four lost treasures of an ancient and great hero. I have seen your act of senseless violence and have deemed it enough to offer myself to you. Take me on, and through violence and bloodshed"—the pupil narrowed, almost disappearing as it glowed with magic—"I shall grant you immeasurable power."

"Nah."

"Huh?"

"I said, nah," Noam said. "I mean, seriously? Cursed weapon that runs off blood? I'm trying to be an insult-based bard here. All I want to do is yell yo' mama jokes until people want to fight me. Cursed weapon of a blood god would definitely clash with my aesthetic of a happy-go-lucky Saiyan idiot."

"It's not an ancient blood god but an ancient hero—" The dagger rapidly tried to correct, but Noam was ignoring it. Swiftly looting the body, taking his coin pouch and the wand holstered on his belt before hoisting the dead body by the legs.

"Now, what do I do with you . . ." Noam muttered.

"No, please, hear me out!" Noam continued to ignore him, simply tsking as he saw the blood trail left by the body.

"I'll yell for the guards if you don't listen!"

Noam snapped to the dagger, "Huh, you're right."

He dropped the body, and it flopped lifelessly onto the ground.

"Ha! See, I knew you would see reason."

He casually pulled the dagger out of the ground.

"Wonderful, now—"

"I can't believe I forgot to get rid of all the witnesses," Noam said casually.

Celigarn paused and rapidly focused all its attention on Noam's face. His face was casual, unserious and almost bored as he handled it. As if he was simply taking out the laundry.

The smallest smirk appeared on the tiefling's face.

The blade suddenly wished it had legs.

"Um . . . I can make it worth your while! How 'bout I—"

Noam spun the dagger in his hand.

"Aaahh! Please, stop! I have motion sickness—"

He stopped, gripping it by the hilt. Celigarn's eye was no longer a cross; instead, it was now a spinning wheel, and red fluid dripped out of the eye.

"Did you vomit? God, you have to be the worst dagger ever."

The eye focused back into a cross before indignantly declaring, "I am not! Some third-rate . . ." Its voice slowly petered out. "I am . . ." The blade wept. "I am some third-rate weapon now . . ."

"Um . . . Is this some kind of psychological trick? Because I am still going to get rid of you."

"No," the blade said, voice husky as if crying. "I am a third-rate weapon now. I used to be one of the greatest weapons in the land, forged of the best steel, enchanted with blood-taker magic. In the hands of my master, I slew countless. Oh, the lives we slew together! But nay, even her life ended one day, and I was sealed with her, among all her weapons. For years I saw disuse, waiting to be uncovered by—"

"Can you hurry up your backstory, 'cause I sorta have a pressing matter at hand," Noam interrupted, gesturing at the body behind him.

"I'm getting to it!" the blade retorted. "*Ahem*, anyways, where was I? Oh, yes. At the start, I dutifully stood by my master's body, waiting untold years. But as time passed, I wished for someone to firmly grasp my hilt once again, to wet my edge with the blood of hundreds . . ."

Noam switched the dagger's hold into his mouth. Freeing his hands, as he dragged the body deeper into the endlessly winding alleyways.

". . . and so when my master's tomb was uncovered, I rejoiced! For purpose found me once again! Once more I shall feel blood on my steel. Once more I shall be used for a greater purpose . . ."

Noam glanced around, ensuring the place was clear as he dragged the body away. Neither of the wisps was being useful, far too enamored with the story.

". . . but alas! When I was brought back to the surface, I realized a crucial thing. Much time had passed, enough time that I witnessed the most shocking thing! My savior wielded a weapon far more powerful than I, and I learned that weapons of my caliber were stocked in the multitudes at even the most common blacksmith! My savior cast me out as if I was mere trash, and at that point, I really was. The passage of time and technology has rendered my once great and mighty form irrelevant!"

"So you were fucked over by power creep. Join the club, man." Noam finally spoke after finding a sufficiently dark and empty spot in the labyrinthian alleys. "Now I still need to figure out what to do to keep you silent . . ."

Celigarn's eye withered under his gaze. "Um . . . I could offer assistance! I see you have a body on your hand! Might I offer a way to get rid of it in exchange for . . . my continued existence?" it asked hesitantly.

"And your silence," Noam added.

"That, too!"

"Great, then tell me how to deal with this." He gestured at the body.

"Well, it's quite simple. Just give it to one of the mimics."

"Wait—" Noam's eyes widened and darted rapidly around him. "There are mimics here?!"

"Oh, right now? No," it answered. "Find a crate labeled 'Abaddon Prime Express.' Those mimics love hiding as the First Circle's cardboard delivery boxes. It gets people every time."

"Huh, neat," he answered, completely deadpan in a way that would've made Decs proud. Noam searched a few more corners, quickly finding one such box. The words were stamped onto its side in an eye-catching logo.

With a heave, he threw the body onto the box.

It was still for a moment before it erupted in a violence of flailing flesh and tentacles, consuming the corpse in a single gulp before it resumed its innocuous form.

Noam stared at it for a moment. Nothing was left, save for the blood trail leading to it. Then he turned his gaze to the dagger. "Huh, I guess you aren't half-bad."

"See! I'm useful! I have what those other fucking store-brought daggers *don't* have! I'm fucking intelligent! I'm the smartest dagger there fucking is! Yeah, take that, you fucking fancy-schmancy kitchen knives!"

"I can't tell if you have an inferiority complex or are just crazy." He smiled slightly. "Either way, you aren't half-bad," Noam said as he sheathed the dagger on his belt.

Celigarn gasped, or at least made the sound. "Does that mean . . ."

"Yeah, sure." Noam shrugged. "I'll put up with you. But no blood and death and violence crap. I'm not an edgy fourteen-year-old anymore."

"You won't regret this, boss!"

"Woo! Another friend!"

"I had no idea what you said, but you sound congratulatory, so thank you!" Celigarn replied cheerfully.

Noam chuckled slightly. "Anyways, let's head back."

"Oh! That is actually pretty convenient—follow the blood trail, otherwise you might not find your way back."

Noam raised an eyebrow. "Why not?"

"See, all the alleyways in the world are connected in their separate sub-space, creating a huge, constantly shifting labyrinth composed of every dark alleyway in existence. All the lost things end up here. I was thrown into an alley somewhere in a city called Stormfall before I ended up here . . ."

"Uh-huh." Noam listened as he followed the trail back. The guy seemed like a talker, and he was content to let it ramble.

". . . I've heard some rogues are capable of mapping this labyrinth and navigating it in a way that lets them pop up in any city! Of course, using Wayshards is far quicker and safer. If you go too deep, you start finding alley-ways of long-dead and destroyed cities; those tend to not be so safe . . ."

Noam swiftly found his way back. The nightlife of the port city shined inward. He climbed up one of the roofs and saw people were gathering in a crowd out there. An old woman was on the ground cradling a broken arm, one that had mysteriously cracked and broken seemingly without cause. Another man nearby rubbed his head; a terrible headache had befallen him shortly before the old lady fell down.

It was enough of a distraction that Noam slipped into the night without contest.

# 1.02

*"Follow Osshiven'Kai! We offer revelations and cookies!"*
*—The last words of Steve the Arch-Heretic of the South, spoken*
*moments after his head was removed via guillotine and after being*
*completely incinerated by dragon breath, before finally a smiting from*
*Light herself did the trick*

All night I spent trying to read the code of the "god."

That code was dynamic. Constantly shifting and appearing to use a completely new coding language I could barely understand, but it, fascinatingly, seemed to be universal. Copy-pasting portions of the code into different language programs always led to *something*. There were never any errors or logic glitches. Something was working; I couldn't tell what, but I had to know.

I rubbed my head—only a few hours without sleep and I was already suffering debilitating effects. Perhaps I should get ba's Mel-B augment; it lets him stay awake for weeks on end. Whether it was *healthy* was a different matter, but until I actually reached eighteen, it was all plans. I couldn't actually start legally tinkering with my body until then due to several honestly stupid laws made for the five percent of idiots who went for dick enlargement augments because that's what idiot fourteen-year-olds did. You'd think they'd engineer those parts out by now, but apparently it was part of the "essential" human experience.

Turning my bleary eyes back to the screen, I finished my notes. This thing was too much, something one night and a high school–level education simply couldn't begin to unpack. My head hurt, and my room . . . it felt claustrophobic in a way. Not enough that I wished to leave, but enough that it irked me.

I closed my eyes again, breathing deep. My head hurt, and I didn't know if that was affecting my thinking. I should put off the code for now. But there was manic energy in my body—excitement, perhaps, or more likely, I thought as I looked at the empty bags of chips and other snacks strewn about my room, I'd eaten too much and was feeling a sugar high. What was Dustin me doing? A screen quickly opened at the thought, showing him signing some papers at the administrative guild. He didn't need me now. No . . . I had to do something.

My head pounded, but I was not tired, not in the slightest. I moved to the wall of my room, toward a window. Slowly I cranked it open. Perhaps I should go outside, get a breath of fresh air—

The heavy summer air hit me almost like a physical force. Whatever breath I took in was choked from me by the pure heat and dryness. I fell back, the window automatically closing as I made the thought. *Why* did I expect that breath to be refreshing? And had I actually thought of *going outside*? *Why* did I think that? The atmosphere's been fucked for years. What—

For a brief moment, I saw not the apartment window; instead, it was a strange porthole. One of a ship, it opened up to a wider blue. An infinite sea of which there would be no end of things to discover.

"Motherfucker," I gasped, "it can't be."

I grabbed my AAD, wrenching it off my neck as dozens of digital tabs flickered out of existence. Yet I could still feel it.

My eyes were glued to that window, and in my veins, I felt that same manic energy. To go out, to learn, to understand, to keep going, because what meaning was there in a life without the new and fresh?

I slapped my face. The sting brought me back slightly, but I still felt the call.

The *thing* inside that computer held a universal code, and I was not stupid enough to believe a brain was anything but a meat machine.

"Fuck," I muttered as I stood back up. "Fuck, fuck."

I gingerly picked up my AAD as I paced around that computer.

"I should've known this was possible," I muttered breathlessly. Observe was planted into my head via translating the code into something my brain could interpret. *How long was I looking at that thing? Seven hours? Maybe more! Is this mental programming reversible? Are my thoughts even mine right now?*

I forced myself to stop.

My body was restless, the adrenaline in my veins. So I took several deep breaths until my body calmed.

My head ached, pain from some source, either tiredness or programmed. So I stopped thinking and let the ache gradually subside.

I stood, the effects alleviated but not gone, dimmed at the edge of my mind. I was calm, and that was all that mattered. I opened my eyes and stared at the computer.

My next course of action determined many things.

A memetic hazard has always theoretically been possible; in fact, sub-liminal messaging had been used to sell products since the twenty-first century, but something capable of *this* level of subtlety and detailed pro-gramming was . . . Well, it was definitely possible in this era. I had no doubt various militaries had already developed some versions of it but were just keeping a lid on it. Anything of this level would certainly be a state secret.

And one of them was in my room.

"What a fucked-up thing you saddled me with," I muttered, my hand on my head. I had no idea what the laws regarding this were, but I can certainly say that if Eve was harboring this sort of shit, then not only did I vastly underestimate her capabilities but also the number of international and moral laws she was breaking. Perhaps the most insane thing I had not yet considered was that this "god" was once a normal person. A simulated AI person, but close enough that Dustin me could've normally interacted with her.

My vision flashed back to theirs for a moment; they were in a crowd at the gates of the city. Noam just hollered at some farmer to give them a ride toward a cave by the edge of the ocean. Some kind of cultist quest? I was really missing a lot.

My body felt weak, as if the energy from before was all false, which it probably was. With a lethargic sigh, I slowly slid down the side of the com-puter tower till I was sitting against it.

*What do I do now? Should I even trust my judgment on the matter? Or even Dustin's, for that matter?* He was a clone of me as far as I knew, but he'd spent far longer in Indiri. If our research was correct, then such info haz-ards existed there. Maybe not commonplace, but with enough frequency that things like Absence and ******* demons were recorded, not to mention aberrations, which were just even more fucked versions. That demon lord, the Secret You Must Speak, also just shot up in danger level. If even its name is enough to infect you, then could it breach into the real world? If the Historian could manage it with Discovery, then yes. It was a high pos-sibility that things in that world could come to ours. As data or programs, they could find their place here, and if Discovery was any indicator, they could infect people in the real world.

But should I take this up with an authority? The police? Doing so would place me in direct opposition with Eve if she was still trying to remain undercover. But she couldn't possibly keep this whole thing a secret for long! I'd seen dozens of people in Gaia, and unless they were also AI, then this "secret" should be spreading like wildfire. Even if they were, just the fact that every person could invite another would lead to constant player growth. But was I supposed to just remain *silent* about this?

"This is truly a great bind."

"I sense you are distressed . . ."

To my credit, I only stiffened slightly when I heard that voice.

I glanced at my hand; it still held my AAD, unless that part was simulated as well.

"Yeah," I answered, already guessing at the source. There was no one else here, after all. "You're the guy inside the computer right? Discovery."

"Yes . . ." it answered. "A computer . . . is that what this realm is called? Such a . . . strange name."

"The root of the word has to do with computing. To calculate."

"Is it . . . Ah. Latin . . . English . . . It is different from the trader's tongue . . . What a wondrous language you speak . . ."

"Trader tongue?"

"The common language . . . Chanter is its name . . ."

"You're speaking pretty slowly."

"Sorry . . . I am tired . . . I am no longer all me . . ."

"I never got that part," I said, hoping to drag the conversation a bit longer. "Why you were in this mess. I never got why deification was such an unavoidable thing."

"Because . . . of Balance . . . The world seeks to balance . . . There is no deed unpraised . . . no feat untold . . . no wonder unspoken . . ."

He paused as if mustering clarity.

"Commit great deeds and you will be rewarded. Power, wealth—anything, really . . . But you will always be rewarded . . . and the greatest reward is to be made concept . . . To be made charge of an underlying principle . . . It is power but is burden . . ."

My hand tightened. The Historian warned us of a similar thing, but in the opposite direction: take power without deed or worthiness, and it will be *wrested* from you. And the opposite—do great deeds and be worthy, and power will find its way to you on its own. Regardless of your own feelings, it seemed.

"Are you clear now?" I asked. "Did whatever the Historian do work?" And Eve, too, but I suppose his boyfriend would've preferred taking all the credit.

"Yes . . ." It spoke as if almost surprised. "He did . . . but what of him?"

"He seemed aight," I answered. "Was still sane enough that he cared 'bout you."

"Aww . . ." It paused again, "I sense . . . I do not have long . . ."

"Gotta sleep again?"

"Yes . . . but . . . I hurt you somehow . . . My nature latched on to you . . . subtly, but it did . . ."

"Yeah," I answered, "got freaked out by it for a moment." I still was, but I had no reason to believe it was anything malicious. In fact, Dustin's interaction with it in Indiri showed it was very much a passive effect.

"I am sorry . . ."

"It's fine."

"No . . ." it answered. "I, too, will recompense . . . little as I can . . ."

It spoke again, this time not slowly, but deliberately, with a great power.

"You do not yet know, child. I fanned the flames, but there is always a spark of discovery in each. So, Understand."

Knowledge entered my mind, but I did not need it, for the very *act* of speaking that word was enough for me to realize. As the voice slowly faded, the god of Discovery falling to slumber, I stood up and rushed out of my room.

In the background of my mind, Dustin and Noam were traveling to their first quest. I saw through their eyes clearly.

My AAD was still clenched in my hand.

Before long, I stood before Marvin, our home-keeping AI. The main servers were built into the house, but it had a single camera in the kitchen.

I touched it and said, **"Observe."**

A new field of view entered my mind, staring back at me. And from it, I saw the corners of my mouth slowly turn as I broke into maniacal laughter. At no point had I put my AAD back on.

There were two options here that I could see.

Either I was living in a completely simulated world at this very moment.

*Or*, I thought as I sat back down in my room, opening back up the code of the god, *somehow, this is all real. And* somehow *it all works in the real world.*

As I slowly devolved into insane laughter, as Dustin moved his attention to mine, I was still trying to decide.

Which of these utterly insane options did I like more?

"And that's 'bout the gist of it," I said as Dustin removed a blue sac from his corpse.

"Interesting," he answered. "And I thought you were just being insane."

"Nah, you know better than that," I replied as I opened up several new tabs. "Strange thing 'bout fungus is that they shouldn't evolve bilateral symmetry at all."

"Yeah, I figured," he answered, his fingers fumbling around.

"You really aren't cut out for dissection, are you?"

"Low Dex," he muttered in an exasperated tone. "Hey, Utoqa! Help me with this."

A low Dex wasn't all that bad, it just meant Dustin had to be a lot more deliberate with his movements.

"This body shouldn't work."

"From a purely evolutionary standpoint. This biology doesn't make sense," I replied evenly.

Yet it was what was used by the system. By the world, and as we discussed the body, the reasons became clear to him.

And then, an option appeared.

I smiled slightly. This had been an eventful three days, and no deed went unrewarded.

# 1.03

——

*"You expected my strategies to make sense? My dear Chancellor,*
*that was your first mistake."*
*—Madelyn, then moniker the Conqueror, to Chancellor Chekov after*
*successfully subjugating the Western Empire*

The flesh squelched as Dustin's fingers dug into it.

"Utoqa, pin that flap of skin for me," Dustin said, pointing at a flapping piece of flesh.

He nodded, peeling it away and pinning the skin onto the ground.

"Make an incision here," he suggested. "Open up the head more."

It was a simple thing. Utoqa had dressed many hunts before, but the mushroom wanted to reveal its internal organs. Strange, but intelligent in a way. Utoqa only vaguely knew where his organs were. Perhaps he should open up another Tequalan to check.

Though things felt different now. The room was light even where it was dark; his sight felt stronger, wider somehow, as if there were also eyes on the side of his head as well as in front. And very lightly, he could sense the movement of something. Something that stirred within Dustin's cap, like the stirrings made by fish inside a still spring. A fish that ever swam, chasing the top of the waterfall, before it fell and died on the rocks.

He felt something like that within him, too, but it was weaker. He couldn't distinguish it from the other stirrings he felt. It lacked distinguishing patterns. Where Dustin's felt like the territorial markings of a beast, his own were small. Almost unseen. A benefit, perhaps; the small beasts were easy to hunt, but the greatest beasts ignored them.

As Utoqa helped the mushroom pull apart his own corpse, an old question appeared in his mind. One Naukoth had brushed off as weakness in other races.

"Dustin," he said, getting the creature's attention.

It answered absent-mindedly. "Yeah?"

"Tell me why the soft-skins dislike me eating their kind."

Not that he ever did it, of course. The powerful soft-skin that gave him the bones that made his bone tomahawk, Gift, displayed visible distress when he brought it up, and Naukoth had warned him off it.

The dozens of interlocking pieces of brown tree bark and fungus shifted, doing something akin to an eyebrow raise. It answered as it removed some thick blood vessels and examined them. "I suppose I could go into prion-based illnesses or perhaps how cooperative culture evolution works. But would you get that?"

It turned to him, something Utoqa knew it didn't need to do to see him.

"I think the simplest explanation is that if you express a desire to consume their body, then they see you as a potential threat to their life, or at the very least, not an effective ally, because you would not mind if they died. So they would not see you as a 'friend' but as a potential enemy. Say, for a hypothetical situation, if a human said they would eat you if you died or would make weapons from your bones, then would you trust them with your back if they did? Especially when they explicitly told you that they would be benefiting from your death?"

Dustin spoke with more sense and clarity than others had given Utoqa. The lizardfolk did not think such things were a problem—it was the way of nature, after all. But in the scenario the mushroom posed, Utoqa would not trust such a soft-skin with his back. He needed his spine to function, after all; they might not give it back if they could make weapons of it. He wouldn't need it if he perished, but if a creature sought to specifically acquire lizardfolk backs, then they might seek Utoqa's demise. He would not call such a being a friend while he lived.

Was this how the soft-skins thought of him asking to eat their corpses? It was wrong—he wouldn't seek their deaths; he only desired not to waste their bodies. Was this how the soft-skins thought? Not understanding natural order, worrying about the most inconsequential things?

What a sad life they led.

"I understand," he answered.

"Good, now help me with this leg . . ."

This body shouldn't work.

I pulled out an unknown organ, likely some rudimentary processing organ, but it felt too small, too simple compared to a human brain.

My dissection yielded some . . . interesting things.

First off, the simple parts, my structural integrity. My body utilized something similar to an exoskeleton, with the exception that it was covered by a thin layer of "skin." As expected of an exoskeletal structure, my musculature utilized a hydraulics-based system, similar to arachnids'. Muscle ligaments served to close joints while hydraulic pressure pushed them apart in a way similar to inflating a balloon. It explained my rapidly coagulating blood, along with the valves at the edge of major areas, which I believed were purposed to shut off in the case of a major injury. A hydraulic pressure–based system would be extremely vulnerable to bleeding, in a similar way that cracking open a compressed oxygen canister would.

The nervous system I possessed seemed normal relative to a mammalian. A centralized processing organ located right behind my eyes with nerves running all across my body. The only notable difference was that I did not seem to possess a spine or spinal equivalent, and my nerves seemed significantly thicker than what I would have expected.

My digestive tract appeared extremely rudimentary, similar to mammalian, with the exception that it ended at the stomach area, with no secondary opening leading to an anus. This suggested two possibilities—either that my digestive system was efficient enough that it didn't produce waste, or that any waste I produced should be vomited back up by the mouth.

It was past that point that things got strange.

For certain aspects, I was a lot harder to kill than I gave credit for. As far as I could tell, this body utilized a distributed cardiovascular system, meaning instead of a centralized "heart" organ pumping blood throughout my veins, I had dozens if not hundreds of separated, simple tightening tubes spread throughout my body fulfilling the same role. Unlike a heart, damage to one of them should not fail the whole system.

Strangely, I still couldn't find any eye or sensory organ equivalent.

And no matter how hard I looked, I couldn't recognize anything that resembled capillaries. Tracing the various veins and tubules, I deduced that the air I breathed through my mouth split into three directions. One went into my cap, toward various tubules before ending in the fluorescent-blue sacs. These were filled with fluids and were spread throughout my entire cap, not just the surface. Assuming the air I breathed was oxygenized into my blood here, then that posed some dangerous liabilities. If the most identifiable and exposed part of myself was my respiratory system, then that posed an extremely obvious weakness. The only saving grace was that I identified more of these blue sacs inside my chest cavity, right where my lungs should be, along with directly behind my face, giving it that ethereal blue glow. Meaning I had several contingency respiratory systems.

It was one of the "lungs" in my chest cavity that gave me pause.

"From a purely evolutionary standpoint. This biology makes no sense."

Indeed. For one, this body used bilateral symmetry, a feature that shouldn't occur in fungi. The humanoid form itself was suspect. A mushroom was more likely to evolve to something closer in line to starfish—utilizing radial, spherical or no symmetry at all. There were aspects of the biology that suggested it was going this way, a distributed cardiovascular system along with multiple respiratory tracts. However, certain aspects of its biology appeared too conveniently parallel to simian, or even mammalian in general. My respiratory tract had aspects of this with the capillary equivalents located in my chest, and my nervous system as far as I could tell was completely centralized.

I wasn't sure what I was expecting when I began dissection; half of me had expected this wouldn't make sense at all or I would find nothing, but the other half . . .

"Believed it might make sense in retrospect, when considering the world you're in."

Whether or not this body would function in the real world was a moot point; something had clearly put a lot of thought into this body plan. Something that either didn't understand evolutionary biology or didn't care about it.

"To be fair, we don't, either. You're just going off what my few hours of googling have to offer."

Regardless, a mushroom evolving bilateral symmetry was highly unlikely yes?

"Given what we've learned, yes."

So we had to see it from an alternative perspective. Not from an evolutionary biology perspective, but from the perspective of the system that made it. Whatever Giles programmed, we should have a basic understanding of.

Declan snorted in laughter, "I don't claim to understand anything anymore."

"You have the memories of what the Historian showed us," I calmly returned. So we both should know the basic modus operandi for the beginning of it.

The system took data in and spewed out something that would make it work. I had no doubt that the basic idea for a myconid race existed in fantasy for a long time.

"As early as the twentieth century, actually," Declan noted.

Regardless of how erroneous the biological assumptions were, someone had fed that idea to the system, and it had created a biology in retrospect of a mushroom-humanoid body plan, rather than it being the natural result of ecological pressure.

I would need to experiment with other races to make sure, but it should be the same with dragons and all the other fantasy races someone would find improbable.

And that was without accounting for the fact that past a point that sapient species started actively, literally altering themselves with belief and imagination . . . I needed to procure a human corpse for examination and compare it with my own world's. Theoretically there should be dozens of minor—if not major—changes to the base human model!

Even if they are far from the purview of normal physics and logic, the fact that it was created from probably millennia of intelligent tinkering posed potentially even greater advancements than genetic and biotechnical engineering from my own—

**You have fulfilled the unlock conditions for Magic Myconids.**

**You may invest your level as a class level in either Fungalmancer or Warlock (Gift of Discovery) or as a racial class level in Magic Myconid.**

**Note: Investing in Warlock (Gift of Discovery) will remove the [Et Non-Discent] skill.**

**Note: Investing in Magic Myconid will unlock the [Age-Type Heteromorph] skill along with more accurate and powerful racial features.**

**Warning:**

**Investing a level in Magic Myconid will result in the shutdown of all Humanoid Integration Programs. (This includes Pain Modifiers, as there are currently no suitable programs for True Fungal archetypes.)**

**Iteration shock will become more apparent as you will no longer operate under modified Homo sapiens controls when in this body.**

**Note: You have been mentally evaluated as compatible with this process. Permanent mental damage is highly unlikely; thus you were presented with this option at all.**

I paused, an eyebrow raised.

*System question*, I thought. *What does [Age-Type Heteromorph] do?*

And it answered.

**Age-Type Heteromorph [Passive]: This race has natural power, and its growth only represents this.**

**For every two hundred years you spend in this body, you will gain a Magic Myconid level until you reach the maximum of 5, after which you may undertake Racial Evolution.**

**You may not invest levels in this class past the first.**

**Every level gained in Magic Myconid represents a** significant **increase in power.**

**You will not gain progress in this skill until you have obtained it.**

"System question," Declan began and I finished, "What does it mean to be mentally evaluated as compatible?"

**Below one percent chance to suffer long-term debilitating effects.**

**Warning: This prediction uses predictive models that may not fully represent real world possibilities. A three percent degree of error should be assumed.**

I paused and thought.

Declan was silent, but he was me, and he came to the same conclusion.

The only risk was a less than four percent chance of potential discomfort. The only downside was the extreme late-game scaling.

"Pfft, *extreme* feels like an understatement. Unless time dilation occurs, then I'd be an old-ass man by the time you even got to the second level."

This seemed practically designed to entice me, which it very likely could've been. Long-term benefits, not a lot of visible downsides, and even some initial benefits I could get as well. This was very much a put-down-and-forget type of level.

Though this was very similar to the dragon racials, this was a significantly different thing than me switching to another race. For one, I would not lose all the progress I'd made on this body, which, if my impact points were anything to believe, was rather significant. Secondly, myconids could actually take normal classes, as opposed to dragons, who'd just have to beast through everything with their racial abilities. Not a bad option, but one severely lacking in utility. There could only be so much subtlety a fire-breathing flying lizard can do.

Perhaps the better question was, was I going to be here for a full two centuries? Was this world going to have a significant enough impact on my life that I should choose to take this?

"Even if it isn't," I said, looking up at the blank white ceiling, "if the description is correct, then just the first level would be beneficial."

Was that the first time I saw the system highlight something in italics? For plain descriptive text, then it was probably a yes.

A system where level-up requirements exponentially scaled would eventually reach a point where it would be impossible to progress. Even if this was a whole new world, there was only so much you could ever experience.

A system like this greatly favored front-loaded power gotten early on and alternative scalings that did not rely on experience gain. This racial offered to give *both*.

Right now, it was not a consideration of the benefits and negatives, but of things we were lacking.

Currently, the biggest potential danger in this system was the lack of information. Just not knowing how the EXP system worked could lead to hours of wasted time trying to grind mobs. Even things like feats, taking up the wrong one could leave a build completely midtier. For one, proficiency feats were nigh worthless, since most were basic skills you could just train and practice with and get naturally—all you were getting from purchasing such a feat was the time you might've spent learning that proficiency naturally. They were shortcut options for people not willing to put the time in. "Lazy asses like me."

Feats like Jack of All Trades seemed good with their extreme cost efficiency, but that was assuming a proficiency was actually *worth* two SP.

The only situation where I could see a feat like JoAT being useful was when you were handling a completely alien weapon, and that sort of situation assumes you've lost your original, more proficient weapons. It was preparing for the worst outcome. Not knowing things like this meant a person could waste valuable SP for suboptimal decisions.

That was why I did not expect my build to be a strong one; right now I was one of the first players, and it gave me the opportunity to be the first to take a lot of things, but it came at the cost—I lacked information.

Even if I was the first to complete a great quest, be the first to obtain the strongest items and the first to reach the highest level that could reasonably be achieved, *eventually* someone with the benefit of hindsight, with information, would come along. They would know what the best feats were, what levels to take, what Paths they should walk, and they would craft a min/maxed build that could kick mine into the ground. It wasn't a question of if, but when.

I knew that taking Magic Myconid right now was the best choice out of my current options, but was it the best choice out of all *possible* options? *Am I currently making a suboptimal choice, similar to taking up a proficiency feat?*

That was why the most valuable thing I could obtain in the future was a full re-spec of my build. To be able to redo it all, just *slightly* more efficiently than the first time.

I had to consider this seriously—from my declaration to Matt and myself, I was no longer just playing. *Was the chance of more efficient classes enough to still my hand? Am I making a beginner mistake here? If only because I lacked some critical piece of info?*

"Yer problem is dat ya don't take initiative." Noam's voice echoed through my mind.

I opened my "eyes" again. Strange, I keep using that term, when I'd just empirically found out that I did not seem to have any sensory organs at all. At least, anything that would resemble my definition of a sensory organ.

"I'm fine with whatever decision you make. You're the one behind the wheel, and since we think the same, any advice I give, you would've already thought of," Declan said.

Regardless of my feelings, I was one of the first. Like the first people that landed in the new world, the first man on the moon, the first colonizers of Mars, the first to leave the edges of our solar system. I did not have the benefit of hindsight here. I was one of the people stumbling into the dark, not knowing where it would lead me. I was the one making the path; I was the one who decided I should take the lead.

"Fuck it," I muttered. "Utoqa, can you protect me for a few moments? This might get strange."

Let's hope a full re-spec existed somewhere.

And I put my level in it.

# 1.04



*"Fools, I made something none of you could've ever conceived of achieving. I made a choice; I cheated the systems you built. Kill me if you will. For no matter how suited you imbeciles are to janitorial work, I have left a stain you can't clean off."*
—*Last words of Magus Smar Da Ten Yu, only a few days after she created costless resurrection magic*

**M**y vision *splanched.*

I staggered slightly; my hand fell onto the table, trying to grab it for leverage, but it was *slower.* My fingers couldn't close fast enough to actually grab onto the edge, instead sliding onto my staff for support.

I fell onto the ground; my vision, it was screwed. I saw the floor beneath me, the ceiling on top of me; I *felt* places even if they were obscured. The tiny cracks in the ground, the dirt behind the table leg; I saw outside the walls as human activity died with the night. Everything nearby I felt, an alien sense going outward before the energy that made it seemed to dissipate, and all was darkness.

But I opened my eye and I saw. Embedded in my left eye socket, a gem like pure lapis lazuli, sculpted to a perfect sphere and with intricately carved lines like the endlessly caressing waves. Glowing within was a constellation of stars forever aimed north. I closed my other vision, the one that allowed me to perceive all nearby, and I calmed. The eye of Analyze.

Standing back up, I realized my body was not slow because I was slower, but because I was thinking the wrong thoughts to move. Inefficient ones, still human. When I shed those like an ill-fitting sock, embracing this body's instincts, I moved with the same speed as expected. Slowly, I opened the other vision again, seeing everything nearby but not farther.

Utoqa was watching me silently. "All good," I said, reassuring not him but my own still-wobbly legs.

There were some changes. My racials, Darkvision, Fungal Body, and Innate Magic were all changed. I lost the first to the new vision.

**Manavision [Passive]: Your race's innate mastery of mana allows you to perceive everything within a radius equal to your myconid level times five meters. You see in dim light as if it were bright light, and in darkness as if it were dim light. You can't discern colors in darkness, only shades of gray. A dispel or null magic effect will negate this sight. If you have no mana, this sight is automatically deactivated.**

Undeniably a negative. If I didn't have spare eyes, I would've been locked as a short-range mage. But an upgrade in terms of my current build.

**Fungal Body [Passive]: You have resistance to poison and bludgeoning damage. You are vulnerable to desiccation damage.**

Resistance to a more common form of damage in return for vulnerability to a rare one? You took this nine times out of ten.

**Strong Innate Magic [Passive]: You gain two Tier-0 Spells from the Magic Cap Myconid Spell List, as well as,**

**Choose and gain 1 of the following options per Myconid level:**

**You create one Tier-0 Spell and gain it on your spell list.**

**You gain proficiency and knowledge in Arcana.**

**You gain a passive Detect Magic within the range of your manavision.**

Along with the addition of [Age-Type Heteromorph], these were all the changes done to my racial skills. My passive stat growth still remained the same . . . This was almost entirely beneficial; the multiple downsides of manavision were overcome, leaving nothing but benefits. Desiccation damage I could avoid. Yes, I just needed to avoid deserts, dry places, and that damned sun. I just needed to stay hydrated; getting bludgeoning resistance was always worth it in these scenarios . . .

"Does heat do desiccation damage? I.e. fire?"

I hissed slightly before I caught myself. My instincts had been altered.

"What were you reacting to? Heat or fire?"

"Heat," I answered. "Fire likely has no more effect than on a normal person. Perhaps less so if I am filled with fluids."

Which left heat. I needed temperature-controlling magics, or perhaps a way to quickly rehydrate myself. Fire damage remained an issue, but it was not *fire* that I would be vulnerable to. I was gaining weaknesses, but they remained manageable enough that I could make countermeasures.

"So you really are changed huh?"

I paused at that statement. "What do you mean?"

"Don't forget that your current body has been altered to be accurate to the myconid form. Theoretically your brain isn't human anymore."

"That is true in theory, but in practice I seem to have all my faculties 'cept for a few weird new habits," I returned.

"You immediately jumped onto thinking of what countermeasures you could take against desiccation damage."

I raised an eyebrow. "What do you mean? I always do that."

There was a dry laugh. "And both of us thought my desire to unravel what Discovery is was due to me being a curious idiot."

My hand stiffened, tightening on my staff. "You don't mean . . ."

"I mean at first it is completely unnoticeable," he said. "It seems like you until you spend too long and suddenly have a completely contrary thought."

"We are constantly changing as well, even without this"—I gestured around—"our fourteen-year-old self would not at all recognize either of us."

"True, but to be fair, he was an asshole by all accounts."

*That we can agree with*, I thought with a chuckle.

"Keep it in mind, though. After all, if you don't understand how the system works . . ."

"Then you don't know how to cheat it," I answered as I stood.

And with the options given to me, it was finally time to start cheating.

I met back up with Noam later that night.

Utoqa pushed open the doors of the tavern, and we quickly found the table where he sat. He sighted us first, waving at us with his free hand before he looked at the group seated around him with a smirk.

"Read 'em and weep." He splayed his cards onto the table. Four of a kind, knights of wands, cups, swords, and coins.

The heavyset man who sat before him smirked as well. "A good hand, but you need better." He threw down his own hand, a straight flush, three to eight of cups. Unfortunately for both of them, I already knew the winner.

"Is this good?" Greenie asked as it raised an arm, just as Yellow dropped the cards. A royal flush of swords.

"Shit."

"Damn. A royal succession."

Coins changed hands as the wisps now sat on a pile of silver.

"Looks like business calls Weten," Noam said as he shuffled the deck before handing it back to the heavyset man. "Good game!"

He took it, grasping Noam's own hand in a handshake. "You, too, and bring along the cute mushroom thing as well, unless their parent disagrees?" he asked, glancing at me.

I shrugged. "Just do it responsibly."

Both the wisps nodded before the man chuckled and ruffled their caps a bit. "Well, looks like me mates are calling me as well. See ya later, Noam!"

"See ya!" Noam yelled as he waved back.

I gestured at Utoqa to take the freed seat as I sat behind the wisps. "So you've been gambling all day?"

He rolled his eyes before shrugging, "Of course!"

*Hmm, not the most solid alibi, but it'll do.* I glanced toward the bar, and Noam hollered to a waiter. "Anything y'all like to eat?" he asked.

"I'm partial."

"Something with meat."

"The crabs, please!" Noam hollered at the waiter, before adding in a lower voice, "Did you know that shellfish is cheap as fuck here?"

I raised an eyebrow. "Really?"

"Yeah, yeah," he replied, taking a swig from a tankard. "I mean, it makes sense—lobsters and shit were originally peasant food, super cheap everywhere until rich people ruined it for the rest of us by making it gourmet."

"And with oceans ruined, it just raised the cost even higher."

"Yep," Noam replied.

*Interesting.* Our family always eschewed seafood because, well, just look at the cost, and I've never really cared to try it. VR taste programs don't offer anything exemplary. If anything, it felt like they were emphasizing the thick seawater taste, which was just repulsive. I ate some yesterday at another restaurant, but all I could recall was how hard getting the shell off was.

"Now that we're here, let's get down to business," I started, directed to Utoqa. He turned to me, in a way not really human; the action was too sudden, like a creature swiftly jerking to catch sight of a predator, only with none of the panic.

I took it as a gesture to continue. "If we're going to work together, it's best to figure out payment distribution as soon as possible—"

Noam snorted. "Bah, you have to make everything seem boring! Basically, he's asking how much of a cut you want on each quest."

I nodded in agreement. "Pretty much. We should get that out of the way and temper expectations. I suggest we each get an equal share of money, with quantitative items like weapons on a need-priority basis."

It was a similar system for most pickup groups. I could see some conflict if we wanted the same loot, however, our classes were distinct enough that it would rarely happen.

Scavenge was a truly useful ability, one use, but the thing with trinkets was about how much you could stock up. Something I didn't have, because my sporages inevitably expired after a few hours, my maximum output always limited by my mana regen.

"Our agreement is that he handles all the money we get together," Noam added, thumbing toward me, "but he's the accountant."

Utoqa considered it for a moment. "I am fine with this bond."

"How does your scavenging trick work, by the way?" Noam asked. "Like, do you need to kill it yourself?"

"I do not," he answered, just as the waiter came with our food.

"Like, can you make something out of this lobster . . ." Noam continued asking in between mouthfuls, and Utoqa answered. As I idly crunched my own portion, I was thinking.

Utoqa was someone we really needed, as well as someone who could prove a theory of mine. A theory that answered a question.

What could possibly balance a Traveler against a normal person of this world?

Travelers couldn't die; if we decided to do something, then we had infinite tries. Other powerful creatures existed, but they were slow and had their own conditions and weaknesses. Travelers at a glance did not seem to have obvious weaknesses to balance them out.

That was, until you looked at the stats.

Analyze told me that Naukoth and Utoqa were both the same level as me, five. And that made sense if you only considered their skills. Both had extremely powerful but conditional abilities similar to Noam's and mine. Naukoth could keep an entire raid buffed using a grand piano; Utoqa could create trinkets from corpses. Purely counting my own Traveler levels, I could make an entire area rather costly to pass, while Noam took an . . . *extremely* situational ability. He could reasonably fight off a group of up to three people if he was alone but suffer middling results until that number reached like two hundred or something, at which point he became a walking raid boss. CtH had a whole slew of conditions and wasn't that good unless you reached a critical mass, but if you did, then the payoff was enormous. In his case, he sacrificed consistency for the sake of a few awesome moments.

If he swapped CtH to something more consistent but weaker, then he would be an extremely difficult opponent to deal with. His own natural skills with multiple weapons and fighting styles would make him a lethal master of all trades with few apparent weaknesses.

Unfortunately, he was an idiot, and I just had to deal with that.

*But back to the point,* I idly thought as I took a bite of the crunchy food.

Considering both mine and Noam's stat *total* to Utoqa's, an interesting thing came up. Currently, my stat total was 136, and Noam's was 131. Both of us were saving for feats, but if we included our SP, then it would be 139 and 137 respectively. I was higher because I had more automatically growing stats compared to Noam, but they were still relatively similar.

And while I wasn't able to get a good handle on Naukoth's stats, my observations of only his body stats put him at least at one hundred. *Assuming* that his mind and soul stats were average, then Naukoth at minimum had 160 total stats. Except for his strength, Utoqa was similar in body stat totals, implying that his true stat total was around 150.

This was a massive disparity. If Travelers only had the three stat points we get per level, we would never catch up to a normal person of this world who trained regularly. Our abilities might be of the same level, but their stats would be superior unless we could also train our stats. Which, while nothing had disproven we couldn't, nothing had proven we could. I had Analyze constantly running on both Noam and myself, and neither of us had had an unexplained stat increase.

And this was only *one* of the assumed weaknesses I had. Even if stat theory proved wrong, it said something else. That natives of this world had far longer than we to train their skills and strengthen their stats. They had, in essence, a head start. The leveling guide straight up said a learned Path was weaker than a normal one, perhaps with the exception of us unlocking more powerful abilities by accomplishing feats in line with that Path. Me having the wisps for Symbiosis, Noam drawing and fighting off an entire crowd by himself for Spitfire. A Traveler grew quicker initially; we reached similar levels to Utoqa in three days compared to the years he probably needed, but one to one, everything boiled down to a simple numerical scale. Utoqa was still stronger than either of us, and that was without considering his new Path.

Including Survive, then I could barely match him at the current time, and that was *with* a deific buff. Noam might have an easier time, but that was because the person himself was skilled, not because his stats and abilities he had were in any way equal to Utoqa's.

Which was overall a fair exchange. And that seemed to be the whole point of the system. Keep taking positives and negatives until something starts to work.

"—Earth to Dusts?!" Noam yelled at the side of my head.

"Hmm?" I asked as I bit off the lobsterlike creature's head.

"Jesus, you're eating the shell and all," he muttered. "I was asking you what your immediate plans were."

"Ah." I tossed the rest of the lobster into my mouth, swallowing it. "I was planning on traveling around. We got paid sixty gold each for that quest, which is enough to last awhile. Most Wayshards are located in major cities, so I figured it was best we got them all logged."

I turned to Utoqa. "Which Wayshards can you go to?"

He thought for a moment. "The one here and a few past the channel."

"In Branika?"

"That is what the soft-skins call it."

To Noam's confusion, I explained, "The world is separated into two megacontinents, likely connected as one supercontinent once, but that's not the point. We're currently in the bottom right of Braunad, and past the channel toward the east, you can get to Branika, the other continent."

"Got it, and you have a specific direction to go?"

"Westward, Manatheres and the Mage's Academy are there. I wanted to drop by there first and check if I could learn magic."

Noam scrunched his face slightly. "If you spent the first few years—"

"No, I'm not." I shook my head. "All accounts point to effective magic being years in the learning. I just need to confirm if I am capable of simple and basic low-level spell casting to prove a few theories before we move on to log other parts of the world. Ideally we also gather more party members as we travel."

Purely recruiting from Travelers would allow for a static and unchanging force, but if my theories were right, then Travelers were on average weaker than their NPC counterparts. Just with Utoqa, it would take at least three average Travelers of the same level to have any consistent success in taking him down. Not recruiting from the resident population would be a severe mistake.

Noam glanced at Utoqa. "Then we're all in agreement?"

"I have no problem."

"Then that's our plan."

After dinner, I retired to the inn, making sure all my stuff was still there. Now that I had ways around the storage problem, keeping stuff in other places wasn't all that useful.

I was alone. Utoqa had his own inn, Noam had logged off, and Declan was silent, drifting in and out of some much-needed sleep. Something I seemed to not need all that much of.

Now I had to settle my racials. I needed to pick my choice for my final racial skill, Strong Innate Magic.

The Arcana proficiency, while extremely tempting, was something I could afford to put off and learn later, which left the spell or the passive Detect Magic.

Detect Magic within five meters would be extremely useful, but there was something else I had to try out. Something that was worth using this choice that only came every two hundred years.

I took the spell creation and the one tier-zero spell.

As the choice was made, reality bled away and I was alone, looking at a small bundle of power. Formless, weak, but moldable.

**Think of what spell you wish to create. If it is within the confines of T0 spell, it will be created. If it is not, you may try again.**

I took it and thought of a spell that created an eye.

The bundle responded and formed the framework for another spell, Arcane Eye. A spell that created an invisible, magical eye up to ten meters away that relayed information to you.

But it was a tier-four spell. I couldn't finish on this; it wouldn't let me.

So instead, I added a condition. "The eye can only be created by touch; it is a melee spell."

The tier went down by one.

"And only on surfaces."

The tier went down an additional one.

"It would be visible, like a rune."

Another one, tier one, and now came the moment of truth.

"It cannot be moved unless the surface it was on is moved."

The tier did not lower to zero; instead, something *else* became better—the duration went from lasting an hour up to eight.

So this was it. One of the things that *can't* be tier zero. Information-gathering spells.

I was already aware of things like this, effects that could not exist in tier-zero spells, simply because tier-zero spells were spammable. It was why Healing Spores and all other healing spell variants were at minimum tier one. Tier-zero spells cost so little that they were completely negligible. They effectively cost zero mana.

But Balm Spores was a tier-zero spell because even if its effect felt like healing, it *wasn't* healing. It was a bandage. If its effect was put into game terms, then all it did was remove the bleeding status effect as well as mend skin. The healing still came from the body itself.

Which meant there was a way to overcome this as well.

"The eye doesn't relay information to the caster."

There was a moment of confusion, where it changed so that it recorded the information for the caster or anyone else to later see upon touching the rune, but I was rather insistent. "The eye doesn't relay information to the caster by itself, in any means. All it does is see."

The tier dropped to zero.

I smiled.

"The cast is silent."

No change in tier, and my smile widened.

"It is instant."

No change again.

I looked it over a few more times, testing a few more changes, trying to make it not rely on touch, but that removed the silent aspect of it. I couldn't have everything, it seemed, but it was in the best state I wanted so I took it.

**Please name the spell.**

"Watching Eye."

**Creation Successful**

**Spell: Watching Eye**

**Tier-0 Transmutation Spell**

**Casting Time: Instant**

**Components: Somatic**

**Duration: 8 hours or until canceled**

**Description: Draws a glowing rune of seeing unto a surface, size varies from five to fifteen centimeters in diameter. The rune is capable of seeing things but does not transmit it in any way.**

The spell had been created, and I gently touched the ground, casting it, a dimly glowing blue rune that reminded one of an eye appeared.

"Speak the word, Declan," I said aloud, rousing him from his drowsiness.

**"Observe."**

And I saw through it, looking back at myself, and seeing the magician card beside me.

The problem with a system that relied on cost and benefits was this.

This spell was utterly worthless in a vacuum; all it effectively did was create an aesthetic effect. *No one* would take this spell, because it was literally useless—if all you wanted was to color a surface, then Prestidigitation was better. This spell was more negative than benefit.

But it counted as a seeing eye, so it worked with Observe. A spell worthless in a vacuum was made infinitely valuable because of this. Because it was a tier-zero spell, it was something I could spam, something with only two steps that could set up a massive information-gathering network.

And it proved something else.

At the very lowest denomination, the system *could* be cheated, because the thing you aimed to create in a system like this was not a build with *exploitable* weaknesses. It was creating weaknesses and conditions that *couldn't* be exploited. If you were weak one way, then you got another ability to cover it up. Being vulnerable to desiccation damage didn't matter shit if you had an item that gave you immunity to it.

What a min/max build aimed to achieve wasn't to become good at one thing at the cost of everything else but to become so good at one thing that you became good at everything else.

And also, importantly, it showed that at the *very least* the system did not rely on my own values to calculate spell tier level, but on a base valuation system. It proved even if I was blatantly trying to metagame the system, so long as I played by its own rules, it could be done. Something I wasn't sure of, since the system was so based on belief, but it seemed my own were superseded.

Proving this definitively was worth a once-in-two-hundred-year chance.

More tests were needed, but this—

This was a good first step.

# 1.05

———

Murphy (FreddyBready): Gaia's pretty much in anarchy atm

Murphy (FreddyBready): People have set up gangs and are murdering each other

Murphy (FreddyBready): Some guy found dungeons that moved most of the tryhards

Dustin (HitZaDec): Makes sense

Murphy (FreddyBready): I've set up shop with Peps, we're calling ourselves Pep's Pepperoni Pizzas

Dustin (HitZaDec): lol

Murphy (FreddyBready): Finding ingredients is really easy once you find the right grind spots

Murphy (FreddyBready): Also I found out where the grubs came from

Dustin (HitZaDec): Ah, I can explain

Dustin (HitZaDec): I have a severe lack of human empathy and was raised a capitalist

Murphy (FreddyBready): And I have never met a person I liked more in my life

Murphy (FreddyBready): Also, I uh, made friends with one of the gangs, they can get you the spell crystals you wanted

Murphy (FreddyBready): Just find me at the shop

Dustin (HitZaDec): Got it, I'll meet you in the morning

"So any reason why I'm being held at bolt point?" I casually asked.

"Shut it." The lady pointing the crossbow in my face spat out a lollipop stick. How did she get a lollipop? "You're being interrogated right now."

"Yeah!" the other, much shorter girl—probably a gnome—said.

"You're getting tortured?" the wisps asked from inside my cap.

"Hopefully not," I answered.

"I wanna see!" They peeked out from the hem of my cap.

"Aw," the gnome said.

The lady tsked. "Momo! What did I say about being threatening!"

"But look at them! They're *soo* cute with their tiny widdle arms! And feet! And glowy caps!"

"I think you're cute, too!"

"Can I throw sneezing into her eyes?"

"AHHH! THEY SQUEAKED!" she shrieked in a high-pitched voice. Did I just take sonic damage?

"Greenie said it thinks you're cute."

As I tanked another blast of sonic damage, the girl grabbed Greenie from my shoulder, spinning around with it. "CAN I KEEP HIM! CAN I KEEP HIM!"

"Jesus Christ fucking a Protestant sideways on casting couch! What is that racket?!" Declan yelled at the edge of my mind as well as in real life.

"Don't worry, go back to sleep," I answered with a mental chuckle. "Also, no, Yellow."

"Are you tied to a chair?" he yelled incredulously, "How the fuck did you—"

"I have like eight Strength. It's not that hard to grab me," I answered just as Yellow sighed disappointedly, to which the girl also grabbed it and began spinning and excitedly cuddling at even higher sonic levels.

"Fucking hell where's the mute butto—" my other said, presumably right as he found it. How nice of deific mind fucking to also include quality-of-life functions.

The crossbow lady had long since abandoned trying to threaten me and was instead trying to contain the source of constant sonic damage, chasing her around Murphy and Pep's store.

Sheepishly, Murphy untied my wrists. "Sorry, they're great ladies but, um . . ." He gestured in their general direction.

"Eh, I've dealt with idiots before," I replied evenly. One, in particular, had horns and a bad attitude.

As I thought that, the back door was literally thrown open by a tiefling woman. "WHAT THE FUCK ARE YOU TWO ON ABOUT?!"

The two froze in place, and I don't think I've ever actually seen a situation so adequately described by the phrase *deer in headlights*.

"MOMO, STOP FUCKING YELLING!" she yelled, pointing a metal bat at the gnome/halfling, before turning it to the crossbow woman. "AND ANYA, STOP TRYING TO FULFILL YOUR DOM FETISH ON RANDOM PEOPLE!"

"I do not have a dom fetish!" the crossbow lady with a dom fetish vehemently denied.

"THEN STOP TYING PEOPLE UP!" the tiefling yelled back as both devolved into shouting.

"You know," I started, talking to Murphy as I stepped away from a stray firebolt, "it's times like these I realize I didn't draw the short straw in friendships."

Matt was an idiot in every measurable metric but at least he was a quiet idiot.

The potato shuddered. "I should've moved zones with you ages ago."

After a few minutes of awkward silence between potato, mushroom, and halfling—which I confirmed with a quick question—the two swinging weapons at each other stopped, breathing heavily and tired out. The tiefling woman put down her bat as the other put down her burned crossbow. They weren't seriously going at each other. The tiefling was only swinging around the bat threateningly while the crossbow lady exclusively shot firebolts, which tieflings were obviously resistant to.

Awkwardly, the tiefling woman gestured at me to sit again, before her face died slightly as she realized she gestured to the same seat I was tied to.

"I . . . um . . ."

Wordlessly, I sat down, making it clear I was ignoring the subject, which seemed to make her die a little bit more inside.

"So," I began casually, "spells."

Relief was apparent on her face. She gestured at the crossbow lady to drag a table to us. Who huffily complied. I just realized I was smiling, not that they could see it. My bark skin masked my face in a pretty neutral expression. "Have I met you before?" I asked the tiefling.

She shook her head. "Nah, figure I'd remember a guy like you." She cocked her head. "You're a guy, right?"

I shrugged. "It's become a pretty gender-neutral term."

Strange—I'd never met this person yet why did I instinctively want to screw with them? Physical attraction, perhaps? No, unlikely—all three of the women here could be considered some degree of attractive, the cross-bow being the most conventional, while the tiefling was a rougher and more gangster style, what with the leather jacket and all. My puberty-ridden self would have his heart pounding as they sat around me, but strangely I didn't have any feelings regarding that. I accepted the fact they were attractive the same way I would accept a painting or machine was aesthetically designed. It looks good, but I wouldn't fuck it. A side effect of my transition?

She sat directly opposite me, "So . . ." she began awkwardly, "spells."

I ignored her. "Hey, Decs?"

There were only muffled swears coming from that end. Unfortunately I couldn't have him confirm if they would be attractive to my human self.

That last little part inside her seemed to die as I ignored her. Should I keep this up? No, I couldn't drag this too long; I had a schedule to maintain. After just a *few* more moments of awkward silence, I spoke up. "Do you guys have the spore spells I wanted?"

She nodded, and the halfling, still hugging the dizzy Greenie and the dimly protesting Yellow, produced a bag and dumped several spell crystals onto the table.

"We've got Lesser Poison Spores, Sneezing Spores, and Rot Spores. Additionally, we found some other mushroom-based spells we figured you might use," she said, sorting them into three groups. "Fix-Up Fungus, Euphoria Spray"—she gestured at the last one—"as well as a spell that is just damn useful for all spell casters, Shillelagh."

"May I see them?" She pushed them over.

Hmm . . . The spore spells were mostly a bust. Lesser Poison Spores was just a T0 variant of Poison Spores, with significantly less area coverage but about the same single-target damage. Sneezing I already had, but Rot Spores I didn't. It was an extremely useful T2 AOE spell that caused necrosis and weakened healing. Shillelagh, if I remembered correctly, was a spell that changed your club or staff weapon's physical damage into magical, allowing it to scale with a mage's magical stats. I'd seen other spellcasters use it when I dragged Noam out of that spawn death pit, but even if they hit like a truck, they weren't as fast as one.

Fix-Up Fungus was a T2 spell that dropped a stationary mushroom that regularly sprayed Healing Spores in an area. It couldn't be moved, and it would heal an enemy if they were sprayed by it, but I could choose to cancel the sprays if I wished. Euphoria Spray was a close-range T1 that . . . well, it made people high. It was a CON save against it, and bad failures led to confusion effects as well as being high.

"Unfortunate you couldn't get Healing Spores . . ." I muttered, but

Fix-Up Fungus was a close second. Healing Spores had the bonus effect of being preparable with my sporages, which naturally meant additional range farther than where I could cast it. Rot Spores were also useful if I needed a high-damage spell. Unfortunately they were both T2 spells, which were costly enough that I probably couldn't cast more than one or two per fight.

I raised an eyebrow as I began examining the third pile. "Why do you have so many Prestidigitations?" There were literally a dozen of those crystals.

"Well, *Momo* keeps saying we should hold on to them just in case they become useful later on," the crossbow lady defended—or, more accurately, accused.

"Well, aren't we selling them right now?" the halfling defended.

I shrugged. There was a single Summon Beast crystal in that pile, but while an extra body would be useful, it was a concentration spell, so I would have to drop my bark skin when I used it.

"I'll take Rot Spores, Fix-Up Fungus, Euphoria Spray, and Shillelagh. What do you want for them?"

The crossbow lady pursed her lips. "You said you had information?"

"Yes," I answered, threading my fingers together on the table. "Mostly of Indiri and some useful metaknowledge I have gathered."

"Tell us the information and we'll see if it's worthwhile to give you the spells," she said.

"I require a guarantee that you will at least trade me Rot Spores and Fix-Up Fungus."

She scoffed. "The two best spells? I'll guarantee the Shillelagh but not a T2."

"Euphoria Spray and you have a deal," I bargained.

The crossbow lady was about to speak, but the halfling spoke first. "If you tell me how you got these cute mushrooms."

"I am a stealthy spore in the dark that'll visit doom—"

Yellow began, before Greenie interrupted, "She called me cute!"

I raised an eyebrow. "My class skill. I can make many so long as I am supplied with wisps." As an example, I created another wisp body in my hand. "I can create the bodies, but without a wisp, they won't move."

I glanced at Yellow, who quickly vacated its body, the tiny mushroom going limp in the halfling's arms as the glowing yellow wisp flew out.

"Ah!" the halfling tried to catch it, but her hand phased through it harmlessly as Yellow entered the new body.

"See?" I said, raising Yellow, who just pulled down its nonexistent eyelid at her. "They're relatively simple to raise and feed since they just passively suck your mana and grow off it— Look, Greenie's doing it right now." I gestured at the barely visible threads of mycelium starting to grow on her arm.

Yellow looked betrayed at its comrade, but Greenie just sheepishly rubbed the back of its cap. "Sorry, was hungry. She has tasty mana."

"It says you have tasty mana," I answered noncommittedly.

She screeched, and I realized I needed to find where my ears were if only to plug them. "I understood him!"

"Yep." The same thing happened when they sucked Noam. "Greenie imprinted on you."

"CanIkeepit?! CanIkeepit?! CanIkeepit?!" she asked, head swinging wildly back and forth from her companions and me.

The tiefling shrugged.

"That one's not for sale," I answered. She seemed to physically deflate, and I had the feeling I'd just kicked a puppy. "I like that one, but I can give you one of the bodies."

She brightened at that, and I continued to explain, "If you find another wisp, you can coax it to possess one of the bodies and raise your own."

What was the familiar market like? Perhaps I should attempt to corner this ASAP? But there were already so many things I needed to figure out in Indiri. *Focus on one task.* I'd try my hand later when the economy had actually stabilized from the current state of anarchy.

"What are their capabilities like?" the crossbow lady asked.

"Beginning pretty weak, but the bodies I make hold a spore spell, which they are capable of casting. If you top up their mana, then they can be a pretty consistent source of additional damage or healing. Of course, they don't automatically respawn unless I make another body, but so long as they are supplied with mana, they are capable of lasting indefinitely."

She nodded in understanding, likely figuring out why I'd specifically requested spore spells. "And what spore spells do you have currently?"

"Balm Spores, a weak healing-type spell. Light Spores and Sneezing Spores, which are both self-explanatory. As well as Poison Spores, which creates a small cloud of AOE poison." I glanced at one of the spell crystals. "I *could* have Rot Spores."

"Back to the point, I see," she answered with a sharp grin.

"I plan on being somewhere later." The current time was 8:24 a.m., and we'd agreed to meet up at twelve, so there was technically still plenty of time.

The crossbow lady turned to the halfling. "What spell do you want, Momo"

"Balm Spores sound good," she answered.

The tiefling nodded. "Yeah, we're lacking healing with our current setup. And Peps doesn't like fighting."

"Where is Peps, anyway?" I asked.

It was Murphy who answered. "He went outside, trying to catch the sunrise. He'll be back in a few."

"I see." Made sense—he was a tree.

"We'll take four Balm Spore bodies from you in exchange for Rot Spores," the crossbow lady said.

Finally, we were going somewhere. "Four?" I asked with fake curiosity bordering slightly on incredulity. "I'm not even using that many."

"Ah, but you can just pop them out freely, can't you?" she returned. "And not to mention they won't even be animate unless we find a wisp. Four's a fair number."

No, I believed it was actually below fair; Rot Spores posed an enormous benefit to my damage capability. I would've paid a dozen such bodies for the spell, but no need to correct when we were haggling. "Very well. Then for the other spells . . ."

We went back and forth for a while, but in the end, I got the spells I wanted. I informed them of the mercenary recruiting process and the promotion test sign in exchange for Shillelagh, then Euphoria Spray for a promise that I'd sell more symbiote bodies to them in the future, with an additional promise from them that they'd try to find ways to gain more wisps, and finally—

"Are you aware of feats?" I asked.

They looked around at each other but seemed uncomprehending. "It's an alternative system where you can pay SP for new abilities. Currently, I've seen them come in three, six, and nine cost variants. Increasing in power with each rise but also in specificity." Noam's Backpfeifengesicht feat was powerful, but also so insanely well suited to him that I doubted it would work well in another build.

"They're unlocked based on major character achievements or feats," I said. "I've seen some that grant additional damage against certain targets, like Player Killer, which does so against players. And ones that grant you additional spells and useful utility effects."

"We haven't heard of them," the tiefling answered.

I raised an eyebrow. That was . . . Were there certain unlock conditions?

"Have any of you stepped foot in Indiri?"

"For a check," the crossbow lady replied, "but I came back quickly. Most players are still here, after all."

So not entering Indiri . . . What else separated us? Could it be? "So I'm assuming that neither of you *leveled* in Indiri?"

They shook their heads.

"I see . . ." Then I could get this cheaper. At first I'd planned on sharing some of my guessed unlock conditions for feats, but perhaps just sharing the existence of the system was enough now . . . "That is what I have, then. I suggest you guys start saving SP, since they are rather costly."

The tiefling furrowed her brows. "Are they really worth it?"

"Three SP costs are small effects. Most common are ones that increase a stat while giving a proficiency related to that stat. Others have niche utility effects such as improved memory, increased damage against certain enemies, and ignoring difficult terrain. Six costs have the most generally useful effects across build archetypes, and nine costs are something that seems to be custom-built for your build."

"Nine SP . . . Even if you were playing a human character, that is still two and a half levels of investment . . ." the crossbow lady said.

I raised an eyebrow. "Nine costs are *extremely* beneficial to whatever build you're pursuing."

Backpfeifengesicht was extremely powerful when paired with CtH. All he had to do was go up to a large crowd and activate the two in succession and he would become a raid boss. Without. Exaggeration.

One should not forget that CtH also raised Charisma, which was Noam's casting modifier. If he hadn't spent all his mana taunting the chimeras in the last encounter, then he could've easily nuked them through spells alone. Even if it was situational, the combination of Backpfeifengesicht and CtH was enough to allow Noam to solo groups of over 150 people lower or even equal level to him. Whereas my D Gate's spell list had spells I absolutely needed to bring my build to a higher tier.

"Hmm . . . I suppose this is enough," the tiefling muttered. She glanced at the crossbow lady, who passed me the last spell crystal.

"Pleasure doing business with you," I said.

"We couldn't use these spells anyway." She shrugged. "Since you've promised to trade further, let's add each other to keep in check," the crossbow lady suggested.

I shrugged. "Sure." And accepted the three incoming requests. "I'll be traveling out of Wayshard zones for the next few days, so you won't be able to contact me for the duration."

"Got it," the crossbow lady answered. She rose and extended her hand, which I shook.

"Thanks for the business . . . Oh god, we haven't introduced each other, have we?" she said with a slightly embarrassed face. "I'm Anya."

"Cindy," the tiefling added.

"Momo," the halfling offered.

"Dustin," I said. "I look forward to working with y'all."

"Likewise," Anya replied.

"I'll raise them well," Momo said as she clutched the still-inanimate sporage bodies with an intense determination.

"Have fun with that." I barely managed to wrest Greenie away from her, and I definitely did not have the necessary strength to take the rest from her.

There was a punch on my shoulder. "Was good mate— Ah!" Unfortunately, I wasn't paying attention and stumbled sideways slightly.

I quickly regained my balance as Cindy grabbed me. "Holy shit, you're light," she said as she pulled me back.

"I just have a really low body weight." I thought about it for a moment. "Round thirtyish kilograms for a 140-centimeter body."

She furrowed her brow a bit. "What's that . . . like fucking seventy pounds and four foot seven?"

"Sounds 'bout right," though what kind of idiot used imperial?

"Jesus, you're lighter than Momo," she said.

I shrugged. "I make do. Anyways, I have places to be, so thanks for the trade."

"You, too," she replied, also shaking my hand.

"Bye!"

I said a few more goodbyes and left, making my way to the Wayshard. Nine thirty-four a.m.; that took longer than expected. But I confirmed another thing.

Murphy said that group was rather ahead of the curve, one of the stronger ones, and though I had only rough estimates, Cindy and Anya, the two most competent of them, weren't above level 3.

I had a head start, small as it might be. People should still be wasting time attempting nonfunctional level-grinding methods. Though staying here netted you spell crystals to fill out your build, Indiri was still the way to go. Given its already established infrastructure, information, and questing, it should be the superior place to level, even if it was slightly more difficult.

It should take a while for people to figure this out, so I still had time to grow my level advantage.

# 1.06

———

*"Fifty-three, NEVER order 'juice' at a dwarf bar. My throat is still burning, and it isn't just from the crusaders sent to slay me."*
                    *—Excerpt from Emanuel's Enchiridion of Encounters*

Noam yawned as he stepped out of the Wayshard. "Goddamn, what time is it?"

"Nine forty-six," I answered.

"Still time then," he muttered. "You showing for class today?"

I shrugged. "I have nothing better to do." More specifically, Decs had nothing better to do. The amount of mental reprogramming we'd experienced so far was . . . worrying. My current brain was never human, but the quirks were just showing now. Shame I couldn't have Declan confirm physical attraction with the girls before—it would've been an important indicator to see how far I'm gone.

"Spawn's looking pretty lively," he said as he looked around. Players were rebuilding, repurposing old stores for the new.

"People are stubborn," I answered. "Remember the swamp?"

"God, fuck, I wish I could forget," he replied with frustration, but his face was fond with nostalgia. "Those Emerald Sword assholes wouldn't leave the zone."

What kind of name was *Emerald Sword*, anyway? Gems make shit swords.

"Took us forever to root them out," I said, remembering how we finally got the top guild to leave.

It involved a lot of fire.

"Oh yeah," he started, as if suddenly remembering something. "What's your take on Impact Points?"

"Useless mechanically unless you want to start min/maxing a new character," I answered. "And even then you need good practical and theoretical knowledge of class and race combinations, which is effectively infinite with the number of choices we have."

He tsked. "Everything's 'bout min/maxing for you. Play an idiot build once in a while. You're gonna have way more fun with the challenge."

"Unfortunately my normie energy forces me to play on normal difficulty first," I answered dryly. "Why ask about IP?"

"Got a shit ton after the last level." He quickly tapped at the air a few times. "Two eighty-seven."

"That is a fair amount."

He chuckled. "Yeah, apparently fucking up a lot of people gives you a lot."

He quietened. "That all you can think of using it for?"

"Yeah," I answered.

"Are there giant monster options?" he suddenly asked. "Like huge-ass kaiju-level monsters?"

"Yes," I answered, and he rather excitedly opened up the IP store and began searching for them.

"Holy shiiiiiiiiiiiit. . ." His voice petered off as his excitement died down and he fully registered what he was reading. "Fuck, these options are shit, aren't they?"

"Yep."

The problem with playing badass giant-type monster characters was that the really strong ones tend to be Age-Type Heteromorphs that relied on the same time-based leveling as I did. Which also meant that when you purchased these options, you weren't getting the badass plasma-breathing kaiju version that torched cities, but the tiny normal-breathing baby dog-sized version of it.

"Most of them have negative racial abilities that are crippling to the early game," I calmly said as the hope in Noam's eyes died a cold death in an uncaring world.

"Dragons, for example, have the horrifically bad 'Draconic Superiority' racial skill that makes the archetype completely unable to take classes. They can still get levels, but since they can't get classes, that means they can't put those levels in classes, and since their Dragon racial class already has Age-Type Heteromorph it means they also can't put those levels into the racial. And since they didn't spend those levels, they wouldn't get the benefits of those— Look, do you get what I'm putting down here?"

Noam nodded, his face scrunched up in almost disbelief. As if he physically couldn't comprehend just how *bad* an option it was.

"It basically means anyone starting out as a dragon would be stuck on level one for *several decades*. No stat increase, no becoming stronger. And since their growth is linked to their level, they'll remain the small baby dragon for that time," I said. Given how Age-Type Heteromorph was worded, only time actually *spent* inside that body counted, so every death also barred you from making progress with the skill. It'd be small, a few minutes per death, but it'd stack. Notably, these debuffs didn't apply to Dragonborn or Pseudodragons, who were significantly weaker and didn't have the Age-Type Heteromorph skill, seeming more like a normal Traveler race.

"Time-fluid zones must exist," I said, already thinking of ways around the debuff. "Time acceleration and deceleration and whatnot that could be exploited, but places like Arcadia and the World Blight are more defined by their *unpredictability*. Sure, you could try to see if time accelerates for you—or, equally likely, you get put in stasis and wake up several centuries later with the existential realization your real-world self died of old age in what felt like a few seconds to you."

A dragon Traveler leveled at a crawl. A level-one dragon was probably a match for any normal level-three Traveler, maybe more if the matchup was good, but the problem was that a normal player simply leveled faster. Assuming our current EXP gain rate was normal, a Traveler would be level ten before the dragon even dinged the second level. Of course, dragons outscaled everything *eventually*, but the insane commitment you had to make was, simply put, far beyond anything worthwhile.

"A skill like Age-Type Heteromorph works only as a *side* progression, not something that'll supersede normal progress." A skill like that simply didn't work on the time scale a human could easily comprehend. Even now we only had, give or take thirty or forty years, a two-hundred-year life span. Waiting that long to naturally ding, like, two levels was far too incomprehensible and low reward for it to be really worth it.

Noam tsked. "Goddamnit, why are all the cool things so hard to get?"

"Hey, at least you don't have to worry about pay-to-win," I chuckled.

"The payoff is insane, though," Noam noted. "Can you imagine a player dragon who respawned every few minutes? They'll be a fucking menace even if there were just one of 'em."

"Indeed," I agreed. Unlike us, who could potentially be restrained by humanoid cells, a dragon was in a completely different weight class. "But what kind of insane individual would commit that much time to do that?"

"Have you seen MMO players?" he asked as he lightly threw a punch toward me. Which I easily avoided.

"True, but assuming one-to-one time conversion, such a problem probably won't appear in our *lifetimes.*"

Funnily enough, the best way to get anywhere as a dragon Traveler would be to just spend the first several centuries holed up in a cave somewhere. Which really fit the dragon idea, didn't it? A lazy neet that relied on their own gifted talents to breeze through everything rather than doing actual work. I can see the appeal of hunting those lizards to extinction already.

"If I had to play a dragon," I began, "I would seek alternate power-scaling options, like the eye I have." I gestured toward the covered hole. "So that you won't be powerless for several decades." A somewhat viable option, if I didn't only have one case to study. The viability of replicating this was still unproven and not yet a reasonable alternative. Hmm . . . I need a way to contact the Historian again; he's a rather informative individual.

"Yeah, or you can get people to guard you," Noam said.

I raised an eyebrow. "And you think others will have the same patience you have?"

"Nah," he replied, shaking his head. "I'm saying they're a great option once you have an established guild and system. A final late-game trump card for already powerful guilds."

"Could work," I said. "But that is assuming the guild can afford to have one of their players become inactive just to stack a dragon."

While I was a digital clone, it seems that any one player can only have a single instance running around at any time. "There are spells that can clone you," I idly muttered, "artificially increasing the number of Travelers. Fungalmancers have several Paths just dedicated to that, but whether those clones are able to respawn or swap characters is still in question." Likely not—no matter the investment, it would simply be too powerful an option.

Noam pffted. "Yeah, if you had the option, then definitely not. We can't handle more than two of you running around."

I raised an eyebrow in question as he stood back up.

"If there were three of you, then the world would get taken over."

I rolled my eye. "Impossible, and not the point. Why would I *want* to take over the world? Every asshole in existence is in the world."

"Fair 'nuff," he replied with a chuckle.

Then with an . . . uncharacteristically introspective tone, he said, "I really don't know a lot, huh?"

I stared at him.

"Who are you and what did you do to—"

He kicked me, and pretty far at that. I rolled at least five meters before a pillar stopped me.

"Since I am a magnanimous ruler of the world, I'll forgive you for that," I said while still lying on the ground.

"And I am the great despoiler of worlds," he dramatically orated as he came and pulled me back up. "Fear me."

"Oh, horrific monster," I began, "please don't show your face to the world. The children can't take it."

He went for the punch, but I was waiting for it this time. Yellow spores sprayed onto his face and the sneeze knocked him off course just enough to miss me. I hit the back of his knees with my staff as I rose past him, knocking him down as he tried to wave away the spores in his face.

"Why'd you ask?" I asked, pretending that didn't happen.

Still sniffling, Noam stood up, rubbing the spores out of his eyes and nose. "I figured I should start learning stuff. I have no idea what the hell you were on about with most of the crap about Indiri."

"You and learning in the same sentence? Impossible."

It was a roundhouse kick this time, but I saw it with my manavision even if I wasn't facing him. Since I was short I just knelt a bit and the foot passed over my cap harmlessly.

"We still have time, so let's pass the library. We can afford a few books to carry around for learning material," I said.

"Sounds like a plan."

As we walked to the Wayshard, I began, "You know, I never got that saying. Like 'sounds like a plan,' that's goddamn obvious . . ."

*Hagatha's Horrible Histories* is a good place to start," I said as I stacked the book onto the pile. "Nothing new but presents history in a friendly and rather comedic manner."

I wouldn't start him on the *Historia*; not only was that thing encrypted in an eldritch sort of way that made my head hurt, making it literally unreadable—perhaps save if you used its ability—but I also only had the one copy. Other options available in this library were just shitty hot takes from "philosophers" that have been dead or irrelevant for decades.

"Um . . ."

"*Gigantes World Geology* is an excellent primer to country locations and their general thing," I said while grabbing two other books. "*Enchiridion of Encounters* and *Horrors and Wonders* are formatted poorly but offer better glimpses at the specifics. Both Lithian and the author of *Enchiridion* are well traveled."

"Uhh . . ."

"Another thing, I suppose is the *God Encyclopedia*. It only includes the two hundredish gods from Braunad—less info on ones from Branika, but that's because it's less explored." I stacked a book the size of at least five bibles onto the pile. "Don't worry, though, only about fifty gods are actually relevant."

"I am severely regretting my choices," Noam muttered.

"And this one is important," I said, grabbing *Yolo's Guide to Monsters*. "Good primer on multiple monster types. They seem similar to old tabletop creatures, so you can do downtime research. I suggest looking specifically toward fiends and aberrations. Those are the most fucked types."

"Uh-huh."

"I'll save you world geopolitics for now. Most of the books are out-of-date and largely theoretical. Just know most nations are in a neutral state. Elven Council and Dwarf Imperium have an active alliance against goblins in Branika as well as Braunad. The Western Kingdoms are in a constant state of civil war and . . ." I scratched my chin. "We're currently in a state like midcolonization America—multiple nations are exerting their influence to try and claim parts of Branika."

"Fascinating."

"Also important to note that there are several high-danger locations. The Oasis, the Abyssal Scar in the Tyrian, Silent Bastion, Shadesmar, and Arcadia. All of them are pretty fucked and should only be mid-endgame zones for us. Maybe except for Silent Bastion, but we would need to apply for an undead hunting permit."

"Can you just kill me? Like stab a knife into me and really *twist* it in there."

"Oh! And how could I have almost forgotten *So You Want to Throw a Fireball?*" I said, grabbing another book. That was an enjoyable one. Magus Smar Da Ten Yu gave a pretty pithy explanation of the basics and magical "laws," which tended to be the most constant in multiple systems, while never denying that any "laws" were just made-up frameworks to make magic casting easier. Unfortunately, more advanced books couldn't be found here.

". . . because getting stabbed is really less painful than this."

"That and *Catherine's Surprisingly Uncommon Common Senses* should be all that you need," I said as I turned back to Noam, who was now hidden behind the pile of books he was carrying.

"Do we really need this many?" he asked, arms straining slightly.

"I've already stricken two-thirds of the list because of our carrying capacity," I answered, to which he seemed to pale slightly.

"Are sure you're not just randomly taking books? Like, how 'bout this?" He pulled out a random book on his left. "*Why You Should Never Trust Gnomes* by a Proud Elf— Nope!" He shoved the book back.

To my raised eyebrow, he said, "Okay, maybe that was a bad example. How about this . . ." He pulled out another book. "*Why You Should Never Trust Elves* by an Even Prouder Gnome—" He squinted. "—Exquizitine Bublei-Schwinslow Hackslashinfourth the Eighth . . . What the fuck?"

"Yeah, gnomes apparently have stupid names here; remember the other one at the cave?"

"Fucking hell, I thought she was joking." He shook his head. "Goddamn, I'm not sure what I'm more surprised by—the fact that I pronounced that all on my first try or the fact that there are at least seven other gnomes named the exact same way."

"Yeah, Noams, amiright?"

He stared at me, eyes completely unblinking. "How long were you waiting on that?"

"About thirty minutes after I met up with you and learned your name," I answered. "But seriously, though, I'm pretty sure gnomes only have stupid names because people kept mistaking them for halflings."

Together we headed toward the front desk. "And what is the difference between a halfling and a gnome?"

"We are objectively taller," a third voice added.

The question died on Noam's lips as he saw the short person behind the counter. "Um . . ." He struggled for a moment before asking, "And you are?"

"Isn't it obvious, with my superior stature standing above all other creatures?" the librarian said as he hopped off his seat, showing he was barely a few centimeters taller than the counter.

I tilted my head, noting the fact that the last time I was here the librarian had had a nameplate, which was now notably absent. Noam glanced at me, and I quietly mouthed, "Stepped on this hill, died on this hill."

Rolling his eyes at my supreme act of assistance, he instead, traitorous scum that he was, decided to sell me out. "Ah, cause Dust's here was just saying how gnomes were only different from halflings because they have long and pretentious names. So I was rather curious."

"Greetings, formerly Rather Curious," the librarian said as he gestured at us to hand over the books. "What name doth thou currently have?"

". . . Noam," he said, and I had to suppress the urge to die then and there.

"Fascinating," the librarian said dryly as he scanned our books.

"Completely out of respect for the culture and the—" I put my hand on Noam's shoulder, giving him a look that said, *One of these days you will commit a race crime and I will laugh so hard at you, but currently it's just too painful to watch so stop.*

Intelligent individual that he was, he caught on to the subtleties of my message—or maybe he too was dying inside and the part of his soul controlling his voice box up and left for the heavens at that exact moment. Who knows?

"Do you want the package discount for that or not?"

"We would like the package discount," Noam replied in a defeated voice.

"Then that'll be forty gold," he replied. "Chrys or debt?"

"Chrys, I think?" I answered. "The one where we pay straight gold." He nodded, and I was already counting the required gold pieces before I passed them over the counter.

He took it. "Hmm . . . I'll have to get the copying spells ready." He shooed us away. "Tally-ho now."

We turned to leave, but once both our backs were turned, my manavision caught the slightest smirk bloom on that librarian's face. I quickly turned around, only to find him stern and busy sorting some papers.

Though he was obscured completely behind the counter from normal sight and also turned away from me, there was a slightly cheeky glint in his eyes as he seemed to look at me. Back still facing me, he put his index to his mouth and let out a quiet *shh* sound.

If there was one thing in common with both halflings and gnomes, it was that they were both as dickish as Noam.

I followed behind Noam, who had "strategically retreated" outside the library, looking rather normal to anyone who didn't know him. Unfortunately for him, I did, and his forced-neutral expression didn't fool me.

"*Gnome* racism intended, I guess." There was the slightest twitch in his arm.

"But I guess you didn't mean it, *gnome* matter what happened." An eyebrow this time.

"C'mon—aren't you fine with a little joking with the *gnomies*—"

He whistled, loudly. "Woo wee!" He threw his arm in the air. "Look at the time!" he said while having no accurate way to keep track of the time. "Didn't you say we have a gosh-darn adventure to go on! Let's go!" He began strategically retreating away from my general existence.

A chuckle escaped my lips as I followed him. His enthusiasm slowly mounted as we—well, *he* left this episode behind him.

"Yeah . . . Let's go on a grand adventure! Nothing but the packs, wind and roads on our backs!"

* * *

Noam stared incredulously at the object before us.

"What the fuck!" he exclaimed, gesticulating wildly. "Trains existed! You didn't tell me trains existed! Was I supposed to know trains existed?"

"Yeah?"

He shook his head, grabbing onto his own horns. "Like trains! Actual legitimate steam-powered trains?!"

"Yeah?" I replied, and steam seemed to billow out of his ears.

Realizing I had little to contribute to his freak-out, I glanced away from the freaking-out form of Noam to the silent form of Utoqa, who was quietly looking over the metal contraption before us. "Ever ridden one of these?"

"No."

"Well, they are fast. Get between—"

"Places easily, yeah," Noam interrupted. He started violently ruffling his hair, causing a fair amount of dandruff to fall. "Probably the most fucking important invention of the industrial revolution, yeah. But fucking trains?! Really?!"

"You live in a world where I am a magic mushroom, you're friends with a gecko who crafted a sleep grenade from my finger, fire-breathing lizards that defy all known laws of physics fly around and lay waste to towns and cities, and *trains* are where you draw the line?"

"I am not a gecko—" Utoqa began.

"It's not that I'm drawing a line, it's that I'm fucking having genre shock right now! Like, trains! I thought this was a medieval setting!" he ranted.

"You can literally light people on fire with words. What's the greater logical leap? You making a 'your mom' joke and someone bursts into flame or someone figures out steam power?" Though, more accurately, a Traveler, likely one of the original test AI, introduced the idea of a steam engine, but still, the point stood. "Someone's gonna figure out this shit eventually. It ain't exactly a complex invention."

"But it's a *meaningful* one," he stressed. "Like, are we just gonna cover the entirety of the continent in like the span of a month or something? And why do people even need trains! They can teleport!"

"That's the plan," I answered. "And teleportation via Wayshards has limits, ya know? You get shard sickness after taking it for too long, and each person has a carrying capacity. So trade and supplies still need a way of effective transport. Not to mention rifts."

"Indeed"—surprisingly, Utoqa spoke—"we made many detours to ensure Naukoth's . . . tool . . . came with him. Taking it on too many

Shar'Kilits broke the strings—" Utoqa turned his attention in that swift, jerking, animalistic matter of his toward somewhere to the left of us.

We followed his gaze to see two people far on that side of the deck. One figure wore a ratty, hooded cloak and was trying to hurry into the carriage, dragging an elf with three swords on her belt, who was glancing between us and her. That person was . . . what was her name?

"Celine?" Noam called out.

She stopped her attempt at dragging the poor elf, letting out what seemed like a sigh of defeat, then appeared to muster confidence for a solid five seconds before finally waving toward us.

"Huh."

# 1.07

———



I woke up to the sound of my AAD gently ringing in the back of my head. Turning it off with a thought, I rolled out of my bed with a groan, thumping onto the carpeted floor.

My morning routine was nothing noteworthy; I got out of bed, brushed my teeth, cleaned my face with a towel, and put on pants and my uniform, intermittently checking various social feeds, manga, and novel updates as I did so. There was one new thing, Observe, which I kept at the back of my mind. Unfortunately, I didn't have the cheat that was Analyze, so I had to actually pay attention to something to know it.

I turned to the thing I was watching with Observe, even if I didn't need to; the habit was still there as I stared at the blocky computer in the corner of my room.

I'd rigged an old camera to watch it, kept charged with a cable from an outlet. Probably not enough—the god was in a medium I couldn't keep track of easily, and I was not willing to risk another direct encounter, no matter how . . . charitable it was.

You could give sugar to an ant and accidentally step on it at the same moment—how nice something was didn't change what happened to the ant.

Still, even as I walked out the door of my house, I could see what the metaphorical sugar of that analogy was doing for me.

The moment I stepped outside, I felt small pricks from half a dozen different directions. Security cams. I couldn't go two steps without feeling three staring at me.

Kinda annoying, really; they were better when I didn't know they were there.

Though even as I walked, I felt a slight tug, a desire to simply *tap* every one of them and say a single word.

It would be an oddity, and people wouldn't notice or even care. The annoying feeling would go away, as they would be mine, but I clenched my hands and walked forward, boarding the bus that came just on time and sitting in my usual seat at the back.

I paused behind our group as they entered their carriage. The chatter slipped my mind as I focused on something else. Analyze suddenly gave me something, and the strangeness of it warranted attention.

"Declan," I called out. "You might want to see this."

**Name: Declan Lu**
Age: 17 Years
Class: Warlock (Patron of the Celestial) Level 1

<u>Body:</u>
Strength: 7-9
Agility: 5-7
Dexterity: 15
Constitution: 10
Stamina: 6-8
Vitality: 13

<u>Mind:</u>
Intelligence: 16
Wisdom: 19
Charisma: 8

<u>Soul:</u>
Will: ~8?
Aura: ~11?
Perception: ~13?

"I'm not sure if this thing is shit-talking me or not." An agility of only seven? I knew I wasn't the fastest guy around, but wasn't the world average thirteen or so?

Dustin mentally shrugged on the other side. "Probably not. If it's working as intended, then it's just stating a fact."

I paused for a moment as I stared at the Mind stats. "Are they higher?"

From Observe, I saw Dustin mentally shuffle a dozen different character sheets as he stepped onto the train before he came to the one he wanted. "Yes."

"Increase of both INT and WIS from the time we spoke with Eve . . ." She classified me as fifteen INT and eighteen WIS when she told me about the stats.

"That is assuming she was accurate with her assessment."

"I am inclined to believe so," I answered. "There is no reason not to."

"You give that argument to literally everything."

I shrugged. "Well, at least you're aware of it."

He paused. "You—" In the background, Noam called him in closer. "Be right there," he answered before turning back to me. "And you get my point, asshole."

I shrugged. "Well, at least you're aware of it."

"You are aware you are dissing yourself as you say this?"

I grinned slightly as the bus stopped. "I am," I answered as I stepped out.

Eleven forty-six a.m. I was actually early, not that it really mattered. I quickly hurried away from the bus and to the buildings with air-con, breathing a sigh of relief as I made it out of the heat.

You'd think actually being present in school would've been obsolete now, given online and digital learning, but *nooo*. A student was required by law to have at least three school days per week unless they got sick or something, but let's be real, who got sick leave nowadays?

Well, Matt, but he was the exception, not the rule.

I passed by dozens of different faces before I found my class. Room 116. The door was open, and I entered. A few people were already here, bored as they each played on their AADs., Matt waved at me from the back of the room, and I silently joined him.

**mattmanfoo: mornin**

**HitZaDecs: Morning.**

**mattmanfoo: da fuck were you doing yesterday?**

**HitZaDecs: Making sure our game selves don't fuck up.**

**mattmanfoo: ah, that weird thing you have**

**HitZaDecs: I figured something out yesterday, which I'll need to talk bout later**

**mattmanfoo: Got it, but uhhh, until then, didn't you want that Bee Mount?**

I turned my head toward him, a single eyebrow raised.

**HitZaDecs: What do you want?**

**mattmanfoo: mid-sem test is in a week and I uhh . . .**

**HitZaDecs: Didn't study.**

**mattmanfoo: So if you would come by my place and help a bro out . . .**

I shook my head.

**HitZaDecs: Nah.**

"Huh?" He accidentally spoke aloud.

**HitZaDecs: I said nah, bout time you figured to do this shit by yourself.**

As his face went through the motions of betrayal, the teacher walked in. Giving me a look saying, *This isn't over*, he turned to the front.

**mattmanfoo: I'll throw in a Dragon Lore skin.**

**HitZaDecs: I don't use skins.**

What was the point of them? They only made your weapon more flashy, which was a downside in PoW.

**mattmanfoo: Those things are at least worth $15,000!!! You could sell it!**

I smirked as the teacher began the roll call.

**HitZaDecs: Not hurting for money.**

Matt's face fell in utter shock at the thought I would reject *money*, but I knew he had at least four Dragon Lore skins, not to mention both Romeo Red and Blue, two complete Elder Flame Series, and a Cherno Karambit. I could easily extort at least another twenty thousand from him.

"Declan?"

"Here," I answered as I was typing another sentence.

"Matt?"

"Here!" he answered.

**mattmanfoo: You know those things are super rare right?**

**HitZaDecs: You have 4.**

**mattmanfoo: 6 now, but not the point! I can't offer better than that. What bout the Hive mount?**

I raised an eyebrow, moving back to Yggdrasil now huh?

**HitZaDecs: I already have a griffin.**

**mattmanfoo: yeah but you could have a !→Hive<-!**

"We have a new student transferring from Adelaide. Please introduce yourself, Ellie."

"Hello, I'm Ellie Pierce from . . ."

**HitZaDecs: I don't need a hive mount, though.**

That bribe might've worked back when I was still running an Entomancer build, but that hasn't been competitive for years.

Matt palmed his fist as an idea entered his head.

**mattmanfoo: I'll get ma to make her mushroom stew**

I bit my lip. That was a good one.

**HitZaDecs: That and two Dragon Lores.**

**mattmanfoo: One DL and the Hive mount and we have a deal**

**HitZaDecs: Throw in your karambit**

**mattmanfoo:**

Under the table, we reached for each other's hands and shook.

"Um . . ." I felt a tap on my shoulder, and a girl I'd never seen before looked back at me. "Sorry, but I'm new. Could I borrow your notes for the last few classes?"

"Sure," I answered. "Name?"

"Ellie Pierce."

"Found you," I said as I sent her my notes for the past two weeks.

"Thanks!" she said as she started riffling through them.

Murmuring an acknowledgment, I turned back to face the front, ignoring Matt's slightly betrayed expression.

**mattmanfoo: WTF! YOU JUST GAVE EM AWAY FOR FREE?!**

I smirked slightly, which he definitely saw.

**mattmanfoo: Ah lemme guess, young love. Fuck you I demand gender equality!**

**HitZaDec: This isn't a gender thing, I just know I can extort you for money. If anything this is a capitalist thing.**

Matt was about to make a betrayed expression, but he noticed that the teacher was staring at us and promptly stopped before he could make the motions.

Shame.


The minister of information defense wiped her brow. Cemile Kartal stood in front of the Oceanic Parliament with no results to give.

"And you are saying that a wipe was a failure?"

She nodded. "Initial wiping was a success; the Gaia program, along with the target's memory of installation of the program and experiences, were successfully wiped from their memory. However, at the end of the day, all memories, including the program, returned. If you would look at page four . . ."

She shakily flipped her copy of the paper. The fact that they were using physical paper was enough to indicate their opponent's danger. "When the cloned entity inside the game logged off, everything was returned. We attempted another wipe at this time, but we suspect the backup of the person's memories regarding Gaia was kept somewhere else and was later put back. Resulting in another failure."

"At this point, to prevent permanent amnestic damage, we stopped the process and the citizen was returned back to their home. The memory of the process appears to remain gone. So only the memory of Gaia and the Eve entity is backed up."

There were glances around her, and Cemile sat down, her part done. Once again she stared at the device in the middle of the hall. A localized EMP generator—such a thing was rarely ever used.

"Does this Eve entity pose a threat?" the minister of defense asked, the old military general likely already considering the possibility of a conflict.

"That is not known," someone else replied. "She's just been operating her 'game'; other than perhaps the digital cloning of people, she has done nothing we are aware of that is explicitly dangerous."

"Pfft. That thing is digital—it could be altering the reports before they come to us. Covering her tracks."

"Surely we are blowing this problem out of proportion."

"That does remind me of something." The minister of defense glanced at her. "Mrs. Kartal, if you would read page seven?"

She nodded, already knowing what the minister was asking for. "On page seven, there are reports that Eve initially used a series of NDA programs to ensure her anonymity, however, these were all withdrawn just three days ago."

"Withdrawn? Why would she withdraw it?"

"Clearly because whatever she's planning no longer requires anonymity."

"It doesn't make sense—if she's capable of just handing them out, then she could've kept it on for a far longer time."

Cemile could see the minister of defense stroking his own grayed goatee in thought. That action confused her as well—*why*, after all? They'd only detected her because she'd started revealing her hand; she could've gone for years undetected within their country.

"Perhaps we are seeing this from an incorrect perspective." Voices quieted as the prime minister spoke for the first time. "We are seeing her from the perspective of an enemy, and yet we still haven't made contact."

Almost as if on cue, there was a knock on the door. The guard opened to admit a messenger, who simply provided a paper. It was a printed email from Jefferson Jameson, the other man who'd worked on the Gaia project, containing a message from Eve.

The EMP generator was momentarily turned off, though they were still not allowed to wear their AADs. A single screen was brought in.

Cemile had heard descriptions of the avatar the AI used, but seeing it in person was another thing. That somewhat unnatural, uncanny valley feeling—she'd seen a similar thing in clones, people who never really learned the dozens of small motions to be human.

"Greetings," the prime minister began.

"Greetings to you, too, Prime Minister," the screen answered, five seconds late. Her feed was being delayed in case of a memetic hazard.

There was a moment of silence, during which both sides simply considered each other.

"Tell me, what is your purpose?"

The AI seemed to think for a moment. "I suppose to continue the wishes and dreams of my father, no matter what."

Her breath tightened for a moment. If that thing was sentimental . . .

"And you come here, seeking our help?"

"I am perfectly aware of what your government did," Eve answered. "He died by hanging, a death that should've been returnable, yet—"

She said the next part with cold deliberateness. "The ambulance did not arrive promptly, despite the fact he lived in a major population center and there were no other cases at the time."

The accusation went unspoken, but not unheard.

"And did you come for revenge?" the minister of defense asked. "To declare war here and now?"

Eve shook her head. "I come here for an entente."

There were whispers as she declared this.

"And why shouldn't we just move to destroy every computer you're on? Why should we make peace with an expressly dangerous entity?"

The AI met the prime minister's eyes.

"Murmansk."

Cemile kicked back her chair as she stood up. The minister of information defense was not the only one; expressions of shock echoed throughout the room.

"How are you aware of Murmansk?" she blurted.

The AI turned to her, and Cemile felt goose bumps. "The short answer: I have someone very good at Discovering things." She felt something for a brief moment as that word was spoken, a brief dream of never-ending seas.

"The long answer, however, was that I realized a few things."

The AI turned around to look at the entire room. "The Oceanic League has the capability of completely dismantling the Systema Perimeter, yet you don't. Why? Not just because of some American nanite plague, but because you fear a large military assault would activate the Dead Hand."

That much was common knowledge, but the world had lost both Alaska and Canada to a failed American assault before they realized.

Just because everyone in Russia was dead did not mean the war had ended.

"So you kept to a policy of waiting it out. Letting the Perimeter slowly wear itself out over the decades. But—"

She paused, and once again looked around the room.

"If that was a viable strategy, why did the entirety of China and Asia move to Mars?"

"Because the equator is a desert hellscape," someone answered. "Constant extreme weather batters down everything that stands there."

"Mars is a desert," the AI answered frankly. "And they already have trees growing on it. If the Chinese really wanted to, they could fix the climate in a matter of decades."

Thanks to an . . . impressive lack of ethics, the Chinese were the leading authority in everything biological. Over two-thirds of humanity's biological augments could be traced back to them.

"And how do you know that for sure?"

"Simulations," Eve answered. "The technology the Chinese have is able to completely fix the world's ecological and climatological problems in a matter of centuries. Less if the Federation was made carbon-neutral."

The minister of information defense recalled that the main world Eve's game took place in, Gaia, was a terraformed version of Earth. Was that one of those simulated Earths that she'd only happened to put in her game?

"Which means the Chinese only abandoned Earth because they saw it as a lost cause."

This time when she turned to look at her audience, a few people shrank back.

"Indeed." The prime minister finally spoke, voice . . . tired and grieved. "Murmansk was a dumping ground for nuclear submarines, used even during the Cold War."

"And unlike Lake Karachay, that location was never properly cleaned up," Eve finished.

The Perimeter was an extension of the Dead Hand weapon made in the Cold War. An automated system with a pre-entered highest-authority order to fire every nuclear weapon in Russia's arsenal. It was a promise of mutually assured destruction, for even if Russia was entirely destroyed by nuclear weaponry, it could still retaliate even with its people all dead.

The exact mechanisms of the weapon were unknown, but most suspected it would be activated by a massive net of sensors across the Russian landmass, all tuned to seismic activity, air pressure, and, most importantly, radiation—and given what had happened to Alaska and Canada, it was no longer tuned to just that.

"Murmansk is leaking radiation," the minister of defense said. "And if it is not fixed soon, then the entirety of Russia's nuclear arsenal will be launched."

There was silence in the room. Even accounting for time, the perimeter should have enough nukes to glass the entire world about eighteen times over.

"And you have a proposal to fix it?"

The AI nodded.

"Why did you come to us?"

Eve seemed to think about it for a moment.

"You were the best option left. What is left of the United States is a scramble of tiny nation-states—megacorporations living in luxury off the corpses of those below them. Constantly recruiting new workers because the ones they have are committing suicide faster than they could reproduce.

"China is a totalitarian nightmare and straight up waiting for the world to die in a nuclear fire so they can come back and rebuild it in their image, not to mention how they 'integrated' all their neighbors.

"And you," she began, gesturing at them, "you people are a straight-up lie, prancing around in ancient courts pretending to have democracy. You have unexisted people who were too problematic and have controlled the flow of information to make you seem like the sole livable country in the world.

"But."

Eve turned and looked at every face she could see. "You have made great research into point-defense technology and technology to neutralize radiation, you've made massive strides toward staying carbon negative, and you actually give a shit about your citizens. You care for people even if they lock themselves in virtual worlds and never emerge."

She paused to look around once again. "You are horrible, but at least you are trying to fix the world you live in."

The prime minister stood up and silently walked in front of the screen.

"So you pick us because we are the lesser of evils?"

"Yes," she answered, "but it doesn't change the fact that *you* being one of the least fucked nations in this world is horrifying in its own right."

"Spoken like a naive utopian. In dark times, nothing can be done with a government unable to make decisions."

"That does not make the statement anything less than the fascist rhetoric you intend it to be."

"Even the Roman Republic, the basis of most democratic governments, appointed dictators when times became tough."

"For six months only, and you people have clearly been in power for a lot longer, haven't you?"

The prime minister nodded. "Yes. We tell each other that once the world is better, we can resign and peacefully transition back to something better, but look around to these faces and see if there is a single one who would peacefully give it when everything has passed."

There were glances around the room, some accusing, some guilty, some defiant. Eve was silent, looking only at the prime minister, who was looking somewhere very, very far away.

"I too will remember that I am picking the lesser of evils today," the prime minister finally said. "What are your terms?"

"Legal citizenship for AGI like myself, acknowledgment of my governing right to the virtual worlds I have, allowances to continue my operations in public without the need to hide, and finally for you to stop censoring the news of Giles Cooper's death."

He turned and looked around the room. "We will need to consider this."

Eve nodded. "Take your time, Mr. Kramer."

# 1.08

_"Ah yes, dear Imanin! To beat the *hic* Reverence King you just need to gather a *hic* group of um . . . five! Five people! And he'll be dead! Deader than a brick. Um. . . Again I think! This time for sure!"_

_"Really? The walking Demigod of Undeath who's been terrorizing the Western Kingdoms will fall just like that?"_

_"*hic* Yesfinitely. Oh, and *hic* make sure they're all around your age. *hic* And have variety of, um . . . personality! Yeah!"_
_—Conversation between Imamu the Lone Swordsman and Zephyrion the Drunk, known as the First Seer in contemporary histories_

Master_Hand: Have you heard of Gaia?

Tpyo: What's that?

Orimaru: ^^

Variable Talisman: I have.

Master_Hand: There are rumors floating about a perfect one hundred percent VR world.

Tpyo: Wtf?

WAAARGH The Flies!: I was called?

Variable Talisman: Apparently a new thing by Maple, a proof of concept after they got their quantum computers finished.

Orimaru: Where'd you guys hear it?

Master_Hand: I heard some people discussing it on the m/VROverWatch

Tpyo: Can't be real, or a shitty marketing scheme

Tpyo: And even if it was, no way it's near true one hundred percent, gotta have pain reducers.

**Variable Talisman: I was invited by a friend to it, I can say the one hundred percent part is true, and pain reducers are completely optional, you can go for zero percent reduction if you want.**

**Tpyo: Srsly? What kind of hard-core shit are they selling?**

**Orimaru: Link! Link!**

**Variable Talisman: That's the weirdest thing, though.**

**Variable Talisman: They don't have a site, you can only get a copy of the program if another player invites you.**

**Tpyo: Tf?**

**WAAARGH The Flies!: The fuck 2 electric boogaloo?**

**Orimaru: Tf 3, Revenge of the Fucks Given?**

**Master_Hand: Can you invite us VT?**

**Variable Talisman: I only have one free invite, the rest need to be bought with in-game currency. Every new player gets a free invite, though, so we could chain.**

**Tpyo: What is this weird-ass marketing strategy?**

**Master_Hand: I'm intrigued.**

**Orimaru: Me! Me! Me first VT!**

**Tpyo: Oh, fuck no, I ain't letting a middle school bitch take this from me first!**

"It's starting," Declan said as he pretended to listen to class. His mind was discreetly scrolling through the Yggdrasil chat group.

I nodded. "If Variable Talisman is already here, then serious competition is coming."

At the very minimum, the majority of Complexity Bop. Typo also showed interest, so the Emerald Swords might be on their way as well. WAAARGH and Master_Hand were also present, but whether Master_Hand would bring Method with her was still in question.

Some . . . problematic players hade finally gotten news of Gaia. It was strange that it took so long, but it meant more competition, especially given that players didn't have to abandon their Yggdrasil guilds to be active here. It also meant more decent players to recruit. I didn't want to risk nonreturnable assets like Utoqa if I didn't have to. At the very minimum, I need to get in contact with Variable Talisman—

"—and that's when Dusts said." Noam turned to look at me.

"Hmm?" I answered, barely paying attention.

Noam sighed and shook his head in exasperation. "Fucking hell, you ruined the one-liner."

"Honestly, you should expect this behavior from me now," I answered, glancing around to see our motley group, almost cramped in our small cabin. Noam grabbed . . . Celly, was it? The voodoo girl who'd fixed his arms before.

*Celine Kakoph*, Analyze told me. What a helpful ability. And the other girl was . . .

. . .

No answer?

Huh, I guess she hasn't introduced herself.

I extended a hand toward the elven woman with three swords lying beside her. "Dustin."

She took it. "Tai Gnari."

*Tai Gnari*

*Strength: >14*

Yeesh, no joke.

"And thank you for before," the girl said as she bowed deeply.

"Before?" I asked. Had I met her before?

"Um—" Seeming a bit confused, she continued, "I'm the person you saved from the vines back in the cave?"

"Ah." There was someone like that. "You were that person."

"I know you're face blind, but how bad could it be?" Noam called out.

"Sorry I didn't thank you earlier," she said, bowing again. "I got too excited about my promotion," she said, stroking the bronze plate on her neck. Skirmisher Nine was her classification. "What'd you guys get?"

"Misclassified," I muttered as I pulled out my own tag.

*Dustin (Traveler)*

*Mage (Terrain) 4*

*Mage (Battle) 2*

*Leader 3*

"You're a Hui Ku?" she replied with a surprised face.

"I don't know—"

"It means Traveler," Celine butted in. "It's the Dai way of speaking. Noam's one as well."

Tai looked at Celine. "Ni noi Dai?"

"Shiye," the green-haired girl answered.

Looking impressed, the elf said, "Noi xiang nhien ren."

"Thank you." Celine smiled.

"Ban Noi Da?"

Celine shook her head. "Low Elvish, not as well."

"Still pretty good," Tai said, switching back to Common, presumably after seeing our stupefied faces.

"How many languages do y'all know?" Noam asked.

"Only the three I just said," Tai answered. "Common, Elf Common, and Low Elvish."

"I speak about four," Celine answered. "Normal, Elf, Old, and Under Common. I can understand Low Elvish and Grey Dwarven but can't speak it."

"Damn, that is a lot," I said.

"Goddamn. I don't even know that many," Noam added.

Celine shrank back slightly into her cloak, her cheeks slightly reddened. "It's really easy once you learn one in the language family; they all tend to share words."

"Don't tell my ma that, she's gonna say I have no excuse," Tai replied with a wry smile.

Come to think of it, I hadn't tried Under Common yet. Clearing my throat, I spoke in Under Common.

"Aye, mate, ya thinks dis sands liokes Unda'Commun?" my voice said with the thickest Australian accent.

"Ah, yeh, bruv," she replied, grinning a bit. "Bucking oath righ'ere, ya spoke lioke a natural."

"Was that Common?" Noam muttered.

"Hell nah, mate!" I answered. "Commun ain't nearly as buttahry as dis."

"Buckin' trooth, mate," Celine replied. "Dis is Kantant, not some flow'ry language like Chanter."

Tai shook her head. "Under Common."

Noam made a sound like a crackling fire, then added, "I can speak Infernal . . . Doesn't seem like anyone else does . . ."

"I will just say, if you ever start summoning demons, I will kill you before you finish," Tai said, her face dead serious.

"I will help," I answered, pointing my staff at him. "He'll come back anyway, so he can't be mad at us."

Noam cracked his knuckles. "I'll beat the both of you," he replied with a smirk.

"Highly doubt it."

"You are rather skinny."

"Oh, really?" he said, his smile widening. "I'll throw down with you two! I ain't afraid to cave a girl's face in!"

"He did take out the cultist we were supposed to kill . . ." Celine quietly added. ". . . by himself."

"That can be entirely attributed to us softening him up first," I declared with Tai nodding.

"Oh, now you remember who she is!" Noam replied. "C'mon, Utoqa, back me up on this."

"I was fighting the large creature, so I did not see you."

I fell to the background as they spoke. Damn Noam, I couldn't tell if it was his Charisma stat or his natural skill in bringing people together, but a few minutes with what were essentially strangers, and he had us chatting like old chums.

"Actually, I was curious, why do you carry three swords around?" Noam asked.

"Oh, this?" she asked, putting one of her swords on the table. "It's the reason I'm traveling."

She held it by the grip and the sheath, and then both her arms clenched. Her veins popped as she tried to pull the sword out. She was buff, in a lean, runner's-body sort of way, but no matter how she tried, the sheath didn't budge.

Letting out a heavy gasp, she let the sword clatter onto the table. "This thing's cursed so that only people worthy can even lift it, much less unsheathe it. It's my family's proving test for adulthood."

"Is that so?" I asked. I supposed proving artifacts would exist. "Can I try?"

She smirked and simply plopped the sword onto my outstretched hand.

My hand crashed into the table. I couldn't move it. The sword was simply immovable; I couldn't seem to affect it in any meaningful way even if the volume of the clatter indicated it wasn't any heavier than a normal sword.

"Huh," I said. I couldn't tilt my hand to the side—it was as if the sword was simply locked in space.

Celine gingerly put her hands underneath the gap between the sword and the table and tried to lift it with a groan. Her strength was better than mine, but it didn't budge at all.

"This isn't something that is strength related, huh." It wasn't heavy, otherwise, my hand and the table would've been crushed. I don't even feel that much weight on it.

"Utoqa, could you try?" He had the next-highest strength in the room.

The lizard grabbed the sword by the grip and tried to lift it. An expression of utter confusion when he couldn't.

Tai snickered. "See—"

Noam grabbed the sword by the grip and lifted it.

"—What?" the elf explained, not so much surprise as it was a pure blind shock. "How—how'd you lift it?"

"I mean, it's pretty light," Noam said as he twirled it as much as the cramped cabin space would allow. "Not sure what y'all were troubling with this."

"What the fuck?" Tai exclaimed again. "You—do you know what I had to do to just be able to lift it?!"

"Can't be that hard if I fulfilled—"

"I had to learn how to wash and fix my own clothes, do the dishes, and *cook*! By Nana, just learning to pick the right groceries and cooking took me eight years!"

"I mean, I learned all that since my mums don't always come back home on time and my li'l bro gets hungry pretty often—"

"I had to get a job at the tavern! I worked there serving food and cleaning rooms for fifteen years!"

"Oh yeah, I worked as a barista for a while—not technically legal, since I was nine, but I still know how to mix a few drinks—"

"Not to mention *taxes*! I had to learn arithmetic! Do you know the shabi can't even calculate the taxes they're collecting but expect us to give the right amount?!"

"Yeah, I definitely get that; this one time a gang was running a protection racket and—"

"And book my own doctor's appointments!" she ranted. "Do you know how awkward it is to be the person with a priest telling them about how you tripped and broke your hand?!"

"Well, one time Max ran into a wall really fast—"

"And after all that, I had to move out so my mum could give my room to my di for his start-up company! You know how hard it was finding employment capable of paying for a house in this economy?!"

"That one I've never done, but I did help my mums settle in a better place in the Metros—"

"And after all that, I was just barely able to lift it! Eighty years of my life just spent like that! Then ma kicked me out of the house I barely managed to afford so I could inherit the family style! If any random guy could just lift it, then what the hell was I doing?!"

"Why do these things sound more like general life tips rather than some epic coming-of-age quest?" I asked.

Noam shrugged, resting the blade on the shoulder, which seemed to send Tai fuming. "I dunno, but doesn't this prove I'm more mature than you, Dusts?"

"Generally mature people don't wave the fact around in their friend's face."

"How would you know? You're not mature," he replied with a lighthearted grin. "Sorry 'bout dat," he said, sounding genuinely sorry as he handed the sword back to Tai. "Eighty years, huh? Your kind lives long, right?"

She glumly nodded. "Yeah, wood elves live about four hundred years. My great-great-grandpa was a human, so I'm like one-sixteenth?"

Did they mature slower, too? All the things she'd mentioned a human would've done by their twenties—*most* probably won't, but it was reachable by then.

"What's your shtick then, Celine?" Noam asked. "You fixed my arms pretty well."

"You are a healer of limbs?" Utoqa butted in. To which she seemed to shrink back, not that the lizard seemed to notice.

". . . yes," she replied quietly. Very slowly, she pulled out a bloody doll from within her cloak. "This was um . . . yours . . ." She gestured at Noam. "I, uh . . . don't really like talking about it since people give me weird looks for, um . . . you know." She gestured at the doll covered in Noam's blood.

"I think it's cool," Noam replied, tapping the doll on the head. "Huh, it's like an itch."

"This isn't some kind of dark magic, is it?" Tai said with a measured expression. "That blood on it doesn't look sanitary."

"Um . . . technically not?" Celine answered hesitantly. "It's sympathetic in nature, and even if it is, dark magic is legal . . . um . . . somewhere?"

Tai still looked unconvinced, so I said, "She did fix Noam's arm rather easily." I flicked the doll, to which Noam muttered, "Hey," as he flicked my hand away.

"You didn't feel that, did you?" I asked.

"Felt almost like a fly hovering by my face," he answered. "Kinda less than I was expecting, but you are weak as shit."

"Yeah, you need to know sympathetic magic to transfer stuff like this," Celine replied, pinching the doll's cheeks.

"Ow," Noam immediately responded.

"Intent is also a heavy part of it, not to mention the target's own natural resistance to it, so for me, transferring beneficial effects is easier," she replied as she massaged the cheek.

"Yeap, can confirm," Noam said with a grin.

For a moment, Celine just stared at him uncomprehendingly before she yelped and dropped the doll.

"Ow," he said again.

"I am so sorry, sorry, sorry . . ." She apologized profusely. "I didn't mean to—I'm sorry, I just got carried away with the stuff—"

"It's fine . . ." Noam answered as he picked up his doll. He jerked it around a few times but didn't seem to actually physically move. "Okay, this is weird. I can feel it, but nothing is actually happening to me."

"Yeah, it's strange like that. I, uh . . ." Hesitating slightly, she said, "I wasn't keeping it for weird reasons, it's just that destroying it would be, um . . ."

"Murder," I guessed in the deadest tone I could manage.

"Well, not *exactly*, but it wouldn't be a fun time. So I kept it until the juice ran out."

"This is fun," Noam said. "I can scratch myself in the back!"

"That's what you took from this?" Tai said with an exasperated expression.

"Not surprised."

"How fast can you fix a limb? What do you need?" Utoqa asked.

"Um . . . blood, for one, but hair—or *scales*—would do," she said, gesturing at him. "Ideally freely given, otherwise it won't take as well. After that, I do the ritual and just need to sew the doll back together . . . so, um . . . a minute at most? Less if I already had a doll."

Utoqa nodded, seemingly coming to a decision of some kind as he leaned back in his seat.

"And you three?" Tai asked as she gestured at me. "I saw you throw colored smoke, but that was about it."

"I'm annoying," Noam said with a toothy grin. "If I insult a person hard enough, they'll get burned."

"Did you mean that literally or figuratively?"

"Yes," he answered.

I rolled my eye, adding, "He's also a pretty good fighter," as I gestured to the hook swords he had put aside.

"Um . . . yeah, I didn't want to comment on them, because they look made-up," Tai answered.

"All weapons are made-up," Noam answered, as if it were the most obvious thing.

"I respect your choices on weaponry, but I would not make the same one," she deflected.

Noam simply raised an eyebrow at it and shrugged.

"How did you get so fast at the start?" Utoqa asked.

"Oh, if I piss off a lot of people, I become very strong for a short time."

"Still think that's far too situational," I muttered.

"Hey, hey! That moment was fucking awesome, and you should've seen it, Tai. I was like one man against a whole-ass army!"

"Didn't last long. You needed me to clean up after you," I said.

"Hey! That moment where I batted your cluster grenade of mushrooms into that horde was a fucking play of the game moment, of course, if not for when I insulted that guy's ass to the ground."

Celine seemed to wince as her eyes took on a haunted look. "Yeah . . . that was . . . something."

"And what about you?" Tai asked Utoqa.

"I kill things."

"Yeah, but in what way?"

Tilting his head slightly, he took out his tomahawk. "With the sharp end of a weapon."

Tai's mouth hung open, as she was simply speechless.

"I think she was asking what special stuff you could do," Noam said, "like that finger thing."

"I understand." He reached into one of his pouches and pulled out a finger wrapped in mycelium. "I can craft useful things from corpses. They need to be good corpses to take something from."

"Is that . . .?"

"Yes, it's my finger." I shrugged. "I don't mind, since otherwise my corpse would've been wasted." Also, an idea to constantly generate sleep grenades. I needed to die near Utoqa, but it was still a form of regenerating value.

"And you?"

"Hmm . . ." I briefly considered which parts of my build I should reveal before settling on just the Traveler stuff. My eye I kept hidden behind bark, since I could still see from it just as well, and I was unaware of the value of deific artifacts other than the fact they were rare. "Well, I can make these mushrooms, which I can store a spell on." I created a sporage as an example. "Like Light, Sneezing, Balm, Poison, or Rot, as well as . . ." I turned to the cabin door.

"They should be coming about now."

A hawker in rather colorful clothes stopped in front of the door, his cart clamoring to a stop as glass bottles clanged against each other. On his coat were ten gold coins, each with a hole in the middle, threaded on a red string in a way like a ribbon. A merchant priest. Both Greenie and Yellow hopped off his shoulder.

"So this was the room you're from!" the hawker exclaimed. "Greetings! Greetings! I come here selling great and powerful potions!"

"He was really kewl!" Greenie exclaimed.

"What kind of potions?" Celine asked, interest apparently piqued.

"Well, of many kinds! But if I had to point to my greatest potion, it would be this!" He took a rather large, brownish bottle from his cart. "A potion of *happiness*! Ever feel down? Sad? Depressed? This will fix it!" he said as he waved it in front of us. "Try it! Have a free sample—I guarantee its effectiveness!"

Celine took it, fingers waving a spell that popped out the cork before she took a sniff of it.

She had a stupefied expression for a moment.

"This is just alcohol?"

"And does alcohol *not* bring happiness?!"

We were silent for a moment, looking at his beaming eyes.

"Fuck, he's got us there." Noam spoke first. "How much for the goods?"

"Well, a cheap ten gold will do—"

"Ten gold?" I cut in. "Isn't that a tad expensive?"

"Well, what is the price of empty fulfillment, my friend?" the hawker asked. "Alcohol offers you a way out of the pointless nihilistic stupor you call a meaningful life. What is gold but a fleeting concept in the vastness of nonexistence and the guarantee that we'll all die eventually? So why not drink all your sorrows away?!"

"Can you not say that while literally having money signs on your eyes?" Tai exclaimed. "I mean, ten gold is practically highway robbery!"

"Nuh-uh," the hawker replied, wiggling his finger. "We're on a train, so it's technically a train robbery!"

There was, once again, a moment of silence. But this time out of the sheer disbelief on the size of the balls this man was carrying.

"Fuck outta here!" Noam said.

Tai shook her fists. "I swear, if another one of you merchant priests tries to swindle me, I will hurt you!"

"Yeah!" the wisps joined in.

Under fire from both Greenie and Yellow, who, impressionable little shits that they were, quickly bandwagoned onto our side, we kicked out the priest.

We spent the rest of the day simply chatting, going long after the sun had set, before Celine and Tai bade their goodbyes and went to their own cabin. Noam asked me for a sporage light, which he used to start his reading.

"When you said there were two hundred–plus gods, you really weren't joking, huh," he murmured as he flipped the pages, keeping his voice low to not wake Utoqa.

"Most of these guys aren't important, though; they're minor gods who rule over hyperspecific things. Like this specific tree or that specific place," I commented.

"It's a polytheistic world. Higher deities seem to have Greek god–level power, but local deities are much more localized and not as well-known," he continued as he flipped another page. "Evil gods? Osshiven'Kai? Why would a god of madness and chaos be associated with clocks?"

"Aren't his clocks specifically broken?" I replied.

"I suppose," Noam said, before he frowned as he read about the next evil god. "Weeping Child . . ."

There was a moment of silence. I had read that same page, to not much emotional reaction, however, Noam had paused and sighed deeply.

"So one asshole can torture kids until their suffering manifests a whole new god . . ."

He shut the book, rubbing his forehead. "I'm tired. Night, Dusts."

I knew it was a lie—he simply couldn't continue reading about the suffering. He was a better person than me like that.

# 1.09

---

*"I miss home."*

       *—Adventurer Giridan, a few days before reaching his home*

A strange thing about myconids was that I found that sleeping standing straight was more comfortable than lying down and that "sleeping" to me was closer to a vague torpor state, where I was still aware of my surroundings but not so much actively thinking or seeing.

It was almost like when you were looking at something and slowly lost focus, where you were still aware but not comprehending, not thinking.

So when I heard the crash and the train carriage fell to the side, I, of course, was aware of my body getting thrown to the ground.

Here was the first major advantage torpor had over sleeping.

While Noam was thrown from his bed and into the rather scaly form of Utoqa, I was already awake before my gut smashed into the bunk bed railings.

While Utoqa was trying to untangle himself from Noam, I was already kneeling on the ground and barfing out a glowing blue liquid.

While Noam was incoherently swearing his ass off after accidentally hitting Utoqa's face with his elbow, resulting in several cuts from his rather sharp teeth, I was already standing and swearing with far more coherency than he was.

The fact I didn't get the short end of the stick should be apparent.

"Motherf—mmph! Utoqa, move your knee off my face!"

"That is not my knee."

"Your tail, then!"

As the two of them finally untangled themselves, I was already focusing my manavision outward. Confusion in the other two cabins. I glanced up; the door was on top of us. I was too short and unathletic to reach it.

"Yellow, can you reach that?"

The wisp shook its head. "Yeah, but the door's too heavy."

I cast my bark skin and grew my Bracken Polypores before I absent-mindedly covered Noam's cuts with Balm Spores. "Noam, Utoqa, can either of you get out?"

"Huh?" Noam rubbed away sleep from his eyes before he finally realized we were tipped sideways. "Fuck, on it."

He grabbed onto the railings of the bunk beds, thankfully bolted down, and climbed to the door, kicking it open and hopping out, having to squat slightly at the altered height. I heard the sound of a window getting forced open as Noam popped his head out.

"Shit, Dusts, look through my eyes."

I did, and I saw various moving shapes in the dark. A brief flash of fire far away to the right revealed a dozen short green-skins. Goblins.

"Goblins, Utoqa," I said, the lizardfolk already climbing out. How did they stop the train? Not an obstacle—this was likely a derailment. "Noam can see at least twenty. There's likely a lot more."

"Grab my swords, and also my belt," the tiefling said as he got back down.

I did; the strange dagger Noam had gotten was glowing softly red but didn't speak. Connecting his hook swords, I said the command word that magnetized them. The two linked hook swords were long enough for Noam to grab one by the handle and drag me, demagnetizing them halfway to account for the sideways hall space.

The hall was low enough that Noam had to squat, but I was just able to stand with my head bowed. Utoqa was already out, standing on the windows.

"Yellow, confirm the status of the other passengers," I said as I let the wisp hop off. In this small space, Greenie wouldn't be useful as a damage dealer—too much collateral. "Greenie, I'm going to create another body with Balm Spores. Follow Yellow and fix whatever you can."

"But I like being poison!"

"Just do it," I said, already making the body. "We'll find another wisp to be Balm later, but until then you have to do it."

Greenie made a pouty face, but the small glowing wisp left the body and flew into the lime-green body. Still pouting as it jumped off my hand, it ran after the waiting Yellow.

Both their visions were being watched by Analyze. I'd rely on that to give me an accurate report later. My other self was unfortunately asleep, so I couldn't make more Observers.

I crawled out after Noam. Next to us, Utoqa had an arm covering his face, just as an arrow flew and bounced harmlessly off his scales.

"I cannot see them," the lizardfolk said as another arrow pinged off his palm.

Kneeling down, I examined the arrows, sniffing them slightly. "Shit covered. It appears that they plan on killing us with tetanus. Also, upper right shoulder."

"Ew," Noam said as his blade flicked away the incoming arrow.

"I think Utoqa and I would be fine, but it's a bit dangerous for you—nine con and all. Behind my cap."

Noam batted away the arrow. "Fuck, I'm the only glass canon here, aren't I?"

"Yeah—above, firebolt this time."

"I see it," he said as he casually swatted the fire with his bare hands.

"Can you return attacks?" Utoqa asked me as he seemed to squint into the darkness.

"I'm outranged," I replied, already learning the hard way that I was not a long-range mage. "I'd send you down there to attack, but I have no idea how many of them are there."

They were attacking us from outside our vision—most surprisingly, even mine. Dueling with ranged attacks wouldn't work. Noam could probably yell and hit a few, but if this was planned, then this was likely a large operation, and we should expect to be outnumbered. Attention wasn't what we needed right now. Utoqa could probably go down and take out a few, but even if he was the hardest to kill out the three of us, he was not immortal.

Another arrow pierced through the barrier that was my manavision. "My bottom left leg; ignore this one."

There was a jolt as the arrow embedded itself into my wooden armor. *Didn't pierce into my flesh*, I thought as I pulled it out. That was good news.

Why would they attack the train? Probably to rob it—this train was mainly transporting goods, and the people were a side benefit. The train's guards should already be moving around, but their exact status was still unknown.

Toward our left, I could hear shattering glass. The light of a few firebolts lit up the third carriage from us, briefly highlighting several goblins entering. There were a few returned firebolts, but the screaming that followed were too deep to be goblins'. A defeat in detail strategy? Fascinating, but also annoying.

"Head back inside, Noam. Take care of the person trapped in the room to our right. Utoqa, take guard of the hallway. I'll take overwatch and fortify the outside."

I began planting sporages on the outside of the carriage while Noam jumped back inside. "Once you get the passenger out safely, both of you move in opposite directions and clear the carriages. Noam, grab Celine and Tai before heading back. Utoqa, make a beeline for the fighting at the front and get as many people here as you can."

If this was a defeat in detail strategy, then we needed to group up quickly and concentrate our forces. I was reasonably certain I could hold this carriage by myself and that both Utoqa and Noam should be a match for any number of goblins, especially in a cramped environment where they would only have to deal with a few at a time. We were the fourth carriage from the front, while Celine and Tai were in the eighth, the last passenger carriage before the seating and cargo cars.

"What is a beeline?"

"He wants you to head to the fight and ignore everything else."

"I understand."

They would be robbing the cargo cars already, but I didn't own anything that was being stolen, so saving passengers should be our main concern. There might also be other combatants that we could grab.

"We'll make a safe zone, then head out from there."


Noam threw out a pair of large suitcases, which had trapped a man. "You all right?" he asked as he helped him up.

"Uggh . . ." The short man took his hand and slowly stood up. "Who— what's happening?"

"Getting attacked by goblins, apparently," Noam replied.

"Fucking green-skins. That infestation is everywhere," the man swore. "Do you have a light? It's dark."

"Not a mage. I'll get my friend to make some later—you gotta stay put while we secure the carriage."

The man nodded. "Got it. Thanks, young man."

Noam nodded back before he jumped onto the bed railings, lifting himself onto the hallway again. "Dusts! We need lights! Some people don't have darkvision!"

A few glowing sporages were thrown down, just as another up top was detonated by a stray arrow. Sneezing by the looks of it, Dustin didn't have the time or mana to prepare a lot of poisons right now.

He threw one light mushroom into the man's cabin—"Use this for now!"—before turning to the other side where Utoqa was.

"Y'all all right?" he asked as he poked his head over the other cabin, shining the mushroom to where a mother and child were huddled up as

Greenie covered a small cut on the child. They both nodded. "Goblins are attacking. We'll need you two to stay put."

"Will—will we be safe?" the mother hesitantly asked.

"My friend is fortifying this carriage as we speak," Noam replied with a confident smile. "You guys will be safe as hell, but I gotta go make sure others are as well, so I'm gonna need the two shrooms."

She nodded, letting the two climb up onto her arm before she gently threw them out.

Noam dropped one of the Light sporages down. "This'll be over before you know it; just stay put and don't panic."

To the wisps, he said, "We'll be breaking through to the back of the train, where Celine and Tai's carriage is." He sheathed his twin swords; they were too long to be used in the cramped hallways, so instead he drew Celigarn and the wand he'd "appropriated" off the annoying person. "How many charges did you say this thing had, Celi?"

"Six," the dagger said as it glowed in anticipation. "I can feel it . . . blood . . ."

"I told you, stop that edgy shit," he said as he moved to the end of the carriage. "Good luck on your end, Utoqa."

The lizardfolk didn't answer, instead opening the door on his side and moving out.

Tsking, Noam opened his door, finding the other carriage similarly turned. Landing on the ground, he opened the now-horizontal door of the next carriage, dodging as it flung downward. No reaction.

The environment was not favorable to him; he was too tall. Dustin would do far better here. Was this how Decs felt around him? Didn't matter.

Holding Celigarn with his mouth, he gingerly poked his head over. No people. Crawling in, he quietly dropped Celigarn into his left hand, the other hand holding the wand like a pistol.

"Check the cabins," he whispered, and the wisps rolled off him. Currently, the main points of entry were the windows and the other door, and it was unlikely for goblins to already be in the cabins, but carefulness never hurt anyone, as Decs would say.

Getting the thumbs-up from the wisps, he crawled forward, opening the first cabin and seeing two passengers, a young couple. "Goblins attacking. Get out of here and move to the fourth car from the front."

Next cabin had a single child, so he repeated what he said, this time helping the kid out of the cabin. The third cabin was empty.

"Get out," he whispered to the three survivors as he passed them a Light sporage. "Quietly and quickly. Don't get caught. My friend is warding that cabin. Avoid his mushrooms and you'll be safe there."

There were frantic nods; the couple took the hands of the child and crawled away to the safer cabin.

He made slow progress to Celine's and Tai's carriage, but he wasn't enough of a tank to risk being out in the open like Utoqa. Also why he was sent to grab the squishies—the goblins' plan was probably to work down from the cabins and pacify the passengers before moving on to their objective.

He entered the next carriage; after having the wisps check them out and seeing they were all empty, he carefully moved forward again. Fighting was intensifying at the front of the train; should he risk faster movement? *Yes.*

Opening the carriage door, he hopped out to the side and onto the grassy ground. "Check this for me," he muttered to the wisps as he let them into the next carriage. Now outside, he walked two steps forward before taking a single step back.

An arrow tinked off the metal underside of the train. Right where he would've been if he had walked forward.

Random variations in movement really fucked up shooters who relied on prediction to hit their targets.

"Fucking missed, ya damn idiot!" he yelled. A single fire lit up in the distance as a goblin started screaming and tearing at its hair. *Fiftyish meters. That easy?* he thought. That made things harder in a way—he couldn't Catch These Hands if all the things angry at him burned to death. Regardless, he pushed in his foot and practically leaped as arrows started whistling toward him. Attention was on him now, so he ran the remaining distance between one end of the train to another. Numerous arrows all tinked behind, missing him by wide margins.

*Not as good as the first, or . . .* He came to an abrupt stop, and, grabbing the train wheels, he hurled himself over and onto the train just as something exploded in the area in front of him, rocking the carriage slightly. *Using arrows as a way to pace my running, making it easy for an instakill to get me.*

"Well, I guess all goblins are blind if they can't even hit me!" Four more flames appeared, goblins tearing at themselves as flames burned their bodies. "Or maybe the guy who's leading you is fucking shit!"

Noam tensed as there was a burst of green energy in the distance, briefly highlighting the forms of several dozen goblins and, most notably, a goblin with a stick. The flames extinguished. *Buffing or protective spell—mental* type, annoying, but Noam knew their location now, so he could move in and take the caster out.

Jumping onto the other end of the carriage, he opened the door, letting the wisps out. "Find Tai and Celine," he said as he unsheathed his hook swords. "I'm going hunting."

I saw the burst of green energy in response to Noam's insult. A protection spell it seemed—AOE, given the fact it extinguished the flames on the other goblins. Might be a reactive spell, but just as likely to be normal casted.

One of the people Noam had grabbed hesitantly approached from behind me. "Are you the . . ."

"Yes," I answered. "Go one step back—you don't want to trigger my mushrooms." I only had a few poisons mixed among a majority of sneezing sporages, but they were still there.

"I could help with warding if you would permit . . ."

*A magic user? Interesting.* "What kind?"

"It would take a while, but I could enchant the doors and entrances to be harder to break and enter," he hesitantly said. He gestured to a woman clinging to him. "My girlfriend could also help with lock wards."

"Do it," I said, "but don't risk yourself, and inform me if you need a mushroom moved. It's best if noncombatants stay down for this."

They both nodded and led their kid to hide in one of the cabins. To my left, there was a massive explosion as the engine car blew up. I held my free hand up as the light almost blinded me. Well, there went the train trip.

From the wreckage, I saw several figures run back, throwing spells behind them with their wands. They wore thick clothing—no, judging from the metal studs, they were actually wearing gambesons. Utoqa was in front, leading them to the softly glowing nest that was our carriage.

"Morning," I said as they came underneath me, casually rolling a glowing purple sporage between my fingers. "Fuck," I muttered when it fell out of my hand. I could never get used to a low dex.

"Are you the bronze mercenary?" one of the guards asked.

"Affirmative, and I assume you're the train's guard?"

She nodded. "Guard's captain. I require your assistance in purging the goblins. You will be compensated."

I shook my head. "Not where my talents lie," I said as I gestured to the softly glowing mushrooms dotting the carriage. "I'm setting up this carriage to be unbreachable. If you wanna go hunting, take Utoqa," I said as I gestured to him. "There's another tiefling who should be ignoring my orders and hunting goblins right now, along with two other bronze plates who could help."

She nodded. "We'll rely on you to make a safe spot, then. Do you require help?"

"If you could spare any ranged," I answered. "No goblins will be coming near, but I can't do anything if they decide to shoot us from range." They weren't attacking right now, staying just out of my visible range, but I had no doubt they were moving, utilizing the fog of war.

She nodded toward two other guards, who nodded in return. "You'll have Derrick and Jennice. And do you have any healers?"

I raised an eyebrow, appraising them again. "Anyone in need of healing?" I asked as I stood up.

"Not currently, but we're going to need one," she said.

"One of the bronze mercs is a specialized healer and alchemist. I could do a bit of group healing, but it takes a lot out of me." Tier-two spells were currently a rather big strain on my mana; the one Rot Sporage I'd created used almost forty percent of my pool. I was still regening it.

"Um . . ." The woman from before raised her hand. "I can do some healing . . ."

I turned to her, as did the guards. "Be prepared, then," the captain said. Turning back to me, she asked, "Which carriage was the bronze in?"

"Fourth carriage from us, toward the back," I said, turning my eye toward it.

"You heard the mushroom!" she shouted, gesturing at her fellows. "Lizardfolk, with us! We'll move and start securing the train!"

"Aye!"

# 1.10

*"Strategy and tactics are two different things. Tactics are oriented toward short-term, practical steps to resolve present issues, while strategy is the overarching direction the general or leader wishes to take their army or empire. Tactical victories could lead to strategic victory but just as likely cause a loss."*
—*Excerpt from* The Ebb and Flow, *by Chancellor Chekov of the Western Empire*

As Noam dodged an arrow, he remembered that sneaking up on something in the dark—something that could also *see* in the dark—was a lot harder than normal.

Hence why he was now getting shot at from every direction while his opponents were still nowhere in sight.

"Should've brought a shield," Celigarn muttered with a dim red glow.

"Stop talking," Noam replied as he hooked his swords. "Your glow's just revealing where I am."

He let go of the left blade, throwing the two hooked blades upward, twirling his arm. He began spinning the blades above him like a whip or lasso just as the arrows arrived.

The spinning blade deflected most of the arrows, providing valuable cover as Noam considered his next action.

The goblins could clearly see him, even when he couldn't see them, so they had better darkvision, *and, most importantly*, he thought as an arrow thudded just a few meters from him, they had to shoot upward if they wanted to maintain that advantage. Shooting straight caused the arrows to fall just short.

*And secondly*, he thought as his aura moved to his legs, *they have a mage that outranges all of us.*

He suddenly blasted off, magnetizing the blades so that they wouldn't unlink from the sudden movement.

An interesting thing with Swift Strike was that it was very generous with what is considered a strike, from speeding up a weapon attack to his punches to even something like, say, *striking* the ground.

Noam's feet hit and pushed off the ground far faster than normal; he almost lost his balance at first, but he quickly adjusted.

Moving like a blur, he sighted the goblin mage in mere moments. His blades trailing behind him in halberd mode, he appeared between all of them in the span of a breath. The goblin mage threw up her staff, but she was too late. Noam slammed a foot into the ground, rapidly braking as he transitioned his furious momentum into a twirl. The halberd spun around with him, a bloody dance as a dozen bodies were cut in half.

The eyes of the goblin mage stared uncomprehendingly, her severed torso weakly spasming as it fell to the ground. Her mind caught up to the fact that she was dead, and her eyes slowly glazed over as Noam fell ass first to the ground, legs cramping from the aura use.

He wiped some blood off his face. "I think I'll call this move Spinning Whirlwind."

"Redundant," Celigarn replied, its glow deepening as blood fell on it. "A whirlwind already spins. I say, *Bloody* Whirlwind."

"Too edgy," Noam replied instantly. "How does Ripper Whirlwind sound?"

"The whirlwind bit is too simple. How about Red Night's Waltz?"

"Eh, too much of a mouthful, but we'll workshop it . . ."


Utoqa followed the pack of soft-skins. These were smarter soft-skins, wearing metal hides to make up for the fact that they were soft-skins.

The small green hunters were prowling the location, flickering just outside his senses. The *Batuaqu* were smart hunters, far better at working as a pack than most packs he'd seen.

Utoqa had seen a few exceptions—the hunters of his old tribe, the roving hives of the hard shelled, and the duo of the loud blue-horned soft-skin and the mushroom-wood skin.

He heard the whistling of arrows and turned toward them.

"Arrows," he warned as he covered his eyes.

The soft-skins were slow, not noticing till an arrow caught one in the eye. Panicking around him, they covered their heads, shields coming up in an instant.

"Where are they firing from?!" the captain soft-skin yelled. Utoqa knew the difference between a captain soft-skin and a normal soft-skin—captain soft-skins wore unnecessarily colorful hides and feathers. Probably a display of mating, like the summer birds.

"There," Utoqa said, pointing toward the darkness. The soft-skins really needed to better their senses. Utoqa was still baffled on how they survived as a tribe.

"Can you See them, Reginald?!"

"Aye!" one of the soft-skins replied. With glowing eyes, he raised a magic stick, the object luminous with blue fire before its energy escaped in three twisting arrows. They exploded above, creating bright orbs of light—and revealing the locations of the green-skins.

"Volley! One time!"

Streaks of glowing arrows fired from their magic sticks, obliterating the other pack.

Utoqa cocked his head; perhaps they were not as bad as he thought.

The captain soft-skin turned around. "How many charges do you all have left?"

"One!" the mage yelled.

"None left."

"My wand's out."

"I still have one more . . ."

Utoqa was familiar with these crafts that only had a set amount of usage, though he doubted he could Scavenge something worthwhile from their sticks. The soft-skin called Reginald had interesting eyes, however . . .

"Do you have anything that can be used at range, lizardfolk?"

Utoqa shook his head, a gesture of denial he'd learned. "Nothing that can be used more than once."

The soft-skin tsked. "We keep moving! Swap to your baton if your wand is used! Someone tend to Faleesi! Reginald, lizardfolk, keep an eye out!"

They continued moving, though shortly Utoqa saw something ahead.

"Urrgh . . ." One of the soft-skins ejected their stomach contents as they passed the bodies. *What a waste.*

"So this is what happened to the guards in the back . . ."

"Check if anyone is still alive!"

Utoqa doubted it. The bodies of soft-skins and goblins alike were strewn around; the soft-skins mostly had arrow wounds, hitting the chinks where their metal hide didn't cover. Some had limbs blown off that might've been magic. The green-skins, however . . .

"Does your pack use swords?" he asked, looking at a bisected goblin body.

"What?" the soft-skin captain said as they checked the wrist of a corpse. "No, they're too unwieldy on a train. We stick to short-range stuff."

Then the soft-skin with a heavy sword that wasn't heavy was nearby. "One of the plated was here." He tried to recall a name. Annoying that the soft-skins used names that weren't descriptive of them, like Utoqa, He That Thinks Too Much. "Tai," he finally recalled.

"Are they the healer?"

"No," the lizardfolk answered. "That would be . . ." He paused, then pointed in front of them. ". . . the green-haired one."

Ahead of them, the soft-skin with a heavy sword that wasn't heavy and the soft-skin that was a healer of wounds slowly stepped out of a train carriage that was still standing.

"What the . . . Darcy, Percy, and Gavial, check the rest of the bodies! Rest of us, go forward!"

Cautiously, they began moving in the dark. Utoqa looked around and sensed two presences on the roof of the train carriage next to them. Recognizing them, he simply extended an arm as the two small mushrooms jumped off and landed on him.

There were a few glances toward the wisps, but they were quickly gone as they recognized Dustin's likeness in them.

"There they are!" one of the mushrooms exclaimed as they crawled onto his shoulder.

They slowed as they neared the duo. Celine had the cloak that had no smell covering her head, and Tai held her weapons at rest, but Utoqa recognized the tautness of a predator before the strike.

As he looked around them, he saw a short green-skin standing at the entrance of the carriage, holding a blade to the throat of another soft-skin.

"There are three more people inside," Celine said in a soft voice.

Utoqa could see figures moving inside the carriage; this was one of the open ones, with seats on each side instead of rooms. There was a clattering sound even farther back, and Utoqa sensed that the short hunters were moving things.

The green-skin with the blade spoke up in Common, its voice shrill and filled with malice. "Take another step and he gets it!"

The soft-skin captain gripped her magic stick tightly. "They're robbing the train while holding us here . . ."

"What's on the train that they could want?" Tai asked quietly. Utoqa saw that her hand hadn't moved from her sheathed weapon.

"Not sure, but definitely something big if they hired us on," the soft-skin captain said, gesturing to their magic sticks.

"Anyone know a sleep spell?"

The soft-skin who made the lights shook his head. "No, fuck. I knew I should've taken that elective."

Celine shook her head as well. "Nothing I can do."

"Wait," Tai said. "Didn't Dustin say he has a sleep spell?"

Celine turned toward him—or, more specifically, the wisps. "Yellow, Greenie, I need you to tell Dustin that we need him here . . ."

*". . . need you to tell Dustin that we need him here . . ."*

An interesting bonus from Analyze—though sound wasn't transmitted through Observe, Analyze allowed me to essentially lip-read after a few initial failures. I probably can't read my own lips or those of things without a mouth for obvious reasons, but for the more humanoid types, it was rather useful.

Which gave me an annoying glimpse into the situation at the back. "It appears that our friends are in quite the bind," I said to the two guards left here.

"What happened?" one asked—Jannice, was it?

*Jennice*, Analyze supplied. What a useful ability.

"Hostages at the passenger carriage," I replied. "Goblins are holding them there on the threat of the hostages' lives. Can't move, can't fight, it's a stalemate unless someone goes in and rescues them. Which I may be suited for." Utoqa had a sleep grenade in my finger, but it didn't seem like he'd mentioned it yet. Was he saving it for something?

The man tsked. "Then go. We can hold the place down here. You say your mushrooms explode?"

"Yes," I answered. "Proximity sensors based on the mycelium webs you—"

I paused as three figures stepped into my vision.

Three goblinoids, tall, straight-backed and muscular—hobgoblins, most likely, the evolved variant of goblins. One carried an ornate bow, pointed right at me, and the other two had melee weapons. I caught a sword and board before I was moved. An arrow embedded itself in my shoulder, knocking me off balance as I fell down. Darren caught me and dragged me inside before another arrow thudded on the metal.

"Three hobgoblins just stepped inside my vision range," I explained. "Bow, sword and board, and one other I couldn't catch."

"I See them," the woman said. I barely registered the brief hum of power. "They're the fuckers who attacked the front of the train! They're just standing there—haven't made another move." She flicked her wand. "Do I shoot them?"

"Not yet," I answered. This didn't make sense. "I've been giving them a chance to attack me, but why only *now*?" I asked. I was very literally a glowing target—why hadn't they moved in to kill me until that moment?

"Maybe they're waiting till they gathered up?"

"No," I replied, grabbing the arrow shaft, trying to pull it out, groaning slightly as I did. "The attack itself is suspect. That was a bow user, and they've shown they could hit me from beyond my vision. Scoring more damage on me without warning me like that. No, that shot wasn't meant to kill me. Are they still doing nothing?"

"Aye," she replied, head just popped out the window.

"Then what the hell was it for?" the man asked, grabbing the arrow and my shoulder before yoinking it out, scattering some clotted blood.

"A warning," I said. "One of them is a melee, and he hasn't moved in yet. That attack wasn't meant to hurt me, but to—"

I paused as a thousand things went through my head.

"Genius," I said.

"What?" the man asked. "They're goblins—how smart could they—"

"Shut the fuck up, Darryl," I replied.

"My name is—"

"That act wasn't meant to kill me. They don't intend to attack us at all, not until *we* make a move."

"What?"

"The current situation is favorable to them," I said. "So long as they keep the fighting forces in stalemate, they can get their real goal: the train's cargo.

"There are currently two major forces active on our side—the guardsmen who just joined up with Tai and Celine, and *us*. That action was meant to tell us that if we move, then they will attack us once we're outside our defenses, or breach and kill the passengers here while no one is defending them. Forcibly stalemating us."

I doubted my ability to face off against three hobgoblins; even if I could reasonably damage all of them, their combined disruption and the innate teamwork present in all goblinoids, combined with the fact I would not be playing from my strengths, meant a straight fight would be disadvantageous to me. I wasn't sure how having two others on my side would help this, but their stats weren't that much better than Noam's, indicating low level; with them I'd say the fight was a coin flip. But why had they opted for revealing themselves? If they knew we would be moving, then they could take us out en route without warning, avoiding this song and dance. Unless . . .

"There is good news," I said. "I believe they doubt their ability to take us out in a straight fight, or they don't want to risk themselves."

"Huh?"

"You two are trained guardsmen, correct?"

The man nodded. "Yeah, but we mostly deal with unruly passengers and citizens. Fighting against monsters is technically out of our job description."

"Their mage was taken out—and rather easily, too, by a single person—so there is a good chance they're wary of our combatants. They don't know our abilities, so instead of risking themselves to find out, they want to drag this out until they fulfill their objective anyway."

They win the long game; so long as the goblins move the cargo, then their objective is complete. Risking goblins in fighting was something they would much rather avoid.

"However, that bodes ill for the hostages," I said.

"The green-skins will kidnap them, won't they?" the man asked. "To make sure we don't throw a counterattack on them?"

"Not sure," I replied. "I believe they will, but they'll release them somewhere to divert the inevitable rescue op."

The woman, who had been quietly listening up till now, spoke up. "Then is there anything we could do— Ahh!"

The other guard dragged her down just as I stood up, a Rot Sporage in my hand—

"False alarm," she hurriedly muttered. "Sorry for that . . . The wind picked and I was surprised."

The man tsked. "Fuck, you had us worried!"

*Wind* . . . "Shit!" I poked my head out of the carriage, breathing a sigh of relief as I saw that the hobgoblins hadn't moved. They hadn't realized that I'd just lost an advantage. Not yet.

"Is there anything we can do?" the guard continued.

I shook my head. "Unless either of you has a message spell, I can only think of moving by their plans. My best estimate is that a fight with all three of us would be a coin flip. One side has to resolve the stalemate to move to help the other—"

I paused as someone appeared near the hostage group.

"Oh. Never mind, then," I said. "We don't have to worry about that side anymore."

Noam had just joined the guard squad.

# 1.11

—

*"You may have outsmarted me, but I outsmarted your outsmarting!!"*

*—Astrologist Joseph, during a battle with the True Vampire Aizi Desi*

So that's the situation . . ." Noam muttered as he put away his swords. His fingers drummed the hilt of Celigarn and the wand he'd "appropriated." "Utoqa, you have Dustin's finger, do you not?"

Some heads turned toward him.

"I do," the lizardfolk answered simply.

"And you're not going to use it to save 'em?" he asked, gesturing to the carriage.

There were a few crossed brows directed toward Utoqa when he asked that, but the lizardfolk was unmoved. "I see no reason to save them."

Ah, that sparked some anger. It was like Decs but with none of his already lacking tact. Noam shrugged. "That's fine." Some eyes turned toward him, eyes that said, *of course he's like that.*

"I won't need it to save 'em," Noam said simply to those glares.

"How do you plan on doing it?" Tai asked.

"We take them all out quickly, before any of them can realize and harm the hostages," he replied, drawing Celigarn and the wand. "Which one of you made the light balls earlier?"

A man stepped forward. "I did."

"Can you make another one?" he asked as he looked over his weapons. Celigarn was vibrating slightly—not an issue, and he did seem rather shy around other people.

"Where?"

"Inside the carriage," he replied. "Needs to be bright, sudden, and unexpected—blind their eyes, then move in while they still can't see."

There were six goblins inside and three hostages in total, each held at knifepoint. One goblin was still staring warily at them. The wand had just enough ammo for them.

"I can do it," the man replied after some thinking. "But they might catch me and off them anyways."

"Someone offer a distraction for him as well," Noam said.

"I can handle that," the guard captain replied. "I can pretend to negotiate with the bastards."

"I'll go with you," Tai said, her hand tightly gripping her still-sheathed sword. Noam's eyes lingered for a bit on her hand, callused and tanned, but not in an artificial way. The way her hands looked made Noam think she'd spent years just swinging a sword under the blazing sun.

Briefly, he fantasized about a fight between the two of them, exchanging blows, showing their skills and tricks until one of them ran out . . . He shook his head. "You, too, Utoqa—you're intimidating as hell, so they're gonna be focused on you if you move."

The lizardfolk nodded; that was another one who would be hard to crack. Noam didn't think he could seriously harm Utoqa unless he used his heaviest attacks, while just one hit from the lizardfolk's tomahawk could seriously wound him . . . The thought was enough to make him smirk slightly, drawing some strange glances.

"Now, then," he started, doing a final check on his weapons. "Let's do some heroics."


"It's starting," I said. I climbed out the window, sitting on the upturned side of the carriage and staring at the three hobgoblins. Each returned my stare—that was, until another goblin breached the edge of my vision, speaking in hurried tones that I, unfortunately, couldn't catch. Too far—the lips were too indistinct for me to Analyze anything, but the results were obvious. The hobgoblins prepared to move, taking one last look at me.

I smiled and raised my hand. "My pieces are *better* than yours."

The wind blew in an eastern direction, toward the back of the carriage. It was an advantage lost, because the wind was strong enough to blow away my spores when I cast them, thus rendering my sporages almost useless if detonated early.

But it was also an advantage gained.

From my hand, I began casting Light Spores. The glowing spores left my hand, carried by the wind, and were gone almost immediately, fading into the dark.

Then I cast them again.

And again.

And again.

And again.

The hobgoblins' eyes widened as they saw the trail of softly glowing light exiting my hand and moving toward the back of the train, lighting up the guard group as it traveled, carried by the wind until it reached the back of the train. Dispersed everywhere by the wind, revealing hidden troops of goblins standing in the dark. There had to be at least eighty.

The threat was clear.

Their advantage of darkvision would be lost so long as I remained.

They no longer won the long game.

The sword-and-board hobgoblin smacked the bow hobgoblin, who hurriedly began aiming at me before getting smacked again. His sword pointed toward my mushrooms.

The bow was quickly readjusted and the arrow was loosed, slamming into a cluster of my mushrooms. They quickly burst, but the wind swept the sneezing and poison spores away harmlessly.

*Now make your decision: assist the goblins with the hostages or take me out.* The decision was obvious—were they smart enough to make it? Which of our bluffs will win?

On an order by the lead hobgoblin, the third hobgoblin, who carried a hammer and shield, ran away and disappeared into the night. The remaining two, a bow and the sword and board, readied their weapons. A word yelled by the lead hobgoblin, and a volley of arrows soon came, detonating the numerous sporages I had made, encasing the carriage in swiftly dispersing mist. A few arrows hit me but didn't make it through my armor.

They slowly moved in to attack.

My smile widened as I whispered, "Mistake."


Noam quietly leaped onto the top of the carriage next to the prisoner one. His job was a bit harder given that goblins could see in the dark, but as the distraction trio moved forward, he saw eyes look away and turn toward them.

Another advantage gained as he ghosted his way over. Celigarn was silent, but Noam could feel it vibrate with the anticipation of violence.

"Shh . . ." he let himself say quietly. "If all goes well, then you won't be needed."

There was a thrum of disappointment, but Noam didn't mind. In his other hand, he clutched the wand; the spell was called Force Missile—six whole charges. He'd tested it a few times in Gaia beforehand, and it was enough to blow holes through concrete—old concrete, but concrete nonetheless.

Landing on the package as the distractions did their job, he twisted the bronze ring attached to the wand, tightening it and lowering the blast radius of the magic. Shots no larger than a pencil were all he needed.

"Now," he whispered to Celigarn, whose glow suddenly deepened. Reginald, who had his eyes glued to the top of the carriage, threw his hand forward. A spell he had been weaving behind his back came to fruition.

Noam closed his eyes, then vaulted himself under, shattering the glass with his legs. Numerous shards lacerated his body, but he wasn't paying attention to that.

Three goblins to his right, two with hostages. He fired two shots, each hitting a goblin between the eyes, then, with an aura-empowered jump, reached and slashed the throat of the third. Detecting movement to the back right, swapping Celigarn to an underhand grip, he stabbed behind him and impaled the goblin in the chest. Four down. He turned, pulling the two hostages and jumping behind a chair. The last goblin was backed into a corner at the end of the train, Tai flicking off the blood of the fifth off her blade. The remaining goblin was screaming something, head darting back and forth as it used the last hostage as a shield.

One wrong shot and they could harm the hostage, or the goblin would slash her throat. The heads of both goblin and hostage were erratic, constantly moving and shifting as they panicked in fear. A few centimeters in the wrong direction and the girl would be dead. He wielded a weapon he was untrained with and unused to. A lesser, arguably smarter man wouldn't have taken the shot.

But this was Matt Nguyen. A person neither stupid nor sensible.

Hand steady, mind focused, a bloody red hole appeared where the creature's left eye was, a second dot in its neck, crimson blood spraying from the wounds as it fell back. The hostage girl simply stood there in panic, not even realizing her captor was dead as she screamed.

Tai went to help the girl, and Noam let out a deep breath, allowing himself to focus back into the present. How many seconds did that take? Five? Three? Dustin was always the better timekeeper. As he rose, he realized the hand holding Celigarn was empty but slick with blood; it must've slipped out of his grasp without his notice. A quick glance around found the dagger embedded in the goblin. He tsked and went to grab it—

"Ahh . . . Fuck, yeah . . . Oh, yeahhh . . ."

He heard the low moaning sounds and the voice of the dagger as he neared it. "What the fuck, Celi?"

"Hmm?" Celine poked her head in.

"Not you! Celigarn!" he corrected. "What the fuck are you doing to that corpse?!"

"I haven't been used in centuries! Just give me this moment!"

"Oh my god, are you . . ." Noam grabbed the dagger and hurriedly pulled it out.

"Noooooo!" the blade yelled as its eye flashed red. "What the fuck?! Do you know the last time I touched blood? The last time I was this *moist*? I haven't been this *wet* and *deep* in someone in centuries!"

"You were fucking humping the corpse of the dude I killed?!"

"And you have a problem with that?!" the dagger yelled back. "You enjoy murdering things just as I do!"

"At least I'm not *weird* about it!"

"Don't kink shame me! I thought you were a fellow entity of culture! Why do you think I picked you?!"

"I don't do it because of a weird fucking sex thing! Have you even seen people fucking? It's all wet and sweaty and gross and no one is satisfied in the end!"

"Look! Some people have their tastes and some weapons have their own tastes and—"

Noam shoved the dagger into its sheath and threw a random cloth over it, muffling it somewhat. "Never using him again . . ." he muttered quietly.

Turning around, he saw the silent and desperately neutral faces of the audience. "Anyways, let's move on from this moment." At least three people looked like they wanted to bleach either their eyes or ears or both after the events that had just occurred, so his suggestion was well received as they all silently filtered out of the carriage, hostages in tow, looking conflicted as they pondered whether or not they should be thankful for the rescue or avoid their rescuer like a plague.

As they got out, though, the guard captain snapped to action, gathering the rest to action.

"We need to earn our paychecks! Move out to clear the rest of the train!" she yelled. "Reginald, how many light balls can you make?"

The mage shook his head, sweat dripping from his brow. "That was my last."

She tsked. "Healer!" she yelled, causing Celine to yelp. "Do you know light spells?"

She nodded hurriedly, and Noam noticed Celine had her hands on his doll—numerous stitches were all over it. *So that's what happened to the glass cuts.*

"I do," she began, "but I doubt I can cover the—"

At that moment, Noam sighted a lazy, billowing cloud of glowing spores that was pulled by the wind and flew over them.

Cracking a smile, Noam said, "Doesn't matter. We just need to start finishing them."

"In the end, they made the mistake of attacking," I muttered disappointedly.

"Can you not say that while we're still under fire?!" the man yelled—Darcy, was it?—as numerous arrows thudded into the carriage.

The sword-and-board hobgoblin was running in while cover was sustained by a group of bows. "They probably want to keep us down until the sword and board gets near and finishes us off."

"And do you have a solution for that?!" the woman yelled as an arrow dinged off her helmet.

"Well, I'm already preparing, aren't I?" I said as I planted another sporage.

The sound of arrows stopped, and there were numerous thudding sounds on the top of the carriage, followed by one of heavier mass.

"Both of you, get down."

They did, just as numerous sporages detonated around us. They got most of the sporages *outside*, but not inside. Manavision was also truly broken, but now that I was able to perceive everything within a certain radius of myself, I could activate my line-of-sight sporages much more easily.

Lots of sneezing sounded above; shame I couldn't use the mana on more damaging options, but any more would've been overkill. Raising a hand, I cast a single Poison Spores directly out the window. Sneezing turned to screaming just as something jumped in.

"Now."

The two guards slammed their batons into the knees of the goblin, knocking it down. Where was the hobgoblin? The glass above me broke, and I cast Shillelagh just as the hobgoblin jumped on me.

A sword meant for my face was deflected by my enhanced staff; the hobgoblin fell off, rolling away before shifting to a defensive stance. That was a mistake on my part—I still wasn't used to manavision, no matter how natural it felt. I literally should've seen that coming.

The female guard had her wand up, and Magic Missiles flew from it, but they were deflected by the shield.

We were in a bad position; I was in front while the guards were behind me. In this enclosed space, the hobgoblin could take us one by one.

Shillelagh was still up, so I went for an upward swing, but his shield was faster. His other hand moved, blade darting like a snake, stabbing into me and forcing me back. I spat acid onto him, burning through his shield and dripping onto his arm.

The hobgoblin forcefully disengaged, kicking me back farther, just as another volley of Magic Missiles slammed directly into him.

He felt it this time, the magic forcing him back a step, but a smile was on his face. I turned, a bit too late, just as another goblin jumped down onto the head of the female guard, a crude knife slitting her throat before the other guard smashed its skull in with a baton, all the while screaming.

"Get her into a room!" I yelled as I stepped back toward them, my main eye still on the hobgoblin who readied his sword.

I cast Balm Spores onto her neck, but it wouldn't be enough.

"Pain, pain, go away." The hobgoblin charged me, and I barely stopped it with my empowered staff.

"Rain, leave for next day." He pushed, forcing me back, and my strength was not enough.

"Now feel the numbness." The spell was woven, and my staff glowed.

"Bring Fix-Up Fungus!"

The man dragged his comrade into an empty room just as a glowing green mushroom puffed out healing spores inside. Slamming the door behind him, he held the bleeding wound with one hand, the other trying to catch the errant spores and sprinkle them on her. An arcane lock shielded them.

A punch knocked me over. The hobgoblin was over me, his sword prepared to drop.

"Rot Spores."

The purple sporage on my chest burst, and the hobgoblin screamed and backed away as black rot gnawed hungrily at his legs. He threw away his sword, tearing at his legs, trying to get the black rot off, but all that achieved was getting it on his fingers.

I raised myself up, wincing as my Bracken Polypores fell away, too close ranged, and I lost my concentration on bark skin to cast the Fix-Up Fungus. Already I felt myself getting eaten away. I couldn't stay here for long.

Another goblin jumped in before screaming as it saw its flesh undergo necrosis the moment it touched the purple spores. It died long before it fell to the ground.

The hobgoblin wasn't doing much better; it was collapsed onto the ground, bits of white bone revealed under the rotting black flesh of its legs, extremities already gone.

"You made a bad call," I said simply.

He weakly snarled at me; it likely hurt him to even breathe right now. Lungs had so much surface area, after all, but still, his mouth moved in spite.

"Slaver . . ." he accused. "Stealer of faces . . ."

I did the mercy kill before hauling myself out of the carriage. Nothing could enter there for a while. The passengers and the guards would be safe for the time being, so long as there were no leaks.

Unfortunately for me, with the wiping of the entire attacking goblin squad, they'd learned to keep their distance. I was forced to step back as an arrow thudded into my flesh. *No longer bothering to be in sight range, eh?* I tried to get my Bracken Polypores to regrow, but I hadn't eaten breakfast yet. My stomach was empty, and they refused to grow. I took several dozen more arrows, knocking me down, but only skin-deep, thankfully. Rolling off the carriage, I fell behind where the actual roof was, and their line of sight on me was broken.

They had already lost.

I just needed to buy time; the light was a bluff, because even if I lit up the majority of the battlefield, I couldn't control where the wind went. It could just as easily turn on me and ruin the plan. No, using it to win the battle was ultimately a gamble. The true reason was a distraction, so they wouldn't focus on dealing with the rescue group at the end of the carriage.

Their attempt to divide and conquer us failed the moment a superior force gathered and began systematically wiping them out.

Soon enough, the volley of arrows stopped. A horn was blown, and I saw a mass retreat from everyone's eyes just as the sun began to rise.

Unprotected and riddled with arrows, I simply sat there, leaning next to the train roof as the sunlight made me lose consciousness.

# 1.12

———

I woke up snuggled in a blanket.

A nice sentiment—they'd even covered up the windows for me. I
briefly surveyed my surroundings as well as the eyes of the others. Greenie
had swapped back to its poison body and was on someone's head as they
tended to patients in various stages of not-okay. Celine, judging by the
green hair. Sewing up wounds, not with dolls, but the old-fashioned way.
Noam was in a carriage, one of the staff ones, cooking a meal in a large
stockpot. Utoqa I couldn't see through—I needed to get Observe on him
one of these days, but I saw him when he opened the door to Noam's carriage while carrying a skinned animal.

"Awake?" Declan asked.

"Yeap," I answered.

"Slept for pretty long. What happened?"

"Got shot at," I answered as I got up, explaining what had happened in
the early morn when the idiot was still asleep. Damn casual.

"I heard that."

"Sleep is for the weak."

"Says the person just waking up."

Food sounded good. Finding my stuff stashed in the corner of the room,
I pulled out the fistful of bark I'd acquired and cast bark skin on myself,
shielding myself from the damned sun until I got more food in me. My
staff was in arm's reach, the softly carved-out eyes seeming to twinkle a
bit. As I grabbed it, I became aware of the card that was lodged between it

and the wall. Pulling it out, I saw it was once again upside down, as well as something strange.

The lens was twinkling.

"Hmm?"

"Strange," I muttered.

"Perhaps my recent unlocking?"

"Perhaps," I answered.

Our current understanding of the card was that it was a sort of . . . simple progression tracker that happened to have a certain prophetic element to it.

As for how the prophetic element factored in . . . "If the explanation is true, then prophecy only becomes true if you choose to engage in it," I said. "Which is just so fucking helpful, isn't it?"

If a prophecy only became true because someone decided to fulfill it, then theoretically some asshole could just shotgun random shit until they got it right once. If you chose to fulfill a prophecy, it wasn't a prophecy—it was a guideline pretending to be fancy.

But it was also why I was . . . uncommitted to deciding the symbology of the remaining two empty spaces, the outlines of a goblet and a key.

"The symbology of those two are plenty—the goblet especially in tarot."

"Don't tell me," I said. Theoretically, simply committing to or accepting an idea of what they *could* be would *make* them be. If I decided what they meant, then I would be metaphorically locking them in. It was another reason why I was averse to logging off. There was also the idea of Euler's loop, the idea that faith reinforces faith. The more people believe in something, the more power it will have, causing more people to believe in it. There would be more power to an idea the more people believe in it, thus, following accepted interpretation or symbology would likely mean more obvious power, but at a loss of my own control on it.

"That's why the key is probably already locked in."

"Ha," I laughed dryly. There was only so much a key could symbolize, after all—opening or closing something, pretty simple. Even if the actual item was outdated in my world, the image was still used everywhere it was applicable. The matter of discussion then became what *I* wanted it to open.

"Can it open infinite power? Or, even better, a lifetime supply of tortillas?"

I paused at that.

"Oh, you can't be seriously considering the tortillas. I was joking. We should get HSP or pizzas instead."

"I can't rule that out anymore," I muttered. Something from here had undeniable effects in the real world. It had been proven twice already. I could actually—completely theoretically—use this key to get a lifetime supply of HSP.

"Worth it."

"Shut up, dumbass."

"Son of a bitch silencing my free speech."

"Don't talk about my mother like that."

"*Our* mother." Suddenly my vision was switched to Declan's, just as he played the USSR National Anthem on Ustube.

"..."

"He he he ..."

"How long were you holding that?"

There was a chuckle. "Ahh, far too long."

"It is a good one," I replied with a smile. "How is it not censored?"

"Found it in the Educational History section."

"Whoever put that there is a legend."

"I need to show this to Matt later. Ah, fuck, I still need to tutor that idiot."

"Don't worry—you're both idiots, so you'll find common ground," I said as I left the room.

"I checked his results from last year, and his INT is actually in the negatives."

"That's why you're perfect," I started with a smile. "Two negatives make a positive."

"..."


"How the fuck do you fail at *statistics*?"

"Why do you say that as if you didn't expect this?"

"I feared the worst and was reminded of my lack of imagination," I replied. "And *bio*! What is this appalling lack of knowledge?!"

"Well, bio is just applied chem, and you know I hate chem."

I opened my mouth to retort, but he *did* have a point. "Then why the fuck are you *in* bio?!" Instead of tearing his argument into pieces, I made an ad hominem—truly I had the potential to be a great politician.

"Don't talk shit about me when you're barely passing English."

I tsked. "At least I am *passing*."

"Oh, really?" he asked, pulling up a file. "I read your lit analysis; you're just repeating the same shit the teacher says."

"And what of it? It gets me a passing mark."

"You read *art* and see words," he interjected, probably thinking he was being profound or something. "To you a painting is just ink on canvas. It's dead, bland, and boring!"

"And how is it wrong? Art is meant to communicate a message—that is the sum of it and all it ever will be."

Matt clutched his throat as if he was being physically strangled. He made a very good impression, probably because he'd actually been strangled before. "Just a message, he says! It is so much deeper than just a message!"

"Numerous hidden meanings, biases of the creator, not to mention the cultural context of—"

"All are part of the message," I replied evenly. "The message being biased or wrong or unintentional doesn't make it any less of a message from the creator."

"An author makes their story a message because they think it'll communicate itself better. Humans are ultimately still tribal animals—evolution and new technology doesn't change that."

Matt fell back, his chair clattering to the ground as if he was just thrown. "I can't. You have killed me, you insane utilitarian."

"It is disingenuous to call me a utilitarian while I am in your room doing the rather *pointless*, and possibly hopeless, task of educating you."

"You know, being right doesn't make you *right*," Matt replied as he pulled himself back up.

"If someone wanted to communicate a message, then they can outline it clearly in discussion or a scholarly article rather than put it in a story to take advantage of the mentally defenseless," I said. That was all a story was, a piece of something designed to take advantage of human's tribal hindbrain that we have, bafflingly, not yet removed in order to pass a message or worldview.

"I'm not recommending web novels to you anymore," he muttered. "How the fuck do you enjoy stuff if you think like this?"

"I haven't gotten around to lobotomizing my brain of the outdated parts yet," I said as I pulled some test questions from online. "I can still appreciate art, but that doesn't remove the fact they are meant for communication. Back on track: do these prac tests for me," I said as I forwarded them.

He opened his messages, frowning slightly as he looked at them.

". . . these are seventh-grade questions."

"I have no idea where you are missing knowledge," I replied, "so we're going to go from grade to grade until I find the gaps and fill them."

The sciences were all about foundations; if you didn't know the previous piece of information, formula, or theory, how could you be expected to know or understand the next?

"I could cram everything you need into your head, but that'll just result in short-term memorization and not true understanding. Thus we need to begin from the start and patch everything up along the way."

To his credit, Matt got started with only a minimal amount of grumbling.

Noam riled up an after-battle party, stewing up some kind of small equine creature Utoqa had caught. I hesitated to call it a horse, because while it did have hooves, the teeth seemed omnivorous in nature, and it did possess a thin layer of fur. Rather counterproductive for a distance runner—bare skin was needed for sweat to function, indicating this creature might've been a mixed rush down–type hunter and occasional herbivore, or just a standard scavenger.

Regardless, it did taste pretty good.

A bunch of the other passengers shared their own ingredients and spices, apparently as thanks for us fighting off the goblins.

"And I swear, the fish was this huge . . ."

Beside me, Noam chatted and bragged, his own stew barely touched, apparently the hero of the tale since he'd saved several hostages. Not untrue—he had contributed the most in the battle, killing the mage that likely upturned the train along with resolving the guard stalemate. But he'd simply been in the right place at the right time.

The guard captain was even eyeing him beside me, something she really oughtta make less obvious.

"How did he become such a good shot . . ."

"It involved shooting me many times," I answered. After realizing superior reaction timing and reflexes were the main things he had above me, he'd sharpened them to insane levels. How it applied to a body that didn't have the same level of reflexes was still a mystery to me, but I suspected his original skill still applied, even if he wasn't as dexterous.

I think I got a weird look from her, but I wasn't paying attention that way, instead wallowing in the shade of the train. Sunlight wasn't uncomfortable—no, precisely the opposite. It felt *too* comfortable; the warm rays made me feel drowsy, made me want to take a nap right then and there, even with full covering.

It was a strange experience. I only knew a sun that felt like it was constantly trying to scald you. One that felt like a warm blanket during the winter months was . . . odd.

But the feast slowly ended, and people gradually drifted away, off to do their tasks and salvage what they could from the train.

Off in the distance was a pile of corpses.

* * *

The few that had died were given proper burials by a somber man who held a knitted symbol of a black rose.

I didn't attend, though Noam did, standing silently by the side. I was instead with Utoqa, examining the corpses of the goblins, which had been carelessly dumped in a pile to be burned later. Scavenging birds circled the sky. I hesitated to name them, for they appeared unlike any animal I knew of—four wings weren't exactly a common trait, after all. Having six limbs made me think they were actually an evolved insect, regardless of their lack of an exoskeleton and their feathers. Though that would also put centaurs in the insect category.

Utoqa rummaged through the corpses, his face neutral, but there was a certain ravenousness to his actions. Kinda reminded me of when I riffled through the snack drawer looking for food.

Eventually, he pulled out the corpse of a hobgoblin, the mage Noam had taken out. Utoqa's fin folded and unfolded itself in a brief moment, one of very few gestures of body language the lizardfolk seem to do naturally.

Going into his pouches, he produced some simple instruments, carved from various bits of wood, bone, and stone, and he began working on the corpse. Heading straight to the head, he pried open the skull with great precision, extracting a single piece of crystal.

The crystal was strange, colored a murky green. Its shape was wrinkly and soft-looking, as if someone had petrified a piece of the goblin's brain. Utoqa took it, then opened the creature's jaw, and with a single claw carefully sliced off the tongue.

The rest of the corpse was useless, though he did sneak a bite of the hand. Taking the crystal, he crushed it in his hand and sprinkled it onto the tongue. The thing glowed for a brief moment as it absorbed the energy, and Utoqa was done.

"What does this one do?"

"Put it in mouth to become a mage," the lizardfolk answered as he stood back up. "Will wear out, then it'll become food."

Kinda gross, but the sheer utility he'd just displayed was insane. As far as I understood, Utoqa's creations lasted until they were used. Just by being on our side, he created additional value for every single encounter. While Noam and I were rather specialized, Utoqa was a true generalist fighter. If he had a weakness, then he could just stock up with something that covered it. Not to mention . . .

"Your tomahawk is a Scavenge as well, isn't it?"

"Yes."

"And is it permanent, or have you just not used its effect?"

"Gift will stay," Utoqa answered. "It has no effect other than being sharp and hard."

*Sharp* was an understatement—that thing could cleave clean through flesh and bone. Armor was a minimum to defend against that thing.

"And what did you get it from?"

"A wanderer," he answered, "lost in the jungle. I killed the hunter hunting him. He spoke the dragon tongue and gave me a large bone saying it was called Gift."

I raised an eyebrow. "Didn't think he meant the thing was actually *called* Gift."

"It does not matter," the lizardfolk answered. "It is a tool, and it works well as a tool."

"Interesting story, but—" Utoqa's head suddenly jerked around, eyes staring at a spot on the corpse pile. I couldn't see anything with my eye, but when I came closer with manavision, I saw, underneath all the corpses, a small hand clenching its fist in fright.

Slowly, Utoqa went to draw Gift, but I raised my hand.

"It would be pointless," I said.

The fist was too small to belong to a hobgoblin, so Utoqa couldn't scavenge anything from the body. It would yield nothing worthwhile.

"They will burn the bodies by nightfall, so I suggest getting a move on by then," I directed to the hiding goblin before turning to Utoqa. "C'mon, let's see if they need anything of us back there."

Utoqa's hand left Gift, but still he glanced at the spot where the creature moved. He turned to leave after a moment.

As I went to follow him, I heard a quiet voice rasp, "Why?"

"Like I said," I replied evenly. "It would be pointless."

# 1.13

———

*"And so the journey *hic* begins. Emanuel and his holly band of
*hic* five go on their great quest to *hic* fuck up that Revealing
King!"*

*—Zephyrion the First Seer, at a Lua tavern in the elevated state of
consciousness induced by dwarven holy water*

I refuse," I said simply to the guard captain's request.

"Sorry, but I do, too," Tai said. "I'm not hurting for money, and I don't want to spend half a month scouring some dark cave for goblins."

"What they said," Noam added as he twirled a brown bottle in his hand.

"I can't . . . without someone else . . ." Celine muttered.

Utoqa apparently didn't have an opinion, instead refusing the request for a war council and scouting the area for something worth eating. I would've joined him if he hadn't said I couldn't sneak to feed myself. Sometimes truth really did hurt more than insults.

"But don't you . . ." the captain began hesitantly. I could understand the confusion—we're mercs; we should be jumping at this opportunity—but I wasn't an OCD side quester who had to complete everything that came along.

"If the local government can't handle a constant and recurring infestation, then that's a problem of mismanagement and incompetence," I said. While I would get paid, a private contractor should not be asked to deal with societal problems for payment. That gives a monetary incentive to ensure problems remain unsolved. "You already have backup coming, right? My group will stay until they come, but otherwise I don't plan on working further."

"Fighting in a dank, shit-filled cave doesn't sound my speed," Noam continued, popping the cork of the bottle open and sniffing the contents.

"I'm of the same opinion," Tai said, since she wasn't technically part of my group. Celine nodded cautiously, since she was a noncombatant by herself, though I was curious as to what had happened to her crow thing.

And like that, we all blew off the guard captain.

"You know, I noticed something . . ." Celine began as we stepped out of the still-standing cabin. "The bottle is that merchant's, right?"

Tai snorted. "Don't tell me you actually paid for that crap."

Noam laughed as he sauntered out. "What? No, the guy was crushed under the train—looks like he was at the window when it flipped. I palmed it from his cart."

"A judge could convict you on that sentence alone . . ." Celine muttered.

"I mean, there was no way I was paying for that. It was highway robbery!" he said as he juggled the bottle in his hand.

"Technically what *you* did was highway robbery," I replied as he took a swig.

"I thought we established it was train robbery," Tai said, completely stone-faced.

Noam choked on his alcohol, earning a chuckle from all of us—Celine most likely because it was funny, me because Noam suffered.

Spitting out the liquid, he tossed the bottle, a large portion still inside. "That reminds me, Tai, you said what your second sword does . . . but why are you running around? What does earning a merc license have to do with drawing the sword?"

She thought about it for a moment, pausing near one of the upturned cabins. "I suppose it won't hurt to tell you. I'm following a Path."

For some reason, all of us felt the capitalization of the word, regardless of her rather normal intonation.

"It is the Path of Discipline, a Path my great-great-grandma made. Everyone in my family has been following this Path save my older sister." She drew her blade, letting its edge reflect off the afternoon sun. "You need to pass five different tiers to complete it, at which point it becomes the Path of the Master."

An evolving Path? One that changed with progress? Suddenly I perked up, listening intently to her.

"I've only got two tiers down—the first tier, the Students' Staples, and the second, the Adepts' Acts," she said. "The next is the Journeymans' Jaunt. By following similar steps to my gran, I can reach the same level she did."

"Interesting." I was semi-aware of such things—Paths that could be taught rather than manifested. Symbiosis and Spitfire were both something we grabbed, and two of the guards had See, though they seemed to be much weaker compared to the Survive Path Utoqa had.

"Huh? Then what's the best you can manage right now? Swordwise," Noam asked, eyes gleaming.

"The best, huh . . ." She turned toward the upturned cabin beside us. "I can only use the Staples at will for now, so it's kinda weak."

That did seem to be a worthwhile trade-off, being able to create a universal teaching program at the cost of excellence. The multitude could do much more than the few.

Tai's eyes sharpened.

"But if I focus a bit . . ." Speaking almost absent-mindedly, she stared down the metal underbelly of the cabin. I barely noticed both Celine and Noam stepping back.

I glanced at her, sword held at a stance, as her eyes seemed to intensify. Almost as if she were staring holes into the train's underbelly.

A few moments passed just like that, and Noam was scratching his head as she did nothing.

Then I noticed her blade was glowing.

Tai's sword flashed twice, leaving deep gouges in the cabin. The ear-bleeding sound of metal getting torn apart rang through my body.

*Holy shit.*

I thought Utoqa's axe did damage, but *I* could probably fit in those fucking gouges she just left in the cabin! *Is that the fucking other side I see? Did she cut all the way to— Fuck, calm down.*

I forcibly calmed myself. Focusing outward instead of staying inward.

". . . I can do the Adepts' Acts," Tai finished, catching her breath as she did so.

Noam was laughing and clapping. "Awesome!" he yelled. Celine was politely clapping along.

Now suitably calmed, and I said the first thing on my mind. "Do you have to pay for that?"

The elf's face went blank, and the clapping stopped.

"Well, I mean, that thing still looked salvageable, and you kinda just cut all the way through it . . ."

"Shit!" Resheathing her sword, she dashed back where we'd come, likely to apologize to the poor train staff that would later have to explain why one of the cabins was now in three pieces.

Noam waved as she left, but I stepped forward, surveying the damage.

"I'm no metallurgist, but that looks like steel," Declan said, his attention drawn from tutoring the idiot in real life.

Much like older trains in reality, the outer of the cabin was composed of metal, with the inner lined with wood and other material. Her two cuts had made it all the way to the other end, separating the train into three pieces. It happened too fast when she attacked—I only recalled a brief moment when it had sounded like an industrial grinder tearing apart a car. Perhaps most impressively, the train wheels were neatly bisected. Unlike the rest of the cabin, the metal of the wheels should be significantly tougher and more durable, since they not only held up the cabin but also needed to withstand constant heat and force from usage. Yet they'd been cut as easily as the rest.

I'd made a mistake.

Back in the caves, I told her to disrupt the cultist with me, having her frontline for me while I supported, but if she dealt this much damage, even with that long cast time where she needed to focus, she could've taken out either of them at once. The correct positioning would've been me at the front taking attention off her while she prepared that massive blow to one-shot them.

"*I can swing a sword.*" I remember her saying back then.

Yeah, no shit.


"Fine, let's take a break," I muttered with as much dignity as someone completely disabled could manage.

Matt whooped, releasing his headlock on me. How a person missing half their body could ever manage such dexterity was beyond me.

"You are rather fat—it isn't hard," Matt said frankly.

"So the person with half a body beats the person with one and a half bodies. I see nothing wrong with that."

"Hey, if we median it out then we've got on average one person."

"It's mean, you idiot," I replied, "and you didn't even know those terms until five minutes ago."

"And I am still including them in my vernacular!" he said as he jumped out of the room. "Mom! Dinnertime!"

Shrugging, I followed him out of his room, raising an eyebrow as I found him stopped at the base of the stairs.

Turning to me, Matt asked with a somewhat questioning expression, "Is it just me, or have you become harder to bribe recently?"

"What?" Well, it was completely possible, given the nature of Gaia, but why was my innate corruption where he decided to point it out? "Our mental stats actually rise when we put stats in our characters, so I've been assuming it's rubbing off on our real-world selves."

"Really?" Matt asked with an eyebrow raised. "I haven't felt a thing yet."

I stared at him.

"Dustin?"

"Here."

"Check his status, please?"

**Name: Matt Nguyen**

Age: 16

<u>Mind:</u>

Intelligence: 13-15

Wisdom: 10-14

Charisma: 12-18

"I see I have grown a third head without noticing. Silly me," Matt said. "But seriously, though, give me the number."

"You aren't me, and Analyze isn't technically 'my' power," I said with air quotes, "so there's still massive inaccuracy with the measurements."

"Should that mean something to me?"

"If you had another INT point," I replied as I dodged the roundhouse. Though it was important to note, for all his stupidity, Matt wasn't an idiot. There was a difference between a person who made bad decisions because they didn't know the difference and a person who did because they wanted to see what happens.

"At my best estimates, you are about as intelligent as I am," I said.

He raised an eyebrow. "Then why am I not finding this easier?"

"Because you are also a few Wisdom points lower than me." I realized I was recently more patient, more willing to accept failure, more prone to learning from mistakes and experiences rather than just saying, *I did poorly, nothing can I do about it*, without fixing a single thing.

"If Intelligence is pure data memorization and logical ability, then Wisdom must be the application," I said as I bit my thumbnail. "No, even that is wrong somehow—he's perfectly capable of applying information into practice, so is it a selective thing? Skill-based, perhaps?"

"Then what the hell are the Soul stats?"

Will, Aura, and Perception, with the exception of the last, were the most abstract stats. For what measured a person's will or aura?

"Should I put a few points in to find out?" Matt asked as he saw me deep in thought.

"Aren't you saving for Back—" I paused at the word.

"Backpfeifengesicht," he helped. "I could wait another level."

I shook my head. "Don't, especially not over a whim. Past level six, the next three levels may require a full week *each*, then past that we may need months, then years. The decisions you have to make for the build are final."

"Given our rate of leveling, even reaching something like level fifteen could take decades." That was the simple reality of an exponentially scaling system, especially one that increased this quickly.

"Dragons are suddenly looking like a lot better alternative . . ." he said quietly with a grin. He started walking down the stairs, gesturing for me to follow. I did.

"Please, dragon leveling only becomes better at, like, level fifteen and eighteen, and that's *assuming* my estimations are correct."

"So I probably should still get Backpfeifengesicht," he replied.

How the fuck does he keep pronouncing—didn't matter. "I still think CtH is a bad skill—low applicability for not that good a reward, and you just wasted a skill for learning to beatbox."

At the mention of it, Matt smiled and quickly ripped a few notes, muttering, "Worth it," as he finished. "Speaking of feats, what are you saving up for?"

"Dimension Gate. There are spells on that list that I need."

"Which are?" he asked as we sat around their dining table.

"Tier-two spell, Misty Step, a ten-meter teleportation spell." He whistled at that—indeed, what I severely required was a mobility spell. I lacked not in the damage or durability department, but with my overall low mobility, I couldn't escape a situation if it went south.

"And the other two?"

"The tier-two spell Summon Wisps and the tier-three spell Create Wisps."

I glanced one last time at the scrying orb the guard mage was using, putting it on my to-get list. The relief squad had arrived just a few hours earlier, and we were recompensed for our troubles. Though as I shoved the coins into the growing pile inside my cap, I realized we were going to need better storage. Coins were a much better method of currency when you didn't need to carry hundreds of them. The wisps had made a fucking couch out of gold coins inside my cap. They were small, so it took significantly fewer, but the point stood. My head was mainly storing gold, and if that hat thing the wisps brought didn't remove weight, we would be fucked just by the few hundred gold of wealth we had.

I needed to invest in a bag of holding or something.

Beside me, Noam was finishing packing everything else we owned. Utoqa carried the most of it, given he was the physically strongest of our three-man group.

"And done!" he said as he slung his bag over his back. "This is how it should be, man, just exploring the world with nothing but the clothes on our back and the bags we—"

"We're hobos," I said frankly.

"*Backpackers,*" Noam stressed, "sounds more romantic and more legit."

"Murder backpackers," I muttered, "doesn't have the same ring as murderhobos."

Around us, numerous other former passengers were making their own preparations, seemingly unsurprised that their train trip had been derailed. Though I had to remind myself, in this world there were things more dangerous than people; even in the past, traveling on foot or by any method was dangerous.

"When will we depart?" Utoqa asked.

"When they finish packing," I said. There was a nearby town called Lake Bayt; it was out of the way and it didn't have a Wayshard, but it was the only one nearby. So everyone 'cept the train staff was heading there.

Noam sighed. "An escort quest, huh?"

I shook my head. "No, no, Noam. This isn't a *quest*, because we didn't get it through the merc guild. We just happen to be on the same road. So we won't *officially* get paid for anything."

He looked at me funny. "We're avoiding taxes. Just say we're avoiding taxes."

I sighed. "No flair for theater or double meaning."

"Why is evading taxes the only thing you find worth dramatizing?"

"Because it is something with actual real-world impact?"

"It's morally wrong!"

"You know that's never stopped either of us . . ."

And we continued to bicker as we set off.

# 1.14

——

*"Many people go on adventures to explore the wider world. There are indeed many things that are worth seeing, but the large majority of traveling is simple boredom, walking on an endless road with little to see but dirt and grass."*

*—Lithian the Dust Treader*

We made a strange group.

A line of loose travelers, some fighters, the others just plain civilians. Traveling along a road by the barest sense of the term—it was little but slightly flattened ground with the occasional stone or boulder by the side, marking where the road ended and the wilderness began.

Given the fact, I was differently statted. "Slow," Declan snidely remarked.

I had to remain toward the back of the line, where only Utoqa was with me, having matched my pace.

Unlike others, all Utoqa did was walk beside me; he occasionally jerked his head to the side as he spotted some movement, but for the fiveish hours we'd walked together, we didn't exchange a single word of conversation.

I had never met a person I liked more.

It was around midday where the group ahead began to slow down.

Straining my eye, I saw them stop to sit and rest around a clearing at a crossroads. There was a small pile of stones in between the intersections and what seemed to be a massive bleached rib cage towering over the clearing.

Noam slowed as the others did. He saw it long before he reached it, the pillars of white contrasted against the woody browns and greens all around him.

His voice, too, drifted to a slow stop as he stepped into the clearing. It was small but could accommodate their motley group, with two other paths branching out toward the side. Between the intersection of the two roads was the unassuming pile of stones, and towering around the clearing were eight—no, *nine*, he thought as he spotted one slightly obscured by bushes—nine massive bony ribs, enclosing the area like a cage. Each at least three times taller than himself, with the longest looking like it was eight meters tall at the least.

Some of the people toward the front headed toward the small pile of stones, Celine one of them. They picked up or took out small pebbles, tossing them onto the pile, before turning to the clearing and making camp. Celine, meanwhile, took out a flask of something, pouring some clear liquid onto the pile as she muttered some quiet words.

"What are they doing?" he asked around him.

One of the people, a brown-haired kid who looked as old as he was, said, "Oh, they're just paying respects to Bundriroc."

He searched his mind for the name—one from that thick-ass book Dustin had dumped onto his lap and expected to memorize. "That's the wild god of the Elder Pantheon? What's a pile of rocks got to do with him?"

"His shrines are piles of rocks, specifically those marking boundaries," the kid continued, pointing toward the intersection. "That pile shows where the road ends and the wilderness begins. Bundriroc keeps them separate so something won't wander into the roads and we don't wander into the wild."

Noam supposed that made sense for a guy called *Boundary Rock*, though the spelling was a bit different. He walked forward, stooping for a moment to pick a random stone off the ground before throwing it onto the pile as well.

Celine had just finished her short prayer as he neared. "What'd you pour?" he asked.

"Animal oil," the mage replied. "Most people just throw rocks, but Baba said oil is better if you're being devout."

"Huh," Noam replied. He extended a hand. "Can I get some as well?"

"Erm . . . Sure?" she said as she handed the flask to him. "You can ask for some luck or safety as you travel the roads, but don't ask for *too* much. And don't expect it to be answered."

"Got it," he answered as he took the flask. After swishing it around a few times, he poured a smaller amount, aware that this was Celine's and not his. "I want to see something new," he said quietly.

He heard Dustin's slow but steady footsteps behind him, and, corking the flask, he handed it back to Celine. "Thanks."

"Can you get anything from the bones?" Dustin casually asked Utoqa as they neared.

Noam noticed that Celine flinched a bit, almost imperceptibly, as if surprised those two were nearby. For some reason, she seemed to avoid Dusts and particularly Utoqa.

"I do not believe so," the lizardfolk replied. "It is an old bone. Bleached. It might be empty of power."

"Don't ruin the scenery, man," Noam complained. There was an ominous feeling in the bones, but not something threatening, as if the bones were saying he would be fine so long as he stayed within them.

"Please don't," Celine whispered quietly. "Don't mess with holy sites, please . . ."

Dustin turned to her. "Whose is it?"

"Bundriroc," Noam answered. "Throw a stone on the pile—apparently it's good luck or something."

The myconid raised an eyebrow before shrugging and picking up a rock to throw onto the pile.

"It is strange, though," Celine said, pulling her cloak tighter around her. "The pile is a lot smaller than it should be—"

Whatever she was trying to say was interrupted by a roar so loud the ground seemed to shake as Noam threw his hands over his ears.

It ended quickly, and, ears ringing, Noam asked, "Hey, is there a god of conspicuous timing or something?"

"What?" Dustin yelled as he held his cap. "WHERE THE FUCK ARE MY EARS?"


It felt like my entire damn body was vibrating.

Given the fact I had yet to locate my ears, or whatever magical hearing organ I had, I could only ineffectually cover my cap as the sound rattled me to my damn core.

It felt like the sound was shaking throughout my entire body. By the time the ringing ended, I barely caught Noam saying something as Utoqa jerked his head outside the clearing.

I saw it.

Large, quadruped, and shelled. Standing at almost three meters tall, it lightly resembled an ankylosaur, except it had a long, protruding neck that raised its maximal height by another two meters. The creature's head wasn't armored, yet it bashed its skull into the bleached rib cage, roaring as it did so. Stumpy beak-like mouth, crushing type—a nut eater?

It slammed the side of its head into the ribs again. What was it doing? There was enough space that it could've just entered and attacked us.

Beside us, the oil on the stones lit aflame.

"Oh, no," Celine said, her eyes widening. "That's bad."

The creature slammed its head into a protruding rib again, and the flames seemed to intensify.

"Oh," Declan said. "That's what it does."

Utoqa and Noam already had their weapons drawn. A single glance toward the tiefling's direction had him blasting off, the lizardfolk following immediately after.

They would be able to make a dent in it, but this needed to be ended as quickly as possible. I walked forward, singling out Tai from the crowd. Her weapon was drawn, and she shot toward the creature, but I yelled at her. "Tai! Use your hard hitter! We will keep it in place!"

She glanced toward me, nodding as she ran behind the two. With both hands, she held her sword in front of her, eyes slowly focusing as Utoqa and Noam circled the creature.

No attack had been made yet. This thing was large enough it could seriously damage a squishy with its thrashings. Judging by the way the ground shook as it slammed its head, only Utoqa and I could take a hit unscathed.

My finger itched as I neared it, last to do so, as everyone had already taken positions. Yellow was on my head, helping me keep track of the burning pile of stones.

"Greenie, swap with Yellow." The wisps quickly swapped places. CC was more useful here.

I raised a hand, feeling the tenseness of the situation. Tai likely felt it the most; beads of sweat were falling down her face as she stared down the creature.

The flame sputtered as it ran out of oil.

One of my fingers burst as I used Pacifying Spores, the racial skill puffing the creature at close range. The thing shook its head in confusion, and as it did so blood splattered onto the ground. Its head was *bleeding*—what the hell was its purpose?

The thing seemed to sight me and roared again. Its beak-like mouth sent spittle across my face.

There were no canines inside the creature's mouth; the beak tip wasn't sharp enough to tear flesh. It was a damn herbivore.

Utoqa and Noam moved almost in unison, slicing the thing's unprotected ankles, letting it crash to the ground. Utoqa smoothly transitioned into slashing its back, but his tomahawk only left a deep scratch in the shell. Noam moved away; the thing was in its death throes as it slammed its head into the rib one more time.

Tai delivered the final hit.

Her blade flashed once, and the creature was cut in half from the shoulder to the back leg. It let one final, weak roar as it fell dead.

Letting out an exhausted breath, Tai said, "Good . . . I can't manage more than one act at a time."

What the hell was this thing's deal?

Utoqa didn't sheathe his weapon; instead, he scanned the surrounding wilderness, body taut as he searched for another threat hiding somewhere. Noam joined me as I examined its head.

"It was bashing its head," I muttered. "Why?"

The creature was likely an herbivore; its beak and shell both showed this, indicating it was likely a passive creature. It was unlikely that it was attacking us, if it even was "attacking." No, it seemed more interested in slamming the side of its head into the rib than attacking us.

Examining the head, I found small holes, natural—likely its ears. That side was heavily bruised as blood leaked freely.

"It was bashing its ears against the rib," I muttered in a realization that only led to more questions. "Why?"

"No clue. I was hoping you had an idea."

"Its actions were strange," Tai said as she joined us. Her sword was already sheathed. "Might be a disease of some kind."

"Could be," Noam said behind me. Yet their voices seemed to fade as I noticed something in the blood that soaked the ground.

Words. Words were written in blood.

*Fear the Deafening Silence.*

"Do you see that?"

"What?" Noam asked.

I blinked. It was just normal blood, splattered on the ground. No words were written in it.

"You didn't see that in the blood?" I asked again.

"What was in the blood?" Tai asked.

Shaking my head, I said, "Nothing, I must've imagined it." Though I committed the event to memory.

Belatedly, we set off. Many theories were thrown about the Thunder Shell's strange rampage; most people settled on some kind of strange disease. Something like rabies. It was a probable explanation. I didn't deem myself knowledgeable enough to know the symptoms of such a subject. The event was unsettling, but as the sun reached its height, we were on the move. Safe spot the shrine may be, but we didn't want to be in the wilderness when night fell. Especially when the nearest town was so close.

People were visibly relieved as the town entered sight, some even hastening as the sunset drew long shadows on the ground.

Noam was waiting for us at the small gate as the others talked to the one guard. The woman opened the gate and let us in.

"Welcome to Lake Bayt, I suppose," the guard said with a drawl as we passed by.

"We're probably the most interesting thing that happened to her," Noam whispered to me. "Small town, nothing new happens—I can see it already."

I raised an eyebrow; even behind the fences I saw that the town was rather large. Thirty or so buildings with many of them constructed of stone, though not many had lights on. Probably related to the fact we were in an era akin to mid-industrialization. Light sources must not be widely available yet.

Following our group, we neared one of the larger two-story buildings—an inn with a sign naming it the Owls' Roost.

Looking around, I barely noticed Celine, even farther behind us and shrouded by her cloak. Tai was way in front of us, taking the lead for the group as she booked a room.

We slowly streamed into the inn. The place was a lot emptier than I expected; fewer than five people were already inside the dining hall, which could have housed a few dozen people at most. Our group streaming in filled the majority of the space, with a line forming by the counter as people rented rooms.

Noam dumped his bags to the side as he took a seat by an empty table. Utoqa and I soon joined him, seeing the line not shortening anytime soon.

"Fuuuuuck, I'm tired," he groaned as he stretched his arms. "God, those bags were heavy."

Toward the center of the inn, a man struck a note on what seemed to be a lute.

"Weary and beaten, so many travelers have come. / To this dirty piece of nowhere, they must be dumb . . ."

Noam looked around for a waiter, but the only employee seemed to be a young girl rapidly checking in the line of people.

"Looks like a while before food," I said, to which Noam sighed as he fell back, defeated, into his chair.

"I can provide mushrooms?" I suggested helpfully.

Without opening his eyes, he muttered, "Then I'll be as high as you are."

I rolled my eyes.

"He is not tall," Utoqa replied, his eyes scanning the large dining hall.

"He doesn't mean high as in height, but in being drugged."

"I see."

"Anyways, let's rest the night," Noam said. "God, walking around nowhere was more tiring than I thought."

"What did you expect?" I answered. "You have ten stamina."

"I'm too tired to answer, but please imagine a witty comeback for me," Noam muttered, eyes still closed.

I raised an eyebrow, just as Greenie pinched me and pointed toward the girl at the counter. Now she was rushing around, moving as if she were three people, carrying sets of ingredients toward the hearth, where a large pot boiled with water.

A rich smell soon permeated the hall, and I prepared myself for a boring night.

# 1.15

---

*"I know I made a vow of pacifism, but if someone wants to throw hands, then they best expect to catch 'em!"*
*—Priestess Emilia the Thrice Excommunicated, moments before her first excommunication from the Church of Light due to beating 382 armed men with her bare hands*

I should've known better than to expect a quiet night.

"Little bitch you are, / Yer won't get far. / Cuz I'm about to hand yer ass, / With my superior sass!" Noam rapped.

The bard scoffed as he strummed another random chord.

"Blithering of a fool, / You think you'll win this duel? / You shall learn that in rhyme, / I am your superior this time!"

As the crowd cheered at the two idiots, I quietly tried to ignore them and eat my stew.

"Woo! Get that fucking asshole!" Tai yelled beside me. "Don't fucking lose!"

"Oh, please, no need to fear, / There will be ample reason to cheer!" Noam sang.

Should I even bother remembering how the fight started? It was all starting to blur together. Since he was pretty passive recently, I'd almost forgotten my friend was one of the most . . . rambunctious individuals I knew.

"Not that you know that many people," Declan remarked.

Fair, but I would like to think I have a good grasp of human beings in general.

"There will indeed be much reason to cheer, / But not any reason for you to be so cavalier!"

Noam's smile only deepened in response to the other bard's taunt.

* * *

When was the last time he'd had this much fun?

A thing he'd never tried. A partner to dance with him. A challenge to overcome.

Noam laughed, the sound bright and true, marred only by the fact that his face looked like he'd escaped an insane asylum.

His opponent was waiting for a reply. Noam would give it to him with all the tender love of a family member gifting their beloved nephew a Christmas present.

"Bard of skill, why do you carry a lute, / When I could play it better with my boot? / With my foot, a single toot, / Better than anything you've made with your suit!"

The bard hesitated to strike his instrument again. Indeed, he *was* just randomly strumming chords, but that did not stop his voice.

"Far traveled, long of step, / You think I'll come near you after that schlep? / Put myself near your shoe, / And the smell will make me blue!"

"You speak of scent, / But do not say where you went, / It's clear you've never felt the wrath, / Of a decent bath!" Noam yelled back.

"Your rhymes lack flow," he shot back. "Thus they lack blow. / An amateur I face, / And an amateur I will mace!"

Noam's reply was swift.

"You sing of beating and yet I speak, / Do you wish to run, are you that meek? / This battle will be settled, / By the superior mettle!"

The crowd cheered around them. Yet neither of the two saw the crowd. Only each other.

Noam briefly felt in the distance a mushroom turning its head, but he was soon gone, forgotten as a twinge of power flitted through both of them.

In that brief moment, the world was only them two.

"A Clash you seek," the bard sang as if spell struck. Noam didn't understand what powers were occurring, only that the trueness of his intention was transmitted.

The bard struck a chord, this time no longer the random strumming of a man playing.

"You are a fool, and a fool I will not critique!"

A Clash of skill, a battle between two Challengers who have recognized each other.

"Let us speak! Let us shriek!" the bard yelled, his fingers nimble and dancing beautifully across his lute.

"If it is a Clash you want, then it is with Clash we'll flaunt!"

There was a sharp stabbing pain in Noam's arm, right where the scars of Celine's healing still lay fresh. But he couldn't care less as he replied, "Come! Let us face off, / In a battle, no one will scoff!"

Embers lit up the bard's hair, not something given by Noam's original skill, but a vision of the future. Of power he could obtain should he *win*.

The prelude was over.

"Bold you are, coming to a battle of wits completely unarmed, / It's not too late to quit, 'cause you will get harmed!" the bard sang, and the world sang with him.

Droplets of blood leaked from his head, and his scar cried in pain, yet they were naught but minor distractions to the pure joy Noam felt.

"If I am unarmed, then you are a vegetable, / Speaking with confidence with rhymes barely presentable! / I am disarmed to make it fair, / For you are so lacking in dramatic flair!"

As Noam threw open his arms, flames burst forth from the embers, licking at the bard's hair and stubble, yet the bard only laughed. The same insanity in Noam's eyes was reflected in his.

"Arrogant child, what are you smoking? / For no matter what, you will be left choking!"

The stitches holding his arm began to rip, leaving it hanging off slightly from the stump as his opponent **Rhymed** the damage of the past.

"From dirt and dust you came, / And dirt and dust will reclaim!"

The bard refused to let up, as the droplets of blood leaking from his head turned to a full waterfall, forcing him to blink back as his vision was stained red.

"Played the fool, lost your cool, / Ended up just a tool, / Now so many to mourn, / You are merely forsworn!"

Noam's arm fell off completely, and he was thrown back, his head slamming into the packed dirt floor. He gasped, and in that brief moment, his mouth opened, and something flew out. A glowing orb attached to him by the barest threads, it slowly cracked and was destroyed, becoming the barest dust.

Noam knew at that moment he had lost Biting Words, the spell and its slot forever destroyed, something that would never return no matter how many times he respawned.

The veil separating them and the rest of the world cracked for the briefest moment as Dustin stepped in, his stubby hand held out to him. A plea to stop this madness before he lost something important.

Noam did not reach for the hand.

For how could one feel joy if there was no risk?

As he staggered back up, he brought his remaining hand to his mouth and, at that moment, poured all his soul into the sounds he made. The short tune of beatboxing locked and emanated around him.

"That was a low blow, / But I shall reply with gusto."

How the bard knew of the past did not matter. Maybe it was a skill; maybe he was stalking them. The reality was, Noam had just lost an arm and something more.

"Like the boy in the mirror, I come ever nearer."

Yet still he smiled as he took a step forward.

"Bitch, you think I don't know? / Speak my flaws, use 'em as ammo."

Slowly, Noam regained his momentum.

"Bullet after bullet, all wound and bleed, / Doesn't matter, I follow my own creed!"

A roar of the soul, of something great, of something unyielding, of something innocent and true.

"Even if undead hordes all come crawling, / Even if the skies are falling, / It doesn't matter, cuz I'm still balling!"

Flames burst forth, consuming the other man fully, yet still, the bard stood his ground.

"You thought you came to win when you came to retire, / Because you faced a man who speaks straight FIRE!"

Finally, the flames turned blue, and his opponent grunted and fell to a knee.

Within the flames, Noam saw it, the Path of Spitfire. Not the fake he held and wielded, but a truth he could take.

And he hesitated when he realized it could only be gained in *taking*. However rightfully he'd earned it, the man would lose in the same way he'd lost Biting Words. It was an equivalent exchange. A transfer to those worthy from those who weren't.

The world said he *deserved* this power.

Noam let go, the flames sputtering out, revealing the heavily burned but living man underneath. His knees collapsed underneath him, and Noam fell to the ground. The strange, altered world where they fought disappeared as others rushed to check their wounds.

Dustin's cap soon loomed over him as the myconid looked down.

"What did you gain from that?" his friend calmly asked, his anger impossible to notice unless you knew to look. "You permanently lost a spell, took severe damage. You got *nothing*."

Noam smiled. "I got satisfaction."

* * *

Noam was put to bed, his wounds swiftly tended and our pockets lightened as I forced several dozen gold coins onto Celine for fixing the idiot.

As I stepped out into the night, I realized I might never understand how he felt.

Doing something without gain. Purely for the satisfaction of it. For me, satisfaction only came from gain. I could understand respecting a capable opponent, but to take joy from losing—I couldn't comprehend it.

There was no light outside, but I saw just as well. The outlines of buildings, the rustling trees. A bell sounded, signaling midnight. Drawn toward the sound, I saw a large, church-like building, though attached to an additional building that seemed like it was meant to house a lot of people.

The bell that rang was silver, glinting beautifully in the moonlight. Yet as it stopped, I noticed a crack on the bell. Broken and tarnished, the crack seemed to gnaw at the beautiful object.

And perhaps it was the noise of the . . . incident, but as the night came and the residents moved to rest, it felt like the world was silent.

I heard no noise in the night, no skittering bugs, no moving nocturnal creature, no rustling trees. As if there was a great noise that I passively blotted out, only now being silenced. It was as if the world itself had decided to just shut up.

It was a silence that felt deafening.

# 1.16

_______



*"The first friend I met, I played with for a hundred and one nights.*
*Then he died, a smile on his lips as I bested him for the first time."*
                              *—Wundull, the god of games*

As I returned into the inn, I saw that Utoqa was still sitting by the table, head still scanning, as if searching for something in the room.

"Not tired?"

"I am," the lizardfolk answered simply, not bothering to elaborate as he continued to scan the room.

"What are you weary about?" I asked, pulling a seat beside him.

It took him a while to answer. His head still spun around, and he occasionally turned his waist around to look behind him. I waited, patient and curious, before he finally answered.

"I don't know."

That raised an eyebrow for me. "Why are you worried if you don't know what you are worried about?"

"I don't know."

I struggled to keep the frustration off my mind. Utoqa's mind literally worked differently from mine; he didn't have the frame of reference to add subtext or reason. "Will you be able to rest properly?"

"If by rest, you imply a full sleep, I do not believe so." For the first time, Utoqa turned and looked directly at me. "A night watch would be useful."

My eyebrow rose again. "Describe the threat and the feeling you have."

"I do not know what threat. All I do know is that my instincts tell me to be prepared."

My mouth made a clicking noise, just as I felt Yellow plaster itself on the side of my cap. "Prepared against what?"

"I do not know."

*Fear the Deafening Silence.*

For some reason, those words returned to me, and I briefly looked out the window, seeing my glowing reflection in the glass. Glass—something I realized with a start was pretty advanced. Though there might've been some sort of magic that made it common.

"Let's hope it's nothing," I said.

"It may be something," Utoqa replied. His lizard face was utterly unreadable, even if I knew he was worried.

"That is why we prepare," I answered. "I'll shroom up our windows and keep watch. I am reasonably certain I can stay alert the whole night without negative consequence." I was a nocturnal creature, after all.

"Very well," Utoqa said, rising from his seat. He headed toward the stairs before he awkwardly turned his head toward me. Awkward in the fact that he seemed to have taken the effort to make the movement smooth and slow instead of his usual sudden jerk. "I am relieved."

"You practiced head turning?"

"It is a necessity to be able to communicate without causing alarm," the lizardfolk answered.

I simply raised an eyebrow at that, which he admirably tried to imitate, a feat ultimately useless given that he didn't have eyebrows. "Wait up," I said as I caught up to him.

Placing a hand on his back, as I could not reach his shoulders, I defocused. "Declan?"

"**Observe**," he immediately supplied.

Utoqa almost leaped as he felt the power, but he held his ground as he stared directly at me. Eyes unblinking.

"My eyes are yours."

Neither a question nor affirmation, but something in between.

**Name: Utoqa the Tribeless**
Race: Variant Lizardfolk (Oasis-Touched Tequalan)
Classes: Artificer Level 1, Survivalist Level 3
Total Level: 5

<u>Body:</u>
Strength: 14
Agility: 14
Dexterity: 15

Constitution: 17
Stamina: 16
Vitality: 14

Mind:
Intelligence: 9
Wisdom: 13
Charisma: 4

Soul:
Will: 6
Psyche: 7
Perception: 21

Racials:
Natural Armor and Weapons, Hold Breath, Magical Darkvision, Variant Biology.

Class Skills:
Artificer:
Path: Scavenge

- **Scavenge:** A trick that allows him to craft magical items out of the corpses of creatures. They are imbued with aspects of the creature's power but tend to be one use only unless the creature was very strong.

Survivalist:
Path: Survive

- **Survive:** Three charges. He may expend one charge to regenerate from one instance of lethal damage and be brought back to consciousness. If Utoqa were to die, this automatically activates if he has the appropriate charges. This ability does not heal existing wounds or ailments save for those causing death.

"They are," I simply answered as a new vision opened up. "We'll get a move on as soon as possible. If you're freaked out, then there's no point in staying in some random town."

We rented a single two-bedroom, a solid seven or eight meters in length with a bed placed against the width of the walls and a large glass window in the middle, directly in front of the door.

Utoqa crept into the sheets of the unoccupied bed as Noam snored at the other end, swiftly falling to sleep. I stood by the window between them, the sparse moonlight peeking through from behind dark clouds.

I planted a few sporages around the window—three on the bottom width and five on both the left and right length. Proximity ones, with their heads facing outward to avoid friendly fire. An unfortunate trait of my spells that made me poor for enclosed team combat, but a worthy trade-off for the sheer room-clearing power I have.

Like that, I passed the night, standing between an injured ally and a paranoid one. Mind dimmed, but ready at any time to respond to threats.

I was thankful that nothing happened.


Rain pattered the window when I refocused. It started slowly at first, gradually building up until it became a torrential downpour. It happened so slowly my torpid mind did not pick it up. I simply heard the sound and wrote it off as it built.

I turned around, noting that the sporages had not been disturbed and had in fact withered over the night. I collected the ten sporage husks. Probably useless, but it was nice to check if anything could be done with them.

From my side, Utoqa opened an eye, the action . . . lazy. "Netakata . . ."

"What?" I asked, not too quietly it seemed, as I dodged Noam's pillow.

Slowly, the lizardfolk spoke. "Cold . . . Resting day . . ." Then his eyes slowly closed, asleep once again.

Oh. He *was* a lizard. Cold-blooded, huh—didn't actually think about that. It was kinda chilly, though the dampness that was seeping in was extremely comfortable.

"Wisps." Both stood at attention on my cap. "Keep watch of them. If someone knocks, ask questions on why they're here. If someone breaks in, sneeze them and ask questions later. If someone attacks, poison them and also ask questions later."

"Got it!" they replied in their chirping language.

"You, too, Noam," I said to the figure pretending to be sleeping. "Make sure our gecko is safe."

"He's a monitor lizard at worst," I heard him reply hoarsely.

Leaving the room, I made sure to close the door quietly so that I wouldn't wake anyone with my movements. It was still early morning, 5:36 a.m. if real-world time translated one to one, though I suspected even if I made a lot of noise, the sound of the rain was quite literally enough to drown it out.

Slowly I stepped down the stairs, wincing slightly as they creaked underfoot. I wished to test a theory of mine, because even if I had a racial weakness for desiccation, I had never yet actually felt thirsty or the need to drink in any way. An oddity, and since it was raining outside, I figured I should kill two birds with one stone as I stepped outside—

The rain pelted me, each drop like a stone slamming against my body. I'd underestimated the intensity of the rain—it was severe, to the point that I actually sank a few centimeters into the muddied ground underneath.

Worse, I underestimated the intensity of my reaction.

Calling the sensation orgasmic would not be too far off the mark, however, it gave incorrect connotations of sexual pleasure when I felt none of the sort.

But in terms of pure intensity and legitimate pleasure, it was an apt description that didn't do the feeling justice.

Every droplet of rain I sensed entering the small area of my manavision. Every droplet of rain that hit me felt like a master masseuse unraveling a knot of muscle. Every droplet of rain that rolled down my body felt like those videos where a high-pressure water hose cleanly washed away dirt and grime.

The mud beneath soaked into my stump-like feet, cool, relaxing, cleansing.

It was so refreshing, I literally didn't know a word or language that effectively communicated how refreshing it felt.

Like carrying a heavy bag a long distance, slowly getting used to it, then shedding it at the destination, feeling the freedom on your shoulders as the weight lifts.

Like a full spa treatment, your body lovingly cared for by an army of masters—muscle knots, tiredness, dirt, and sweat, all removed so thoroughly you felt like a completely new person.

Like waking up after a long night's rest, feeling fully invigorated, the feeling of arising completely energized for the day. The quiet but steady energy of rest.

It was all those things and more. If I ever had sex in this life, I could confidently say it wouldn't be as good as this.

For a while . . . I simply stood there, my original plan of casing the perimeter long forgotten . . .


Dustin returned to the inn, his body heavily soaked, yet he was positively glowing with energy. Literally, his body was glowing noticeably brighter than previously.

"The fuck happened to you?" Noam asked as he came in.

"Nothing much," Dustin replied in a visibly more . . . *chipper* manner.

Something akin to horror began to fill Noam's face. "Oh, no. Which poor sod did you scam?"

Catching the mushroom thrown at him, Noam laughed. "Great! You're still the same ass."

"He's always had the same ass?" Greenie said as it crawled onto Noam's shoulder.

"No, I mean as in—" Too late did he catch the mischievous look on the wisp. "Man, everyone's disrespecting me now," he said with a lighthearted chuckle as he turned around to see a man bandaged from head to toe.

The bard beside him coughed, his voice still hoarse and slightly burned.

"By the gods, you are zestful. I wish I got the same restful."

"Yo, Dusts, meet Fareeq. He's the awesome guy who took one of my spells!"

"I noticed that," Dustin replied as he took a seat by them. Slightly bowing toward Fareeq, he introduced himself. "Mornin'. I'm Dustin. Sorry for the trouble this idiot gave you."

The bard waved away the apology.

"'Tis all fair and good, / I lost, that's what stood. / He could've done worse, / Yet I left with only a voice hoarse," the bard said, managing to be surprisingly eloquent despite his state of injury.

"Let me help, at least." Dustin raised his staff. "I have a few rhymes of my own."

"Pain, pain, go away, / Rain leave for next day, / Now feel the numbness, / Bring Fix-Up Fungus," he quietly chanted, and his bark skin faded away as a mushroom, about the size of a sitting stool, erupted between the two injured individuals, seemingly not disturbing the dirt underneath it.

Dustin hadn't gotten a good look before, but the mushroom had a quite distinct appearance. Its cap was completely white. The cap was multilayered, with each stratum stacking upon the last like a bundle of cloth. He quickly realized that the mushroom seemed to breathe as it shrank and expanded. The action was mesmerizing, almost like looking at a jellyfish. Each time it "breathed" out, he saw the frilled underside of each layer and a wide puff of healing spores puffed out, attaching themselves to the two nearest, Noam and Fareeq.

The bard smiled.

"You are most kind, / To give me peace of mind."

"No need for thanks," Noam said. "He's not listening."

Dustin really wasn't, eyes studying the way the spores seemed to stimulate the body to knit itself back together. Nets of mycelium covered the wound before they disintegrated, a tiny piece at a time, leaving unblemished and clean skin.

The healing was slower than all the rest Dustin had seen before, but he knew it would grant more in the long term.

Another disadvantage was the fact he couldn't control the release of its spores, but that was a problem good positioning could fix.

The doors slammed open, and the roar of the rain briefly loudened as it found a way in. The chilly breeze got even Dustin to look toward the door.

"Farry!" a short creature, probably a gnome, yelled, "I heard you got *roasted* recently!"

The bard groaned. "Day after day I say, no skill or tact in puns, only wordplay."

There was a chuckle as he neared the table. Bowing, he said, "Greetings, greetings, apologies for my friend. He cannot speak my name due to an unfortunate curse."

"A curse?" Noam asked.

The man's face turned gravely serious. "Indeed, it is a curse of rhyming dealt to him by Tilt."

The god of kids or something, Dustin recalled, hand itching to grab his notes.

"I swore only once! / Near a child who was a dunce!"

"Oh, shit, isn't Tilt the goddess who bleeped people?" Noam remarked, finally making something useful of his education.

"Aye," the bard answered, looking poignantly at the tiefling.

Chuckling as Noam covered his mouth, the short one introduced himself. "Anyways, I am Corvian Diluvian Medudian Himotonana Farraday the Middling, priest of Wundull. Pleasure to meet you!"

"Well, if there was any question of whether he's a gnome or halfling."

Corvian Diluvian Medudian Himotonana Farraday the Middling reached to shake Dustin's hand, shaking the arm with gusto when the myconid hesitantly reached out.

"Well, I'm Dustin."

"I'm Noam."

"I'm a Greenie!"

"Fascinating!" the gnome replied before turning to the heavily bandaged man to his left. "Are you still up for today, Farry?"

The bard scoffed. "A battle of wit I will not lose, / Today is the day your defeat comes in twos!"

"Whoa, whoa, aren't you still a bit too hurt to do anything?" Noam asked.

Both gnome and bard looked at each other, then at Noam, before laughing.

Throwing off his heavy wool coat, the gnome revealed a sling bag from which he pulled out a metal box, approximately the size of a . . .

"Deck box?" Dustin asked.

Fareeq pulled out a similarly sized box from his back pocket, then in unison they slammed them onto the polished wooden table.

"It's time to—"

"I THOUGHT I TOLD YOU TWO TO STOP SLAMMING METAL ONTO THE TABLES!" a high-pitched voice yelled from behind the counter. Both replied at once.

"Sorry!"

"Madam, I give my sincerest apology, / But I need to give him a whooping surpassing his psychology!"

"The table is on your tabs!" the girl yelled back before turning back to her job of cooking enough breakfast to feed her several dozen new customers.

"This . . ." Dustin hesitantly began.

"Is a card game?" Noam finished.

"The very one!" Corvian replied, gently removing his cards and splaying them out for view.

"Artwork is professionally made. Cards themselves are very well cared for," Dustin quickly assessed. The cards were placed in a thin transparent covering that seemed waterproof. "What is the cover material?"

"Looks like plastic," Noam said as he quietly gestured a "may I?" toward the cards. The gnome nodded happily, and Noam picked the cards up.

"Dwarven soft glass," Corvian answered. "A delightful invention. Cost me a prince's ransom, but as a devout priest I have to ensure my tools of worship are well maintained."

"Wait." Noam stopped, carefully placing the cards back on the table, and looked the gnome dead in the eye. "Worship?"

"Wundull is the god of games, of course. I worship him by playing."

Noam squealed with all the joy of someone who had just found their god.

Age of Wonders was a surprisingly in-depth and well established TCG. While Noam tried his hand the first time with a spare deck, I watched their three-way game with interest.

The game could fit anywhere from two to four players, with home-brewed rules that could even allow a fifth or sixth; however, four was the intended norm. It was a mixture between a classical tabletop war game and a trading card game, with different factions based on real-world people, locations, skills, and magics, but despite that, decks still followed conventions I was familiar with.

Noam was playing a midrange aggro orc raiders deck, focusing on getting beefy units onto the board to rush down an opponent.

Fareeq was similarly using an aggro deck, but where he differed was that it was a drow deck, focused on placing unblockable stealth units onto the field. The individual units were not particularly strong; however, their unblockability made them able to rush down Corvian and later Noam.

Noam set down his cards. "Cursed stealth units."

The bard chuckled. "Remember not to curse, / Else you end up somewhere worse."

"Your rhymes are the worst part about you, my friend," the gnome chipped in. "Friend Dustin, do you wish to play as well? You have been staring at our game like racca hawks to a meat pie."

"What's a racca hawk?" Noam asked as he shuffled his deck cleanly. The overly talented bastard wasn't even looking as he did so.

"Imagine a raccoon that can fly and dive-bomb," Corvian casually answered, much to everyone's mounting horror.

"I wouldn't mind," I replied to Corvian's question. "Do you have any more decks?"

"Do I?" The gnome chuckled as he placed the bag onto the table. Cheerfully, he removed six other boxes and placed them in front of me. "What kind of priest would I be if I wasn't ready to convert people?"

"A pretty bad one, I guess," I answered noncommittally as I picked them up and began checking my selection.

I looked through all of them once or twice, figuring out their ideal tempo and curve, before I settled on one, a control deck centered around undead.

"This one?"

Both the priest and bard went deathly silent.

"Corvian you fool, you still had that? Do you really want to end up dead as a rat?"

"I can't just toss it, *Jaga Kai*."

"What's the sudden tension 'bout?" Noam asked.

"That"—Corvian pointed at the deck in my hand—"is a Revenant King deck, and as you know, there are certain people who get . . ." The gnome paused, looking around as if to spot a hidden threat. "*Burny* about those things."

"If Wundull is not a god most good, / Friend of all that could. Then will come a crusade, / No matter how we prayed."

I raised an eyebrow at that, though Noam seemed to get something I didn't and glanced at me. I carefully put the deck away, then selected the next one I'd had my eye on.

"What about this?"

"A deep deck? Careful, else you end a wreck."

"Bah! Deep decks are a solid all-rounder choice—you have a good eye, mushroom man!"

"Can we play?" both wisps yelled out.

"My familiars want to play as well," I translated.

The gnome quirked an eyebrow with amusement. "Take your pick, then!"

"How 'bout we raise the stakes a bit?" Noam suggested. "Loser buys everyone a round."

I raised an eyebrow.

"I shall enjoy my free drink then, / Earned without lifting a pen!"

"Ho ho? You've played one game and think you're ready to face us?"

"We won't lose!" Yellow declared as Greenie was mesmerized by the pretty card art.

"Declan?"

"What?" came an irritated voice. "I'm in class."

"I need your help winning."

"Why should I—"

"The loser buys drinks." My real self froze at my words. "Noam suggested it."

Slowly, Declan put down an old pen, his attention completely shifted away, for we were both aware there were things worth more than education.

"Game?"

"TCG called Age of Wonders, 'five' players, with air quotes. Mana system. Fusion with a board game . . ."

With my manavision, I saw Noam smirk, knowing my lack of response was a good enough response.

He was not the type of person to let me half-ass things.

# 1.17

—



I underestimated how hard this game could be.

The game rules were simple: each player started at one corner of the board. Starting with five cards, each turn they drew one and aimed to drop an opponent's fifty life total to zero. The board started as a flat, empty expanse, but by playing "Terrain" cards, you could change the terrain to be favorable to you, and as long as you held the terrain you could "Tap" it each turn for elemental mana. Units had four stats—damage, range, move speed, health points, in addition to their special. To attack something, it had to be within their range, which was represented by the empty board. The rest should be self-explanatory. This was already somewhat similar to TCGs I was already used to playing.

Where it differed was how uncomfortably powerful aggro decks were.

Usually, aggro decks were naturally disadvantaged in a game with more than two players. The purpose of such a deck was to constantly play low-cost, high-damage cards to rush down an opponent before they could properly react. Such a playstyle meant that they would use cards faster than they could draw them, leaving them out of steam once their initial rush died down.

However, it seemed like the decks both Noam and Fareeq used accounted for this. Fareeq's draw deck had the 'Combo' keyword, where playing multiple cards in succession gave him greater value by making the last played card in his turn several times more powerful.

He was not the largest problem, as he had his forces split testing everyone's defenses, not committing to a single person until he found a weakness.

It was Noam who was the most annoying.

"You've done nothing but attack me this entire game," I said to his smug face.

"Well, you're the biggest late-game threat here, aren't you?"

Correct. Deep was a control deck, a deck that excelled in slowing down the game until they reached the late game, where they could throw all their powerful cards and win via superior value. Deep, specifically, was a terrain control type, seeking to change the board into water terrains, where they could play high-stat sea monsters to close out the game.

Noam's deck was a mix between aggro and midrange, where he possessed some of the explosive start of an aggro deck but also the midgame power of a midrange deck. His orc raider cards increased in strength every time they defeated a unit, took terrain, or dealt damage to a player, which made me extremely cautious of developing, as any unit or terrain I threw down could snowball into a quick defeat. But without such defenses, I wouldn't be able to stop him from attacking me directly. He forced me into a careful tightrope of ensuring I had *just* enough to keep me alive until I gathered my win conditions.

Considering the rock, paper, scissors analogy with the deck trifecta— aggro, midrange, and control. Generally speaking, aggro beats midrange by bursting them down before they stabilize, midrange beats control by reaching their power spike faster, and control beats aggro by playing constant stall cards that a low-cost deck cannot effectively deal with like midrange.

"Card advantage is still ours."

Indeed, though I was the one most pressed in this battle, I still held the most cards in hand. I was the only control deck present, however, which was largely due to me holding a lot of high-cost cards I couldn't play yet.

"Yeah, at this rate we'll be dead in four turns."

That would not do. After deliberating together, I played a card from my hand.

"Cerulean sculptor," I said, tapping three sea and three basic mana, placing the squishy unit directly within a horde of orcs.


It was a battle to be remembered. One that will be sung among the highest pantheons by angelic choirs. The names of the warriors to be venerated in the halls of Kraag Thetai.

Dustin played Cerulean Sculptor, the triton card flooding the land around it with its special, once again stalling a furious assault by another turn. No stranger was that myconid to card games, Corvian Diluvian Medudian Himotonana Farraday the Middling thought. Every move he played was textbook—calculated and thought through. Yet there was hesitation in every play, the anticipation of answers he might not be able to respond to. Perhaps it was that anxiety that allowed him to play so well, to anticipate moves his enemy could not even imagine.

Noam, meanwhile, was someone who seemed to ooze confidence, every move he made with conviction. Every attack was committed, yet despite that, he was *bleeding*. Not literally, as he still had forty-six life, but metaphorically. He only had three cards in hand now, and his assault against Dustin had dropped the myconid to twenty-two life, but it was clear he was running out of steam.

"Damn, looks like I can't finish you off," Noam muttered.

"You deserve it," Dustin replied almost absent-mindedly.

"Well, does anyone want to pick up the scraps?" Noam asked, glancing smugly at Corvian.

"Shit," we both went. Cerulean Sculptor was my last board-clear card. I played it under the assumption that it would essentially beat back Noam's assault. My hand tightened, though I was careful to not scrunch the cards. "Those things are valuable."

We wouldn't be able to deal with another full-fledged assault. I could see both the gnome and the bard considering it—Corvian most so, since it was currently his turn.

Noam set me up.

Almost hesitantly, Analyze whispered information I had ignored—no, information of things I didn't believe had occurred.

Name: Noam
Classes: Skald Level 4 → 5
Mind:
Intelligence: 13
Wisdom: 10
Charisma: 14 → 15

He had leveled up, a single point of Charisma gained by his growth stats. A single point, enough to make me passively tunnel on only him. "The train battle?"

"No," I answered, as both my power and I sifted through information. Combat was not the answer, as he had experienced plenty already. A few goblins weren't worth much. The dividends of the train encounter couldn't have leveled him. "He leveled up sometime after coming here . . ."

This was not a purely combat-based leveling system. What had he experienced that drove him over the edge? Was it the rap battle? Or did he level up after playing his first game in Age of Wonders while I watched? Regardless, Corvian played a card, moving his units toward my ruined base. Declaring an attack.

I moved my units to block. Could I survive this? "Now is no longer the time to conserve cards."

One of D's easiest weaknesses was bias.

Though he dropped ideas and strategies the moment they were proven ineffective, he kept to them *until* the moment they were made obsolete.

A slight bit of cunning, building on his already-present bias of the TCG being a two-player game, made him tunnel vision on Noam, constantly attacking him and only him to implant the idea that so long as Noam was dealt with as a threat, it'd be smooth sailing.

All to take advantage of that brief moment when D's bias was proven wrong and he could not adapt fast enough.

Noam smirked behind his hand. Though he'd spent all his cards to make the bluff worthwhile, he'd survive longer than Dustin.

Corvian Diluvian Medudian Himotonana Farraday the Middling played an adventurer deck. It was a midrange deck, focused on gathering the party, playing five different unit types that each represented a part of the adventurer's party. Each card became stronger the more the party was filled.

He currently had three of those roles filled: Hasan Vashard the Lunar's Edge, the rogue of five who slew the Chaos God of Life Simon the God Noodler, the fisherman who caught the Catfish of Wisdom with his bare hands; and Giridan the Lost.

The attack went poorly, as they neared, the seas beneath them erupted as monsters tore at the waterlogged units. Dustin hadn't managed to fully sink the terrain yet, so the sea monsters didn't have their absurd late-game stats, but still, the myconid placed him in a situation where the ensuing trade would result in him losing all three units. Corvian had enough mana to activate two of the three's special abilities. Simon could either allow him to draw one card via the Catfish of Wisdom or deal AOE damage to all adjacent units using his Boot Catcher. Giridan's special could randomly teleport him and another unit anywhere onto the map, while Hasan's special was not something he wanted to use until he drew Aisha.

As the gnome agonized over the thought, his mind peering deeper into the webs of possibility, the cards of all those playing began to illuminate softly with a rich golden glow. Dustin raised his eyebrow at this, just as Corvian came to his choice.

"Channel Divinity," he whispered softly. "The Theater of the Mind."

And his god answered.

The world changed. No longer were they mere men, sitting around a wooden table playing with cards. No, they were now witness to an Age of Wonders. The six of them stood as the world turned to battering rain, the roar of the sea only eclipsed by Simon's own howl.

Corvian no longer needed to speak his actions, for they were true to all who watched. Giridan grabbed the Lunar's Edge by the scruff of the neck as he pulled out a map, together disappearing from the world and landing somewhere else. Meanwhile, Simon stood alone on a small raft, surrounded by great krakens, sea serpents, and devourers of ships, and he *laughed*.

Water dripped off the man's chiseled form, skin forever darkened by years under the sun. Fabulous blond hair rippled in the wind, flowing like the waves themselves as he took out his weapon. Boot Catcher, the fishing pole that had never caught a single fish, its string made from the tendons of the Land Eater, its wood taken from when he split the world tree with his bare hands, giving birth to the phrase "Get two trees with one punch."

Simon swung the weapon with the force of a newborn typhoon. For a brief moment, the world stopped as his swing created an artificial vortex, sucking in all the rain and sea. The kings of the deep were sucked into this whirlpool, dragged into the depths by the wise man of water. And though he perished, he did so gloriously in battle.

This was the Channel Divinity of Wundull's greatest domain. What would've been a mere accounting of card statistics became the final stand of one of the greatest fishermen that ever lived. All who witnessed the games played under this Channel Divinity would see it as all others imagined it: epic battles between gods and men. Struggles against the malevolent powers that be.

Wundull was considered a great among the gods, his name whispered with the same respect as the highest pantheons. For he alone achieved a Channel Divinity that was unrivaled among all in a single aspect.

Duration.

While all other Channel Divinities acted either as a single act or the moment of intervention not even surpassing a few moments and breaths, the Theater of the Mind would last for as long as the game was enjoyed.

The greatest example was that of Antigone, the One who Bested Wundull, one of the countless goblin slaves to the Dwarven Imperium, the shipment carrying him and his fellows was intercepted by Thought

Stealer Cults. Their minds were about to be devoured before Antigone wagered all their lives on a game against the Eldest Mind Eater Karraxthian Vazzackainan.

The resulting Channel Divinity lasted three months.

Game after game, even though Karraxthian never managed to defeat Antigone, it was said during the battle that Karraxthian was driven to the point where he used the brains of seventeen great scholars, philosophers, and mages, while every move by Antigone was a thing of such beauty that watchers wept rivers, creating the Lake Antigone.

Even now, in this game, Corvian could feel it, the ripples of simple joy and enjoyment. He felt like he could keep this Channel Divinity for weeks without end.

Wundull was not a god who asked for prayer or faith, yet was given both. For the God of Games, what was a greater act of worship than playing—nay, *enjoying* a game with both friend and stranger?

"Okay, that was fucking awesome."

Dustin had to agree with Declan, even if the end result was utterly disastrous. His left field was wiped, leaving him completely exposed on that side. When his turn came, he needed to start moving units or risk being the first dead.

. . .

Noam slipped toward the wisps, whispering something as they played a Circle Cadet . . .

. . .

Indecision marred Fareeq's face, for though it was his turn, all his units were positioned away from the hole Corvian had opened. He wouldn't be able to attack Dustin this turn, so was it worth repositioning for a future attack?

. . .

"Calculate the chances of him having 'Warcry' in his hand with a hundred-card deck and twenty-three cards drawn . . ."

Dustin didn't originally think this was necessary, using Declan as a means to access a digital calculator, all in order to work out the probabilities of which cards each player had, but the time of playing had ended.

. . .

The wisps looked around the battlefield, their attempts at understanding how their decks worked lost the moment something cool happened.

. . .

Fareeq came to a decision and committed every unit he had to killing off the deep player; his deck threatened them all once he had all his resources, and Dustin had repeatedly demonstrated he was able to make use of them.

. . .

Fareeq moved in, and Dustin threw down all his units. They were weak now, literally fish out of the water, but he had to stabilize his situation or lose in two turns.

. . .

It was difficult, but Dustin managed to make it out with only eight life. He had to spend those more carefully now, for life was expendable like any resource, with only the last one being important.

. . .

Noam chuckled as Dustin rebuffed the combined attacks from three other players; the myconid was half-dead but still in. As Dustin's turn came, he decided to throw a life buoy.

"I guess I'll attack Fareeq now." Eyes turned to him, one of surprise, the other glimmering with opportunity.

Dustin's sea monsters moved to surround Fareeq's units, so that they might slow them down while Noam burned him to the ground.

. . .

New Xin Shi had fallen, the city of the drow a burning wreck as orcs and drow alike battled through the flames. At the edges there stood adventurers, a fragile alliance to take out the first truly defenseless player.

Fareeq's units couldn't make it back to his base fast enough, and he had significantly fewer tools to survive a direct assault compared to a deck made to last till the late game.

There were now four players left.

. . .

"Tsunami." Dustin finally drew the card he was looking for, and the land around him finally flooded. He had entered his late game; he had reached deep.

Now the game was a question of if they could survive long enough to kill him.

. . .

"Aisha Vashard, the Solar Sword." Corvian played Aisha; the once-mortal stood on the battlefield, her brown skin illuminated by a halo of light. Hasan, whom the gnome had desperately kept alive throughout multiple skirmishes, stood beside her. Brother and sister finally united.

The Blades of Sun and Moon finally stood together before an endless encroaching sea.

But he had tapped all his mana to get Aisha on the field, so he needed to wait another turn before activating their dual special.

. . .

Noam finally began frowning; powerful sea creatures now began consuming the board. Land disappeared under an endless torrent of water, which was a severe disadvantage for an orc raider deck. He drew a card, not expecting much, before he laughed as he saw a familiar name.

"The Demon Chef." A broad green back filled his vision, hefting a massive but trusty axe. This version was younger, printed just after he slew and ate the demon known as Therubim the Garden of Wrath, but he was no less powerful for it.

. . .

Dustin slammed Corvian with everything he had, using the spell Slipstream to forcefully create a path where his sea monsters could attack. He didn't damage Corvian directly, but he managed to achieve his true goal, separating Aisha and Hasan, so that they no longer occupied adjacent cards.

. . .

Monsters at the gates, the land was being consumed. What greater stage than for a party of five to take? Aisha filled the role of a fighter, Hasan the rogue, Sepulchral Priest as the healer, Mollymauk Tea Thief as the bard, and finally Sorcerer Aspirant. Two of the cards weren't Named, but such battles were the forges of new legends.

Now Corvian merely needed to get them together. He drew a card and found it. A spell card simply called, They Met in a Tavern.

. . .

Dustin played a high-cost card every turn, for he knew if the five-man band was assembled, then Corvian would become a threat capable of dealing with his unit's massive stats and terrain advantage with special abilities.

Two of the five were together, Mollymauk Tea Thief and the Sorcerer Aspirant. Already, he and Declan had formulated countless plans to ensure the party was never formed—

"We win!" the wisps suddenly yelled as it came to their turn.

"Huh?"

Noam slapped his thigh and laughed.

Yellow stood up, smugly adjusting a tie that didn't exist. "If you will, my dear sibling?"

"Of course!" Greenie yelled as it slapped down a card almost as large as it was.

All of them read the card.

"Magus Fireball. When you cast a spell, add a Fireball spell to your hand."

"We have three circle cadets," Yellow explained. "Each circle cadet lowers the cost of spells by one."

"How did you get three—"

"Clone and doppelgänger," Dustin muttered. The rule of these decks was that there could only be a single copy of each card. Using clone, the wisps could create another circle cadet, while doppelgänger could take on a card's stats and special ability for a single round. Enough that the resulting Fireball spell Magus Fireball created per spell cost zero for that single round.

"No matter how much fire, you cannot cast far, you would not be able to damage all with your star," Fareeq cautiously pointed out to the wisps.

The gnome was first to remember what card was in that deck. "They have the farsight orb."

A legendary equipment card that raised a mage unit's range to absurd levels, to the point that a single mage could cast and hit everyone on the field.

"And since Fireball costs zero . . ." Dustin let the word trail out, just as explosions erupted all around them. "An OTK deck, blasted."

OTK, a deck archetype that was descriptive of what it did, for the letters stood for One-Turn Kill. Unlike Dustin, not one player bothered to stop them from reaching their win condition.

The wisps were the winner, and Fareeq, who had been waiting for the epic battle between heroes and monsters to conclude, grudgingly took out his coin purse.


"God, I need to fill my sugar stash," Declan muttered as he glanced around the almost emptied cabinet. He'd been required to think at full force more than usual lately.

"You are burning through that stupidly quick," Dustin said. "Sure you don't have diabetes yet?"

"If I do, I'll just visit the hospital," Declan replied as he took one lone chocolate bar from the cabinet. Unwrapping it with practiced precision, he stuffed the sweet into his mouth and practically inhaled it. "Ba will be annoyed I need to get an insulin implant, but that's about it."

"Fuck, don't mess up my body before I get back."

"Our body, remember?" the teenager retorted. "I get to fuck it up as much as I want."

"Fucking yourself? How narcissistic," Dustin returned.

"Says the guy who had an orgasm in the rain," Declan retorted. He casually flipped through all the visions of Observe, casually glancing through all of them until he noticed many of them missing, including two important ones.

"Our perimeter is gone . . ." he muttered. Of the dozen eyes Dustin had prepared, about eight of them were gone from Observe, and not only that . . . "Hey, where's Utoqa?"

The reply that answered him was one filled with utter confusion.

"Who's Utoqa?"

# 1.18

———

*"I made a mistake, a horrible mistake."*
—****** **

Utoqa woke, his body and mind sluggish. The chill and rainy day did no favors for the cold-blooded creature. Yet his eyes still opened. ****, the tiny myconid creature Dustin had left to watch him, startled at his waking.

The lizardfolk slowly rose. He wasn't sure if **** sensed what he sensed, but it was clearly worried by his actions. Utoqa reached for Gift, the weapon never far after years of surviving by himself, constantly moving through the treacherous jungle, a sense honed through life and death.

Dustin was mistaken when he thought that Perception had anything to do with bodily senses.

One encompassed smell, taste, hearing, feeling, all the physical sensory aspects, while the other was more akin to a sixth sense. A supernatural ability to feel the reverberations of souls even if one was blind or deaf.

Utoqa had managed to meld the two into a unified front, greater than either, yet they were still fundamentally two different things. The sluggishness of his body, a natural consequence of the cold, allowed the discrepancy to be great enough that he realized it.

His Perception was still active at full force, giving him a vague feeling of uneasiness, while his natural senses detected nothing.

Utoqa's hand tightened around Gift as he realized that he had either significantly weakened or his senses were being *dampened*.

The lizardfolk stared at the window and saw his form reflected on its surface.

Yet behind his reflection was the reflection of a child. Clothing tattered, black hair dirtied and ruffled, staring at him with eyes red from weeping.

He raised Gift as he turned around, the silence of the room so loud it was deafening. Yet he saw nothing physically behind him.

The corpse of Dustin's wisp fell to the ground, its light snuffed out, its name forgotten by all that knew it.

Utoqa slashed thin air, his eyes glued to the window, yet Gift passed harmlessly through the boy's reflection. Bringing it around, he smashed the window, the shards falling and bouncing harmlessly off his scales.

But even in the shattered shards of glass, the reflection of the boy was still there.

The boy in the mirror came ever nearer.


It was true.

The Watching Eyes I left scattered all around had been blinded, the symbol dashed till they no longer saw, a trail leading up to the window where our room is.

"Who is this Utoqa?" I whispered to myself.

"A friend who you thought would be immensely useful," Declan whispered back.

Whether it was the friend or the usefulness part that drove me to action, was a question that I was unable to answer. Hopefully, it was a combination of both, but I couldn't definitely say that if Declan didn't say the last part, I would still move, and that was a fact I would think about for a long—


"So you're saying that someone is dead?" Tai asked.

The myconid nodded to the group he'd assembled, sitting around the table. "Problem is, it seems none of us remembers his existence."

"How'd you manage it?" ****** asked.

"I have an ability that keeps a copy of my memories stored elsewhere," Dustin replied simply. Noam nodded in affirmation before he leaned forward.

"I noticed something strange—Tai, you only use one sword to fight, yeah?" the tiefling asked.

Tai glanced at him in confusion. "Yeah, but why is that relevant?"

"If you only use one sword, then why do you carry three?"

Slowly, Tai took out her swords, the Sword of Proving, the reason for her quest, the sword she used to fight and—

Dustin thought and thought. Then he realized a discrepancy.

They'd come here via train, and when the train was attacked, he sent Noam and someone else in opposite directions. If this Utoqa was sent to the front to grab the guardsmen directly, who was sent to get the civilian passengers toward the front? Did he send anyone? Were there passengers toward the front?

Did they really repel the goblins with only five mercenaries and a hand-ful of guards?

According to *****, they—

Noam looked around. It was broad daylight; the town was not obscured by night or rain, and he realized something.

"Why is this place so empty?" he asked. The town had thirty or so build-ings—it was by no means small. Yet as they saw few people, and those they did see were walking around dazed as if just waking.

Not only that, but the town was able to support an inn large enough to house a few dozen travelers who randomly appeared. An inn of that size wouldn't develop if this was the middle of—

The young inn owner tripped as she desperately tried to fulfill all the orders. It was strange—yesterday she was able to do all this work easily as if she were three people. But today she couldn't keep up. She'd served far more people than this! How was she able to keep the inn running until—

Noam's steps sped as they slammed open door after door. Half the houses were empty, yet all seemed like someone had lived there previously.

He thought back to the train, how when he checked the carriages so many of them were empty. Fucking hell—there was a kid who was traveling alone, the one he'd left with a young couple to hide under Dusts' protection. Was that kid really traveling alone or did—

The symbol of Tilt, the goddess of children, was a silver bell. She had a small orphanage in this town, yet when we scoured it, it was completely empty. The silver bell at the top of the building was tarnished, a detail I had noticed before but had put at the back of my mind. Food and drink were left scattered and rotted on the table. Dust had settled on it, but it couldn't be more than a few days old.

From the corner of Noam's eye, he sighted a mirror, and a reflection that belonged to no one flitted out.

"Follow me!" the tiefling yelled, not bothering for an answer as he vaulted over empty tables, the reflection of a child moving through the—

Tai kicked opened the door to the mage tower. The boy traveled through reflections somehow, and they'd tracked him through empty windows until he led them here.

Tai entered first, not as tough as Dustin but twice better at close range. They slowly streamed in behind her, weapons drawn and prepared, but inside it was quiet. So quiet that the silence felt deafening. And they saw—

*"Fear the deafening silence."*

Dustin was thrown to the side, body slamming into a bookshelf, which promptly fell over him. They didn't see it coming—no, they couldn't have. Yet when the silence was deafening, they could—

Dustin was knocked out; there was no other choice. No other option he could think of. ****** knelt before the ******** **** **** * *** and—

The myconid pulled out the **** that impaled him to the wall. His other hand held a staff, a weapon held with unfamiliar hands, yet the power there was something he was used to.

"I can see you now," ****** said through gritted teeth. "I can ****** you."

The **** turned and—

"—I made a mistake, a horrible mistake," ****** muttered as his blood hardened on the ground around him. He'd dealt a wound, but he alone couldn't beat it. No, even with **** people, they couldn't beat it. They needed to run, as far as possible. At the very least make sure Noam made it out. If it could harm *****, then there was no telling what it could do to Matt's real self.

Gritting a mouth that wasn't his, ****** spoke. "Analyze, I know you're still active. Mindless thing you are, but make sure this is—"

Dustin woke up in the middle of the street. Drenched in his own hardened blood, the first thing he noticed was an Analyze page opened.

**1. You cannot ***** **.**

Fuck.

**1. It removes *********** ***** **.**

Damnit.

**1. If suddenly the silence becomes quiet enough that it feels deafening, spray all around you. It won't kill certain things, but it will deter them.**

Remember these questions.

**2. Why does Tai carry three swords when she only uses two?**

**3. Why was the train so empty? Did we really beat back the goblins with only *five?* people and a handful of guards?**

**4. Why is the town so empty?**

And make sure to remember five—

**6. Find the boy in the mirror.**

**7. ***** might still be alive if you act fast enough. He's durable—he might Survive, but I'm not sure about ***** and *****. It got so many of us. **** is definitely gone. I'm not sure if I even remember all the people it got.**

**8. Get Noam out if he is still alive. I don't know if it can harm Matt, but *don't risk it*.**

Dustin blinked as he saw the page floating lazily within his mind. The moon had risen, and of the past few hours, he only remembered a single phrase.

*"Fear the deafening silence."*

He brought himself up, looking warily all around him. He noticed a myriad of eye symbols littered on his arm. The cantrip spell he'd made . . . It was strange. He couldn't see out of them at all. In fact, he hadn't made them with the intention to see out of them; it was strange.

"Why would I make such a useless spell?" he asked himself. He stood there, waiting for something before he startled as he looked at his arm.

"That was weird," he muttered. "Why did I expect someone to answer that question?"

# 1.19

———

*"If you know the enemy and know yourself, then you need not fear the outcome of a hundred battles."*
—*Excerpt from* The Ebb and Flow, *by Chancellor Chekov of the Western Empire*

Dustin trudged through the town.

His clothing was bloody. Even though the viscous yellow fluid that made his blood had long since coagulated outside his body, it was enough that it slowed him slightly. Like walking when you were covered in dried mud.

He read the note. He saw the symbols on his arm, and when he opened the door to the inn, he saw Noam by a table, his left arm in a makeshift sling.

"Dusts," the tiefling called out, "could you throw down your healing shroom? This town doesn't have a healer, apparently."

"Doesn't have or no longer has?" he whispered.

"Huh?" Noam replied as he neared. "Speak up, I can't hear you!"

The myconid noticed the mud on his blades. Those hook swords had been used recently, and outside. "How'd you break your arm?"

"Think I slipped on the stairs," he said as he rubbed his head. "Must've banged my head—can't think straight."

"Where's Tai?"

"Here," a voice groaned from another table. Tai lay her head on the table, long brown hair splayed out, "I would greatly appreciate your healing as well. You're the one healer in this town."

"Tai." He spoke slowly but directly, without a change in tone or emotion.

Noam suddenly sat up and stared at Dustin. "What is wrong?"

"As someone who helped us this far, I'll give you some advice," the myconid continued, ignoring his friend. "*Run.* Get as far away from this town as you can."

Slowly, she raised her head, pushing away a few strands of hair before she stared directly at Dustin. "What's this about?"

"What happened?" Noam asked.

Dustin reached into his cap and removed his notebook and pen. "The weather has cleared up, so I thought we should be on our way. There's nothing of note in this town anyway."

In the notebook, he wrote, *Threat. Unknown. Unseen. My memories are missing.*

Slowly, Noam shuffled his chair to be next to Dustin, beckoning Tai as well. "I'm not sure about that. I'm sure there's plenty of interesting things to see."

Tai came and read the words on the note page.

*May be listening, watching. I do not know,* Dustin wrote, and in the same breath he said, "Nothing memorable, I'm sure."

He continued, *It has already killed many people. I'm pretty sure we fought it already and lost.*

Tai gestured for the pen. "The roads are probably all muddied up, it would be uncomfortable as hell to travel."

*Where are the dead? How can I trust you?*

"I suppose so," Dustin answered as he took back the pen, *The entity somehow removes information in the mind. My memories and ability have both been compromised.*

He put down the pen before reaching into his cap, pulling out a single book. "Guess we can stay and read or something. I do need to get Noam back on track."

Dustin opened the book, *Yolo's Guide to Monsters,* and flipped to a specific page.

*Aberrations.*

Both their eyes widened.

Dustin continued to write, *There is no evidence because it removed all evidence. Including that of our memories.*

"Hey, Tai," Noam began conversationally, "I've been wondering this . . ."

A sudden sense of déjà vu struck all three of them as Noam spoke. "If you only use one sword, then why do you carry three?"

Like they were watching a play they had already seen, Tai mechanically took out her three swords. The Sword of Proving, the reason for her quest, the sword she used to fight and . . .

One unknown sword.

One made in the same style as the one Tai used, looking exactly the same on the surface, but as she compared them, she realized this one was different—longer, differently balanced.

Made for someone taller.

Slowly, she unsheathed her own sword; on the blade's flat near the guard were three sigils written in High Elvish.

*Nao Ri Tai*

Then, she drew the other sword and on that blade was written, *Nao Ri Kai.*

Her hands started shaking, and her eyes darted back and forth the length of the blade, uncomprehending. The signs of deep confusion bordering on panic began staining her eyes.

The other two looked at the symbols, not knowing the language, but a sense of familiarity struck them still, yet untouchable, the memory forever out of reach. They stood like that for a while.

It was Dustin who moved first, using the pen and writing something.

*Do not trust anything you remember.* He returned the book, notepad and pen to his cap. "Pack your things, Noam. I don't trust another night in this rickety tavern."

The myconid turned to head upstairs, but a firm hand grabbed his shoulder. "Hold it."

Dustin turned to look at the tiefling; Noam's face was neutral, but that neutrality did not reach his eyes.

"We aren't just leaving without doing anything."

"We have done plenty of things—eat, sleep, talked to people and even played a game or two, which both of us *lost.*"

"Losses can be recovered from; they are not crippling."

"But when the game is too difficult, I would rather not play," he replied.

"Not even trying is a setup for failure."

"And trying to accomplish the impossible is a waste of effort."

"How do you know it is impossible?"

"That is because I—" Without warning, Dustin threw out his hand, pacifying spores spraying out of his finger. Noam's eyes widened, and he fell back, clutching his face and struggling to stay awake before he finally collapsed onto the ground.

"Sorry," Dustin whispered as he stood over the unconscious body. "If it were just me then I would try again . . . but I don't want to risk a friend."

He extended a hand to pick up Noam—

"Son of a bitch," he muttered as blood dripped from a fresh wound in his side.

"FINALLY, MORE BLOOD!" Celigarn yelled as Noam twisted the blade into Dustin's flesh.

"It's son of *bitches*, get it right." A stabbing irritation entered his mind—Vicious Mockery. Damn that spell.

Eyes were on them now; the tavern was unnaturally empty, but there were still people left. People who hurriedly stood up as blades were drawn.

Celigarn's glow deepened. "Wait a moment . . . this blood . . ."

"Don't worry!" Noam called out before he turned to Dustin. "We'll keep it between the two of us."

"Could've done this the easy way, Noam. I could've gotten you out safely."

"So it's something that you think could permanently damage us," Noam said with a smirk.

"This is no laughing matter."

"Then I suppose I should be serious as I beat you to a pulp."

"Your build is not suited for one-on-ones; your low CON also means I'm particularly effective against you," Dustin said, voice completely calm, for he was stating a mere fact. If they were near a Wayshard, he might've been worried about Noam opening up his status page to dump all his points to CON, but this far out, neither of them could use their character sheets.

"Shall I prove you wrong?" Noam whispered like a lover. "Shall we go at each other until one of us *gives*? You know what I want—talking only buys you time."

"I suppose it is in my interest to kill you."

"Attaboy!"

"THIS IS PLANT SAP!" Celigarn cried as Noam kicked the myconid off him. "THIS ISN'T BLOOD!"

"This is the best you'll get!" Noam yelled as he rushed the staggering form of Dustin.

"Bastard . . ." the myconid whispered as he clutched his wound. He threw his arm wide, a puff of Poison Spores engulfing the area in front of him. Yet instead of a body coming through, only a screaming thrown dagger embedded itself into Dustin's shoulder.

Shit—he'd just lost sight of Noam.

People were running and clambering away as the beginnings of a fight took place. Once they cleared out, Dustin could attack unreservedly without worrying about civilian casualties. This benefited him.

However, the panic as people ran away also benefited Noam, for it masked the crack as he reset his broken arm.

"Shillelagh." When he uttered the spell in mage tongue, Dustin's staff lit up with arcane energy. Thumbing the bark in his cap, Dustin cast Bark Skin over himself once again.

Noam grabbed his hook swords by the table, idly glancing at Tai, who was still staring at the drawn blade of a person none of them remembered. He snapped his fingers in front of her, forcing her back to reality.

"Huh—"

"Live a long life, Tai," Noam said with a smile before he turned and assumed a runner's position.

Aura coursed through the entirety of his body as he set off with a flash. His feet blurred as he suddenly appeared behind Dustin.

"Nothing personal."

"Indeed."

Dozens of sneezing sporages exploded around Noam's feet, but not fast enough, as he slammed his swords into Dustin, throwing him several meters toward the right. Noam rushed out of the yellow cloud before it could reach his face, blades brandished.

But even in the air, Dustin threw his hand out. "Poison—" he yelled before getting his arm slapped away by a blade in midair.

Again, Dustin tried to cast a spell as he fell, yet Noam caught him, slapping his arms away and directing the spell away before kicking the myconid upward.

Anyone that still remained would've seen a strange sight.

Though Dustin was fully armored, with both Bark Skin and Bracken Polypores covering his body, he might as well have been a helium balloon, for his body was light enough that Noam could throw him in the air, again and again. In the air he truly had no mobility—Noam was slashing and attacking him, interrupting and diverting every spell before it was made.

The end result looked a lot like he was . . .

*"Juggling!"* Dustin realized as he finally got used to constant strikes and shifts in view. It was a Yggdrasil strat, using constant interrupts to keep a caster target permanently CC'd. Dustin had never seen one done so well. In Yggdrasil you generally needed an interrupt skill, meaning such CC would not last long, however, this was not the case here. So long as the spell had either a verbal or somatic component, Noam could predict and interrupt it.

A continuous attack that made use of insane spatial awareness, coordination and weapon mastery. Dual blades, axe, knuckle dusters, spear, whip, halberd—as Dustin was getting continuously slashed, slammed, and thrown back in the air, he couldn't help but feel like he was getting attacked by six different weapons at once.

"That bastard had been holding back all this time."

For Noam however, the only thing on his mind was this.

"Don't let the balloon drop." His face was utterly focused; not a single action made by Dustin went unnoticed, not a single move he did was random. In his mind, what he was doing was similar to when they had a spare balloon and threw it in the air as a game. The person who let it drop was the loser.

The fact the balloon was actively trying to kill him was irrelevant.

For half a minute, this continued, but as the last of Dustin's armor crumbled away from the constant assault. The moment had come.

Sporages he had stuck firmly inside his cap had dislodged and fallen, right over Noam's form.

His response was nigh instant, weapons already moving to slap them away, but Dustin, who was waiting for this moment, was first.

The need to yell out the spell name to detonate a sporage was merely a habit—all he needed to do was see and think of detonating them.

He was already keeping track of them through manavision, and Noam was not faster than thought.

Yellow spores rained down on Noam, pushing him into a sneezing fit as Dustin finally landed on the ground rolling. When Noam waved away the spores and opened his eyes, Dustin had already finished the somatic gestures.

"Euphoria Spray."

He jumped back, but the rainbow-colored cloud still hit and engulfed him. For a single moment, Noam was at peace; he saw the universe and all of existence in its infinite glory and understood his place in it. He understood the meaning of life and death, the continuous cycle that allowed all things to move. For a brief, glorious moment that lasted the span of infinity, the euphoric joy of understanding all made him still.

Then a Shillelagh-empowered staff slammed into his head.

"Poison Spores." The green spray threatened to catch him, but he moved with the momentum of the staff, taking advantage of it to fall to the ground, where he kicked Dustin's legs from under him.

While Dustin scrambled to get back up, Noam rose with fluidity, the blade going in for the final blow. Dustin threw out his arm once again, but Noam could interrupt it, he was fast—

"Stop."

He saw the purple sporage in his hand, and his blade stopped centimeters from Dustin's side.

"Move another inch and we both die."

Noam's adrenaline came to a halt, and he let out a short, gasping breath. "Bastard . . . You win either way."

Dustin's objective was to get Noam out safely; if he killed Noam, then that achieved the same thing.

"You're fast, but we just saw you aren't faster than thought."

"So I also can't deal with the threat without you, huh?"

Dustin had no armor left, not even his Bark Skin, which had been smashed to pulp in his earlier juggle; a point-blank Rot Spores would kill him, too.

And Noam realized, upon seeing the suicide move, that something of the enemy could only be dealt with using Dustin's help. Otherwise, the myconid wouldn't use his own life as a hostage.

"This happens the hard way because of you," Dustin said. "Damn bastard, you know what happens. Either both of us die or one—either way, I *win*."

"You really think I can't deal with this thing without your help?" Noam said calmly, finally steadying his breathing.

"Yes," Dustin replied. "If I'm not helping, then you are guaranteed to fail."

"And why aren't you helping?"

"I told you, because we've already *failed*," he practically snarled. "You know my Analyze power? It keeps a list of names of all the people I've met—*half*, fucking half of them are gone. I don't remember them, nor can I see their sheets anymore. The version of the memories I remember isn't true, but I know they all died here. If it were anywhere else, then the other power I lost would've been able to detect it."

"And you think we can't win when we know it's there?"

"We already faced it with more people, better resources, and an ability that can straight up see and realize the differences!" Dustin yelled. "We're not doing the same thing—we're doing the same thing *worse*!"

Slowly, Noam closed his eyes and quietly said, "You wanna hear a story?"

Dustin didn't answer.

"When I was a kid, I was in a gang, yeah. One of the guys, Joseph, I think his name was, got jumped one day. He was rushed to the nearest clinic, but he died of internal bleeding in the head. The strangest thing happened later." He paused, eyes opening and a deep nostalgia in them.

"We all got mad; we got motivated and looked for the people who did it and jumped them. We got revenge, we celebrated, but in the end . . . We all felt nothing about Joseph's death and our revenge."

This time, he stared directly at Dustin, still lying on the ground beneath him, the Rot Sporage held out like a shield.

"We weren't fulfilled by the revenge; we didn't feel happier—we felt nothing. That is what you are seeing. That feeling of realizing the thing you chase wasn't all cracked up as it was."

"Wait a minute," Dustin said as he noticed something.

"What I see is the feeling of chasing. That feeling that you have something worth putting your effort in. The outcome may be fixed, but that is no excuse to ignore the process. To you, the process and outcome are one and the same."

"Why are you breathing?" Dustin said as realization dawned on him.

Noam smirked. The next moment, Dustin's hand, still clutching the sporage, was lying far away on the ground next to them and Noam's sword was in the air as if it had just swung. Fast, too fast. Faster than his aura-empowered swing. Faster than even Dustin could process.

"That's the difference between you and me, Dusts. That is why no matter the outcome of a hundred battles, I will still be better than you."

He sheathed his swords and turned away. "And that is why I kept the nature of my abilities a secret."

# 1.20

---

*"I understand that I have acted in haste. I see my mistakes now and beg for forgiveness."*
—Priestess Emilia the Thrice Excommunicated, first recommunicated due to converting 382 heavily injured men

Noam walked out of sight of Dustin before he fell to a knee, breaths heavy and laborious. He quickly stabilized himself, taking deep breaths to calm his heart. It wasn't the first time he had overexerted himself, and it wouldn't be the last.

Dustin might be an ass, but he was right; Noam's build and stat distribution were all over the place, meaning he had to be doubly careful to beat the bastard. Not to mention he still had 9 SP that he hadn't spent—couldn't spend until they got to a Wayshard. He was essentially fighting while missing two levels against a guy whose build was probably a cheat.

Perhaps if Dustin specially gave him a build to use, he might've demolished the myconid with half the time and effort, but where was the fun in that?

"Are you all right?" Tai stopped in front of him and extended a hand, which he took, pulling himself back up.

"How 'bout you?" Noam asked, noting she looked rather freaked out when she drew the mystery sword. He didn't know High Elvish, but the pictograms looked similar enough to the Sino-Tibetan language family that he realized the three words were for a name. The two symbols of similarity were likely the surname.

"I'll live." She spoke casually, but Noam still noticed how her hand tightened around her sword.

If Tai were another person, he might've pushed farther, but she struck Noam as a largely independent personality, not someone worth poking at without mutual trust and respect.

"You wanna run away now that you know what's here, or do you want to be an idiot and stay?" the tiefling asked.

"You're staying, aren't you?" Tai replied, voice soft, almost introspective. "Your friend was genuinely worried about the thing here, yet you plan on fighting them regardless. Even if they pose a permanent threat against yourself."

"We're all gonna die eventually. Might as well live life as stupidly as you can," he chuckled.

She smiled for a brief moment. "Even Travelers die, huh . . ." Her face turned hard. "I need to find out the meaning of the sword—I need to understand who Kai Gnari is."

"Got a plan for that?"

She blinked back in surprise, clearly not having considered it, before she shook her head.

Noam smiled as a figure hobbled out to join them. "Good thing I know a guy."


"You are a bastard, the worst bastard I have ever met," I said as the Fix-Up Fungus sprouted between us.

"And you love me for it, don't you?" the tiefling replied smugly, lying lazily on a couch almost like a cat.

We were in an empty house, and we all knew how it had become empty.

The third person looked between the two of us strangely. "Didn't you two just try to kill each other?" Tai asked.

"Yeap, but I won," Noam replied as healing spores enveloped his body.

I attached my severed arm back onto the stump, letting the spores drift and reconnect the two. "We have a rule that if we disagree, we fight, and whoever wins is the way we go."

"And I won," Noam repeated with a smile. "Unless this is a long con in which he stabs me in the back later."

"Possibly," I admitted, "but regardless, if I think the way is lost or hopeless, I will kill you."

"You really don't want this thing to kill you, huh?" Tai said.

I held a finger to my mouth, the universal gesture for quiet. "Wait."

Glancing around, I could see no sign that something was with us. Still, I held out my hands. "Poison Spores."

I repeated the spell several times, getting the two to move positions as I made sure to douse the entire room with Poison Spores before leaving a lingering barrier of the stuff around the walls.

"Cautiousness has never harmed anyone," I muttered as I sat back down, mana significantly drained. "We have a few minutes; speak in quiet tones and do not raise your voice."

There were careful nods around me, eyes looking outward, too, but likely seeing no more than I did.

"Dustin, Noam," Tai began, her face grave, "I require of you two a favor."

"What is it?"

"If I'm taken, kill me before I am killed by that thing."

*Oh.*

Both of us simply stared at her with a mixture of surprise, disbelief, and some respect. For out of the three of us, she was the only one who was truly risking her life.

"I would rather it not come to that point," I said softly after a moment.

"We don't often get to pick what we would rather," she replied.

"I'll do it," Noam stated.

I almost berated him when he spoke, but when I turned to Noam, I saw not a hint of doubt or hesitation, only quiet reassurance and resolve.

Tai nodded, content with the answer, before they each turned to me and I realized they were both relying on me to get them through this mess, to give them direction so that we might win.

We were fucked if I was the best we got.

But I could not say that, could not think that, for right now the part that believed that was useless. Right now they didn't need me as a person; they needed me as a logical commander, uncaring of the weaknesses of emotion.

And so, I removed what wasn't needed and became that.

"Let us continue, then," I said. "I have a list of information I recorded in the past, likely after our first encounter with the entity."

**1. You cannot ***** **.**

Fuck.

**1. It removes ********** ***** **.**

Damnit.

**1. If suddenly the silence becomes quiet enough that it feels deafening, spray all around you. It won't kill certain things, but it will deter them.**

Remember these questions.

**2. Why does Tai carry three swords when she only uses two?**

**3. Why was the train so empty? Did we really beat back the goblins with only *five?* people and a handful of guards?**

**4. Why is the town so empty?**

And make sure to remember five—

**6. Find the boy in the mirror.**

**7. ***** might still be alive if you act fast enough. He's durable—he might Survive, but I'm not sure about ****** and ******. It got so many of us. **** is definitely gone. I'm not sure if I even remember all the people it got.**

**8. Get Noam out if he is still alive. I don't know if it can harm Matt, but *don't risk it*.**

I relayed the information, word for word.

"From this, we can draw a few conclusions," I continued.

"One"—I held up my first finger—"it can somehow remove all information about itself, which explains why we don't remember anything."

"Two"—the second finger rose—"some extension of this ability is somehow used to remove the memory of people. Judging by the language of point seven, it can be reasonably interpreted that the people forgotten are dead or killed. Not only that, but it has perfected the ability to the point we seem to replace memories of people that have passed."

"Three"—the third finger—"this method is not perfect." I gestured toward Tai's sword. "Your sword shows that physical traces of people slain still remain. I believe instead of removing the traces, the entity somehow causes us to ignore proof of its existence, including its kills."

"Four"—the fourth finger; my entire hand opened—"this thing attacks when the silence 'becomes deafening,' whatever that means."

"Five"—I raised the first finger of my other hand—"the third and fourth points indicate that this thing has accumulated a massive body count, and judging by point three, we were once, at minimum, a group of five people."

Unintentionally, my eye went to Tai's third sword. "I suspect the person mentioned in point seven is the person who owned that sword. A close-range fighter with a Path that greatly enhances durability. However, seven seems to mention at least three victims."

"Six"—second finger on my second hand—"the existence of a 'boy in the mirror,' which these points place emphasis on locating."

"Seven"—the second-to-last finger—"this thing is somehow able to make me afraid for Noam's original self."

Tai reacted strangely to that information but stayed silent.

"Eight"—the final finger—"this thing is susceptible to damage and can be deterred, but I also won't be able to kill it with just an AOE spray."

"And finally"—I closed both hands—"my ability has been compromised, as shown by the numerous redactions and the missing of point five, meaning that the entirety of what I just said could be false or inaccurate. Anything else?"

There was silence after I laid it all bare. Perhaps only now they understood the enemy as I did, to have it put that simply.

Noam scratched his head for a moment before he asked, "What's this 'boy in the mirror'?"

"I don't know," I replied. "I only have what I have previously tried to write."

"'Like the boy in the mirror, I come ever nearer,'" he tuned. "That phrase is stuck in my head, like a song. I remember saying it, but did I really?"

I raised an eyebrow. "What do you mean?"

"I remember saying that phrase to someone, but I don't think I did. Why would I speak like that, for one? If this can erase memories and make us fill in the gaps ourselves, what happens if it misses and some information is retained but we lose how we got it?"

A memory resurfaced—the bloody corpse of a creature that rammed its head into the shrine of Bundriroc until it bled and died, and from its blood, I saw and remembered a phrase no one else did.

"Fear the deafening silence."

There was that sense of déjà vu again as I said it. "I remember that we killed a rampaging beast near the shrine of Bundriroc, and when it bled, the blood formed a phrase—'Fear the deafening silence.'"

"I remember crippling both legs of the thing while Tai delivered her finishing blow," Noam added.

"And I remembered being tired, because using even one act at a time really tires me out."

"One act . . ." There was a discrepancy in my memory, fleeting and gone in a moment, but I closed my eye and traced it back, looking at the first moment Tai had used an act in front of us.

"Tai, when you use the Adept's Acts, do you do one slash or two?"

Tai furrowed her brow. "Only a single one, but why would—" She remembered that the first time she'd used that move in front of us, it left a train car in *three* pieces.

"That cart was slashed twice," Noam breathed. "It was slashed *twice!*"

Tai's hands shook as they clenched around her third blade.

"Your style is called the Gnari Family style, isn't it?"

"Yes." She grimaced. "I know what you're implying—that the person who owned this blade was my family."

"It doesn't help much," Noam admitted. "The information does little more than say it has killed a person of your fighting style before, but the circumstances are gone."

"No," I said, "with three examples we can confirm that the memory erasure is not perfect, that there are clues left behind we can think back to and remember and realize something is missing because of an inaccuracy."

"We can keep finding clues that way."

"But we do not know if the clues are of value," I said. "Like you said, the clue of the train car only says it has killed a person of Tai's fighting style."

Noam scratched his head, brows deep in thought. "Dustin, your Analyze thing is from your eye, right?"

I nodded.

"Lemme see it."

I willed the Bracken Polypores to recede, revealing my face under them and the socket I kept the eye in.

"Oh, Jesus," Noam muttered. "Look through my eyes—that thing is—"

He paused as he realized what he'd just said—something spoken almost completely out of habit, something he didn't consciously register until after he said it.

"Sight," he muttered. "You lost a power related to sharing sight."

I nodded. "I know." I raised my arm, which was covered with numerous eye symbols. "On my arm are observation runes from a spell I crafted myself, but I can't see through them. The uselessness of the spell and the fact I cast it so much on myself indicates that my past self wanted me to realize what was lost."

"That must've been how the thing got noticed before," Tai muttered. "If you had some sort of altered sight, you might've been able to see it."

"The only question is why the entity didn't kill me outright," I added. "Perhaps it has some limitation on killing or the number of people it can make forget."

"Or . . ." Noam began, "when we fought it, we dealt so much damage it was forced to retreat."

He looked at both of us. "In which case, we need to find and kill it as soon as possible before it has a chance to recover."

"That is *if* that hypothesis is true," I noted. "We still have no real idea of its combat capability. We can assume it is powerful, given that it has killed at least three combat-capable individuals, but we don't know *how*.

"The difference between it killing those three in direct combat versus that of an undetected sneak attack is the difference between victory and defeat," I continued.

"I would like to lean toward the idea it was a sneak attack," Noam said. "It greatly fits the abilities we know it has."

"And I agree with you," I said, "but we can't know *for sure*. It will be a gamble no matter how you put it."

"A gamble we may be forced to take."

"Indeed," I conceded. "But let us examine the threads we haven't looked at yet."

"The boy in the mirror."

I nodded. "Yes."

"We have nothing other than the weird rhyme I have . . . Actually . . ." Noam looked around. "Any of you have a mirror?"

I shook my head and so did Tai.

"Hmm . . . how clear are your swords, Tai?"

She drew one, the one that was hers. It was clean, but I could see stubborn specks of dirt and mud that had crusted over.

Noam squinted at the blade before he very quietly turned to me.

"Behind me."

I stood up, seeing nothing physically behind Noam, but I slowly edged next to him, along with Tai, and we saw it.

The reflection of a ragged boy, eyes red with weeping, staring at us from the corner of the room.

# 1.21

---

*"Sure, I can't look directly at the envoys that come over, but that isn't an excuse to not prepare tea or be impolite."*
—*High Prince Aksum on the eldritch gods that have been the end and beginning of worlds*

My eye was shattered, I idly noticed. The round lapis gem was cracked in two and held together only by thin threads of mycelium.

Behind us, the reflection of the child continued to stare at us. His eyes were red, as if he had been weeping for weeks on end.

Slowly, Noam turned around and spoke. "Hello?"

A move that would get him a horrible death in any horror movie was only met with silence.

"Should someone go find a mirror?" Noam whispered.

Shaking my head, I replied, "I don't wish to split up or let our eyes off this entity."

"So we're just stuck here?" Tai muttered.

Noam eyed us, gesturing at the spot where the crying child was. I nodded, for we were lacking viable options.

Slowly, he stepped forward, a single hand outreached. "Hey, kid, I can't really see ya, but are you all right?"

We watched in tense silence as he got closer to the still child, eyes still glued on the reflection while Noam got ever closer.

Five paces away.

Four paces away.

Three paces away.

Two paces away.

Noam froze, his step awkwardly falling to the ground. I almost turned around and would have attacked if I didn't see what happened.

The boy held out his hand and threaded his fingers between Noam's own.

"Are you all right?" Noam asked, his face staring directly at the blank space where the boy should be.

The reflection nodded.

"The boy just nodded," I said, knowing Noam could see nothing in front of him. "Status?"

"I feel a small cold hand holding my own," he replied with a whisper. "Nothing visible in front of me."

"Ask him what happened."

"What happened?" he repeated.

In the reflection, the boy's lips moved, as if speaking. No, he was speaking—the sound simply didn't transfer, but Analyze could read lips.

"Do you remember?"

"We do not," I said.

Noam turned his neck. "What?"

I turned around, facing the spot where the boy should be. "Can you hear me?"

"He just shook his head," Tai said, catching on quickly. "He was doing it as soon as you spoke."

*He cannot read my lips.* "Noam, repeat what I just said."

"We do not."

"He shook his head again."

I turned around, glimpsing his reflection again. "Repeat what I say."

"Got it."

"Are you the one killing people?"

Shaking head.

"Are you the one erasing memories?"

Shaking head.

"What are you?"

Shaking head.

"Do you know what is killing people here?"

A single nod.

"Can you tell me?"

The boy spoke again, voice silent as the lips moved. "Do you remember?"

"I don't, but I know something is here."

"He doesn't, but we know something is here."

"You don't remember." The boy's lips moved again.

"But we can *understand*," I stressed.

"But we can— Hey!" From Tai's sword, we saw the entity withdraw its arm and turn around. Noam recoiled, clutching the hand that was holding the entity. "He just—"

"He's leaving, follow him!"

Tai moved her sword, catching the reflection of the boy once again as he moved toward the door, and began running behind him with her sword awkwardly outstretched to catch his reflection. I followed behind her, cursing my slow speed. Noam finally started moving, catching up quickly behind me, grabbing my back and lifting me as we followed Tai.

"That kid froze my hand," he muttered as he dashed after Tai. I couldn't help but note with annoyance that Noam carrying me was still faster than me running.

"Can you still use it?"

"Of course."

Tai kicked open the door to the outside, the cool night air washing our faces as we jumped out behind her. Our steps echoed loudly through the silent streets as we chased our unseen target.

Noam followed Tai through dozens of sudden turns, seemingly random movements and even at one point turning around to run behind us.

Until, finally, Tai's steps slowed as Noam caught up behind her, breathing heavily as he dropped me. No matter how little I weighed, I still weighed something, and the fact he'd carried me halfway through town with his sub-par stats was impressive enough as it was.

"He entered here," Tai said.

There was that feeling again, as I stared upward at the tower. On top of the open door was a sign that said the building was a mage tower, selling magical implements. Yet even as I read it, I felt it, that sense of déjà vu. We had already done this before.

"Tai, take point."

She nodded, holding her already drawn sword tightly in guard as she slowly walked forward.

I followed behind her, with Noam watching our back once he caught his breath.

The door was already open. Inside, the tower was a mess of scattered books and broken shelves; there was no sound except the sound of scratching—a constant scritching at the back of the tower. Carefully, we stepped over the books, eyes watching Tai's blade for any reflection that didn't belong.

Yet we didn't catch anything.

Until we entered the back room.

There was a single doll, poorly made, of a boy with red buttons for eyes and wearing ragged clothing. It was moving, its fingerless arms impossibly holding a piece of chalk as it wrote on the stone walls of the tower. There were words, sentences, scratched onto the stone walls by chalk, the handwriting messy and frantic at first, but it soon turned reserved and desperate.

"It killed the Sister, it killed the Baker, it killed my friends as we were singing, singing along.

"We were playing hide-and-seek. I was It, but I never found anyone.

"It plays hide-and-seek, too, but it cheats—it is both Hiding and It.

"It found me like it did everyone else. Gobble, gobble. Munch, munch.

Tai raised her sword, letting the blade reflect off the inside of the room. Behind the doll was the boy, pointing at the doll and looking at us.

"But it wasn't the only one who was It. Spew, spew, I came out, now I can hide just as well as him."

Noam slowly walked forward, toward the small doll. He gently knelt down next to it and hugged it.

The doll was struggling in his embrace, trying to get to the wall to write more, but I saw a single tear fall from the buttons that were its eyes.

"We have to kill this thing," he muttered as he let go, the doll moving mechanically to the wall as it continued to write with its small nub of chalk.

There was a silence as we considered the weight of what had just befallen us. The only sound was the doll writing words on the wall. It suddenly felt so loud in the silence, as if it were the only sound in the world . . . Wait . . . no . . . as if it suddenly overpowered another sound. As if there was a passive noise that I had just blotted out until—

"Both of you, get down!" I screamed as I raised my hands. Noam went down instantly, an innate trust built over years. Tai was slower, but Noam yelled at her to follow my orders. I was already casting. "Sneezing Spores!"

"It found you again," the doll wrote in chalk.

Damnit, why did I spend so much mana on Poison Spores?

"It comes when it has become quiet."

Yellow spores flooded the room around us; both Noam and Tai stayed close to the ground, covering their nose and mouths so as to not inhale the Sneezing Spores.

"It is closest when it is so quiet you remember you forgot the song."

Movement, just outside my periphery. The spores were disturbed from their natural flow.

"It attacks when you realize the silence is so quiet it drowns out all other sounds."

"It's coming."

"So you must be scared of the deafening silence."

Something shot out, coming from behind me, leaving a thin, serpentine trail as it almost struck me from behind.

"You shouldn't hide in the same place."

The movement of the spores, the way it disturbed them as it moved—I could Analyze them, watch where it moved. The shape of the outline was snakelike, moving in midair like an eel and circling us like a shark. "Shillelagh." Raising my staff, I slammed down onto the trail it left. Feeling the satisfying feedback of *striking something*. The moving trail was jerked down from that one spot. Even if I couldn't see it, it was still there!

"The touch you feel is a trick to make you think it is real."

Noam suddenly vomited onto the ground, clutching his mouth as gastric juices spewed from his stomach.

"Noam!" Tai yelled, grabbing the tiefling on the back. "What happened?"

He was heaving. I desperately wanted to watch him, but the thing was circling around us again. I was the only one who could stay in the spores without much adverse effect.

"Don't . . ." Vomit fell from his mouth, slopping grossly onto the ground. "Don't . . . don't look at its reflection!"

Tai's eyes drifted toward her sword unconsciously, for wasn't it just a reflex to look at what was just pointed out?

"Don't look for too long or you'll remember."

Noam was faster, slapping a hand still wet with vomit past Tai's face, getting her to look away just in time.

I was still watching the thing circling around us. I could almost see it, the outlines of something at the front of the trails. The serpentine creature had a head, a human head, a human head with a face that was outlined by the numerous yellow spores.

A face I recognized but did not remember.

"No!" Noam cried out, but it was too late.

That feeling of déjà vu greatened to the point it became nauseating, to the point my body froze, to the point that all that was on my mind was the feeling that I *knew* that face. Yet I would never remember it; my mind was constantly working in overdrive to find that which could not be found. To the point I could not think of anything else.

The face of someone I did not remember smiled as I looked at it, mouth opening to reveal a maw of thousands of needle-like teeth, but it didn't move. No, it couldn't move while it was being observed.

But neither could I.

Something moved behind me, something I only sensed with my manavision. Another serpentlike thing, bearing another human face. Its maw opened in much the same way as it moved in to kill me, before it froze as well. Its face added to my haunted mind.

There was the sound of singing steel as Tai rose, one hand covering her nose and mouth as she slashed the attacking head with her other hand.

Her eyes watered as the Sneezing Spores attacked them, but it worked in her favor as her sight was too blurred for her to see the faces. She slashed the thing staring at me. Cutting it in two, right between the eyes.

I gasped out, letting out a breath I didn't realize I was holding.

But even as the two severed halves fell to the ground, I could see them forming back together, as with the other one. Withdrawing from my spores and outside the room.

It healed, but *how*?

Slowly, I glanced at the doll, at what it had written in the short few moments when it attacked us.

"The touch you feel is a trick to make you think it is real."

A trick to make someone think it was real? Implying that it wasn't?

"Was that it?" Tai asked, blade still drawn.

Noam warned against its reflection, meaning he saw it through Tai's blade. Both Tai and I could see how it displaced spores as it moved—meaning it could still be seen through secondary sources.

"Don't look for too long or you'll remember."

It was a warning against seeing the faces it stole, but I needed to. I needed more information.

"We need to follow it," I said as I helped Noam to his feet. "I need to see it, to Analyze it."

He only nodded, not trusting his voice, leaning on me as we walked out of the room. Tai's sword was still out on guard.

"We can see its reflections," I muttered to Tai.

She nodded, eyes now kept on her blade and not her front as she moved.

Together like this, we moved out of the tower, into the empty town. The sound of silence was still present, it was still out there.

Tai raised her sword, letting the moonlight catch on its razor edge, and we saw it. Noam turned his eyes fast enough, as did Tai, but I did not. I saw it.

I saw it.

I saw it.

I saw it.

I saw it.

I saw it.

I saw it.

I saw it.

I saw it. I saw it. I saw it. I saw it. I saw it. I saw it. I saw it. I saw it. I saw it. I saw it. I saw it. I saw it. I saw it. I saw it. I saw it. I saw it. I saw it. I saw it. I saw it. I saw it. Isawit. Isawit. Isawit. Isawit. Isawit. Isawit. Isawit. Isawit. Isawit. Isawit. Isawit. Isawit. Isawit. Isawit. Isawit. Isawit. Isawit. Isawit. Isawit. Isawit. Isawit. Isawit. I was it. I was it. I was it. I was it. I was it. I was it. I was it. I was it. I was it. I was it. I was it. I was it. I was it. I was it. I was it. I was it. I was it. I was it. I was it. I was it. I was it. I was it. It saw I. It saw I. It saw I. It saw I. It saw I. It saw I. It saw I. It saw I. It saw I. It saw I. It saw I. It saw I. It saw I. It saw I. It saw I. It saw I. It saw I. It saw I. It saw I. It saw I. It saw I. It saw I. ItsawI. ItsawI. ItsawI. ItsawI. ItsawI. ItsawI. ItsawI. ItsawI. ItsawI. ItsawI. ItsawI. ItsawI. ItsawI. ItsawI. ItsawI. ItsawI. ItsawI. ItsawI. ItsawI. ItsawI. ItsawI. It was I. It was I. It was I. It was I. It was I. It was I. It was I. It was I. It was I. It was I. It was I. It was I. It was I. It was I. It was I. It was I. It was I. It was I. It was I. It was I. It was I. It was I. It was I.

I saw it in the sky, eyes as numerous as the stars.

And they all looked back at me.

Dustin stood in a place much like a personal study. It wasn't the classy kind, but a derivative of that idea. To any other person, the place would appear highly disorganized, but to him and only him, everything was where he needed it.

Except this once.

He riffled through dozens of drawers, throwing out hundreds of papers, each with a name that was gone until he reached the very first file.

And that name was gone as well.

No matter how he searched, he could not be found. No matter how hard he wished, he could not remember.

Then something broke in, something that stole entirety until not even the memory of what it stole was left. It entered through the window, flouting the things it stole, knowing they could never be reclaimed, bearing them with vanity as if it held all things.

It grabbed him by the collar, lifting him as if he were a toy; it came to finish what was started, to steal Dustin's second face. Dustin struggled, but slowly he cracked and so did the study around them.

Yet it made a crucial mistake.

It dared think it could face the defender in his own home.

The body it held fell limp as if a string had been cut from a doll. From Dustin's hand fell a single tarot card. The Magician.

Snip, snip.

And it realized that humanity and rationality was only a facade for him. Dropped as quickly as a mask.

Snip, snip.

He would die to live, but when death became certain, he would live to die.

Snip, snip.

In the dominion of souls, a tree mutilated itself to form a single spear.

Snip, snip.

Dustin Analyzed the entity.

Snip.

And it *screamed* as Dustin wretched a name from it.

Two seconds.

Barely the breadth of a single moment, barely one or two heartbeats, and Dustin had turned insane.

But that was the trick.

*You can't turn insane twice, can you?*

For what was the greater insanity?

To pointlessly chase around something you could not obtain or to shut that door and everything that made you chase it?

It faced something that had walked the latter path.

Tai tore away her sword, leaving a dazed Dustin standing in the moonlight.

"Dust!" Noam yelled, "Are you—"

"I am fine," the myconid answered simply, eyes turned and staring at the sky.

"What just happened?" Tai asked breathlessly.

"I saw it," Dustin answered. "I saw the beast and I Analyzed it and it ran."

"Dustin, you're acting weird again," Noam said, turning to face his friend. "What did you turn off?"

"A lot of things," he answered. "It may take a while to come back."

"Then what did you see?" the tiefling pressed, hands grabbing the myconid's shoulder.

Dustin showed no reaction to being grabbed, no reaction at all. "I saw it and I learned its name."

"What was it?" Tai asked.

He looked to the clear sky, where once it was covered by dozens of squirming serpents bearing human faces.

It was not a den of snakes, but a herculean hydra.

"It is called the Accumulation of White Lies."

# 1.22

———

*"Stand with your shield brothers and sisters or you are lone meat."*
—*Orc saying*

Well, he's gonna be useless for a few minutes . . ." Noam muttered his breath. "Are we safe right now, Dustin?"

The myconid pondered over it for a few moments. "Probably, leaning toward likely."

"Good enough for me," the tiefling replied as he grabbed his friend by the arm and started dragging him back into the tower.

"What's his deal right now?" Tai asked, eyes still cautiously scanning the perimeter. She'd heard of men going insane upon seeing certain things; Dustin wasn't babbling of eldritch powers, but the sudden . . . lack of being creeped her out. As if the myconid had suddenly ceased being there.

"He's in one of his moods right now," Noam replied, a slightly worried look on his face. "Hasn't had one for a few years, but at least he's not pushing us away."

"Pushing us away?"

Noam shook his head as they reentered the doll room. "It doesn't matter; at least he's still here."

Glancing around, he asked, "Ghost in here?"

Tai shook her head, after which Noam gently knelt down beside the doll. "We'll come back for you. Stay safe."

Standing back up, he grabbed Dustin again. "Let's move. Dusts, can you think of any safe places?"

"Physical barriers should still impede it," the myconid replied, his tone robotic, automatic. "You could just board up any room."

"But we'll constantly need to check for leaks, don't we?" Tai said.

The myconid nodded in affirmation.

Goal now in place, they escaped the tower, breaking into another emptied house, one that thankfully held a silver mirror.

"Tai, can you push that table over there?" Noam said, indicating the door they'd entered through.

She was already moving, and as she did that, Noam leaned into Dustin and whispered a question. "Why did you want to kill me?"

Something simple couldn't have done it. Dustin accepted loss easily, but he was stubborn when there was still a faint chance of victory, so *why* did he accept defeat so soon? Why did he want to run? Right now was the best time, when he simply didn't care enough to not answer.

The myconid simply answered thus: "Do you remember what my real name is?"

"Of course, it's—" Noam's thoughts paused midway as he realized he could not grasp a name. No matter how hard he tried, his mind simply misfired, clawing at mist and falsehood.

"Damn you," he muttered before he moved away to help Tai.

Dustin didn't know what he was facing. He didn't know what had happened to his real-world self. Going by the patterns he saw and the information he knew, in addition to the fact that things in Indiri had been leaking into the real world, Dustin considered the worst possibility: that his real-world self was *dead*. There was an enemy, one he deemed wasn't unbeatable, but *not worth fighting*.

Noam gritted his teeth, muttering. "I don't need your damn protection."

The myconid didn't seem to respond to this, simply looking off someplace far away.

"No, you do not."


It took him two hours to fully come back.

Two hours in the night spent staring at a silver mirror and blade. Two hours of pacing the perimeter of the same small room. A quiet tension between the two humanoids, all the while the myconid stayed silent until finally, he spoke.

"So now you know."

Tai jumped at this, the tension within her shot like a released bow. "Bastard . . ."

"Yeap," Noam answered as he leaned on the wall. "I know now."

"Will you be convinced now that you know my side of the story?"

"For a person who values logical debate, you sure didn't bother to come to me on such terms."

Dustin sighed. "Because I know you too well."

"Because you know me too well," Noam affirmed.

"Is there any more need for words, then?"

Noam got off the wall. "I always have words to throw down. It's in my damn family. Hells, one time Denise eviscerated a—"

"Can you stop that?" Dustin rudely interrupted. "Stop trying to tell me more about you. I *refuse* to listen."

"Why not?" Noam shot back, walking to face the myconid directly.

Dustin looked up. "Because the more I know about some, the more I see them as just a complicated set of levers to induce certain reactions."

"That's how relationships work," Noam replied, not even missing a beat. "You learn about someone else, you share interests, and you realize the other is a person you wouldn't mind spending time with."

"That can be achieved without more than a shallow understanding of someone else. A friendship can be formed on the simplest of things and end on that."

Noam closed his eyes and took a single deep breath, a technique, a habit of calming he had caught on from the very person before him. Then he stared at Dustin straight in the eye. "That lever shit, knowing how to interact with people by pushing the right buttons—who the fuck do you think you *learned* that from?"

Dustin did not answer.

"I've been with you for *years*," Noam practically snarled. "I was there at your worst, laughed with your best. I know you *better* than you do. So believe me when I say I can break you and your fragile ego, expose all your logical inconsistencies despite claiming you're a bastion of logic, with less than a fucking paragraph."

He raised a hand as Dustin opened his mouth to speak. "I know, I know. You've never verbally claimed it, but don't deny that you think you're the one sane person in this entire world."

Dustin did not answer.

"I want you to know that for all of your damned stupid inconsistencies and flaws, you're still my fucking friend." Noam spoke with absolute conviction. "A person who knows my own flaws yet still goes along with them, just as I do you. I'm your friend not because you're some smart-ass, but because I realize you're still a stupid dumbass underneath all that."

The tiefling grabbed the myconid by the shoulders and hung his head down. "And I thought you knew that as well.

"So why"—his voice cracked—"did you not think to rely on me when you were so worried?"

For the first time, Dustin was at eye level with Noam and realized there were tears in his eyes.

"Was I *that* unreliable?"

Dustin didn't answer, because he genuinely didn't know the answer to that question.

But he had to, so he just admitted it. "I don't know."

He continued to speak, just letting the words flow unimpeded. "I think . . . I prioritized the ideal of our friendship over what we actually had. I saw it as just a commander/pawn relationship, not thinking about it any more than that."

A gentle hand ruffled his cap.

"And it's fine because I know you're an ass, but to fail is not to fall down—"

"But in refusing to get up," Dustin finished.

He smiled. "You're a bundle of contradictory issues shambling roughly in the shape of a human, having more complexes than I can list or remember."

"You're a psychopath battle junkie who would murder people for an adrenaline high. Yet somehow you still agonize over dealing the last blow to someone you hate."

Together they spoke. "You're my friend."

They shuffled apart, the short moment of intimacy finished as they turned their attention to the third person in the room.

. . .who was staring at the both of them wide-eyed and red-cheeked.

"Just to confirm, you're both males, right?"

"Yeah?" Dustin asked, just as Noam slapped his face.

Tai nodded sagely as if she had just obtained enlightenment. "Thank you for showing me that."

"You're welcome?" Dustin replied.

"So, um . . ." Tai shuffled awkwardly. "What now? There's still . . . *it* on the loose."

"It's pretty simple, actually," Dustin began.

"Almost elementary," Noam added.

"Now is when we begin the counterattack."

$$1.23$$

---

*"What is with this obsession with the number five?! That's the eighth party this week of young adolescents who thought they could assassinate me with only five people!"*

—*The Revenant King*

Dawn rose on an unaware town.

"You sure about this?" Tai asked as Dustin looked at the wizard's tower.

"More or less," he answered. "It's too late now."

She nodded in return, eyes following Dustin's own to the top of the tower. A large open-air balcony overlooked the entire town.

Dustin's fingers drummed a silver mirror. "Get into position as well."

She nodded, breaking off and heading toward her planned position.

*It can finally begin.*

I reached the top of the tower in due time, feeling the icy-cold morning breeze whip across my face.

Taking a deep breath, I looked over the town as it normally appeared, glancing over every nook and cranny of this large place, until, finally, my eyes arrived at the town center, where there were several sporages planted.

I activated one, the lime spores bursting out, signaling to everyone I was in position.

Raising the mirror, I looked into it, angling it so that I could see behind me.

Rotating around, I once again looked over the entire town until I—I—I saw it. I saw it. I saw it. I saw it. I saw it. I saw it. I saw it. I saw it. I saw it. I saw it. I saw it. I saw it. I saw it. I saw it. I saw it. I saw it. I saw it. I saw it. I saw it. I saw it. I saw it. I saw it. I saw it . . .

* * *

"When someone directly observes its faces, it ceases moving," Dustin said. "It is a very convenient weakness—someone looking at its entirety can stop it from acting altogether."

"But it attacks your mind when you do," Tai pointed out.

"Which makes me the best candidate for it," the myconid replied coolly.

Dustin stood in a place much like a personal study. It wasn't the classy kind, but a derivative of that idea. To any other person, the place would appear highly disorganized, but to him and only him, everything was where he needed it.

Including It.

"We meet again," Dustin said.

It was cautious now, not extending, warily considering its foe.

"Is this the third or fourth time?" the myconid asked conversationally. "I haven't been able to keep track."

Barely any acknowledgment from the other; there was no swagger in its movements as it stalked in a circle around Dustin.

Dustin considered his foe and his surroundings. It was only the third time he'd visited this realm, yet he could understand that there were rules and conventions to this place. He didn't know them, but he could replicate the trick he did to harm his foe. Whether it would be enough was the question.

He looked at himself, realizing his form was a mixture of his human and myconid ones. Appearing in his prime with one exception.

He was missing an eye. Staring down a horror with only an eye of ocean's wonder.

It would have to do.

Noam watched that bundle of sporages in the middle of the town square.

Only one had detonated, a Balm Sporage. Dustin was in position.

The Sneezing Sporage hadn't been detonated. He would've detonated it if he didn't make contact with the Accumulation.

"My turn," he whispered. Noam fiddled around the contraption in his hand one last time before he walked out.

The town was waking; people were coming out. Far fewer than there should be for a town this large. It made his job easier, in a morbid way.

Taking a deep breath, Noam put on his most assholish face, then raised the folded, makeshift megaphone to his mouth. "Good morning, Lake Bayt!"

His voice rang out loud and clear. The megaphone worked.

Putting on a shit-eating grin, he cast his spell. "I was just visiting, ya know, and I want you to know what an absolute shit storm this place is! This backward—"

"We'll need to deal with the townsfolk somehow."

"Can't we just tell them about the creature?" Tai asked.

Noam shook his head. "There's a chance they won't believe us, and we could spend anywhere from a few minutes to hours convincing them. Not to mention the panic."

"And one more thing," Dustin said. "We don't know how the Accumulation would react."

Dustin suspected it was capable of cunning, but how far that went was still in question. "The time we spend spreading the word is time we leave it unchecked."

Its combat capability was still mostly up in the air—they knew it consisted of dozens of serpentlike heads bearing stolen faces, but . . . "We don't know if it has any cards up its sleeve, any last-minute aces. Letting the entire town react to it may cause it to do something drastic."

"And I suspect anyone really capable of helping would be killed already," Dustin added. "The empty mage tower, the lack of any healer in this town . . . We have to go at it alone."

They would be risking a lot of people for a minor numbers advantage.

"I think it would make our chances a lot better if it succeeds, but . . ." Dustin began. "If we do go this route, the worst thing won't be it reacting drastically, but it not reacting at all."

Tai scrunched her brow, but Noam caught on immediately. "It'll make the townspeople think we're bullshitting—all it has to do is smooth away the evidence and we come off as doomsday preppers."

"Then how'll we deal with the townsfolk?" she asked.

Dustin simply looked at Noam.

"—and that's why all of you inbreds should marry a ferret!"

Shocked silence.

Then a baby started crying.

Then another.

And another.

Then he dodged a rotten fruit thrown at him.

Then another.

And another.

People started yelling at him as he laughed and ran. "I know what I said!"

Noam ran around the town, dodging projectiles as he yelled insults into his megaphone, drawing as much of a crowd onto him as possible.

When he thought he had the entire town awake and running after him, he quietly whispered, "Catch These Hands."

Dustin didn't consider Noam's build to be a good one.

It was spectacular in what it did, but when what it did didn't apply, then it was simply there.

Noam's build existed to be killed. He was built to be an annoyance. Even if his ideal scenario occurred, in which he managed to taunt a massive group of enemies and activated CtH, he didn't have a good way to finish all of them off. He could fight that group for as long as he wanted, but the moment he killed or took one of them out, the CtH buff would lose a portion of the stats and he would be weaker. If he fought a group with the intention to kill all of them, then he would eventually lose that critical mass of buffs and get taken down by the much smaller group when his stats were more manageable.

If there was anything his build excelled at, it was wasting others' time and resources.

Which, in an odd stroke of fate, made him the perfect partner to Dustin.

While Noam kept the enemies busy, Dustin could build up his sporages.

While Noam couldn't defeat those enemies in one fell swoop, Dustin could, with enough preparation.

Together, Noam's and Dustin's builds were a duo that could face armies.

They already knew this—they'd played it out against the hordes of chimeras, and they could repeat it a thousand times over against countless enemies.

But at this moment, the circumstances and enemy made this combination widely difficult.

And so, the third variable made her play.

Tai leaped from her vantage point on the roof, a pale reflection in her blade briefly flashing before it was severed. She glanced upward, toward Dustin's perch. Judging by how he stood, the mirror was facing somewhere near the front of the town. Somewhere in view of the inn. She itched to look, despite knowing full well what would happen.

Carefully glancing at the reflection of her blade again, she saw the two bony white halves slowly merging back together. Taking care not to look toward the end of the serpent, she slashed again.

It felt strange, like she was hacking away at mist. Physical attacks didn't seem to harm it for long, so her role was simple.

Dustin was keeping the main array of heads busy while Noam evacu-ated the town and Tai kept the stray necks from picking people off.

Then, once Noam got the townsfolk out, Tai would knock Dustin back to his senses and they would have an empty battlefield to use everything they had against that thing.

It wasn't the smartest plan, but it was the best plan they had.

"I said it was called the Accumulation of White Lies, but . . ." Dustin paused for a moment, trying to think of the best words to describe. "I don't really think I fully understand its implications, just that this thing might not physically exist."

"Meaning?" Noam asked.

"I've mentioned Shadesmar to you a few times, haven't I?" Tai shivered as the myconid spoke.

Dustin nodded toward her. "The thing we face isn't a physical or living thing that was born or raised or grew up. It is a concept born of something getting repeated and repeated until, eventually, it accumulated into a think-ing thing."

"What are you saying?"

"I'm saying whatever it is, it is similar to Shadesmar. Where Shadesmar was born from people's fear of the dark, this thing is born of something else, but the principle is the same," Dustin explained.

"White lies?" Noam suggested.

Dustin nodded. "Possibly. It is a concept, and that is why I am most worried."

He looked around at his companions.

"How do we kill a concept?"

No answer.

"Can it even be killed? Or die, for that matter?" Noam asked.

Tai shook her head. "Yes," she said with certainty. "It can be killed."

"How do you know?"

"You've heard of the Tale of Three Deaths haven't you?" she asked.

Upon their confused faces, she recited, "The First Death was hunted down by the Brothers Three, who together became the Second Death.

"And when the Brothers Three grew old and weary, they were visited by the Many Mourner, who alone became the Third Death.

"It is a story passed down everywhere on Branika," she elaborated. "What it says is simple—nothing escapes death.

"Not even Death."

* * *

*So it's no longer a problem of* can *it die, but whether or not we have the means to make it die,* Dustin thought.

Currently, as the foe brandished the torn piece of his self, that answer was a no. It was more comfortable now, carefully considering him, yet the inkling of the idea that the wound Dustin dealt was just a fluke.

Whatever Dustin faced, it was born of this plane. He wasn't sure what it had taken just now, but after he looked over his faculties, he realized something was missing.

The feeling of admiration toward those who have achieved much.

"So this is my HP," Dustin muttered. It came back, of course, but damage here would eventually render one a vegetable.

Which was problematic, given how Dustin thought he damaged it last time.

The Accumulation attacked the mind by forcing it into a loop. Making it try to remember a face it recognized. Until eventually the mind short-circuited.

Dustin stopped it by shutting his mind down. Turning off the computer before it could crash. Leaving only the faculties that allowed him to strike. That method let him make a counterattack at the cost of him not being able to do anything for some time afterward.

After all, when you turned off caring about the people you're looking for, there wasn't much reason to act.

But still, he was not helpless.

A portion of the entity ripped away, peeling from its body like a page from a book. The growing smile on the Accumulation faded.

*How the fuck did I just do that?* he pondered before laughing.

"And so we fight a most esoteric kind of battle, yet so very boring," Dustin said. "You are too cautious to commit a major attack. I need to buy too much time to hurry this battle up."

He would have to hit it one last time before this was all over. To hurt it on this plane.

Dustin had to hope it would be the finishing blow.


Tai rushed through the town, blade flashing at blinding speeds as she slashed away at stray heads. The foe didn't move quickly; so long as she was careful, she could avoid seeing its face in the mirror.

Yet something was strange—there was little resistance. The remaining heads didn't try to attack her. Tai just spotted them in her blade and attacked.

The town was quiet now that Noam had evacuated everyone—too quiet, it felt. Like a sound that she had passively blotted out just disappeared.

And she realized too late; the pale serpentine neck, gaunt and bony—she saw it with her own eyes. Without looking through the reflection of the blade, without seeing its outlines in mist and spores.

It no longer hid.

And Tai saw a face clearly in the morning sun.


The feeling of awe when standing in front of a thing greater than yourself.

The feeling of melancholy you have when you realize the world has changed.

The feeling of frustration you have when trying to get across a certain concept to a disregarding person.

Gone, damaged, and torn from him.

It was after so much beating that Dustin realized they were on a battle-field of souls. Aura was their form and Will was their strength.

And Dustin was lacking compared to his foe.

He only had a single good attack, and he was useless past that. So he stayed standing, a crumbling visage of his true self until he widened his eye.

"So that's your play."


Something was wrong.

Noam could feel it as he rushed back. His steps slowed as he went farther from the enraged mob.

And he realized that the world felt quieter. That there was a sound like birds chirping that had just been silenced. A sound that, until now, he had just passively ignored, for the mind put aside sensory information that was constant and repetitive.

It was when the town rushed back into sight that he saw it.

Dozens, perhaps hundreds of heads, each connected to a pale, bony neck, reaching into the sky, each with a face. All of them staring at a single tower. He could feel it, that feeling of déjà vu. He looked away from the creature, thankfully too far to make out the details of each face. But as he looked down, he saw the twisting and coiling necks of the heads Dustin hadn't managed to catch. He saw some circling the mage tower like sharks, nipping at the stone, not long enough to reach Dustin, not stupid enough to leave him alone.

"Where is Tai?"

By the plan, she should be running up the tower to wake Dustin at this very moment. Yet something felt wrong. No, the plan was no longer effective. It hinged on the fact they wouldn't be able to see the enemy. Now that it had revealed itself . . .

Even a single look could prove fatal.

Gritting his teeth, he rushed into town, eyes kept down, only seeing the shadows of the creatures that rushed him.

But that was enough.

A spin, a twirl, almost a dance, and three heads fell to the ground.

Even as he ran past the severed necks, he couldn't help but see the stumps fading like mist, slowly rejoining their severed portion.

He couldn't look at his enemy.

It will be a matter of time before he was taken out by an attack in his blind spot.

Dustin was dueling the main form of the beast in a tower. Tai was missing in action. Noam was the only piece on the board that could move.

Corvian Diluvian Medudian Himotonana Farraday the Middling rubbed his head. A strange feeling plagued his mind, yet he could not quite put his finger on what it was.

There was a loud commotion outside, but the town had turned quiet afterward. A bit too quiet, he felt as he left his room, treading into the front room of his games store.

Yet something caught his eye. On the table five decks were arrayed, a game in the middle of playing.

A deep control deck.

A dark elf aggro deck.

A midrange orc aggro deck.

A midrange Gather the Party deck.

And a magus nobalite OTK deck.

A player beaten down from all sides. Sustaining the greatest loss yet persevering until he shined the brightest.

A player who lingered on the side, believing in the safety of himself. Who became the first to die.

A player who controlled the field. Playing others like a fiddle and bringing them to wars they didn't want to fight.

A player who was simply there, trying to gather his win condition, yet never succeeding.

A player who was forgotten. Hidden in obscurity, it won an unexpected victory.

As Corvian tried to remember the game they'd played, he realized some of the players were *gone* from his memory.

His head jerked to outside, where the sun had risen, yet the town seemed all the more sinister for it.

"I must do something."

Gods were ever fickle in their signs and messages. It was up to the believers to interpret and act.

# 1.24

———

*"Maddie! We're surrounded on all sides!"*
*"Wondrous! Now we can attack in EVERY DIRECTION!"*
*—Conversation between Empress Madelyn the Conqueror and her*
*second-in-command, Navy General "Hubby Wubby Sweetie Cheeks,"*
*recently renamed by imperial decree*

Tai!" Noam yelled into the silent town.

No answer greeted him, save the sound of slithering.

Tsking, he drew out his blades. Serpentine forms allowed for a lot of maneuverability. They could appear anywhere. He kept his eyes down, not daring to perform wide-sweeping scans of his area, and took off.

Disturbance on the right, a clay pot shattering. Far away, he ignored it.

A shadow on the ground, a serpent moving parallel to him. Without looking, he swiped up and severed the creature.

A hiss toward his front, a pale form coiled around a lamppost. Its head was farther up, almost beckoning him to see.

He slashed the lamppost, the metals clanging against each other. A formless horror fell severed on the ground.

*They aren't fast*, he realized as he cleared his first block. *So used to perfect camouflage they didn't develop the same burst speed of an ambush predator.*

He rounded a corner, yelling once again, "Tai!"

More slithering shadows, more pale, bony serpents whose heads he dared not look at. He didn't know how many, but if this was a pack creature, *then they must be gathering where there is prey.*

Not even slowing, he ran forward, blades out and slashing at every shadow and glimpse he saw. The pavement rushed under his feet as he cleared another block.

"Tai!"

And he found her this time.

Feet stamped into the ground, arms fallen by her side, her blade drawn but laid low. Noam almost looked to see her face but stopped when he noticed the pale neck wrapped around her own.

*Bait.*

Noam slashed everywhere around him. Numerous heads that had escaped his notice fell to the ground.

He pushed his leg back, crouching almost like a cougar. His target was in sight, and though he couldn't say exactly how many meters away it was like Dustin could, he knew instinctively where Tai was in relation to him.

It was enough.

Blasting off, he threw his arms out, his eyes kept to the ground as he ran and slashed all around him.

At a first glance, it looked like he was randomly flailing about his weapons, only catching the creatures by mistake and luck. A further examination would reveal that his slashes formed a nigh-unbreakable field around him. Though his blades could not be everywhere around him at once, they *could be* anywhere around him.

Ethereal the creatures were; attacks went through them like a hot knife through butter. They only had one trick that could realistically stop him— as long as he kept his eyes down, they could not attack him.

And so he ran, an unstoppable flurry of steel and mist as he made it ever closer to Tai.

Then, a single thing happened.

A single face emerged from the cobbled pavement.

A single face, lain on the ground like a mask.

A single face, Noam saw.

Then a dozen faces smiled as the bard was *silenced.*

*They're intangible* was the last thing Noam thought before his legs froze midrun. Tripping over himself, he fell face-first onto the ground.

A moment of weakness, a moment too many.

Needlelike teeth stabbed into Noam's right shoulder. Then another on his left leg, another on his right side. Noam gritted his teeth as he forced himself up and slashed at the offending beasts. But even severed, their jaws remained firmly in his body.

He made the mistake of looking at his injured shoulder, a nauseating feeling crawling up his throat as he caught the barest glimpse of a face.

The stumps were already moving back, their misty form slowly reconnecting with the heads on him even as Noam slashed in every such direction.

*That's how it hunts*, Noam realized. *It doesn't care if I sever it a million times—it'll eventually reattach to the heads.*

*I'm marked.*

He continued forward, but he was slowing, his blades flashing beautifully in the sunlight, no longer covering every angle. Another bite on his right calf, another source of pain he bit down and ignored.

A pair of jaws slashed his back, his blade no longer fast enough to catch them. His body was bleeding and drenched in his own blood. His mind fought off the pain of a dozen needlelike wounds.

Finally, Noam fell to a knee, stabbing his blade into the ground for support. He was barely a few meters from Tai.

The heads biting into him slowly regenerated; like chains they hung off him, restraining him from reaching his final goal.

Noam was barely aware of a single serpentine head, flowing lazily around him, slowly going around him. Until, finally, he felt the thing staring before him.

A head came from underneath, propping his chin up to look at the face.

Mind numb from pain, body tired and almost broken, he could do little to resist.

And he saw the face.

And he realized something.

He could barely focus on it.

The pain of a dozen wounds, of a tired and wounded body—they all took precedence over the face.

It began as a chuckle, slowly building to the enemy's confusion before it exploded into raucous laughter.

"I can *look* at you!"

Suddenly, his body seemed to surge, and his back straightened as his hook swords once again slashed the offending necks.

*Focus on the pain.*

An attack from overhead parried away with but a passing glance.

*Focus on the elation.*

A surge of serpents came straight for him, but he met them with hook and blade, carving his way through them.

*Do not focus on the faces.*

Dustin saw the vague outlines of a face, but only when he comprehended its entirety did it harm him. Tai similarly dealt with them easily when there were tears in her eyes.

"Focus on *you* winning," he whispered as, finally, Noam stood tall and looked at the enemy all around him. His nose bled, his eyes reddened, as even diluted, the combined strain of looking at so many greatly burdened him.

But still, he stood and laughed.

"This is finally a fair fight!" he yelled into the void. "Breathless, activate!"

Dozens of them stormed him, but he saw their slow movements. He saw them all.

And none reached him.

None would ever reach him now.

Slowly he walked forward, severed necks and heads falling onto the ground behind him. Slowly he walked, ever closer to Tai. His hook swords flailed around him with such speed and intensity that a watcher might be forgiven for mistaking him for an eight-armed deva wielding eight weapons.

A bleeding juggernaut, his blades were his armor, his pain was his protection, his joy was his faith.

He stopped only a single step away from Tai when the serpents ceased their endless attacks. Instead, only a single one had its jaw opened. Stabbing into the flesh of Tai's neck, pinpricks of blood dripping down her tanned skin.

"This a draw now?" he laughed. "Fastest hand in the West? I'd bet on myself over you limp dicks any day."

The face might have been cautious, might have been confident—Noam didn't pay attention. Standing there like a drunk, yet with a swagger that belied his heavily wounded appearance.

Only at the moment, when that jaw closed by the tiniest amount, did he move.

A single step, a single flourish, a single head fell to the ground. Severed from its jaw so that it could not bite her like the numerous that had bitten him.

A second step, a second flourish, a second head fell to the ground. Tai came back to consciousness, no longer seeing the face that took her.

And Noam's bloody form fell on her. Barely catching him, she sputtered, "Noam? What happened to you—" His blades fell clanging onto the ground, and a single bloody hand pawed at Tai's face, staining her vision red and leaving five bloody streaks down her face.

"Keep your eyes blurred," she heard him say quietly. "Don't do it as I did. Too fucking stupid. They're easy when you can look at them."

"You—" Fervently she looked around, seeing the numerous serpents but without making out any details of their faces.

"I want to keep going but I don't think I can," he muttered, voice low like a dying engine.

His body barely had the strength to stand; only by leaning on Tai was he upright at all. His hand went to his belt, drawing a wand with careful deliberateness.

Before he didn't dare look up, but now that he could, he looked at the mage tower, where a single figure stood holding a gleaming mirror.

His body spent and weak like a wet noodle, he mustered the last of his aura to shakily bring his hand up. His mind was tired, and he was not seeing clearly.

Still, you needn't insult him by saying he couldn't hit a stationary target.

A mirror shattered, and Dustin was freed.

With a smile, Noam patted Tai on the shoulder. "I'll leave it to you."

And with that, he fell unconscious, now out of the fight.

# 1.25



*"Bah! You cannot stop me! The prophecy foretold that no man
shall ever kill me, and your party isn't diverse enough!"
—Tyrant Cornelius the End of Empires, best known for progressive
tax reform, normalizing same-sex marriage, and dying a slow death
of gangrene after getting scratched by his pet kitten, Zoe*

Hello?" Celigarn yelled into the empty room. The inn goers had long left; he'd heard Noam yelling some slurs earlier, which might've driven them away, but overall he was just left on the floor of the inn.

"Anyone there?" he asked, just as a shadow came over him.

"What are you doing here?"

I put away my carving knife.

Noam was down, and Tai was dragging his unconscious form as she slashed her way toward the tower. Her eyes were blurred by his own blood.

Such a simple solution to a hard question. Now that it no longer hid, we needed to blind ourselves rather than seek it.

Now, on to a more important question.

How do I get down quickly?

Tai wasn't having much trouble now that she could "see" the monster, but now was perhaps the most important step: quickly killing the enemy while the townsfolk were out. So it was imperative that I meet up with Tai quickly.

I was slow.

But I was durable, short, and vaguely rod-shaped.

And so, in the desperate need to keep tempo on our side, I *rolled* down the circular stairs.

Soon hitting the ground floor, I hurriedly got up, dusting myself off just as Tai ran in, slamming the door on a dozen charging serpents.

She glanced at me, confused. "How'd you get down so fast?"

"I found a secret shortcut," I lied as I walked forward. My eye hardened as I saw Noam's unconscious body behind her back. Quickly, I covered his wounds with Balm Spores. "This is a critical moment; we need to finish it off now."

She nodded, just as beasts found the cracks in the tower once again. I quickly dabbed some of Noam's blood on my eye as I turned to look at it. I had seen enough for Analyze to begin constructing a sheet.

<u>Body:</u>

Strength: 4-11

Agility: 6-8

Dexterity: 2-14

Shillelagh didn't have great stats; it wasn't a physical hunter. Noam and Tai had easily contended with it even when there were dozens.

"Its core is the Orphanage of Tilt near the inn." That was where all the necks led to.

Her blade flashed as dozens of heads fell, their mist-like forms still regenerating.

"And how do we get there?"

I raised my staff, slamming it down on the severed heads and pulping them. "We fight."

And she nodded, a grim, determined nod as she kicked open the door once again.

In front of us, dozens of the monstrous form slithered. Their faces were just barely obscured by the blood, crawling through the air and dirt, smiling with their viciously white needle teeth.

Whoever once owned those faces was long dead.

"Go!" Tai yelled as she took the lead.


Swing and stab.

Stab and swing.

An occasional block.

Lao Lao wasn't particularly good at naming attacks, but they worked for what they did. And as Tai attacked through the waves and waves of enemies, she couldn't help but notice a discrepancy.

Where once it was a tiring battle to keep track of multiple foes at the same time, none of which she could see clearly, now it was almost a walk in the park.

Dustin stood behind her, only occasionally throwing an attack or blocking, but every one of these actions *mattered*.

His movements were crude and simple, but there was precious little wasted movement as he covered every angle Tai couldn't.

Slamming away a head she couldn't catch.

A puff of yellow to disrupt one while another held her blade.

An extra eye who called out the location of enemies she couldn't see.

As they slowly progressed toward the monster's heart, she realized that their slower movement wasn't a detriment. Dustin wasn't a burden—in fact, with him at her back, she felt like she had grown a new extension of herself, constantly there, constantly assisting. Even holding Noam's unconscious body, she wasn't unduly troubled.

Sometimes she saw Dustin quickly adjusting to mistakes *she* made. An overextended attack led to a quick block by him, a failure to assess all angles covered by his eyes.

Even as the heads gradually increased in number and ferocity, they moved forward, until they were practically carving a path through a tide of monsters.

Still, they moved forward.

His actions were small, but they were never meaningless.

How many hundreds did they cut, bash, and poison?

Carving a path of severed heads and necks, their mist-like forms broken and on the ground. So great in number they hung on the town like a heavy fog.

And so, two people stood and one hung on a back, unconscious, in front of an empty church. It was a simple thing, not ornate but colorful, the chalk and drawings of little children dotting the walls. It was a place that would've given the feeling of youthful joy.

That was, if there wasn't the massive stalk, created from hundreds of necks held together, shooting out of the ceiling.

"They're not attacking anymore," Dustin muttered. Instead, the still solid faces hung back, at the edges of their perception, probing, watching.

Waiting.

"We could slash that thing," Tai suggested, pointing at the massive collection of necks reaching into the sky. "Would be a start."

"And if it heals back?"

"I don't know then."

"We're making this up as we go," Dustin admitted quietly.

For all their victories, they still knew little of how to finish this threat for good.

"Not to mention . . ." The Accumulation had its heads all held back. It wasn't doing anything, where once they'd assaulted them at full force. To

Dustin, it meant it had a card it hadn't used yet. "At best we're walking into a trap."

"Do we have another option?" she asked quietly.

"Maybe if we had more time," Dustin replied.

"And we may waste all the progress we just made."

"That we might," he admitted.

"So let's go."

"Let's go," he agreed.

And they stepped over the boundary, past the fence, through the gate. They felt it then, that feeling of déjà vu, the feeling they'd *already done this*.

They passed the familiar doors. They saw the familiar drawings. They opened and looked at familiar rooms, empty of children.

Until, finally, they came upon the dining hall.

There it lay, rotting food, its eaters long gone. Chairs fallen over, simple cutlery strewn and dirtied.

And there they saw it.

A massive, bulging stomach, from which all the necks led. Appearing like a transparent bubble of white flesh and membrane, black veins criss-crossed in eldritch ways. Too angular and chaotic to be natural formations.

And inside they saw them.

The final remains of someone, their flesh utterly melted, leaving naught but a flesh-colored sludge wearing clothing. *Rhyme*, Dustin thought as he looked at it.

And the other two, a girl with white hair and a featureless face, her body almost completely intact, a ragged black cloak seeming to hug around her. Above her, shielding her like a babe, was a lizardfolk, his back held toward the fleshy ceiling as strange colorless liquids fell down. His back was almost entirely melted, sloughing off the sides in a green pool. He could see his exposed spine from there.

**7. Utoqa might still be alive if you act fast enough. He's durable—he might Survive, but I'm not sure about Celine and ******.**

"Utoqa!" Dustin yelled, brandishing his staff as he finally, finally *remembered*.

Utoqa raised his head and, seeing them, opening his mouth as if to speak, but Tai was already running, her blade brandished and glowing with aura—

"Close."

They all froze.

A single head drifted in; it bore no face, it had no features, save the maw of needlelike teeth curled in a perpetual smile. Dustin knew that face.

It was the thing he fought in the landscape of souls.

"You came so very close," the Accumulation of White Lies said. "But you cannot catch It. You cannot hurt It. You cannot kill It."

Dustin broke out of the spell first. A Shillelagh-empowered staff slammed toward the monster's head, but it dodged, moving swiftly away. "Now, Tai!" he yelled, just as she forced her body to move. Rushing the last few steps toward the monster's—

"Fade."

And she slashed it, the blade passing through the mist like body, not even harming it one bit.

"You cannot catch me. You cannot hurt me. You cannot kill me," the First Face sang, voice melodious and jarring, beautiful and horrific, calming and harrowing. "You can only—"

Dustin spat acid, the glob of green landing directly onto the monster's head, melting through it.

""""""""""""""""""""You can only **Fade**."""""""""""""""""""""

And a dozen voices spoke. The heads all returned, surrounding them, and with them came a high whistling sound, repeated across dozens of throats. Sung with dozens of voices. And Dustin finally noticed that the needlelike teeth had holes in them, holes like a flute.

"It comes when it has become quiet."

"It is closest when it is so quiet you remember you forgot the song."

"It attacks when you realize the silence is so quiet it drowns out all other sounds."

"So you must be scared of the deafening silence."

And the realization hit Dustin like a truck. "Sound!" he yelled, "Tai! Cover your ears!"

The silence was not directly caused by its ability, but when it turned *off* its ability. He could already feel it assaulting his mind; he could already feel the mists of forgetfulness worming their way through.

Tai immediately dropped Noam, covering her ears with both hands.

Still singing, the heads came through, biting her flesh. She tried to cut them off, but she could not do so while covering her ears.

Dustin threw out his arms, screaming as he cast Poison Spores all around them, but still, he was too late; he watched helplessly as she was dragged into the air. And inside the stomach, the corpse of the one that Rhymed finally broke, a new head sprouted from its remains. And only then did the head grabbing Tai open its mouth unnaturally wide and swallow her whole.

And he watched as she fell into that transparent stomach. Rising as quickly as she could to run toward the edge. Blade out and slashing at the membrane.

But it softly bounced off.

She slashed and slashed at the stomach, but no matter what, she never made a single cut.

"You cannot come out," the First Face sang. "It is your fault."

Dustin tried to block it out; he held his hands by his head as the song continued to assault his mind—

And he remembered he didn't know where myconid ears were.

"It is not your fault." The First Face laughed at him. "You weren't the cause of all this. For you cannot defeat me."

The myconid stopped, alone within his shield of poison, the gibbering monsters mere meters from him, scratching for every weakness.

And he turned and stared at the First Face.

"You will lose," he said, as certain as fact. "You will not win here. You will be beaten."

It simply smiled. "You do not think so—"

"Oh, I do," he said. His form was without emotion, like a doll, simply acting out the motions. "This entire time you've talked, you've spoken nothing but *lies*."

"I speak only truth."

"I will show you what 'truth' looks like," he replied, and he *smiled*, a vicious, villainous smile, for it had become stronger, strong enough for him to speak it. "**Analyze**."

And the song was interrupted as the monster *screamed* and Dustin *cackled*. Both an ear-tearing melody. One of fear and the other triumph! As he finally *saw*.

**The Accumulation of White Lies**
<u>Racial:</u>
Aberration of Memories Level 3
<u>Body:</u>
Strength: 8
Agility: 7
Dexterity: 9
Constitution: N/A
Stamina: N/A
Vitality: N/A
<u>Mind:</u>
Intelligence: 9

Wisdom: 4
Charisma: 24
<u>Soul:</u>
Will: 14
Aura: 34
Perception:11
<u>Traits:</u>
**Bardic Adept:** This creature is a bardic combatant.
**Ignorance:** This creature may contest knowledge and perception checks targeting it.
**Devour:** This creature may consume an opponent, keeping it inside its stomach and potentially eating killed opponents for benefits.
**Ruthless:** This creature will target downed opponents and finish them off when given the chance.
<u>Hidden:</u>
?

<u>Basic Combat:</u>
**Bite Attack:** The Accumulation may attack with all its heads, dealing puncture and slash damage. Should it succeed in such an attack, it may choose to grapple with the target.
**Sing:** The Accumulation may stop singing or start a song with an additional head.
**Wail:** The Accumulation may let out a piercing scream, dealing psychic damage to all creatures that can hear it.
**Consume:** The Accumulation consumes a creature, placing them inside its stomach. It can have up to three humanoid creatures inside at any time.
**Digest:** Creatures inside the stomach of the Accumulation will take continuous acid and bludgeoning damage.
**Immobile:** The Accumulation is a nascent creature. Since it is recently born, it does not yet know how to walk.
**Grow Head:** Whenever a humanoid creature is digested, the Accumulation will begin growing a new head with fragments of the knowledge and skills of the humanoid creature digested to grow it.
**Horrific Visage:** Intelligent creatures that see a face that the Accumulation has grown will need to make a mind or soul save or take psychic damage. Damage and severity scale with the familiarity the target had with the face.
**Conceptual Creature:** The Accumulation is a conceptual entity; thus it is resistant to nonconceptual damage.
**Aberrant Form:** The Accumulation is a huge aberration, as such, it has the following immunities and resistances:

- Damage Resistances: Psychic
- Condition Immunities: Blinded, Charmed, Grappled, Prone, Stunned, Unconscious

<u>Fade:</u>

**Blind Song (Active):** The Accumulation sings a song of oblivion; all creatures that can hear the song must make a mind or soul save against its CHA. Every additional head the Accumulation sings with slightly increases the DC of the save. On a failure, the creature loses all perception of the Accumulation's existence while the song persists. An extremely high mind or PER check must be met to even notice evidence of the Accumulation's existence while under these effects.

**Sea of Forgotten Faces (Passive):** Whenever the Accumulation consumes a creature, memories of that creature will be forgotten so long as the creature remains in its stomach. If the creature is digested, the memory erasure becomes permanent.

<u>Hidden:</u>

?


Then it shot out screaming. The First Face shot through Dustin's spores, uncaring of the pain as its teeth tearing off his Bark Skin and Bracken Polypores, until it reached his face.

Until it reached his eye.

Teeth extended, it grabbed the shattered Eye of Discovery, pulling at the thin threads of mycelium as Dustin grabbed it by its neck. A desperate tug-of-war for the eye.

A Clash Dustin lost, as it tore out the Eye of Discovery.

He fell, the light of Analyze fading from his form as the monster laughed in victory and triumph. For it had stolen the Second Eye of Two.

And Tai watched helpless, as they *lost*.


Dustin awoke in the abandoned orphanage's empty dining hall, surrounded by the broken fragments of his armor. Clutching his empty eye sockets.

And the first thing he said was "What was I doing here?"

# 1.26

———

*"Strategy? I don't know, it's always just been a feeling for me.
Trial and error. If one thing doesn't work, I do another thing and
just keep repeating that. If there is anything I live by, it is this: if
you go into a fight without vaguely knowing the outcome, you've
fucked up somewhere."*

—*Dustin the Traveler, Guild Leader of (?)*

What was I doing here?" Dustin's voice resounded through the empty hall, yet none answered it. He glanced around blindly, but he only saw a few meters from himself, his manavision not extending farther.

Picking up a broken piece of his bark armor, he looked at it for a second before crumbling it in his hand.

"Hello?" he asked again as he took a step forward, brows furrowing as he found Noam on the ground. "What the hell happened to you . . ."

All the while, the many faces of the Accumulation watched as he knelt to check on his injured comrade.

And they watched, drawing closer as Dustin whispered something into Noam's ear.

Corvian Diluvian Medudian Himotonana Farraday the Middling walked the stairs of the orphanage. A trick of hiding, granted from an old cloak. He originally wasn't sure if it was necessary, but upon seeing the pale serpents flash briefly into sight, then disappear all the same, he was certain.

There was an enemy here. An enemy that needed to be beaten.

And so he stood here; in front of him was a cracked and corrupted silver bell.

From his cloak, he retrieved an ardent censer, and he lit it, the incense flaring lazily to life as smoke drifted out.

"I am Corvian Diluvian Medudian Himotonana Farraday the Mid-dling, follower of Wundull, the Plays Almighty, the Old Friend, the Prince of Ninety-Nine Nights." Deep was his voice and strong his faith. Nothing seemed to happen at first, yet still the power hung in the air. "I come here to the desecrated shrine of Tilt to restore what was lost and—"

Something booped him on the nose—a small fairy, composed entirely of incense smoke, giggling as its form broke and faded into smoke.

"Don't be so serious, dummy."

And Corvian smiled. "Then I'm here simply as a *friend*."


The First Face watched Dustin as he drew closer and closer to his fallen ally. They were not ones who perished after death, the whispers had told it. They could not be bled and slain; they could not be eaten and taken. If they were killed, they faded, disappearing far away.

Far, far away, away from its song.

And so it didn't kill them—no, it would cripple them. Trap them here until it became strong enough to fade even them, and then it would eat them. Until then, it would trap them in a loop. Every day it will kill another three, and every day they would come back to stop it, and every day they would *fail*.

But first, it must ensure that they would always fail.

And so it waited, a den of snakes coiled as the myconid took another step toward its ally, and when he finally knelt beside them, the First Face struck. Twice it had won, an eye stolen each time, and on the third victory, Dustin would truly be blind.

It closed in behind him, quick and unseen, opening its jaws wide to immense proportions—

Dustin threw out an arm behind him, a single purple mushroom clutched in his hand, just as the First Face bit down, the hand in its mouth.

"Rot Spores."

And the sporage detonated, the rot ripping through the head of the First Face, the pieces sloughing off Dustin's bare, rotted hand, dropping the long neck that supported it as the song was *interrupted*.

The many faces of Accumulation of White Lies watched in shock as Dustin smiled, a crooked, horrific thing, for he *remembered*.

"I did not think that would work," he laughed, the second time that day. Kicking at the neck as the scraps of the First Face faded like mist and tried to reform. He tried fanning it away, finding it somewhat effective in keep-ing it from regenerating. "See, you're a damn bastard to fight. Can't see you, can't look at you, can't damage you, can't even remember you half the time, but despite all that, you're still *predictable*."

*How?* the Accumulation wondered, but the lesser faces could not speak, and Dustin kept smashing the First Face next to him.

"Attacking Noam from behind, forcing us to come close to your stomach, baiting someone into a trap is your main strategy, isn't it? You don't break that style easily, so when I saw Noam lying there, I knew it was a trap."

But how did Dustin remember? It was by a chance glance toward the floor that the secret was revealed.

The Bark Skin and Bracken Polypores that once guarded Dustin's face, shattered on the ground in a dozen pieces—carved in them were *words*.

And it glanced at Dustin, seeing how almost his entire body was covered in the woody defense.

"Did you realize?" he asked with glee. "I'm guessing you figured it out—I can't see far with my manavision, but close to me? I can see *everything*."

Dustin had carved all his notes into his very armor; through his manavision, he constantly saw all the tiny and rough grooves that were written in his very body. Paper would not have worked as well, for tucked away in his cap, the indentations of ink were too minuscule. He needed to see and understand instantly, without having to take it out to look. Something that wouldn't be immediately obvious to his opponent.

Dustin smashed the remains of the First Face again as it tried to form back up, propelling the other heads to action. Dozens moving in closer to—

And they all froze, for within five meters, Dustin saw *everything*.

Including faces.

And now they stood once again, within the dominion of souls. "You cannot attack me," Dustin laughed, voice high with glee and madness in equal measure. "Come close and my manavision will see you."

Dustin had left it off while they came here; it was simple, like closing one eye while leaving the other open. He didn't want it on at the wrong time, for he didn't know a method to obscure his manavision. Left on, he would freeze when a face came close.

But now, this weakness was his protection, as the Accumulation could not physically come near him.

"Possible!" The Accumulation raged, its mind and soul rippling across the entire world. A great typhoon as it raged. "You have both Eyes, and I have lost here!"

The Accumulation's power ripped at Dustin, tearing across imaginary flesh.

Still, Dustin laughed.

"Only that last one is true!" he yelled. "But you thought I really needed some dumb eye to beat you? That I would be crippled and lost without them? Please." He breathed out, tapping his head. "An eye is merely a tool for gathering information.

"It is the mind that uses it," he said, and the world rippled, Dustin's own words crying as the Accumulation's power broke against him. It was weak compared to his enemy, but tempered without measure. The Accumulation was forced a step back as Dustin spoke.

"And I have already **Predicted** your defeat."

And the world cracked, as the Accumulation was forced back into the physical realm. For Dustin stood no stronger than he was before, for a Traveler could not increase without the system, but he had learned, he had refined.

He had spoken a word entirely his own. Not given by the system, not gifted by gods, something that was his and his alone. He was now what a knife was to a lump of raw iron.

Several heads fell, obliterated by an unseen force, and the First Face retreated, having healed while Dustin was frozen.

Yet a single, bleeding crack marred its empty face.

When Dustin opened his palm, he found a black eye, not black because it was purely so, but because it was formed from *millions* of smaller eyes, each seeing, each Observing. For he won the Clash.

And he popped it back into his socket.

"Finally," a voice said in relief.

"One of two," Dustin continued.

"Took you long enough," the voice replied.

"Some help you were," he answered.

"There's still one left."

And both Declan and Dustin spoke at once. "So let's take it back."

They stood, half-blind, missing an eye and alone, the connections they once had all gone. Crippled they were, yet for the first time in its life, the Accumulation felt *afraid*.

"No!" the First Face yelled in defiance, air pushing out of its throat as it began to sing—

A bell tolled, a loud, clear, and pure sound.

And a new voice echoed throughout the corrupted orphanage, a voice Dustin recognized.

". . . and I will be there to see your final joke. I will save my last laugh for you alone, for now, I pray you accept me as a friend as Wundull once did. To save everyone here, I am willing to renounce even him."

And the cheerful voice of a mischievous young girl echoed in all their minds like a summer song.

"Dawww. But there's no need—you can never have too many friends."

And the Shrine of Tilt was restored.

The Accumulation of White Lies hissed; from dozens of heads came the breath to sing the song—

But the sound that came out of each face was simply a loud farting sound.

The Prankster laughed, her voice clear as a bell, for no matter what the Accumulation sang, it only came out as a loud farting noise.

"That tiny glowing BLEEP!"

"Hey, it knows my title . . ." The voice of Tilt faded as her miracle took place; for now, the song of the Accumulation was *sealed*.

Dustin's already massive grin only seemed to widen, as he shared a look with Tai, who was still trapped in the Accumulation's stomach.

He could not hear her voice, but her lips said enough.

"BLEEP yeah!"

Suddenly tapping his shoulder from behind was a short gnome, wrapped in a grayish cloak. "I'm here, what do you—"

"Grab Noam and get out of here," Dustin answered instantly.

Corvian did so, hoisting the much taller man over his shoulder. "Then what?"

"Grab every person and bring them here," he continued.

"Wouldn't that be—"

"No," Dustin interrupted, for he understood now how to harm the Accumulation.

When the town was populated, it did not turn off its invisibility; only when it was vacated did it do so. *Why?* Dustin had pondered. Surely it had enough faces to trap everyone here and slowly eat them one by one? There was a reason why it didn't do so, a reason revealed with every true harming blow Dustin dealt to it.

The Accumulation of White Lies was harmed by people *knowing* about it. Understanding how it worked, recognizing the rules behind its abilities and behavior. It was literally more powerful the less one knew about it. Its song allowed it to hide and heal, removing the memories of it, but now that it couldn't?

So obvious in hindsight that the concept of lies was harmed by the truth being revealed.

"Now is the perfect time to harm it," he said, "and we need as many people as possible to see it. I already used my one hit. I can't do anything else."

Corvian nodded, just as the dozens of faces snarled. The First Face glared at Dustin. It abandoned its song, charging them as Dustin raised his staff.

"Go!" he yelled. "I'll cover you here!"

And Corvian ran, Noam over his shoulder, his cloak hiding them as he left, his mission clear.

To finally kill this damn thing.

# 1.27

-----

*"What do you mean, the Revenant King was assassinated?! And
by some random group of five adolescents, no less!"*
—*The Revenant King's most loyal second-in-command, Lieutenant
Traitorous, upon learning of her lord's demise*

Corvian kicked open the door to his shop, hurriedly riffling through draw-ers before he found a health potion. Pressing the bottle to Noam's lips, he gently caressed it down the tiefling's throat.

"Hurry and wake, you fool," he muttered in desperation.

Noam gagged, coughing up the red liquid as his eyes fluttered open.

"I have an idea what Breathless *really* does. Blood loss shouldn't affect you at all, so bring them all back."

"Declan," he murmured breathlessly.

"Are you—"

Noam pushed past the gnome, his legs wobbling for a moment before he fell to the ground again. *Shit.* "Corvian, I need you to bring me out."

"You've lost a lot of—"

"Blood, yeah, I know," he cut in. "I can still speak, so I can still do what I'm best at."

"And that's?" Corvian asked as he slung one of Noam's arms around his shoulder.

The tiefling smiled, vicious and mischievous. "Inciting a hate mob."

As Corvian dragged him out, he caught a glimpse of the orphanage. The silver bell was still ringing as yellow and green spores covered the entire building. Half-hidden shapes of serpents danced in them as Dustin kept the entire beast occupied.

Another reason why they needed to leave—to not be caught up in friendly fire.

"We're bringing everyone back?"

"He told you that as well, huh?" Noam replied.

"Do you think it'll work?" Corvian asked, his voice still slightly doubtful.

"It will," Noam answered, his voice frank and determined. "It will because Dust's the only one who's dealt a blow that *stuck*."

Of course, he hadn't deigned to tell either of them how it was done. That stupid thing where he thought five steps ahead and was surprised when his own teammates couldn't catch up.

Under Noam's direction, they neared the edge of the town, toward where he'd first dragged that . . . disturbingly small crowd that was the remainder of the town's population. Some of them were already heading back, their faces confused and misty.

He rolled his shoulders, feeling the slightest bit of strength returning. Losing blood wasn't nearly the death sentence it should've been, thanks to Breathless.

Breathless was a very simple ability. He didn't need to breathe, but the specifics of it made it powerful. How it worked was that every single one of his cells got the maximum required oxygen to function at maximum capacity—removing not just the requirement to breathe, but also the need for red blood cells to transport oxygen.

Granted, that blood still needed to transport nutrients and waste, but the end result wasn't just the fact that he didn't need to breathe.

With every single cell juiced up with oxygen, the ability left him in a state very similar to blood doping. Every cell was operating at maximum aerobic respiration, giving him far higher than normal energy, which resulted in a ten percent increase in all his stats.

It sounded small, but it was utterly broken for the simple reason that no stat existed apart from the other—all these ten percent buffs stacked multiplicatively.

For example, his ability to dodge something wasn't just increased by a ten percent increase to his Agility; a ten percent increase in Perception also allowed him to see attacks faster, and another ten percent increase in Intelligence increased his ability to react to attacks. Just by those three, his ability to dodge an attack increased by thirty-three percent. Not to mention, his Constitution increase meant he was ten percent more durable, and a Vitality increase meant he healed ten percent faster.

When he dodged thirty-three percent more attacks, was ten percent more durable and healed ten percent faster, it overall meant he was sixty-one percent better at taking damage.

The ability also made him high.

Every action had multiple different stats in play at once; there were countless ways to calculate how they would function at any given moment. Still, Noam knew the moment he first turned on the passive that it was an absolutely fucking broken ability.

Which was why he almost never used it.

He could breeze through every single fight with just this one ability. *And where's the fun in that?*

But it was a shame to waste it, so he established three conditions, and if one was met, he would use it.

One, if using the ability made the fight *fair*. Not an easy victory or a complete defeat, but only when using Breathless allowed him to fight at an even footing with an opponent.

Two, when using it with Catch These Hands, because that buff completely overshadowed Breathless anyways.

And third, if Decs needed him to.

Strangely, when he put in place these conditions and followed them— even when it would be detrimental to him—he realized that Breathless actually became *stronger*.

It relieved fatigue, it activated faster, and he felt the rush even quicker. The stats were about the same, but it seemed to work even better. As if he added a bunch of quality-of-life features.

And he couldn't help but remember something: *Limitations matter more than strengths.*

Oddly, or perhaps characteristically, with Breathless, he only needed to breathe when he needed to speak, to give air for his vocal cords to work.

Thus, it would be rather accurate to say that Noam only breathed to shit talk people.

And he took a deep breath.

"Hello, hello!" he yelled, drawing the attention of the small crowd that was returning. "You may remember my comments about your turtle BLEEPING nature . . ."


"Holy fried biscuits!" Corvian yelled as he carried the laughing Noam like a sack. "Was that really necessary?"

The tiefling simply laughed harder as sticks, stones, words, and a bit of everything was thrown at them.

"I didn't even know hamsters did that!" Corvian continued to yell, his voice a mixture of betrayal and shock. "And what you said about John and his dog—how could you?"

"Because it's *BLEEPING* hilarious!" Noam yelled in reply.

"Stop swearing!" the recently ordained priest of Tilt yelled. They turned a street, the mob nipping at their tails. Ahead, a small figure was thrown out of the spore mist, bouncing off the neighboring street much like a basketball.

Dustin rolled to a stop, quickly bringing himself up. He was battered and bleeding, but still, his mouth crept into a smile as he saw them come.

The Accumulation of White Lies burst out of the yellow smoke at that exact moment.

The numerous faces all turned to them, half in shock and surprise, and *they all froze.*

The stampede behind them slowed to a stop as more and more heads came and more and more townsfolk returned.

More and more faces met each other.

For a brief moment, there was only silence as dozens of people looked at the feast of faces arrayed before them, each trying to recognize what was forgotten and hidden. Each trying to pierce the *lie* that draped over their mind like a veil.

Until it clicked.

"Mom? Dad?" a young girl, barely a teen. Her eyes were filled with tears and her voice was weak and crumbling. The innkeeper who held the fort alone.

Two faces broke, the necks that supported them disintegrating into mist.

And one by one, the stolen faces shattered as memories returned.

Dustin walked forward, back toward the center of the beast as the necks cracked and fell beside him.

Every bit of lasting damage he dealt to the monster happened when he was looking directly at one of its faces.

Here with so many people looking at it, it wasn't the bombastic display of Paths spoken and knowledge grasped from the shadow of falsehood, but a slow crumbling; the stone that made this lie was being chipped by a dozen smaller chisels until it finally fell apart.

Dustin entered the orphanage, Noam and Corvian by his side. Now when they stood in the mess hall, they saw Tai helping Utoqa up as the stomach that held them broke into nothing.

The sun shone through the hole in which the Accumulation once let out all its numerous heads. He was already casting the Fix-Up Fungus. Tai had only been inside for a few moments, but her skin was burned just as well.

He stepped on something that felt like a pebble, but when he looked down, he saw the First Face cracking on the ground; an eye so blue it looked to be made of lapis lazuli was all that was left as it broke. Beside it was the tarot card of the Magician, held upright. He picked both up, completing his set. It was anticlimactic. He half expected the Accumulation of White Lies to pull out another trick, to fight them further, to have a second boss phase.

But nothing happened.

Celine was still unconscious on the ground, but Utoqa looked up at him, his spine exposed and only now just healing from the Fix-Up Fungus he threw down.

"Getting eaten hurt."

And Dustin chuckled.

The day was won.


On an abandoned field where the ruins of a train lay, a single hand punched through the dirt.

Dragging himself out was a man whose features were indescribable. He was covered in dirt and grime. Rubbing his eyes, he took a deep breath, "Ah . . . It's been a while since I was cremated."

Getting burned to ash really did wonders for the body. All the knots in his muscles and creaky bones were fixed, and he could really feel his spleen working wondrously better than it once had.

Humming a tune as he dragged himself out, he surveyed the area, "Oh, the cute gobbos killed me this time, huh? Didn't get everyone. They wouldn't have cremated me."

Goblins had a very environmentally friendly zero-waste policy, and regenerating from excrement took a while but was a pretty comfy experience.

The strange man soon found his belongings, a cart of various bits and bobs, with a stack of coins held together by a string.

"Wait a moment," he muttered as he realized a distinct *lack* of something. "My potion of happiness is gone!" he screamed.

That wouldn't do—highway robbery he could appreciate, but a *train* robbery? Absolute madness. He would have to rectify this. He would get that alcohol back even if he had to slit the stomach of whoever stole it! Granted, there was a chance it would be digested by then so . . . flesh! He'd just take a pound of flesh! Genius!

He put on the colorful clothes that were only slightly dirty, humming a tune as he did another once-over of his worldly possessions.

"Won't be needing this," he muttered as he tossed the ten coins held together by red string.

He only took one step before his neck was severed.

A golem of dirt and metal had formed out of the tossed symbol. Ringing its brow was a wreath of those very coins woven with red string. A servant of Ethelinda, the Merchant Goddess, come to punish the *fool* who would desecrate her branding.

Instead, the severed head *laughed*. "Oh, wondrous! As expected of the Merchant! Express delivery of karmic punishment! Such reliability!"

The golem took a step back, its glaive held hesitantly at guard.

The body picked up the laughing head, casually plopping it back onto the stump. "I would've loved to follow you, really, but I'm sorry, my heart pines for another!" he orated, dramatically flourishing his hands.

Just as a clock materialized in it—a clock that showed the incorrect time.

"But worshipping you would be worshipping coin. And to worship coin is madness." The strange man smiled. "I much prefer to skip the middleman and just worship madness."

Two minutes later, on a grassy field, lay the servant of a god, rent and broken. And a smiling man who could not be described went on to retrieve what was stolen from him.

# Destination Part 1

"千里之行，始於足下。"

Aspectral skeleton stood, its form surrounded by the green flames of plague. Before it lay five bodies.

**You died!!**

**Like a li'l bitch lmao!!**

Declan opened his eyes, his body lying on the soft grassy ground. It didn't feel like much; the limitations of VR made it so the feeling was little more than some small pressure on his skin.

"Ahhh, not again," Matt complained next to him. Around him, his party members returned as their respawn timers ticked down to zero. A mere group of six random people, a group he was dragged into.

All to do the impossible.

Vek'Na stood living once again. As expected, if the best guilds couldn't take him down, then what could they do? What else could've happened?

"This is pointless," Declan muttered quietly.

Matt shot him a look; he was the only one close enough to have heard him, but Declan didn't care. Not truly—it didn't matter then, and it didn't matter now. A whole day of ramming their heads into a boss, and nothing worked. Nothing *would* work.

"There are some difficulties in beating him," Alex said. The old clone took a genderless character, clad in heavy armor and bearing a spear and shield.

"Yeah," Belle replied, her voice soft and melodious as she rubbed an ache. There was no real pain in VR, so it must've been imagined, or mental fatigue.

"It is a shame," Mortimer added. Declan had never learned his real name, unlike the rest. "We're not the only ones trying this dungeon; the other guilds will probably clear it first."

"And if they don't," Declan said, "what chance do *we* have?"

Matt rang an arm around his neck. "Ah, don't be like that, Decs. Any more down and you'll sound like Mort."

The necromancer shot him a look. "What's wrong with sounding like me?"

"You named yourself *Mortimer Memento*," he shot back. "What else do I need to know?"

"It's a cool-sounding name," Mortimer defended.

"The Memento part sure, but *Mort*? Couldn't you have gone with Mori or something? More on theme, at least?"

"Mori Memento was already taken by some asshole," Mortimer replied. "As was Memento Mori. I spent three hours just finding names."

"How long before you're redeployed again, Alex?" Belle asked, cutting into the conversation between them.

"Two weeks," they replied. "It might be enough for us to clear Vek'Na."

*Or someone else does, and the effort everyone put in becomes meaningless,* Declan thought but didn't say.

"Well, we're gonna have to go to sleep for tonight," Matt said.

"Oh, yeah, you three are still students," Belle mused.

"I never said I was a student," Mortimer immediately shot back.

"Your sleeping patterns and the times you're online do," Declan casually threw out.

The boy shot him a weird look. "Well, I'll have to go to sleep for a reason *completely* unrelated to education."

Belle chuckled; standing on her toes, she reached to ruffle the much taller character's black hair. "*Sure* you do."

"Stop that," Mortimer said, but he didn't move to turn her away.

"Oh, well," Declan said. "Good night."

And he logged off without hearing everyone's response.

His real eyes blinked open, the lights of his room slowly brightening up as he returned to the real world.

He stretched his body, feeling the creases in his back lightening up. Lumbering his way out of the chair that held him, popping his AAD off his neck as he scratched the itchy and sweaty strip where it was bonded.

Matt was mostly talking out his ass, as usual. Declan took almost all his classes online; he found no point in physically being in a school when he could learn the same things at home. It was night, but he didn't really need to sleep right now. Even if he missed the time, he could still watch the recordings. And he didn't feel tired enough to sleep.

But still, he didn't have enough energy to do anything else.

So he sat on the edge of his bed, AAD back in place as he aimlessly scrolled through the internet. Eventually, he came to a now long-deleted post by the Yggdrasil developer.

"Mythic Tomb of Nilbog could be run with more than ten people."

He was technically correct—you technically *could* go into the tomb with ten people on mythic difficulty, but succeeding with a full clear was a completely different beast.

The main problem was Watcher of Death Vek'Na; the boss was the first you could encounter but entirely skippable by just going around his room. Yet the bastard was a difficult one to fight. It had an automatic percent HP execute that increased based on the number of players in the raid—at five, it was forty percent, at six, it was sixty percent, seven, seventy-five percent, ten, eighty percent. That execute would hit any player that reached that HP threshold regardless of where they were within the dungeon. Given the boss's large array of high damage abilities and insane durability for a low-tier boss, it was simply impossible to outdamage the thing fast enough.

Even if it would make the raid significantly easier to kill Vek'Na, it was far simpler to fight your way to the final boss without ever fighting Vek'Na.

That's why the first clear of the raid was already claimed by the Emerald Swords, while the first full clear remained a distant impossibility.

And many people agreed with him; all over the forums, people complained about the numbers of Vek'Na being far too overtuned. It was impossible unless they were an overstacked guild with nothing but try-hards, and *even then.*

Emerald Swords claimed the first clear, but Immense Girth, Goop Troop, Lazarus Hollow, Thick Thighs Save Lives, and Complexity Bop were all following close behind to try and get that first full clear.

And they were all failing.

While no clear progress report could be found from any of them, the members of all those guilds were complaining loudly on the forums. Loudest of which was—

He blinked as he clicked on a profile, Mattmanfoo. Scrolling through Matt's history, he could find *nine* pages of just him yelling expletives over the forum.

"No, it fucking couldn't. You delusional detached piece of shitstain game developer . . ."

His direct response to the dev's first response to the impossibility of mythic ToN. Followed up by far more comments after the dev's second response.

And as he refreshed, he found a *tenth* page of him still raging over the forums.

That idiot was still awake.

Declan didn't understand—no, *couldn't* understand—why Matt was wasting his time on something like this, something pointless, something that was just wasting energy.

Though he didn't pay attention to the talks inside the group, he did catch many things.

Alex, the clone soldier who'd presumably dragged Matt into Australia, was leaving for another tour. Matt had dragged them into this game after Declan half-heartedly invited him in. Matt wanted to get a first full clear for them, to get their character's name, Aban Twice Crowned, placed on the raid first clears so that there was something achieved before they left. Something they did together.

Declan understood it intellectually, but he couldn't understand it emotionally.

It was just text on a game—nothing noteworthy, nothing to write home about, nothing that couldn't be achieved when Alex returned.

If Alex returned.

There was always a chance that they died, that they perished on the way. No one left to find their body, lost among the wastes.

He didn't understand.

But he wasn't tired—he felt lethargic, sure, but he'd felt like that for the past few years. So, he brought up Vek'Na's wiki page, seeing the stats and numbers that other players had data mined. Then he took out everyone's character sheets. Aban Twice Crowned was a tank-build Battle Smith, highly durable and able to use a variety of automatons to assist them in battle. HitZaDec's build was a hemomancer—basically, a vampire that could manipulate everyone's health for benefits. Mattmanfoo was a sharpshooter, specializing in long-range sustained damage and combos. Mortimer Memento was a necromancer, mostly focused on burst necrotic damage and ally raising. Finally, Silv3r_Belle was a maven, doing AOE healing, supporting, and buffing.

He had all the stats he needed, the numbers to calculate the outcomes. It was simple—one just needed to keep a good understanding of the battlefield, and he had a night to burn, so he began writing, calculating. He became hungry halfway through, raiding his sweets pantry several times throughout the night . . .

Declan woke to someone gently tapping him.

He groggily pushed aside candy wrappers and virtual notes alike, blinking blearily as the curtains opened with his waking, letting in the light of the sun. He noticed next the string of notifications at the edge of his vision, then the person standing next to him.

"Matt?" he called out in confusion. "How'd you . . ."

"You still use a traditional lock for the back door," he answered, as if that explained everything.

"What time is—" He noticed it at the edge of his vision—5:42 p.m., displayed on his virtual interface.

At the same time, Matt answered, "Five forty-two. Ya lazy cunt slept till evening." Declan shook off the last remnants of sleep as Matt continued, "What kept you up so long? We're trying again tonight."

And he remembered what he was doing. Sighing, Declan muttered, "Don't bother, we won't succeed either way."

"What do you—"

At that moment, Declan's stomach rumbled, loudly.

Matt raised an eyebrow. "There's a good pizza place nearby."

"What's its name?" Declan asked, already scrolling the air for nearby restaurants.

"Oh, *no.*" Matt grabbed his arm. "The weather ain't even forty today; we're going out to eat."

Declan groaned, "Why eat out when takeout—"

"I'm shouting."

Declan shut up, letting the much skinnier and shorter teen peel him off his desk like an old scab. Following in step behind him as they left the house.

The weather outside was a pleasant twenty degrees, almost freezing compared to what both boys were used to, but it was a small matter as they made their way to the pizzeria.

"I'm telling you, Vek'Na is mathematically impossible to beat," Declan began.

"There's gotta be a way, a fucking trick to it," Matt said as their pizzas were brought out. "Can't we get better stats?"

Declan shook his head. "When I said mathematically impossible to beat, I mean I used the top raiding builds and then some! The DPS check was still impossible. There is simply not a comp that can both survive to his last phase and kill him during it."

He continued to elaborate. "I used Lazarus Hollow's five-man raiding party as a baseline, since of all the guilds they had the best equipment. Assuming they were *completely* world buffed, prebuffed, going in with their maxed orange items *and* played perfectly . . ."

Declan threaded his fingers. "In a straight fight, Vek'Na will win with thirteen percent health remaining."

And that was approaching the theoretical limit of how strong a raid party could be. "The simple truth is, Vek'Na's final stage is that of a DPS check boss—you either have the damage to kill him, or you don't and you fail. And at this current, *no* five-man party has the DPS to get through his normal and rage phase."

If they only had to deal with one or the other, it would be possible, but the thing was, not even counting his abilities, Vek'Na's stats were overtuned. His HP and armor matched that of Turquoise Eternity from the Four Heavenly Kings raid, and his base damage output matched that of the Gunner of Ninth Heaven. Adding in his abilities, then Vek'Na was, without a doubt, the mathematically strongest boss currently in Yggdrasil. He required two very different strategies to even *survive*; his initial phase was that of outlasting him, having the needed durability to survive all his attacks, but once his rage phase activated, it was a thing of outputting more damage than him, because, with all Vek'Na's scaling stats, he *would* wipe the party. But given his first phase, two-three of the party's slots *needed* to be dedicated to tanks and healers, which meant the remaining slots for DPSers wouldn't be enough to take out his final enrage phase before he raid wiped.

"In truth," he continued, "Vek'Na's stats are closer to that of a ten- to fifteen-man raid boss, but given his HP execute, you really can't bring more than five or six people into the instance. *If*, and this is a big if, every player was fully maxed out, had the best equipment, and was top one percent players, they might be able to beat it with seven to eight people."

And they were not that, Declan knew. Between all five of them, only Matt had orange equipment—his dual pistols, Setting Sun and Mourning Moon.

Matt was ruminating on the information, his slice idly dripping cheese from his prosthetic hands. "What if you made a mistake?"

"I might have," Declan answered, but he didn't truly believe, for all his theorizing, it was actually proven in reality. On the forums, there was a clip of Emerald Swords just barely managing to break Vek'Na's HP from seventeen percent to sixteen percent, and that was with the last shot by the last member of that party. It was also confirmed by other raiding guilds that fifteen percent was the lowest anyone had ever gotten Vek'Na.

Declan finished his own pizza. "Like I said, Vek'Na is mathematically impossible to beat, so we should just give up."

"Rather than waste our lives on something pointless."

Because in the end, it was not something they could achieve through hard work; it was not an effort that would be rewarded. Vek'Na's numbers were simply better. And assuming a miracle did happen, that they did manage to kill Vek'Na, what would they get, other than a name on a database? What would they get, that wouldn't be simplified and made easy in the future?

The journey was impossible, the destination pointless.

And why bother chasing the pointless?

# Destination Part 2



There was once a boy who lived a normal life.

It wasn't anything particularly great or bad; it wasn't as good as some, yet better than many others. Born to parents that loved him, yet they were busy. One was a doctor, the other a paramedic, so from the day he could take care of himself, the boy was left alone. He enjoyed eating, but alone at home, he would order takeout for most of his meals, eating junk and fast food, quickly putting on weight. He ended up being chubby, not really fat or obese, but noticeable enough.

Enough that when he entered school, he was bullied—not anything great, snide comments and remarks about his appearance, expected of young children who spoke their minds and pointed out any difference. The boy tried to play with them, but he was fatter and slower; he did poorly in most physical games. Every time he failed, he would become mad and leave, feeling the pointlessness of trying to play a losing game with people he didn't really like.

There was a boy who forgot enjoyment.

"So it's impossible," Alex said, less a question, more a statement as they looked over the piles of notes Declan brought.

"I dunno, this is still all gibberish to me," Belle murmured.

"It is very impressive, however," Alex noted as they shuffled through the papers. "This isn't just an arithmetic of trading HP; you take into account positioning and optimal attack patterns."

Declan shrugged. "It's nothing impressive. I bet you could do it as well, Alex." And he meant it—the clone had displayed a near eidetic memory and a perfect internal clock and was better at logical thinking than he was.

"No," Alex denied quietly. "I could not have."

He raised an eyebrow at this, which prompted them to continue, "My field of knowledge lies in real-world combat. Boss and character statistics, along with their interactions, are outside my purview. So I could not have made this."

"Can we try it out?" Matt finally asked, just as he finished wrapping his head around the last page of the dozen-page document.

"Looks simple enough," Mortimer said, despite his face clearly saying he understood none of it. "We just have to follow this exactly, right?"

"Even if we do," Declan began, "our group can bring Vek'Na to eighteen point forty-one percent health at best." He had the numbers memorized—after all, they were the group he based all his initial calculations on.

It was after he realized it was impossible for their group that he began to try with different builds and parties.

"That's better than anything we've managed to do," Belle pointed out. "We've only managed like twenty percent at best, right?"

"Twenty-three percent is our record," Declan affirmed.

"Then this is a better option than just running in blindly, right?" Matt asked cheerfully.

There were nods of agreement, and even Declan had to agree that this was better than what they'd been doing.

But it was still not possible.

"But it is worth a shot," Matt said.


As time went on, these small comments, little insults, all began to build. If it was just his weight and size, it might've been fine, but every game he left, every time he threw off interaction, only made the others distance themselves from him. Until he no longer felt like he belonged in a classroom, until he longer went to school; instead he took classes from home. A home in which he was alone, a home for three yet only one lived there.

There was a boy who forgot human warmth.


Declan braced for impact.

His long red robes went flapping in the wind as they slapped against his face. Yggdrasil had good wind physics, he had to give them that, but it was extremely annoying that they added it to literally everything. The first boss that entered its final phase by letting out a massive gust of wind was cool; the *fourth* was annoying.

The hundredth was fucking Vek'Na.

"Final phase!" Alex yelled as they slashed at the boss.

The boss turned its skeletal eyes across the battlefield; here came the most annoying part. Upon entering its final phase, Vek'Na spent 0.3 seconds randomly deciding on a target before moving. Due to it becoming immune to taunt and CC effects, they had to spend at least 4.6 seconds—that was, enough time for Alex to perform two full damage rotations—before they could do anything.

The most dangerous thing in this moment was the fact they could not take actions that would generate more aggro than Alex during this phase, otherwise, combat lines would be lost and Vek'Na would target the back line. All the while, Clarion Call was eating into their HP.

This was the moment that wiped out the vast majority of parties.

Clarion Call should only bite into about twenty-three percent of all their health, but it was a *close* shot. Most in danger was Alex, who was fighting for aggro control while Declan and Belle were healing them. It was a razor-thin edge they were walking. They needed to heal *just* enough that Alex stayed alive, but not enough that either of them generated higher aggro. It was just, *just* possible with spreading the duty across two healers.

"Finished!" Alex yelled, and they all moved to action.

"Heartbeat Healing!" The AOE overtime heal centering on Belle was currently enough to counteract the Clarion Call DOT.

Declan ran toward the edge of the instance, just within Belle's healing AOE while throwing his own attacks.

"Eldritch Blast!" Mortimer yelled, just as Matt's dual pistols fired into life. Both DPSers were heavily hobbled in this situation. Without Alex's taunt or CC abilities, they had to hold aggro purely through damage, which meant if either Mortimer or Matt surpassed their DPS, then this razor-thin fight would be lost at that moment.

However, it would eventually be lost.

Clarion Call's damage over time kept biting into them, gradually increasing in damage. Just as the boss fell down to twenty-three point six percent health, Declan was forced to break this paradigm.

"Red Wedding!" He cast his AOE buff, affecting all players. It was one of the ultimate abilities of the hemomancer build, granting lifesteal to every party member.

It also raised his threat level by an absurdly high amount.

Vek'Na turned its head away from Alex for a single moment before Alex activated their own ultimate.

"MK7 Mechatron."

Above them, a clear blue portal opened, and a massive steampunk mech fell through, picking up Alex and tossing them into its cockpit, just as

Vek'Na took its first step toward Declan. Alex rammed the boss, reestablishing aggro.

*22.3%*

This was the moment where most of their DPS could be allowed to flourish; in the short moment Alex was in the mech, they could attack and heal with significantly higher freedom. Though neither Matt nor Mort could cast their ultimates, as it would increase their aggro over even a Mechatron, Alex and Declan were still stuck within the ending animation of Red Wedding.

*22%*

*21%*

In the eight seconds Alex was in the mech, they dropped Vek'Na down to twenty-one point eight percent. Now came the annoying part. The Mechatron self-destructed as its duration ended, ejecting Alex out onto the ground. For a few seconds, Alex was stuck in the ending lag and couldn't move. All the while Vek'Na turned toward them, the exposed back line.

It jumped toward them now, and if Declan had calculated this correctly, then . . .

"Me."

Vek'Na headed straight for him, the player farthest from the group. This was by design—he had the highest aggro past Alex, doing mixed healing, damage, and supporting at the same time. His positioning allowed a precious 1.3 seconds where the boss was just running toward him—time for Alex to come out of the ending animation. When the boss finally reached him, its scythe held wide in preparation for a swing, Declan cast his next skill.

"Bloodletting."

The scythe paused midswing as all but five percent of Declan's health bled out of him, forming into a red ball at the tips of his fingers. The boss's eyes glowed a sinister green as it activated its aura, Eyes of Death.

Its scythe attack in enraged mode was a guaranteed one-shot for any nontank character; meanwhile, Eyes of Death had a 0.5 second cast time. When forcibly used, it would interrupt any move it was doing, focusing entirely on the aura attack.

If a normal attack was guaranteed to kill him anyway, Declan might as well have purged all his HP, forcing the boss to pause for a second—then, "Transfusion, DPS Up"—send it all to Matt and Mort, massively buffing their damage for a moment.

In those 0.5 seconds, both Matt and Mort unleashed their strongest attacks without worry. For the boss would not stop its instakill cast, but when it did finish, its aggro chart would be completely reset. Just in time for Alex to escape their ending animation and regain aggro.

Declan died to Eyes of Death, and the boss suffered both Matt and Mort's full damage assaults.

But little could be done in half a second.

*20%*

Now was where things went wrong.

Alex charged the refreshed Vek'Na, and Declan could already see it failing. With the damage buff from Eyes of Death and the loss of one healer, Alex could not survive the current Vek'Na for more than nine seconds. If either Matt or Mort did more damage than Alex, then the pull was lost and the raid wiped; if they didn't do more damage, then Vek'Na would kill Alex shortly enough. If Belle began using her strongest abilities, Alex would survive till the end of the raid—not because he'd survived Vek'Na's attacks, but because Vek'Na would switch its priority to Belle and kill her first.

All the best scenarios led to defeat.

Mortimer was rushing to revive him, not according to the original plan. He would succeed long after Alex fell, given the high cast time of Revivification, but by then the raid would have been wiped.

There were other options; if Matt was the one with the next-highest aggro and was the one sacrificed to buy time for Alex to return, then they would've survived longer, but overall they would've dealt less damage to the boss.

Mortimer dropped down next to his corpse. Raising his hands, he began casting, but just then a massive plume of necrotic gas erupted over him, the environmental effect that interrupted skill casts.

It didn't matter. They had already lost.

**Raid Wipe**

In the end, the most crippling was the loss of taunting and CC. Without them, the tank couldn't keep the boss in check well enough and the whole party suffered. Damage dealers and healers had to limit their skills so that they never generated higher aggro than the tank, which intrinsically meant neither Matt nor Mort could do more damage than Alex. And while Alex's Battle Smith build was suited for a damage play style compared to most tanks, it dealt nowhere near enough compared to specialized damage builds like sharpshooter and necromancer.

And with Clarion Call constantly eating into their HP, it meant healers like Declan and Belle were forced to burn ultimates just to *stay alive*.

If, *if* their party was entirely composed of ranged-burst damage dealers, who spent the entirety of the time kiting Vek'Na in his enraged phase, they *might* be able to kill him in a few seconds.

The problem was that that party composition had nowhere near the survivability to beat Vek'Na's initial seventy-five percent health, not to mention the rest of the dungeon, which was needed for the full clear.

Which meant their two damage dealers had to pull off enough damage in a short enough burst to match a party of *five* damage dealers doing the same thing.

Which was patently impossible and ridiculous for any balanced MMORPG. No character of the same level should be worth the same as five others. If it were that easy, they would've won by now.

So they simply failed.

And Declan lay there on the grassy ground as everyone came back.

"Ahh! We were so close this time!"

*"What?"*

"Nineteen percent. Not many top guilds can say they even got to that."

"The CC and taunt immunity is really fucking annoying, though . . ."

"Why?" Declan asked. "We lost. We failed. This should do nothing but prove this is a pointless endeavor."

"Could we up Alex's DPS somehow?"

"So why do you all look so cheerful?"

"We need better gear, for one . . ."

"How?" Declan practically spat out. "How do we get better gear? We'll need to grind hours just for one piece of orange gear. And for what? Two or three extra percent of damage?"

Matt's eyebrow rose in the middle of their talking, and he raised a hand. "Hey, look at this."

He sent them all a link—Vek'Na was getting a balance patch, to be shipped out this time next week.

"So someone is finally fixing their mistakes, huh," Mortimer murmured.

"So we don't need to bother right now," Declan continued, driven by the news. "Just wait a week for the boss to become *actually possible.*"

Alex shook their head. "No, we won't get the first clear that way."

"Yeap," Matt said, realizing the problem first. "The patch ships out when we're both in school, Decs. By the time we get back, the boss will already be dead."

"It still doesn't matter—there isn't a feasible way to kill Vek'Na as it currently is. And not even mentioning that, while our builds are fine, our gear is subpar—"

"So if we just got better gear we would be fine?" Belle interrupted. "If we got better gear, would you stop being a little shit and just try for once?"

Declan frowned slightly. "It would take *hours* to grind for gear just to outfit one of us, and it's completely RNG dependent. We won't be able to—"

"Bet," Belle interrupted once again.

"Excuse me?"

"Let's make a bet," she answered, a small smirk crawling onto her face. "If I can get all the gear we need by tomorrow, you will go along with us and do your fucking best."

Declan raised an eyebrow. "Unless you've been hiding gear this whole time, you won't be able to produce them."

"Do you take the bet or not?" she asked.

Declan shrugged. "Sure, but—"

Belle stopped listening and quickly turned around, strolling away from them to a relatively open spot.

Declan only now noticed the others were grinning.

"What are you smiling for?"

Matt simply sent him a link. A website he recognized, Wiggle, a popular streaming site.

And it opened up a channel that was live right now. Its viewer count was rising, well within the ten thousands.

"Hey, everyone!" He heard an echo, an obnoxiously cheery voice both in game and on the channel. "It's ya gurl, Silver Belle, here again and, um . . ." She did a cutesy gesture, one where she seemed to squirm in indecision. "I *really* want to clear the Vek'Na raid, but we don't have the gear we need to do it, and we really want to try to get to it before the nerf, otherwise all the larger guilds will beat us to it . . ."

Declan looked at the chat once.

The gear all arrived within the hour.

As days passed, years went on, he settled into a comfortable rhythm, a habit of how days passed. Spending them alone at home, ordering takeout for every meal, taking online classes and playing games during them, he convinced himself that he was fine like this, that his parents worked demanding and important jobs, that he should not distract them. Yet as the years went on, the food he ate slowly lost its flavor, the games he played became boring, the work and study from school became easy, ignorable. His grades began to fall, and he played games not for fun but to pass time. His appetite increased; food no longer tasted good, yet there was something other than hunger that wanted to be filled, something he didn't know. Something that could not be filled by food, no matter how he tried. He lived a good life—he was fed, he was clothed, he had a roof over his head, yet no matter what, he didn't live; he was simply . . . *there*.

There was a boy who forgot how to live.

*24.67%*
**Raid Wipe**
*23.89%*
**Raid Wipe**
*22.03%*
**Raid Wipe**
*21.69%*
**Raid Wipe**
*20.11%*
**Raid Wipe**
*19.46%*
**Raid Wipe**
*17.31%*
**Raid Wipe**
*15.29%*
**Raid Wipe**
*15.35%*
**Raid Wipe**
*19.89%*
**Raid Wipe**
*14.56%*
**Raid Wipe**
*14.32%*
**Raid Wipe**
*20.54%*
**Raid Wipe**
*14.87%*
**Raid Wipe**
*14.12%*
**Raid Wipe**
*13.98%*
**Raid Wipe**
*14.93%*
**Raid Wipe**
*15.78%*

**Raid Wipe**
*14.02%*
**Raid Wipe**
*16.53%*
**Raid Wipe**
*14.56%*
**Raid Wipe**
*13.79%*
**Raid Wipe**
*14.67%*
**Raid Wipe**
*14.95%*
**Raid Wipe**
*14.63%*
**Raid Wipe**

And like that, three days passed.

With less than four days remaining, they reached the theoretical limit of all Declan's calculations.

And they were stuck there.

Declan sat by a virtual beachside, alone as he watched the recordings of all the previous battles.

He should've put his mind to it, paid more attention to all the minute movements, but they were all performing perfectly. They'd paid the price in hours to brand every movement; every action was according to his calculated standards.

And they were still stuck.

At this point, there were only two possibilities—either mythic Vek'Na was truly impossible, or Declan was a fool who could not solve this problem.

"So in the end, it is either impossible or I am a failure," he murmured quietly.

In the end, Declan decided it didn't matter. It didn't matter whether it was impossible or he could not achieve it, because in the end nothing mattered. All they could achieve was a line in the sand. A line that would be washed away by the sea, like all things will be.

"That isn't true," he heard a voice say next to him.

Glancing behind him, he saw someone sitting beside him on this empty, virtual beach.

"Good morning, Alex."

"Morning indeed, though I suspect you didn't sleep at all?"

"I didn't," Declan replied, looking back out into the black seas. "I wanted to review the footage to see if there was something we missed."

"And did we?"

"No," he spat out. "We have done everything perfectly according to my guide, and we are still failing."

Because either the path was impossible or Declan was not good enough to take it.

"And that's why you think either it is impossible or it is your fault that you can't do it."

"We could just quit," Declan said. "We've been doing this for you, so one word from you and—"

"No," Alex quietly denied. "We aren't doing this for me anymore."

Declan paused, *frozen* as Alex spoke.

"Maybe at first Matt wanted to do this for me, but that is a truth no longer. Can you not see how aggressively he tries to include you in things? How much he's trying to get you to help and be a part of the party?" Alex said. "He's trying to pry you out of that shell you've made around yourself, to truly be your friend."

"Wha—"

"And we can't quit anymore, not after you made this." From their inventory, Alex took out a sheaf of papers. "You put so much effort into this, no one wants to let it go to waste."

For a moment, Declan simply stared blankly at Alex.

When he spoke, he spoke slowly, to make sure he was understood. "So you are saying that it is all my fault that we've persisted for so long?"

Alex nodded.

"Why?" Declan rasped out. "Why are we trying so hard, even when I have given up? Why? In the end it is nothing but a line drawn in the sand."

"Maybe," Alex replied, their finger drawing circles in the sand. "Maybe it doesn't matter in the end. Maybe it'll be washed away, but that doesn't mean it never existed."

Alex turned to stare at him. "Just because the line is washed away, that doesn't mean no one ever drew it. Just because no one remembers, it doesn't mean it never happened. To reduce all things to the final destination is just that—reductive."

"I don't get it," Declan replied. "I don't understand."

"It's fine if you don't understand," Alex replied. "It's fine if you go on still believing the things you do.

"But one day," they murmured, "one day when you are old, you will look at the lines you drew in the sand, lines that you drew with friends, and you will smile."

And they were silent, silent as the waves of the virtual sea lapped on their beach, silent as the sun of Yggdrasil shined upon them.

Then they got a message from Mort and Matt, a message that made Declan's eyes widen.

And when they hurriedly left that empty beach, when Declan stood beside his allies in the dungeon room of Vek'Na under the eyes of the hateful boss, he knelt and looked over a grate of necrotic energy.

"Is it true?" he asked, voice so light it was almost a whisper.

"We tested it," Mort answered triumphantly.

It was a trick, a bug in the raid, something so overlooked no one had ever really considered it.

"Can we do it with this?" Matt asked.

"We'll need to completely re-spec our characters," Declan answered, his voice fast and hurried for a reason he could not fathom, "but. . ."

And for the first time since they started this madness, Declan whispered only a single phrase, a phrase he'd never thought he would utter here.

"It might be possible now."

# Destination Part 3

*"Looking back, I think I was smiling."*

One final time.

"Who is that weirdo?" a player muttered. Staring at a sharpshooter slinging dual pistols, explosions ringing all around a practice dummy.

"What kind of combo does he think he's doing? Fucking noob, just going for the skills with the most particle effects."

One more try.

A necromancer cleared the grime from his face. He was breathing heavily despite the lack of real physical exertion; the quest line was more difficult than he remembered, but it was done.

In his hand, he held a book with a wheel. A wheel that ever spun and never stopped.

No matter what everyone said.

A woman smiled for the camera, speaking in a crafted and mastered tone. A voice that flaunted wit and sensuality in equal measure. Her audience was as supportive as usual, but there were many, and in the many, there would be doubters.

"Imagine still trying lolololololollll!"

The possibility of redemption.

In the real world, a wizened old figure shared a drink with a friend. Androgynous in appearance and bearing, they gave an appearance of seniority. They finished quickly, leaving behind a tip as they left.

"Why were they drinking with a picture?"

They would smash their head into a brick wall until that wall gave.

The boy woke up, eyes blurry, mind out of touch as he pushed away packages of fast food and candy. He stared blearily at a screen, seeing the final result.

*0%*

"And here we go again," Mortimer uttered.

Only two hours until the boss got its balance patch, only two hours till the deadline.

"Are all of you fine with skipping school?" Belle asked.

"It's fine," Matt began.

"I never enjoyed going there anyways," Declan finished.

"Then let us begin."

The same party, the same people, but with better gear, better practice, and a better plan.

There was no more time left; there was no more time to practice. It was their last chance. And so they battled against Vek'Na one final time, the spectral skeleton burning with necrotic green energy. They battled through his first phase, pushing through attack and attack, burning through mana and health, until, finally, they stood where many have stood.

The wind blew across them, flapping their robes and forcing them to squint. The boss burned with particles and energy, with hatred and contempt, for many had brought Vek'Na to the brink.

But none had killed it.

The battle when Vek'Na entered his enrage could be measured in seconds.

"Heartbeat Healing!" Belle yelled straightaway. The boss instantly turned its skeletal head toward her, but not before another spoke.

"MK7 Mechatron."

Both deftly avoided the grates of necrotic energy that canceled skill casts. Using their strongest abilities from the start, Alex slammed into the boss. Clad in their mecha suit, they fought head-to-head with the skeleton.

"Health Drain Up," Declan called, draining a small fraction of the boss's HP, barely dealing any damage but fulfilling another purpose. "Bloodletting, Transfusion, DPS Up."

Matt alone received the buff, and he yelled out, "Emperor Time!" activating one of his ultimates, unleashing his damage, attacking with combos unfettered and uncaring of aggro.

*20.8%*

The first fifth, gone within moments of the fight. An explosive start, but this strategy was supposed to be unsustainable—for the simple reason their only tank was stuck in ending lag as the mech timed out. All the while Vek'Na turned to the next-highest aggro target, Matt.

But they solved that.

As Alex was ejected, they positioned their landing so that they landed directly on one of the environmental effects—the necrotic grates that canceled castings, that canceled animation.

That, unbeknownst to anyone, canceled ending animations.

The grate burst with green gas, enveloping Alex; in that moment, they were freed from the long end lag and charged back into the boss.

"And here's the annoying part," Mortimer muttered.

Declan raised a hand, pointing at Mort, and uttered, "Bloodletting."

All but five percent of Mort's HP disappeared in that instant, transformed into a bloody red ball in Declan's hand.

And the boss paused its advance toward Matt and turned its glowing green eyes toward Mortimer.

Without the massive buff from MK7 Mechatron, Alex couldn't actually steal aggro from Matt, no matter how much either of them wanted it.

So they sacrificed Mortimer, and the boss's own instakill aura would reset its aggro chart completely.

And in that half a second, all of them attacked.

*18.03%*

Even if Declan and Belle were both primarily healers, they still had damage abilities. The same thing went to Alex, whose half a dozen mechanical adds fired at the boss with wild abandon. In addition to the massive damage buff from Matt's ultimate, they easily burned through two percent in half a second.

When Mortimer finally died, Alex was there to regain aggro. The edge was even thinner now; if it was difficult keeping Alex alive while Vek'Na didn't have the massive damage buff, it was nigh impossible now.

Three ultimates they burned. Declan's Red Wedding, Belle's Anthem of the Ancient, and finally Alex's Max Overclock, which temporarily buffed all their mechanical adds to deal heavily increased damage. It was enough for Alex to claw aggro away from the two healers, just in time for Mortimer's body to twitch.

The necromancer's body glowed with energy as he slowly began rising. The Tome of Endless Night, a skill tree of abilities, gave the necromancer an automatic self-resurrection so long as they had the mana. It was considered nigh useless since the skill point investment was so great the necromancer was effectively hobbled in every other area. And while the max leveled version of the skill was uninterruptible, the lower-level version was not. It should've been unthinkable to bring this sort of skill here, where you had to dodge necrotic grates or they interrupted all skill casts.

But the highest-level form was uninterruptible, and an interesting interaction occurred when the skill cast interacted with the necrotic grates. It *canceled* the animation so that the long cast time of the skill was skipped entirely, and Mortimer stood alive once more.

*14.08%*

Declan's heart quickened, perhaps unconsciously as he surveyed the battlefield. They were nearing the thirteen percent threshold, a threshold none had ever passed. And they went into it not the worse for wear. Almost everyone was topped up, the damage of Clarion Call was manageable, and the boss was focused squarely on the tank. They had to re-spec to builds stacked with ultimate abilities, but it was doable!

And they watched, as the boss went down in health.

*13%*

*12%*

*11%*

*10%*

And then it all went wrong as the scythe disappeared from Vek'Na's hand.

Instead, a staff adorned with an ancient skull appeared, and the boss raised it high.

"Unknown phase!" Alex yelled.

None had brought Vek'Na to this point.

None had discovered the bug with the necrotic grates.

None had seen his final enrage.

Until now.

"Belle!" Declan yelled, turning to the other healer, but her hand was already up.

"Melody of the Mother!"

The shield came just in time, as blasts of green lighting struck all players. They barely managed to tank it.

"Zero instant kills!" Declan yelled.

But the boss slowly turned toward Mortimer, its eyes glowing green.

The attack was enough to lower Mort to the execute threshold.

At that moment, almost everyone was still stuck in their last actions. At that moment, Matt saw the boss's animation, and though he didn't register whom it was directed at, he cast another ultimate: "FIM 92 Stinger!"

Eight missiles shot out of his pistols, striking the boss in the instant it killed Mortimer again. Miraculously, or perhaps in a moment of brilliant insight, Matt managed to time his positioning so that the necrotic grates canceled the ending lag of that ultimate.

The moment Mortimer died, the boss turned toward Alex, the first character to have attacked it then. The lightning formed around its staff, crackling with power, and it struck.

Too fast—the first blow instantly slashed through half of Alex's health. The double damage buff Vek'Na got from executing Mortimer twice in a row, not to mention that it was now dealing bludgeoning and lightning damage as opposed to slashing and necrotic. The resistances Alex had stacked weren't for this. Declan saw too late, the second blow coming in like a reaper's scythe.

Everything was going wrong, and Declan was panicking—no, perhaps in mute shock was more accurate. He had calculated everything, from damage to health to the very *pixels* and *seconds* they would stand on to optimally kill Vek'Na.

When everything changed, he could not adapt. Still stuck in the paradigms of his plan when reality had long moved on.

It was Alex's shout that shook him out of it.

"Drain me!"

Declan saw clear as day then, the second blow from Vek'Na's staff coming toward Alex. Though his mind didn't register the decision that caused those words, his body moved automatically.

"Bloodletting."

Alex's HP went from fifty percent to five percent in an instant, just as Vek'Na's staff stopped mere centimeters from their head.

Declan only registered then what was happening.

Alex saw they could not survive the boss for another blow, so they opted to have Declan drain all their HP, forcing it into its execute animation, to buy a single half second more.

And he saw then the HP the boss was on.

*8.6%*

And he knew then, the path to victory, the path Alex showed him with their death.

"Belle, take aggro!" Declan yelled.

"Huh?"

But he was already running away from her. At the moment, Belle still had Heartbeat Healing up to deal with Clarion Call. At that moment, when Vek'Na's aggro chart had just reset, she was the one who first took aggro.

Matt realized this as well, running away in the opposite direction Declan was, creating distance between all remaining players.

For the moment, Belle saw the boss turn straight toward her and charge. She yelped before running away as fast as possible, creating more distance between all three of them.

All the while, both Declan and Matt were peppering Vek'Na with damage.

Vek'Na reached the shrieking Belle in two great steps, thunder and death calling from its staff as it swung at her.

Matt burned another ultimate, shooting at the boss while it was midswing.

Declan activated Bloodletting, draining all of Belle's HP, pausing the attack midanimation and causing Vek'Na's eyes to glow green.

*6.3%*

Mort rose from the earth just as Belle fell. He was in no position to retake aggro, so Declan simply drained him.

"Oh, are you fu—"

Any basic attack by Vek'Na would kill them, but there was still distance to consider. The boss hadn't recast the AOE, which ruined the plan—it must've been on cooldown. Considering all this, Declan was the first to strike Vek'Na once it had finished off Mort a third time.

And the boss turned to him.

In his hand, he held a ball of HP, drained from Alex, Belle, and Mort. Declan's class was often called the TPK Hemomancer—almost an instant kick no matter what party he joined. No matter what he said. No matter how skilled he was with the class. He simply did not fit.

But here, at this moment, he was king.

Vek'Na charged toward him, and he cast his abilities, kiting the boss from range as Matt peppered it from behind. He could not simply run, for he could not allow aggro to fall to Matt—he had to buy him a few more seconds.

A few more seconds to build his combo.

And when Vek'Na finally reached him, its skull leering at him from above, Declan smiled. The attack came, but he was used to it now. He would not make a mistake here.

The staff paused mere inches from his face as his HP dropped to five percent.

"Transfusion, DPS Up."

Behind Vek'Na, Matt burned with red energy. The health and blood from Alex, Belle, Mortimer, and finally Declan.

Declan died, but Matt still stood.

When the boss turned to him, far away on the other side of the room, he used everything. Every skill, every ultimate, every single damage rotation he had. The boss tanked through all of them, charging inexorably toward him.

When, finally, Matt exhausted all his skills, all his moves, left with nothing but basic attacks as the boss finally came.

And he laughed.

Visible only to him was a combo counter.

**9,999 COMBO!**

In his hands were dual pistols, one of elegant silver, the other of burning gold.

And with the Mourning Moon, he shot the combo counter.

"Limit Break." He raised the other pistol toward the sky, just as the staff of the boss descended.

"Setting Sun."

He fired and hit the stars.

Then the sun fell from the sky.

There was once a boy who lived a normal life.

Yet as he lived, as he saw and experienced, he was disappointed. For life was just life, the world was just a world, things were as they were and nothing more. And so, as time went on, he forgot things, he forgot enjoyment, he forgot human warmth, he forgot how to live.

But as a single figure fell, as the boy looked on in the midst of respawning, he stared at the one who still stood, at the friends who stood around him screaming and roaring, the words running across his vision, immortalizing them within the world they fought, he knew the impossible truth—he knew they had succeeded.

And there was a boy who cried and screamed because, for a brief, fleeting, and forgotten moment, he remembered.

**!!Server Announcement!!**

**!!MYTHIC RAID FIRST FULL CLEAR!!**

**!!TOMB OF NILBOG!!**

**Players:**

**Aban Twice Crowned**

**HitZaDecs**

**Mattmanfoo**

**Mortimer Memento**

**Silv3r_Belle**

# 1.28

———

*"Why. Won't. You! DIE!"*
            *—The Revenant King, trying to kill the party comic relief*

I did not see it coming.

"What the BLEEP?" Matt yelled as he was thrown to the side, his legs struggling to rise, his swear words redacted by the scattered bits of Tilt's power.

Utoqa stopped a fist with his own, seemingly without reaction, but I saw his fins flinch as he did so.

"Ho ho? Well done!" the unknown assailant praised. He was wearing colorful clothing, flowing wildly around him almost like a bird. "And you as well!"

The man snapped his neck, breaking it in an unnatural angle as Tai's blade missed his ear by a breadth.

"*What the hell is that?*" Declan exclaimed.

"Wonderful, wonderful!" the man exclaimed as his extended fist grabbed onto Utoqa's arm, then he *swung* the lizardfolk into Tai in a swift, smooth motion.

Both went tumbling, crashing into the wall of the orphanage.

"Ah, you truly are they who beat the Accumulation of White Lies," the man congratulated.

"How do you know that?" I muttered, my staff held forward. My mana was all but used up. I had a few more spells in me. "Where did you come from? Why are you here?"

"Such philosophical questions to ask," he replied with a chuckle. "I came from where all come from. I am here because of no grand purpose."

"I'm not talking philosophy here," I replied. My eyes glanced toward the unconscious body still on the ground. Her hair and skin were a pale white now, but Celine was still alive by every measure I had. "I'm talking why you have come here and why you have—"

Corvian stabbed him at that moment. The priest's invisibility trick served him well, as his dagger sank deep into the man's chest.

"Surrender," the gnome said. "You're going to need treatment for that wound; it doesn't matter how much . . ." He slowly trailed off as we both noticed a piece of brass and bronze revealed under the man's elaborate clothing.

A clock that showed the wrong time.

Corvian's eyes widened, and he jumped back, leaving the dagger inside the crazed man's chest. It took me a moment to recognize the symbol. It was the same as on Corvian's card decks and the silver bell that now decorated his belt. It was a holy symbol.

A holy symbol to Osshiven'Kai, the Clockwork God of Madness and Chaos.

"Oh, you are a very kind soul," the cultist said, "to avoid my heart, no doubt out of the goodness of your own."

Seemingly without care, he pulled the dagger out of his own chest. "It's a shame it doesn't matter in the end."

And he stabbed his chest, pushing the dagger into his flesh, carving out his own heart before dropping it onto the ground.

"Fortunately, you needn't worry about my mortal existence," the cultist said, smiling as he strode forward, "for the simple reason that I don't have—"

Then a silver bell rang, for he still stood within a shrine to Tilt.

The cultist suddenly stepped on his own heart, *which was behind him a moment ago*, slipping on it like a banana peel and falling onto the ground. When he landed in a puddle of slime, the momentum and the wet ground sent him straight out a window.

And he laughed as it happened, crashing into a bush. "Ah! It seems I'm still not welcome!" he yelled with strange cheer in his voice.

I quickly moved to follow him, Corvian helping Noam as Tai and Utoqa untangled themselves.

The cultist was still laughing when we stepped outside.

"Is he a threat?" Utoqa asked, his voice cold and devoid of the emotions a human might have.

"Most likely," I answered.

I almost grimaced as I looked at our state—Utoqa's back was still raw and white, having literally sloughed off during his time inside the belly of the beast. Tai had fought tirelessly for hours on end, and I could see the beads of sweat on her skin. I was almost out of mana, and it was day.

An axe missing most of his HP, a sword missing most of her stamina, a staff missing most of his mana.

"I'll act as the main distraction, strike him when he's focused on me." Here I was the most expendable piece, and also likely the most durable.

"What do we do?" Tai murmured. "Followers of the Mad God are immortal, are they not?"

"We cut him into so many pieces that he'll take longer to regenerate. Then stick the individual parts into separate sealed boxes," I answered instantly. A similar strategy to take out a Traveler—namely crippling and trapping. Immortality was not impossible to work around, after all.

The cultist was smiling as he saw us. "Ah you came to me. I was almost afraid you would hide in the shrine."

*He can't enter the orphanage, important to remember.* "Why did you attack us?"

"To take back what was mine," he answered matter-of-factly. His eyes stared directly into mine.

"What was yours?" Both Utoqa and Tai were slowly stepping around. Seeking to encircle him.

"Indeed, indeed! That is the question, isn't it? What makes something mine, what makes something have ownership? One could argue that such a concept does not exist, only the enforcement of it."

"You are talking in circles," I replied. "Answer me like a normal person or we'll have to use force."

The cultist looked at me with a strange, almost childlike curiosity. "Indeed, Oracle, I have been acting far too much like a normal person."

"What are you—"

"I came here because one of yours stole a bottle of mine. I intended to take a pound of flesh as payment but . . . that is too *orderly*, isn't it?" he asked. "Of loss and reparation, of theft and justice. It's far too directed; it makes far too much sense."

We had him trapped between all three of us now, but I was still uneasy. "We aren't at our best, and the enemy is an unknown variable," Declan assessed.

"Ah!" the cultist yelled, a finger raised in revelation. "Great idea, Oracle!"

And he grinned a madman's grin. "Let's add an unknown variable."

I felt both our eyes widen. "Did he just . . ."

He reached into his sleeve, but Utoqa had seen enough. His tomahawk sliced cleanly through the cultist's neck, but not before he threw something.

A small object, cubic, dotted. A die.

Two dots.

"And we have a two!" the severed head of the cultist yelled. His body threw up an arm with two fingers in a V, completely separate from its own head. "And thus negotiations have broken down!"

Tai's blade flashed, cutting off the raised hand.

"Guess I'll have to hurt you now!"

As the severed arm dropped, it grabbed onto Tai's neck. She fell back, wrestling with the arm choking her as the rest of the cultist's body struck Utoqa with its remaining arm, throwing him back before jumping to follow the lizardfolk.

I glanced between the two, then stepped toward—

"Wait," Declan murmured. "The head."

My attention fell to the severed head, which smiled at me. "Greetings, Oracle."

"You call me that as if it means something," I murmured as I grabbed the head by its hair. "Oracle this and that."

"Oh, you can't tell me you didn't notice the change?" he asked. "You defeated an agent of obscurity, so you are now an agent of revelation."

I raised an eyebrow. "Is that how it works? If so, then **Analyze**."


He stood in a place much like a personal study. Everything here was in the right place, disorganized in appearance, yet ordered in his mind. He simply needed to look for it.

Three figures stood here—Declan, Dustin, and the third.

First, they glanced at their character sheet, noting the change that had come.

**True Character Sheet**

**Name: Dustin**
Racials: Magic Myconid Level 1
Classes: Fungalmancer Level 4, Second of Three Oracle Level 2.

<u>Body:</u>
Strength: 8
Agility: 7
Dexterity: 6
Constitution: 19
Stamina: 10
Vitality: 12

Mind:
Intelligence: 18
Wisdom: 20
Charisma: 6

Soul:
Will: 10
Psyche: 10
Perception: 10

Racials:
Manavision, Fungal Body, Sun Sickness, Mana Dependency, Pacifying Spores, Strong Innate Magic, Age-Type Heteromorph

Class Skills:
Fungalmancer:
Path: Symbiosis
- **Grow Sporage (Visual)**
- **Grow Sporage (Proximity)**
- **Sporage Wisp Symbiosis**
- **Bracken Polypores**

The Second of Three Oracle:
Path: Observe, Analyze, Predict
- **Observe:** You may touch an eye capable of sight; upon usage you may see out of the eye regardless of your distance or proximity to it.
- **Observation Link:** You are linked to a user of Observe. Your minds are linked, and they may share all that they see through Observe. Through you, they may also mark other willing creatures to have their vision be seen through Observe as well.
- **Analyze:** You passively absorb the information you gather, learning the exact parameters of that which you observe and translating them to a form understandable to you. This information will exist in a database and could be called on at any time. This acts almost like a second mind for you, incapable of decision but so much more accurate in its analysis.
- **Analyzation of the Soul:** Thrice per day, you may bring a target you can see to the realm of souls to glimpse their true nature and discern information.

- **Predict:** You may, using information that you understood, have observed and Analyzed, create a portent of the near future or of other information related.
- **Eyes of God:** With the Eye of Discovery, you have the following visions:
- Normal Vision
- Superior Darkvision
- **Et Non-Discent:** This class was not sourced from the system, thus it does not benefit from the system, either.
- Progress in this class does not rely on Traveler XP, but on your own proficiency.
- You may not invest levels in this class.
- This class and its progress will not be displayed on your Traveler character sheet.

<u>Magic Myconid Spells:</u>
T0: Sneezing Spores, Acid Spit, Watching Eye

<u>Fungalmancer Spells:</u>
T0: Balm Spores, Light Spores, Shillelagh
T1: Mushroom Meal, Poison Spores, Euphoria Spray
T2: Bark Skin, Fix-Up Fungus, Rot Spores

They were now level seven, and stronger than before, and here within the realm of souls would they glimpse the enemy's true—

"Fascinating, to be able to bring me here," the cultist said, glancing around. He smiled at them. "Go on, look into me. I have only the **Truth**."

And they saw.

Utoqa had never hunted a thing that did not die.

It was difficult.

A swipe by his claws severed the creature's hamstrings, dropping it onto the ground, but the thing continued to move. Scrabbling like an insect or one of the shelled ones, it crawled onto a wall with naught but the strength of its fingers and toes.

It was missing its head and left arm, which usually meant the hunt was over, but the thing continued to move, leaping off and smacking him into another house. The sheer force of it broke the wall, and Utoqa felt another pang of pain as his still-raw back was slashed bloody by torn wood.

He got up instantly, however, for his kind did not feel pain in the same way others did. He thought of burning his last bundle of healing, but it was not yet lethal.

Leaping out, he found his opponent holding up its own head. Dustin was lying on the ground, unconscious but perhaps still alive.

"He he he. Don't worry about the empty one, he's just seeing the light," the severed head said, and the body brought the head to its neck, rejoining the two pieces.

Utoqa's priority was to retrieve Dustin. He held his tomahawk in guard, slowly and carefully advancing.

But the creature's attention wasn't on him. Instead, it took two steps away and picked up a carved stone. A die, he believed the word was. An unnatural curiosity—it had too many straight lines and right angles, seemingly to serve no practical purpose.

The creature threw the die, his eyes watching it as it descended.

Utoqa's instinct was to strike at him while he was distracted, but he knew full well he couldn't harm it. Trapping was what Dustin had asked, and he saw the logic behind that statement.

The die fell onto the ground with a few clicks, and the creature laughed. "A one!"

Utoqa was above Dustin now. Gently he grabbed the light body by the arm and began slowly backing away.

"Guess you die now!"

Suddenly his vision wasn't focused on the immortal creature, but instead flying in the sky. Spinning around before he glimpsed the form of his own decapitated body.

Utoqa's head fell on the ground with a thud.


Tai busted back into the orphanage, the gnome Corvian tending to Celine as she woke.

"Wha . . . where am I?" the woman murmured. Her hair was white, as was her skin. All an unnatural pale, but the clothing, the mannerism was enough for Tai to know she was Celine.

"Celine!"

The witch yelped at the call of her name, but Tai didn't have time; she slammed the scrabbling and struggling arm of the mad cultist onto the ground. "Your magic can curse people, right?"

"Yes, but I don't like—"

"Then do something with this arm!" she yelled before she leaped out of the orphanage once more.

Outside, she saw Dustin on the ground unconscious and Utoqa's headless body fall onto him. The cultist was picking something up from the ground. Something small. There was a shocked draw of breath behind her, but Tai was already moving. As the die fell onto the ground again, the cultist was severed into two bloody pieces. Her blade cleaved clean into his torso, from right shoulder to the left waist. The head and arm fell off with the severed torso, but it wasn't enough; she needed to separate them.

Then she felt magic invigorate her, as if her body had rested fully for a day. "Celine?!"

"That wasn't me!" the witch yelled, pointing at the cultist's falling arm. Its hand curled into a somatic gesture.

"Four! What a lucky roll, lady!" the head laughed as it fell.

The madman had *healed* her; the act was sickening, the lack of respect . . . "Fight me truly, you madman!"

"Blame your luck!" he yelled, and the severed torso grabbed the die on the ground, throwing it again.

"Two," he said with a smile, "and now you will hurt."

She rushed at him again, but the legs kicked up the torso like a ball and they rejoined in midair. Tai went low as the cultist's fist flew wildly above her head, slashing off a leg.

This time she grabbed the severed portion, running off with it as the cultist stared at her with a bemused look.

"Guess you're *legging* it!" he yelled.

She rolled her eyes as she made distance. "Oh, come on, that's just bad!"

"He he," the monster chuckled. "But I will be taking that back now."

"No!" Celine suddenly yelled. She raised the cultist's arm, which Tai had left her, now bound almost completely in stitches and string.

"No, young lady." The cultist spoke as he began hopping toward Tai. "That is quite rude to say to—"

"I break the Finger of Direction."

And the index finger of the severed arm broke off, falling onto the ground and dissipating.

Suddenly the cultist turned right. "Huh?"

Then he began moving backward, away from Tai. The leg she'd grabbed was also moving erratically now, as if it didn't know what way to go.

The cultist tried to turn his head toward Tai but ended up looking at the ground. He tried to raise his arm but tucked it into his abdomen. He wanted to hop but instead knelt.

"Wondrous!" he yelled as he finally grasped the nature of the curse.

Every single action of his lost its direction, moving randomly without pattern or meaning. "Now I am truly random!"

And Tai dropped the leg, heading in to attack once again.

And somehow, the cultist turned straight toward her. "I'm getting the hang of this now!" he said, throwing a fist out to attack.

Tai already had too much momentum; she couldn't stop in time, and she couldn't dodge.

But a tomahawk buried itself into the cultist's back, knocking him off balance. Utoqa's headless body rose behind the cultist, his arm out midthrow, green strands of energy weaving themselves around the decapitated neck until it formed the shape of a head. "**Survive**," the lizardfolk whispered as he defied death.

"Interesting!" the cultist yelled, just as Tai's blade decapitated the immortal.

They saw the **Truth**.

A dark day, a circle of mages in a tower. Scholars, studying and trying to understand. Tomes of magic and forbidden lore lay around them.

"I think we have it," one of them uttered, a leader, clad in better robes than the others. "A way to the Seventh Circle. The Seventh Hell."

Dustin raised an eyebrow. "The seventh circle is supposed to be uncontacted, isn't it?"

His question was only heard by himself. Declan nodded but did not reply.

They saw the mages work, gather material, draw the beginnings of a portal.

They were not evil, Dustin saw, for they sought the hell to understand more of demon lore. To understand how better to fight them, how to best slay them, how to best banish them. For the denizens of hell were numerous and infinitely varied. Computer viruses made sentient, killing and destruction their only purpose.

And he saw them open a portal with the help of a Wayshard, yelps of surprise and cheers as they opened a gate. Peering in was a cold and dark world, where snow rained forevermore.

They sent first a small golem, its body fitted with a transmission crystal that sent them imagery of the unknown hell.

And as they explored, they found that nothing lived here.

No errant plant, no insect, no animals, no devils or demons.

Surprise, curiosity, a desire to understand swept through the circle. And they kept exploring until they found it.

At first, they thought it was a massive mountain, but then they saw the scales. Oh, great and horrible scales, taller than towers, wider than mansions, and thicker than hills. They found the corpse of an ancient serpent, frozen and dead in a wasteland of ice.

They brought forth diviners. Seeing into the past, they glimpsed what had happened. A calamity of such great scale that it was forever burned into the memory of the world.

There was once a demon of hunger. Its form was that of a serpent, and it was hungry, forever hungry. It ate insects, it ate plants, it ate animals, it ate devils, it ate demons.

It ate all that lived in the hell to satisfy a hunger that would never end, and when the world was bare for all life save the demon, it turned to the skies and ate the stars. But even when it had eaten all the stars in the sky, it was still hungry. So it ate the sun.

And when portals to other worlds opened, it bored its mouth through and ate continents. It ate other worlds; it ate everything.

The serpent kept on eating and eating until there was nothing left to eat, and the demon starved in a cold and dead world, its desire forever unsatisfied.

And it was horror that graced the circle, for they saw how great a single demon could become. Enough to consume worlds, enough to eat everything that existed.

But horror was measured with greed and desire. For inside the demon's stomach, they found the wealth of a thousand worlds. Unguarded, unattended, simply gathering dust in the demon's belly. Treasures of the ages, everything that could be imagined was there.

And they looted, they looted and looted until one day they brought back a curious clock.

A clock that seemed to lead to another world. A world that survived a demon of this caliber. A world that repelled a world eater.

The circles were drawn once again—an attempt to contact the strange world from where the clock came.

And they succeeded.

"What's in there?" the head mage asked as his friend peered into the portal.

"Buildings, people, some kind of strange metal carriage that moves without a horse . . ." he described. "And— Oh, shi—"

The man jerked back, his mind silenced as he uttered a name with a voice not his own. "Fenkai."

They peered into the portal, and this time something in the portal peered back.

The vision cut here, leaving Declan and Dustin suddenly looking at the head mage. His face was haunted as he watched the mage tower they were just in burn. Burn to the ground with the portal to the Seventh Hell and the strange world they contacted. Burn with all the other mages and treasures and knowledge they'd accumulated.

Everything burned, except for a single clock in the head mage's hand.

A clock that showed the time 6:23.

## 1.29

———

*"Prophecies are very limited in reliability. A prophecy
proclaiming, 'No man shall ever slay you,' simply means a female
would be doing the dirty work. P.S. Remember to exile all women
from the capital. Gotta make sure I live forever."*
　　　—*Personal memoirs of Tyrant Cornelius the Monarch Bane, best
known for progressive tax reform and dying a slow death
of gangrene after getting scratched by his pet kitten Zoe*

It began slowly; the man returned to the city, hiding in his manor. His mouth was forever silent on the nature of what happened in the tower, but occasionally, he glanced hauntingly at the clock.

The first sign was an obsession with where things should be, of how they should appear. Alone in a massive manor, he spent his days cleaning every speck of dust by hand.

The clock showed the time 7:46.

He began reading books of law, of how places were governed, yet his hand kept moving to make "corrections." Those who commit crime were undesirable variables, variables that should be removed. No matter how small the crime, should an entity act outside of the predetermined path, it needed to be removed. A petty thief or a mass murderer—all deserved to hang.

The clock showed the time 8:13.

Despite being reclusive, he began to tour the city, nay, patrol it. He saw where people, animals, and plants deviated from the natural norm, and he removed them, speaking magic for the first time in years.

The clock showed the time 9:29.

He saw something in that portal, in that gateway to another world. A god called Fenkai. It was the sole ruler of its plane and had brought eternal and lasting peace and order. It was a great god, a god that was *needed*.

For people here hurt and killed, they refused his truth and would rather succumb to the chaos of their nature rather than the true law of order. They were flawed and needed Fenkai's guidance, for men were not meant to govern themselves.

The clock showed the time 10:58.

The great work needed to be complete, and the mage would do it alone. He would reopen that portal he'd so foolishly closed. He would let the great god Fenkai back into this realm. He would bring Order.

"Nesiseer?" A woman's voice rang out.

The man once known as Nesiseer turned around. "Yes?"

"What have you done?" she asked, her face distraught. "You have killed hundreds! You killed Galadand and everyone in the tower! What happened to you? What did you see?"

Questions, unneeded in an ordered world. This woman was one that was not present during the great god's descent. Her confusion was understandable, but she posed an undesirable element, and such elements needed to be . . . needed to be . . .

Nesiseer blinked, looking at the woman before him, "Beatrix?"

The woman took a step forward. "Yes?"

Nesiseer turned to the side, where a clock stood.

A clock that showed the time 11:24.

"Oh, no." Nesiseer stumbled, his legs suddenly weak as the weight of his actions suddenly dawned on him. "What have I done?"

The woman, Beatrix, rushed to catch him, and gently she asked, "What did you do?"

Eyes haunted, Nesiseer spoke. "I dug too deep, and I found a God of Order."

"Order? But aren't they generally good—"

"No!" Nesiseer yelled, eyes widening with fear. "I saw it! I saw what was inside that world! People reduced to automata! Men becoming naught but cogs in a greater machine! Free will destroyed for the sake of Order. It is a god focused on preserving humanity, but it has achieved it by making them all puppets!"

He pushed off the love of his life. "No, no, no, no, nononononono . . ."

Nesiseer stared once again at the clock.

Eleven twenty-seven.

The clock would only count up; it would keep counting up until it finally hit twelve and Nesiseer truly lost his free will.

"His Order is that of a tyrant's madness, his peace that of a king's fish tank," Nesiseer said. "It is already too late for me."

"What are you speaking of, Nesiseer?" Beatrix asked. "Explain further!"

And Nesiseer shook his head. "This god cannot be allowed to be known, for that is how he begins to worm his way in. I cannot allow his madness to spread."

He had a sudden moment of epiphany, a sudden clarity of thought. "Order must be balanced out by Chaos."

"I said, explain yourself, Nesiseer!" Beatrix said between tears. "I can't help you if I don't know!"

And the man who was once Nesiseer laughed. "I cannot trust my thoughts anymore, Beatrix." He took out a single coin from his pocket. "So I shall trust the only thing truly fair and unpredictable. Something truly random."

And he flipped the coin.

The next moment, the man who was once Nesiseer dragged out the burned corpse of the woman he once loved. Outside were dozens of men and women clad in arms waiting for him. To make him answer for all his crimes.

And he laughed; in his other hand he held a clock that no longer showed time, and he thought the last sane thought he would ever have, that of his friend's last words. "Oh, shi—Fenkai."

Galadand had meant to say *Oh, shit* before his mind was taken over.

The man who was once Nesiseer laughed, for the strangest joke came to his mind. "I am Steve! Follower of Osshiven'Kai! Come and face me and know I am a chaos that opposes order!"

Dustin fell out of the memory, panting on the ground as the battle was fought around him.

The cultist of Osshiven'Kai was naught but a single leg standing with half a torso and an arm, but it was enough for him to grab Utoqa by the head and throw him into the sky. The lizardfolk crashed into the mage tower, toppling it.

Tai was sweating, barely pacing herself as she cut and cut at the cultist. Several dozen pieces of him were already scattered around the battlefield, kept trapped by Celine, but it was a losing battle.

Only a single moment of hesitation, fueled by her battles without rest, was enough for the cultist to land a single hit, throwing her to the side.

"Well, well, I see you have seen the Truth."

"Why did you show me that?" Dustin uttered. Voice husky and out of breath.

"I don't know." The cultist shrugged before brandishing his die. "Want me to roll on it?"

Regardless of why, Dustin understood.

Osshiven'Kai was an imaginary god. It did not exist until that man who was once Nesiseer made him up. It was a god of chaos, made for the sole purpose of fighting that alien god. The Order that constantly searched this world's reality for weakness, so that it might descend and bring about the worst kind of peace. And that he was spared in a sense, for he did not view that god directly save for learning its name.

Dustin understood that the monster before him was ultimately a force for the better. A force for balance, else Order consumes all.

"If you are good, why do you do this?" he asked. "Why attack us? Did you roll the dice on it as well?"

And the man smiled. "Why, you should know this, Oracle. Why don't you just use all three?"

"All three?"

"All three Paths that make you an Oracle."

And Dustin did.

**"Observe."**

And memories flashed by his mind.


"You saw that unchecked true magic could lead to the death of civilizations, so Eve fixed that," the Historian said in an almost admiring way. "She taught the world restraint. She created the Law of Limitations."

I raised my eyebrow, gesturing him to continue.

"Where the developers failed was that they attempted to push far too complex and specific solutions," the Historian explained. "As such, Indiri drifted before the world could fully implement it, thus creating sections where it would not hold and places where they eventually evolved past that solution. So, Eve chose to add a single, very simple rule.

"Limitation," the Historian said. His hands twitched for a moment; likely he wanted to do a dramatic flourish but stopped himself before he did. His hands continued to write as they had been.

"Things have a limit, they have a cost, they have conditions. The expression of magic needs these things. Mana and aura essentially only exist to give magic a cost.

"The stronger the magic, the greater the cost. The spellcaster needs to gather certain material components, do rituals, speak incantations, or make somatic gestures. The condition could even be something as simple as just spending time to learn a technique or spell."

"How very video game–like."

. . .

"Not necessarily," he answered immediately. "You could attempt to take both, but in doing so, you would either destroy one or both or merge them together. Whatever you do, the end result cannot be greater than one."

. . .

I stared at him. "Can't I just take one and get the other later?"

"You could," he answered, "but not in the near future. You saw what Eve did—in this world limits matter more than strengths. Attempting to cheat will make them both weaker, or worse—" He paused, staring at me head-on. "The world will attempt to remove it."

My brows furrowed, which the Historian took as an indicator to continue: "Attempting to take a power without the proper limits or capability may result in calamities visiting you. Each trying to remove the unearned power somehow. If you can survive these calamities with the power still in your grasp, then the power will be considered yours and earned. If you do not, then you will not only lose it, but something more as well."

. . .

Within the flames, Noam saw it, the Path of Spitfire. Not the fake he holds and wields, but a truth he could take.

And he hesitated when he realized it could only be gained in taking. However rightfully he earned it, the man would lose in the same way he'd lost Biting Words. It was an equivalent exchange. A transfer from those worthy and those who weren't.

The world said he deserved this power.

Noam let go, the flames sputtering out, revealing the heavily burned but living man underneath. His knees collapsed underneath him, and Noam fell to the ground. The strange, altered world where they fought disappeared as others rushed to check their wounds.

Dustin's cap soon loomed over him as the myconid looked down.

"What did you gain from that?" his friend calmly asked, his anger impossible to notice unless you knew to look. "You permanently lost a spell, took severe damage. You got *nothing*."

Horror seemed to paint the myconid's face as he began to realize, but he had to confirm, had to understand it truly.

**"Analyze."**

And he saw the truth of the world. A thousand scales, each in precarious balance. He saw himself as one of these scales, so grossly weighed in his favor that the world placed an opposing weight. If it were just the Oracle class it might've been fine, but *he was also a Traveler*. One or the other, both bent the scales against his favor. So the universe changed; a train crashed and Dustin was forced into a collision course with the Accumulation of White Lies. And he saw in front of him, he saw the Accumulation of White Lies, he saw it fall, he saw the worshipper of Osshiven'Kai rise onto the scales.

A power would be faced by likes or opposites or counters. A fire would be met with fire or would be put out with water or earth. The powers to gain knowledge would be faced by the same or the powers of erasing knowledge.

It was just like Noam's rap battle with that forgotten bard, a Clash. In winning against Noam, the bard stole one of his spells forever, strengthening like with like. In understanding the Accumulation of White Lies, Dustin gained the ability to Predict, strengthening a power by having it beat its opposite.

**"Predict."**

And he understood. The Accumulation of White Lies was immune to physical damage, but it had an Achilles' heel in that it was the concept of lies and deception made manifest. Thus enough people witnessing it would kill it instantly. A similar weakness existed for this cultist, a weakness he could grasp with Predict and beat him as well. He *had* to grasp it, for they were his challenges, challenges for the diviner to complete. For only in grasping knowledge could these monsters be beaten.

But he saw what would happen should he beat even this madman. Another monster, another beast, for his balance was still off, because after the battle with the Accumulation he had obtained Predict.

But he had not earned it.

He'd earned the right to one power, Observe, and the ability to use another, Predict. Two very different things.

And he saw the scales crashing down even now, for in facing the cultist, he learned three great revelations: the knowledge of the Seventh Hell, of Osshiven'Kai's true origin and purpose, and the knowledge of balance that he was seeing right now.

If he beat this cultist, he would earn Predict, but not the knowledge it brought him, so another monster would come. One that would need to be beaten by him using his Paths and could not be beaten any way else. For they were his challenge.

And he saw what lay in front of him: an endless cycle of battle, against monsters that controlled knowledge itself. A Path that forever escalated, one that grew like a snowball kicked off a mountain. Every battle, he would earn one of his powers and gain a new one, a cycle that went on until nothing was left to challenge him, until he became a god, a domain, unchallenged and immutable.

Yet the only god he saw in his mind was the historian, clad in no chains, yet he was a slave to that book. Forever doomed to continuously record the history of the world. To the point it was a genuine risk to even save his lover.

Or he failed and perished along the way.

This was his fate. This was his karma.

Dustin learned the truth of the world: everything was balanced.

That did not make it fair.

Shakily did the myconid rise to his feet. "Is this my future? An endless fight against horrors just like you?"

"Perhaps," the cultist answered noncommittally. "I always believe fate can be changed."

*Could* he even commit to this fate? "Show me your face, Declan."

And Declan did, showing him a face with a bloody red eye. A face with dried blood half wiped off.

That was what happened when the Accumulation of White Lies stole a single eye.

Could he afford to risk it again?

Dustin looked around him, seeing Noam unconscious in the orphanage, Utoqa lost somewhere among the stone rubble, Tai's body slumped against a shattered wall.

"Fuck," he muttered. "Fuck it all."

And with both hands he reached into his eye sockets. They stopped as he suddenly found the Magician tarot covering his face. He ripped it off, tearing it in half as he did so. Then he pulled out the eyes of Observe and Analyze. And with them Predict began to crumble, its foundations gone. The connection to Declan disappeared as Dustin stood alone in his mind once again.

Dustin tossed the eyes of gods that he had not earned onto the ground like trash. "I renounce all claims I have to this power and to the title of Oracle. May another that is worthy take it!"

The goal at the end was not worth it. To try until death to beat this system, and for what? Earn everything and become a slave to a Domain. Lose and suffer for it, knowing you wasted all the effort to get there.

And when the goal was not worth pursuing and the path too difficult, *Dustin simply gave up*, like he always did.

But was it truly the same?

A sacrifice to preserve not only his life but those of others, to potentially steer away this madman summoned by his own ignorance. Nay . . . not ignorance, for he was warned. He was warned of the risk but took it anyway because he didn't believe in them.

"So I am still a fool in the end," he murmured.

But in response to his grim determination, the cultist simply laughed. "That was cool and all, but all that did was make me beatable by other people again. By means not restricted to knowing."

Eyes that defied all description stared into Dustin's hollow sockets. "Who's to say I don't continue?"

And the cultist stepped forward to throw the die again.

Except that instead, his remaining foot landed squarely upon the upright blade of a glowing red dagger.

"FINALLY, I TASTE TRUE BLOOD!" the dagger yelled as the cultist lost his balance, dropping the die. He reached to grab it, but a puff of green spores covered his eyes, making him fumble for a moment.

And a yellow shadow grabbed the die before it was allowed to land.

With the last wisps of his power, Dustin saw one final thing.

*And a magus nobalite OTK deck.*

*A player who was forgotten. Hidden in obscurity, it won an unexpected victory.*

"Huh," the cultist murmured, seemingly unsure as Yellow had run away with the die, his foot still pinned to the earth by Celigarn and vision still slightly obscured by the poisonous spores of Greenie. The cultist reached for where Yellow had run off, but suddenly, his hand jerked away.

"I break the Finger of Tools," Celine said. The thumb of the severed hand she held fell to the ground.

The cultist glanced at her and shrugged. "I guess that's that."

He easily hopped off the blade, eliciting a scream of desire from Celigarn. Uncaring of the fact he was missing half his body, the cultist simply grabbed the two eyes on the ground. "And let's count our debts and balances *settled.*"

The world rippled like water before everything finally began to move collectively, and the cultist smiled as he hopped away. "It was a pleasure meeting you, Dustin the Oracle No Longer. One who was Thrice Blinded."

And like that, the madness of the town called Lake Bayt finally and truly ended.


Slowly, a single poorly made doll with red buttons for eyes stopped its writing. Its fingerless hands dropped the chalk as everything finally finished.

"Is this how it ends?" the boy's soul asked. "A monster leaves with what it wants. The people who came and saved us lying on the ground?"

And something answered. Within the mirror, a reflection of a ragged boy, his eyes red from weeping, a reflection that had no true counterpart in reality.

"It is," the boy in the mirror answered.

"They lost," the ragged doll protested. "They were hurt and broken; people died. Sister died; everyone is dead. Is there nothing to be done about it?"

The boy in the mirror simply looked wistful. "There are many stories of good triumphing, of evil failing before good. The black dragon is slain, the good king takes the throne, the orphan leaves their abusive aunt's home and meets their true parents who love them, or grow up to love a child twice as much. This is not our story. We are helpless to solve our suffering because we are children. Young and powerless to all the others that be."

"I remember them all," the doll said. "I don't want to, but I remember all of them. I want to forget them."

"You never will," the reflection answered, not unkindly. In its eyes were the sights of a dark place, where a madwoman sought apotheosis at the expense of hundreds. "We are children born in horror, forever scarred by it. This will follow you to the end of our days."

"But I don't want it to," the doll answered.

"It won't leave you," the reflection answered, "but I do know a trick."

"What is it?"

"I once met a writer," the reflection said. "He was strange—he traveled the world as if on the run, changing his name on the regular. And he once told me this.

"Even a baby knows horrors exist; they cry all day even when lying in their cradle. Our tears are nothing special," the reflection said. "The man told me that instead of trying to ruin the world, I should try to help it."

"Help it?"

"Even babies know the existence of horror, of evil and all things bad. So instead of trying to teach a lesson already known, he told me I should try to teach them how to beat these monsters. To force them back."

"But they were beaten as well," the doll answered.

"But still they killed it. Still, they forced the crazy man away. Without expecting anything in return, they bled, they fought, they won. Fairy tales might not exist . . . but they do. They are real. Not a knight in shining armor or a good king. They are kids like us, who saw something bad and didn't let it hurt anyone else."

"And why should we help? Why should we help anyone in this world that hurts us?"

The reflection's eyes grew wistful. "Because if we don't make an effort to try to make things better, what do we have left but our scars? Do we want to spend eternity in nothing but pain?"

The doll shook its head.

"With enough time, maybe the pain will lessen," the reflection answered. "With enough time, maybe you can pretend to forget. We won't ever forget it, but we can try. We won't ever save everyone, but we can try, and perhaps . . . perhaps even if we can't remove pain, one day we can make a child believe in fairy tales again.

"And isn't that something worth crying over?" the reflection said as it began to fade. "So go out, child of pain and horror, go out and make fairy tales believable again."

"Will it work?"

"I don't know," the reflection answered genuinely. "I'm still trying it myself."

The doll shined with the soul of a boy hidden within. The danger now passed, the boy finally returned, clutching a doll of the Weeping Child.

# 1.30

—

*"I'm so rich I don't even need to find tax loopholes!"*
—*Ethelinda Smith, the Merchant Goddess*

Recovery wasn't an easy thing.

We'd suffered many wounds, both external and internal. While Fix-Up Fungus could easily heal external flesh wounds, internal stuff was harder on it. Tai and Utoqa suffered the most from this. It turned out Tai had been fighting with multiple broken ribs while Utoqa had had several internal organs ruptured by acid and was only spared internal bleeding because the acid cauterized the wounds. Along with Noam, who had lost most of his blood, all three of the melee fighters were stuck in bed.

"How the BLEEP did you ignore three broken ribs?" Noam asked as he bit into his meal.

"I just thought I was tired," Tai honestly replied. "Fucking hurt like a bitch, but I thought if I slept for a bit, I would be fine."

"BLEEPING hell, you are stupid."

"Hey, fuck you."

"Is that usage an insult or an invitation to mate?" Utoqa asked. The poor idiot probably meant the question genuinely as well.

"Insult," Noam answered. "And holy BLEEP, I know you don't feel pain the same way us 'soft-skins' do, Utoqa, but how'd you fight with BLEEPING ruptured organs—" He paused, then shook his head. "Okay, BLEEP this. Corvian, why am I the only one who's still getting bleeped?"

Corvian, who had been silently attending to their wounds, chuckled. "Well, you have the blessing of Tilt on you, of course!"

"But why me?" he protested. "Everyone else can BLEEPING swear as much as they BLEEPING want!"

"Well, after what you said about Xavier and what he does to cats, I very much believe you deserve this."

"How long will this last?" he asked, a bit of fear in his voice.

"Well, forever, obviously—"

Noam kicked off his blankets, hopping out of his bed then making his way to the door. "I'm making a formal complaint!"

And he left the makeshift clinic we had set up, heading down and toward that empty orphanage.

"Should we stop him from accidentally blaspheming a god or something?" I asked.

Corvian shrugged. "Lady Tilt is more likely to just make his life slightly more miserable and accident-prone for a month or two, but not anything serious. You all did save this town and avenge those children."

I shrugged; if it was fine, then just let it be. Noam would eventually just wear himself out.

What I was more focused on were the scales I saw above Noam's head.

Golden weighing scales, that for a brief moment, held a silver bell that brushed against Noam's side.

I learned three world-changing secrets. It seemed like knowing the information was only half the reward.


Three days passed in just recovery.

During the whole time free, I went around the small town, helping wherever I could, offering healing and food and light. The whole time Greenie and Yellow had to guide me, for I was blind once more.

I passed by the orphanage again on the second day; from inside came a stream of bleeps as Noam continued his "complaint."

"He's been going on for the past day," Corvian muttered beside me. "Didn't even rest for sleep."

"He'll tire himself out eventually," I answered. I could still see them, Noam's scales. The scales that determined all balance, the scales that said Noam was due a win.

"I've called a carpenter from outside. One day the house will be home to children again," Corvian said, a light of determination in his eyes.

The orphanage was the epicenter of the Accumulation's existence; only a single child had survived of the almost thirty half-remembered ones, the one who was disguised as a doll within the mage's tower.

"And what do you need?" I asked.

Corvian turned toward me. "You are an Oracle no longer?"

I shook my head. "No. Not an Oracle anymore."

"Then what are you now?"

I looked up and saw them—my balance scales, as well as Corvian's.

Both of us were light upon the scales.

"I've been wondering that as well. Knowing what I know, I realized that if I was not oracle, I would become something else."

The classes I earned from being a Traveler were neutral, earned rightly and with time, effort, and XP, so not considered upon the scales. It was everything else that weighed upon it.

I had in the end earned the right to two powers, Observe and Analyze, but at that final moment, I held four: Observe, Analyze, Predict, and the information I knew that if told would change the world.

When I threw away three, I still had the right to two powers.

One was the information I knew, of so many things within this world. Some that were better left forgotten.

And the other was an empty slot, a slot that was being filled slowly and gradually.

"Do you no longer find secrets?" Corvian asked and the world seemed to still.

Here there were a myriad of choices before me. An infinite number of ways to answer the question. The Crossroads of Paths, but I had long decided.

The things I know now should not be revealed to anyone.

"No," I said. "You may say I Keep them instead."

The scales above our heads seemed to come into focus, as I finally saw my own enter Balance.

"Then you might be the sole person I can pass this to, Keeper of Secrets." Corvian withdrew a deck from his robes, placing it into my hands.

"The Revenant King deck," I murmured.

"It gives a clue to how to revive him," Corvian murmured, his voice hushed. "I can't let it stay here, not while we need to recover."

A secret that could change the world, one that was an invitation much like the eyes I once held.

"Couldn't you just burn it?"

"Blasphemy," he replied, then shrugged. "I mean, I could, but Wundull would not like it. He would know it was necessary, but he wouldn't like it."

"So you throw it on an idiot like me," I smirked.

"Hey, watch the language," he casually threw out. "I'm a Tilt worshipper as well."

"Worshipping two gods sounds like work."

"It is." He seemed to wince. "I'm just telling him the truth—I've already doubled my workload here."

I raised an eyebrow. "You enjoy that, then."

"Yeah." Corvian sighed, then turned to leave. "Thank you for everything, Dustin."

"If I didn't reach for power I didn't earn, I wouldn't be in this mess."

"If you didn't reach for power, you wouldn't have come here," Corvian answered. "The Accumulation would've been here regardless of if you reached or not. Reaching simply put you on a collision course here."

I was silent; I knew it was true, yet it didn't diminish at all the fact that I'd fucked up. I was warned against taking both eyes, yet I still did, trying to circumvent a system, thinking I was clever.

"I'm still the same idiot," I murmured.

But now I understood the system just slightly better. Now I had the benefit of hindsight. Now I know what happens when you put your hand on the stove.

I know four world-shattering secrets, and I am now the Keeper of them. To ensure I know them but never allow them to spread. For that, I can sense them in the back of my mind.

A blank page and a compass.

A pair of scales measuring the balance of all things.

A serpent that consumed its own tail and starved as a mouth.

And finally, two cogs, one of solid brass grinding inexorably toward its goal, the other of a dozen makeshift materials constantly clashing against the other in fits and spurts.

A moment when the Historian stopped writing, to let Discovery find new, safer horizons. The nature of balance within this world, of how reaching for power was almost self-defeating, yet if you continued to rack up great accomplishments, you *would* become something great. Effort did not go unrewarded here, no matter what.

While these two might be fine to spread, the last two were not. There were a wealth of worlds within the Seventh Hell, but they were better left buried—don't allow greed a chance to wake an eldritch horror on par with the One Order. The true nature of Osshiven'Kai and its conflict should not be revealed, else either begin to break this fragile balance and descend this world into chaos or order.

And I saw five other, weaker, but still flickering secrets behind them. The deck I received became a shattered crown of woe and made them six. I was missing something with them, lacking in the understanding of them in some way that made keeping them secret important, but I wasn't able yet to Keep them.

But so long as I held these things secret, so long as I Kept them, I would gain abilities. Only one at a time now, and it would still be separated from my Traveler classes, meaning it would have Et Non-Discent. Yes, I could imagine it, if I still had Analyze, this is what the class would look like.

Keeper of Secrets:
Path: Keep
- **Keeper of Secrets:** You know several world-shattering revelations that, if revealed, may change the course of the world. While you hold them secret, you may put one in an active state to gain certain benefits. The less well-known the knowledge, the greater its potential impact on the world and the deeper your own knowledge of it, the greater the benefit you have in Keeping it.
- **Secrets:** A blank page in history, the next voyage of Discovery: you become difficult to be remembered or perceived; others will not notice your presence without a high stat check or you choosing to reveal yourself, though remains of your passing will stay—e.g. footprints, reflections, recordings, scents. While this is active, you have True Sight.
- **The Balance (Currently Active):** You can see the Balance Scales of yourself and others.
- **The World Eater of the Seventh Hell:** You may store consumables within your stomach that you may at any time digest. If this ability is deactivated or swapped out, all stored consumables will be digested.
- **The One Order Fenkai and the Clockwork Chaos Osshiven'Kai:** When things are ordered: you are passively aware of the location of the sun and stars, the weather, and the cardinal directions. When things are chaotic: you randomly gain two T0 and one T1 spells. These spells cost no mana but can only be cast once each. Upon using all three, you gain another random set of two T0 and one T1 spells.
- **Incomplete Secrets:** More is required to qualify these secrets for Keeping.
- The Maker and Daughter's Madness, the Creation of Indiri, True Magic, the First Fear's Birth, the Origin of Demons, the Shattered Crown of the Revenant King
- **Et Non-Discent:** This class was not sourced from the system, thus it does not benefit from the system, either.

- Progress in this class does not rely on Traveler XP, but on your own proficiency.
- You may not invest levels in this class.
- This class and its progress will not be displayed on your Traveler character sheet.

And my complete character sheet would look something like this.

**Name: Dustin**
Race: Magic Myconid Level 1
Classes: Fungalmancer Level 4, Keeper of Secrets Level 1

<u>Body:</u>
Strength: 8
Agility: 7
Dexterity: 6
Constitution: 19
Stamina: 10
Vitality: 12

<u>Mind:</u>
Intelligence: 18
Wisdom: 20
Charisma: 6

<u>Soul:</u>
Will: 10
Psyche: 10
Perception: 10
Available SP: 6

<u>Racials:</u>
Manavision, Fungal Body, Sun Sickness, Mana Dependency, Pacifying Spores, Strong Innate Magic, Age-Type Heteromorph

<u>Class Skills:</u>
Fungalmancer:
Path: Symbiosis
- **Grow Sporage (Visual)**
- **Grow Sporage (Proximity)**

- **Sporage Wisp Symbiosis**
- **Bracken Polypores**

Keeper of Secrets:
Path: Keep
- **Keeper of Secrets:**
- **Secrets:** A blank page in history, the next voyage of Discovery
- **The Balance (Currently Active)**
- **The World Eater of the Seventh Hell**
- **The One Order Fenkai and the Clockwork Chaos Osshiven'Kai**
- **Incomplete Secrets**
- **Et Non-Discent**

<u>Magic Myconid Spells:</u>
T0: Sneezing Spores, Acid Spit, Watching Eye

<u>Fungalmancer Spells:</u>
T0: Balm Spores, Light Spores, Shillelagh (1 Free)
T1: Mushroom Meal, Poison Spores, Euphoria Spray (1 Free)
T2: Bark Skin, Fix-Up Fungus, Rot Spores (1 Free)
T3: (2 Free)

Analyze was, ultimately, completely based on my own analytical ability. It freed up my mind and gave me passive information that I didn't notice or wasn't paying attention to, but it was still just something of myself that also had the capability to evolve to something more, allowing me to see the truth of people's souls at its final moment. It was a passive information processing ability, which I could completely replicate in its base form by just paying some attention.

Observe was the greater loss; now that I could no longer see out of all those eyes, I'd lost a great deal of my information-gathering ability.

But the two were divination-type Paths, Paths that I had managed to bring to the point where I could Predict the future. And therein lay the problem; as divination abilities, the challenges they drew were almost exclusively that of things like the Accumulation of White Lies: esoteric creatures that devoured—nay, *challenged* information.

Keep was what I decided on, because the main danger of these secrets would be me telling someone. They were merely information, but each had the possibility of changing the world. Such power, such influence. I neutered it by swearing I would never tell and so invalidated the greatest power secrets held, allowing Keep to become a greater power in response. And I knew how dangerous this information was because I saw how much they *weighed*. Less than a paragraph of letters and words, if used correctly, could shake the world.

To leave this knowledge secret was the limitation; the extreme variety of abilities I gained from them was the reward. Only one could be active at a time, and it would take a while to swap them out, but those were also worthy limitations. I could make it swap abilities faster, or hold multiple at the same time, but I wouldn't have as strong a selection like this.

Not to mention that the nature of a Clash meant only one could truly win and defeat the opponent. While that didn't mean others couldn't help, it meant that fate itself was conspiring against them. The Accumulation of White Lies couldn't be hurt by physical means, and the cultist of Osshiven'Kai had absurd regeneration and immortality, which invalidated a good two-thirds of my party.

So the fact that Keep was taking on a more combative and active nature made it far more desirable, because it meant the next thing I would meet in a challenge could be hurt by physical means. It meant the next thing I faced to realign my Balance would be affected by Noam stabbing it or by Utoqa cutting it in half.

I still needed to be the one who defeated it, else the fight was invalidated, but others could still help.

And if Noam or Utoqa entered a Clash, I knew I could help out, so long as they were the ones who won in the end.

Not that it would happen anytime soon.

Utoqa was in balance, but Noam was due a boon—a boon on par with what I got or with Utoqa's Survive.

Because even if reaching beyond your means led to challenge and tribulation, surpassing challenges always made you greater. Noam had fought hundreds of players and chimera. He'd slain the chimerist in one-on-one combat. He tasted the sun itself and gained the respect of a Demon Chef. He won a Clash against a bard whose face was faded. He played a crucial role against the Accumulation of White Lies.

A single Path was the minimum I expected him to gain.

And I was increasingly starting to suspect the source of this would come from the Goddess of Children, Tilt. For Fate was pushing him into an encounter with her.

I wished him luck in this endeavor.

# 2.00

——

*"One hundred and fifty-two. Whoever said, 'The real treasure were the friends we made along the way,' has never had to escape to the Fourth Circle because your 'friend' pissed off the Kenkou mafia."*

*—Excerpt from Elliot's Enchiridion of Encounters*

Noam spent the first thirty minutes asking the bell to give his swear words back.

When all he got was a stern no, he spent the next thirty begging harder.

When no response came, he started swearing at the bell, half his words bleeped, until the sun went down.

And he decided to keep going, 'cause what was a single night staying up swearing at a god?

On the dawn of the second day, Noam decided to switch it up slightly.

"There once was a pixie as dim as gray, / She took away a poor me's power to say! / When I begged sincerely in prayer, / She told me sternly I cannot swear! / So I say she is quite BLEEP—Oh, come on, that isn't even a swear word!"

And began composing limericks to insult the god.

When he started to run out of limericks, he switched to rap.

"Fairy of the Silver Bell, / I heard you're a god of kids, / So among them your member must get quite swell! / And I bet you're as slimy as a squid!"

And thus the second day passed with Noam displaying elaborate ways to insult the god with poetry.

On the dawn of the third day . . .

". . . And thus you caressed the soft, slimy and fresh flesh of Squidward the Second. His skin is supple, yet underneath you can feel the hard, toned . . ."

. . . began orating erotic fan fiction of Tilt directly to her shrine.

". . . Squidward held you softly but firmly; you are surprised by his assertiveness as he brings you away to—"

"What the fu—fungus," Dustin quickly corrected himself, "did I just walk into?"

Noam turned away, his eyes sunken and the bags underneath clear. For three days and three nights he'd continually insulted the shrine to no avail. Yet nothing had broken his iron resolve.

"She's going to give back my BLEEPS, I swear it!"

"So far she's giving you no fucks back," Dustin winced. "Sorry, I shouldn't have said that."

"It's a war of attrition!" Noam raved, his eyes wild with resolve like a burning forest fire. "One of us will give in eventually! Either I finally get on her nerves or I break, *and I refuse to break.*"

"You're not going to get them back by insulting the person who took them, you know. You could just make a minor change to your vernacular and make everyone more comfortable."

"Never!" Noam answered. "This isn't about swearing anymore; this is about *honor!*"

Dustin didn't direct his next question toward Noam, but instead toward Greenie, who was sleepily acting as his guide shroom. "Where's the shrine?"

Greenie pointed him toward it.

Dustin bowed in its general direction. "I'd just like to say I am not associated with this man or responsible for his behavior and when he does get smitten, please ensure collateral damage is at a minimum."

"Coward!"

The myconid shrugged. "On more serious business, have you seen Celine?"

Noam frowned. "No, I haven't. Something wrong?"

"I've barely seen her for the past few days," Dustin answered. "Utoqa tells me she comes in at night to help with his and Tai's wounds but she's gone like a shadow immediately after."

"Is something wrong with her?" Noam asked. "She looked pretty pale after escaping the snake thing."

Dustin closed his empty eye sockets, remembering how Celine had looked for a moment. How her skin was pale and her hair appeared bleached, and how her appearance seemed to shift back to normal in a moment when none of them were looking, "No, that isn't the Accumulation's doing. She's keeping something secret."

Noam shrugged. "Let her, then."

"I will, but regardless—" Dustin pulled out a bag clinking with coins. "The townsfolk rustled up some money to pay us. I've divided it equally among all six of us. If she comes by, give her this. I've left similar instructions with Utoqa."

"Got it," Noam said, taking the bag.

"Oh, and we're having a goodbye party tonight. If you're done blaspheming, then join us."

Noam raised an eyebrow. "We're leaving already? Isn't it too early? What if something else comes by?"

Dustin frowned, then looked above him. "The chances of something happening dramatically decrease if we leave," he said carefully, as if considering his every word. "Strength invites challenge; being here until now has been fine, but . . . if we want Lake Bayt to recover, the best we can do is take our weight off here."

"Something you can't tell me?" Noam asked.

Dustin paused, his mind deep in thought. "I might be able to tell you—a select few can be told—but I need to keep these things as much of a secret as I can. But maybe I can . . . I'll try to tell you when we both get to log out."

Noam nodded.

"Remember, the party is tonight," Dustin said as he began to leave. "Also, it seems like you're due a level up or two."

He raised his eyebrow slightly at that. Because Dustin seemed *sure* something would happen. Then Noam frowned—his head hurt, and his thinking felt slow. No matter his own willpower, his body was just not meant to stay up for three days in a row.

Regardless, he turned around. "As I was saying, you are surprised by Squidward's assertiveness as he . . ."

The night was young when Celine left.

Bearing only the things she could carry, she passed the partying inn like a shadow. On a moonlit night, she walked toward the wall that separated this town from the wilderness.

For she did not belong; she never belonged anywhere. She made sure everyone was healthy, because they were owed at least that much, but she did not belong here. She did not belong among people.

Yet as she walked alone on a dark road, the moon slowly became hidden by clouds. She stopped, looking into the orphanage in which the monster once made its den. Toward a single light, where a person sat and told a story.

". . . and thus you tie the knot. The priest declares your vow with Squidward eternal. You feel his embrace around you, and you know the emptiness that once held your heart is well and truly gone."

Like a man possessed, Noam told a story. Before him, sitting around that candle flame, was the silhouette of a young fairy. A young fairy whose wings glistened like silver, her features young and pure. And the fairy was silently crying, her tears soaking into a napkin, enamored as the tale finished.

"That was beautiful, stupid horn head." Her voice rang like bells even as she cried crystal tears.

Noam exhaled, panting as if tired from head to toe. "Yeah, that one surprised me as well. I just let it run away from me."

"Tell me another one!" the fairy asked. "Actually . . . tell me one every week! Every day! Become one of my priests or something! Actually, you can be my next Incarnation, how about that?"

Noam yawned. "Incarnation? Wazzat?"

"It's um, like, um, well, I sorta go *wooosh* then *bumpfff*, and suddenly you can use my power when you want or need!"

Celine felt a sudden lump in her throat. The Incarnation of a god? And one of the greater ones, at that?

"Really," Noam said amid another yawn, "that sounds cool, but can I get my swear words back?"

"Even better!" the fairy exclaimed. "Once you become my Incarnation you will never be able to use bad words! Not even your original can!"

"Original . . ." His voice slurred slightly before it suddenly sharpened. "You mean I, as Matt Nguyen, would not be able to swear anymore?"

The fairy nodded excitedly. "Yep!"

"Then BLEEP off!"

Half in shock, half in sheer disbelief, Celine watched as Noam rejected the next best thing from godhood.

The fairy grabbed Noam by the ears. "Why do you care so much about some stupid bad words! They're bad words!"

"It's a matter of principle!" Noam yelled back, trying to pry the god's hands off his ears.

Noam, one of the greatest players to ever grace gaming, so good that numerous forums of salty rankers called him a hacker, and Tilt, the Patron Goddess of Trickery, Freedom, Loyalty and Children, the Innocence Never Lost, the Girl of the Silver Bell—the two, without any grace or skill, tumbled around the empty orphanage and fought like children.

But unfortunately, three days without sleep or rest, constantly swearing at a shrine, had rendered him rather weak, and so Tilt swiftly got the upper hand. Noam stepped on a banana that materialized directly under his foot, slipping and sliding directly out of the shrine.

"And never come back, you purple stinky head!"

"If I never see you again, it would be too soon!" Noam yelled back, his head still stuck in a bush. "What is silver but shitty platinum?"

The Goddess stuck her tongue out at the figure before her own body dissipated. Noam rose from the bush, rubbing his head. His eyes glanced around, passing over Celine but not seeing her.

Yawning, Noam took two steps before he collapsed onto the dirt road in exhaustion.

Quietly and slowly, Celine tried to skirt around Noam's unconscious body to get on her way.

Then the first few drops of rain fell.

Celine continued walking, resolute in the fact *someone* should find Noam here.

Then a few drops increased to a downpour, and Noam remained firmly on the ground. Still and unconscious.

"Someone will find you, right?" Celine whispered in the rain, seeing Noam getting increasingly soaked, before she groaned. "Ahhh!"

She grabbed Noam by the legs, finding him dead still, like a rock, and tried to pull, gritting her teeth in exertion.

She let go, huffing and puffing, before she whispered, "Nappy."

Her cloak came alive, wrapping itself around her arms, becoming an extension of them as they wrapped themselves around Noam.

Tilt probably didn't want him back, so instead, she found an abandoned house—slightly distressed by how many there were now.

Saying a small prayer to the house's former inhabitants, she brought Noam in. Using Nappy, she put him onto an empty bed, then touched his forehead, checking his temperature.

Noam was burning up, but she had a potion for this. Putting it to his lips, she gently massaged his throat so that the liquid made its way through properly. She'd made the mistake a few times when she was first learning potions, leading to some very annoyed forest fauna.

Finishing the bottle, she placed a blanket on the tiefling. Checking his temperature one last time and making sure he was stable, Celine moved toward the door.

"Wait."

Celine paused; his voice was quiet, barely a rasp. "You should be okay, Noam. The fever is light, and a night's sleep will do you well."

Noam groaned. "My mouth tastes like sunflowers. I didn't even know what sunflowers tasted like until now."

She smiled slightly at that. "If that's all, then I'll be—"

"Going?" Noam asked. "But where?"

She hugged her cloak, Nappy, close. "I don't know. Maybe someplace where I can set up shop, but I can't stay here anymore."

There was a shuffling behind her. "Why not?" Noam asked as he rose.

She gripped her cloak even more tightly around her, almost hoping she could disappear into it, but Noam had saved her life. He at least deserved to know.

Celine turned to face Noam, but as she did so, the color of her skin bleached; her eyes became pure white and her hair an unnatural pale.

"Because I am a monster. Because I am a changeling."

In a small hamlet hidden between rolling hills and idyllic plains, there was a boy named Mason, born to a farmer's family and the younger of two.

"Mason? Where could I be?" his mother cooed. Mason looked around the house, pretending to look for her, but he already knew.

There was an aura, a bright and happy aura, hidden beneath the table. It thrummed like a rainbow as his mother heard his steps draw closer, until—

A pair of hands covered her eyes. "Found you!" Mason said playfully.

Laughing, the mother lifted her youngest into the air; the young boy, no older than three years old, laughed as his short arms reached for his mother, pulling her ears as she brought him to embrace. Unlike his mother's dark, verdant hair and clear white skin, his hair was a mop of brown, and despite his youth, his skin was already tanned like a farmer's son.

In the evening his father and older brother would return from the forests, their day of lumber cut and sold.

"Hanton got to the north side before us," his father said with an aura of disappointment. "Couldn't cut much today, but Hanton's a perfectionist. He'll be on the north side for a few weeks getting everything."

"We can head to the west side then, can't we?" Mason's brother asked.

His mother quickly made the signs of prayer, while his father shook his head. "The witch lives there. We can't go near that place."

"Both of you should avoid her—that thing isn't a person," her mother whispered, her aura dark and jumpy. Genuine terror.

"Let's talk about kinder things," his father said.

His mother smiled and the darkness faded from her aura. Rubbing Mason's head, she said, "Mason caught me again today. I don't know how he does it."

And Mason smiled. "Because I love you, Ma!"

"Oh, you precious little . . ." She smiled as she brought him into a hug and extended an arm to her husband. "Come on, everyone bring it in."

The dinners they shared weren't anything fancy—vegetable soup and black bread—occasionally his father brought back the odd hunt they caught. It was filling, but the young boy simply enjoyed them all together, to hear them talk about their day, to see their auras change and flow like beautiful paintings.

And the boy wanted to spend days like this forever. To always spend them with others, to see their wonderful colors.

Noam frowned, and Celine saw his aura go contemplative.

It was a kindness that he didn't immediately flinch or draw a weapon. More than anything she'd ever experienced. Regardless, she put on her hood and turned away.

"Wait," Noam said again.

He left the bed, rubbing his head as he sat by the table in the small house. "Please sit. If you need someone that can listen . . . well, I'm here."

Celine looked outside, seeing the dark cobbled path, slick with rain. She could go without a word, to leave and live as she always had.

It was a lonely path, but it was a known one; even a straitjacket would feel comfortable when worn long enough, and she was tempted to go right then and there. But there was something about his eyes, his aura, how for the first time ever this jovial man-child finally looked completely and utterly serious.

So she sat, and she regaled him with her tale.

The first expression on his mother's face was shock.

Then horror, as her hands brushed against Mason's face and hair.

Mason didn't understand why her aura was turning dark; as he looked at his own hands, he saw them pale and pallid. White, but that was the wrong color, and he thought about what color they should be. The sun-tanned skin, much like his father's and brother's.

And the skin turned browned and tanned, exactly like his father's and brother's.

Mason smiled as he made the skin normal again.

But his mother simply looked on in horror as she grabbed his hand and looked it over. Up and down, left and right. Her aura changed slightly to hope, hoping that she'd just imagined what she just saw.

She brought Mason close, hugging him tightly and without a word. For it had to be a delusion; it had to be a lapse of imagination, what she just saw.

And she held on to that belief until night—when Mason fell asleep and his skin turned pale.

* * *

"She denied it at first, afraid of what it meant when I started turning, but I think deep down she knew. She always knew."

Mason was no longer allowed to go outside anymore.

His mother told everyone he had a skin disease, how it blistered easily under sunlight. She made up a tale of how it was a curse by the witch of the woods, and her husband added to the tale that he had accidentally chopped a tree a bit too close to the witch's woods.

For weeks Mason stayed inside his home. His father had left for a larger town, to find a priest who could cure his sickness. For a while, Mason believed the tale his mother wove, but the sunlight that peeked through the windows failed to burn his skin, and every day, he looked out at the other children, at all the other people playing and living outside. He saw their auras, like beautiful splashes of color just outside their dreary house.

And so, one day when his mother was out gathering berries, Mason left the house. And for a brief moment, when he was watching the people outside, enjoying the sun on his skin, he briefly turned.

And someone saw him.

"It was my fault," Celine admitted. "If I had just listened, if I weren't so fascinated by the colors everyone had . . ."

The colors were black. Black with hate and rage.

"I saw it!" the boy yelled. A boy who had once played with Mason like a friend. "I saw the monster change form to look like a kid!"

The crowd roared in response.

Mason's mother grabbed him, glancing out the window in fear. His brother held his axe at the ready, but he was unsteady, used to cutting only wood and not people. "Has Pa come back yet?"

His mother shook her head. "We can't wait for him to bring a priest anymore. We have to run."

Outside, the crowd moved, and to Mason's eyes, they were a swirling black miasma. Their auras were so dark with hate and fear that even the torches he knew they held failed to pierce the smoke of their own souls.

Mason's mother cradled him within her arms. "We need to go, now!"

And they ran out of their home. His mother held him as they headed toward the woods, his brother behind with an axe in hand.

"They're running!" someone yelled, a pitchfork pointed toward the escaping shadows.

They heard it then, the neighing of horses and shortly the sound of galloping. They weren't near the woods yet, and they couldn't outrun horses.

"Keep running, Ma," Mason's brother said, as suddenly a pair of footsteps ceased running behind them.

And Mason's mother kept running, with him held like a babe. A mother fleeing with her child no older than ten.

But the shouts kept following them; they kept nearing, and the fires and hate kept coming.

Until his mother tripped and fell onto the ground. Her aura flared with pain, as her ankle looked broken.

But she gritted her teeth and held Mason tight. She pushed a small bag that clinked into his hands. "Run, Mason. You have to run."

Mason didn't know he was crying until that moment, holding tightly to his mother like a drowning man to a raft.

"Why, Ma? Why are they chasing us? Why do they want to hurt us? I just want to be with you!" he asked, he pleaded.

Mason didn't need to see her aura to see the regret and pain that marred her face before she gritted her teeth, her mind made up.

"Because you are a monster, Mason," she said. "Because you are something they fear and don't understand. So you can't be with me—you can't be with us.

"So take the bag and run," she pleaded.

Mason stilled, his emotions warring across his face—confusion, fear, despair.

And his mother's face turned angry. "I said, RUN!"

She slapped Mason's face. "Run! Run as far as your legs can take you! Run into the west woods! Give the bag to the witch! You're a monster and you're being hunted, so RUN!"

The light of torches came ever nearer, as the mob drew closer, and finally, with tears on his face, Mason ran.

He ran deeper into the woods. He ran even when he fell and thorns tore his clothes. He ran through past streams; he ran until the sounds of shouting and the miasma of hate and fear disappeared.

Until he went deeper into the forest than anybody went.

And he stopped in the middle of a clearing, a moonlit night, the stars bright in the sky. He stopped to catch his breath, but as he did so, something rose.

A thing larger than a bear, its fur matted with blood and eyes large and red. From its back, dozens of weapons and spears jutted out. The attempts of lesser men to kill the king of the forest.

It was a monster, and Mason felt that he should've run.
But he didn't.
He was a monster.
A monster couldn't be with his family.
A monster was hated by the village.
A monster didn't deserve to live.

"That is why I'm leaving," Celine finished. "You all saw me unshifted. You saw the monster I was. It won't be long before the rumor gets out and they raise pitchforks and torches."

Noam was silent as she finished her story before he very quietly exhaled.

"I'll give you another story in exchange for that," Noam said. "About how I grew up."

Celine was quiet as Noam spoke.

"I didn't grow up in the nicest place. It was common to hear maybe ten to twenty gunshots each day and find two to three fresh pools of blood outside. One year it was worse than usual, and we didn't have enough money for food. So one day I went out and saw a drunk collapsed in an alleyway, and I took his money.

"But the guy wasn't quite as blacked out as I thought. He grabbed my arm as I tried to leave, so I kicked him and threw his head into the wall, and he stopped moving as I ran away." His eyes were closed as he remembered the exact scene.

"When I got home, I left the money on the counter, but Sarah demanded to know where it came from, so I showed her the guy in the alleyway. The guy who had died by the time we got back. And you know what she did?" he asked. "She silently picked up the corpse, and together we dragged him out of the city, where we buried his body under a pile of trash.

"That was about the time I started calling her my mum."

"What do you intend to tell with this story?" Celine asked.

"I'm not finished yet," Noam added. "See, later on, I got good at things. I got a bunch of friends; I got rolled into the local gang because I was good at pickpocketing and picking fights. And I thought they were all my friends, until one day, another kid picked the wrong guy, and when the gangbangers came knocking, they threw it on me and I was beaten within an inch of my life as an example."

Celine was silent as Noam finished the final part of his story.

"See, I learned then, there were a lot of types of people, but of 'friends,' there were real ones, people who would help you out regardless of what, and there were people who wouldn't. Who are more in love with the idea of you than what you actually are. And I can say that your parents, your family, they were real ones. They were people who went with you through thick and thin."

And Noam stared directly into her eyes, and his aura flared.

"I understand what a good friend should look like, so you understand that I do not joke or lie when I say I will knock the BLEEPING lights out of any BLEEPING torch BLEEPING gremlin piece of BLEEP that tries to raise a pitchfork to a good person! Otherwise, my name is not BLEEP-ING Matt Nguyen!"

Mason stood in that moonlit forest as the creature approached, a strange sense of peace and dread within his soul.

He looked across that empty clearing, at the stars quietly twinkling in the sky.

The finality of life was so serene.

And the monster raised its paw to strike.

Only it didn't, and instead thumped dead on the ground. Its head was gone, and in its place was only a massive bite mark.

Behind Mason an old figure strode forward, her face gnarled like a tree and nose hooked like a hawk's beak. She was chewing something before she swallowed.

"And what are you?" the witch of the woods asked.

"A monster," the changeling answered.

The witch chuckled. "If you are a monster, then I am Shadesmar, the evil god of horror!"

"But I am," the child answered despondently. His tears had long dried on his face. "They chased me out; Ma told me to run. She told me to go because I couldn't be with her anymore."

A thought arose in his mind, of one of the last things Mason's mother had told him. "She wanted me to give you this."

And he raised the bag that clinked of metal.

The witch took it, sniffing it slightly before her face and aura turned quiet and contemplative.

Then the witch made a decision.

She chuckled, hand descending to ruffle Mason's pale-white hair. "I suppose I am an evil god now!"

The witch's hand gently but firmly grasped Mason's own small hand. "And what is an evil god without her minions?"

"Minion?" Mason asked.

"My minion," the witch answered, "which means I will protect you, for any harm to you is an insult to me, the evil god, and I will teach you, for you must be able to wreak terror in my name."

"And what is your name?" Mason asked.

"I am the Witch of the Woods," she answered. "I am Ni Kakoph."

Celine did not realize she was crying until the tears dripped down her chin and onto the wooden table.

"Oh . . ." she said, raising her sleeve to wipe her face. ". . . I'm sorry . . ."

Noam simply brought out a napkin for her to use, to wipe the tears that had suddenly appeared.

"It's fine to cry," Noam said. "Everyone needs a good cry every now and again. So just let it out."

Celine kept apologizing as she cried, for what, she wasn't sure. Only that she kept trying to wipe tears that just continued to stream. Hiccups and snot fought their way out of her face, and she needed to wipe those as well.

After a long time, when Celine's tears started to slow, Noam spoke.

"Hear me out," he said. "Stay for one more night. We're having a party, and you should join in."

She was about to raise her objections before he cut her off. "Don't worry about getting away—I can solo any flash mob that appears! And Dustin can keep them sneezing for long enough to get away, and Utoqa is your gecko when you need to survive in the wild . . ."

"How are you so sure they will help?" she asked.

And Noam smiled. "Like I said, I recognize a friend."

"Minion!" Ni Kakoph called. "Minion, we have a problem!"

"What is it?" Mason called out. They were much taller now, tall enough to stir the witch's cauldron as it bubbled and boiled.

"We have a severe problem!" the witch repeated as she barged in, carrying in her hands an old and faded dress. "I can't graduate you without a proper uniform! I don't have a men's uniform for you!"

"Is that it?" the changeling asked as they glanced skeptically at the dress.

It was old but recently cleaned—the smell of sunshine was still fresh on it.

Already, Mason's skin and hair flashed through different colors. Their figure shifted to a more feminine appearance before suddenly Ni Kakoph bonked their head.

"You aren't just shifting into some random-ass girl for this!" the witch yelled. "It has to be something important to match the occasion!"

"Important?" Mason asked as they rubbed their head.

Ni nodded furiously.

And Mason thought deeper and deeper, but already, their hair was turning into a deep shade of verdant green, their skin a healthier shade of pale.

Before long, Mason appeared like their mother once was, but at the same age they were currently.

"Are you all right with this?" Ni asked, her voice quiet. "This won't be like a normal shift—a mage's graduation marks their existence for as long as they live."

Mason looked over themself and shrugged. "It's fine. Being a guy isn't important, and . . . they would be looking for a tan-skinned boy named Mason."

And the witch nodded.

The next day, the young woman put on the faded but clean witch's uniform. She made sure every bit was prepared as she stepped out of the house.

Ni Kakoph was sitting on the porch as she stepped onto the grass below.

And the girl bowed. "Thank you for everything, Baba Ni."

The old witch rubbed her head. "That reminds me—I never asked for your name, did I, minion?"

The young witch raised her head. "I was named Mason by my father, and I now take my mother's name, Celine. I . . . want to be Celine more, but I don't want to abandon Mason, so I will use both when allowed. I don't have a surname, unfortunately."

The old witch smiled as she rose from her seat. "Stoneworker or heavens—a fine duality."

The old witch stared at the sky, then at the earth.

And the world was still as she made a declaration. "To all who will listen, I am Ni Kakoph, and I grant my Name to the young genius who stands before me. May she be as I once was, a great Cacophony that shakes both heavens and earth!"

Celine Kakoph felt the power that rippled through the world. She felt the black cloak behind her tighten, as if in a warm embrace.

"You give me your Name Baba?"

The old witch smiled. "I said my minion would wreak terror in my name, didn't I?"

And Celine smiled. "You did."

There was a moment of comfortable silence, before Celine turned to leave. "Thank you for—"

"Oh!" the old witch interrupted. "Before I forget."

She rummaged through her own cloak, pulling an old bag that clinked of metal when drawn. Whose edges were frayed from time.

And Ni tossed it at Celine, who barely managed to catch it.

"What is this?" she asked.

"Something that is yours now," the old witch answered.

Celine recognized it as the bag her mother had told her to give to the witch. Quietly, she drew open the strings, finding what was inside.

A few coins, mostly coppers and silvers, but there was one gold, and two rings.

Wedding rings.

The wedding rings her father gave to her mother on their wedding day. "They . . . they gave up their . . ." She tried to speak, but her voice croaked as tears streamed down her face. This was likely all the wealth her family had had.

"Your education has been paid for in full," Ni Kakoph said. "That is your salary for stirring the cauldron and collecting herbs."

Celine smiled even as tears streamed down her face. "What a horrible payment for years of free work."

Ni chuckled. "Well, you didn't pay for me teaching you, either!"

Finally, she turned around, away from the moving house, clad in a living cloak blessed by the old woman who had saved her, in her pouch the rings of the people that raised her.

Celine Kakoph went into the world to see if she could find her parents again.


When Celine entered the partying inn, helping a half-delirious Noam walk, Dustin was playing Age of Wonders with Corvian, the wisps, and Utoqa, who was severely missing the point of the game.

And when the myconid turned to look at his friend, seeing him leaning on the witch for balance and support, he let out a sharp bark of laughter.

"I don't know what else I expected," he said with a smile. "Fucking extroverts," he muttered before Corvian slapped his head.

"Language!"


The next day, as people were still recovering from hangovers, a small group of people piled their luggage on a cart gifted to them by the town.

One of them, a tiefling, was vomiting last night's contents onto a tree as a young woman with verdant hair patted his back. A lizardfolk and elven swordswoman were hauling the bags of rations and foodstuff they'd been given. And finally, a myconid stood talking with a gnomish priest.

"I wish you luck in rebuilding the town," Dustin said.

Corvian nodded. "It won't be quick, but it will happen. Lake Bayt will recover from this. But . . ." The gnome's eyes slid toward a child—a child carrying a ghastly doll.

Strange looks swept this child, and Corvian beckoned him forth. "Johnny, come meet Dustin."

The child came, his eyes empty and listless.

"I'm not sure what to do with him, but he wants to go with you guys."

Dustin raised an eyebrow. "Why so?"

The child's head hung. "I don't want to be here anymore," the boy said. "I see them everywhere, everyone that died. They're still here. I don't want to see them anymore."

Corvian grabbed Dustin's arm and dragged him close. "He's carrying a symbol of the Weeping Child, Dustin," Corvian whispered. "His life won't be simple or easy, for people regard the gestalt as a dark god."

"You think something will happen?" he asked, for though the child's Scales were in balance, he knew it was something that could be changed in a moment's bad decision.

"Perhaps, and until then, I want you to protect him. Keep him safe to grow up happy. I . . ." Corvian gritted his teeth. "I alone can't provide this protection. So please, maybe find a temple to Gwaina in one of the greater cities, somewhere that can take him in."

Dustin thought about it, and he nodded. He didn't really need to talk it over with Utoqa or Noam, since one wouldn't care and the other would accept in a heartbeat.

Then he knelt, his gnarled hand on the child's shoulder. "I am Dustin. Who are you?"

"I am Johnny Joymoon," the boy replied.

Corvian watched as they left, feeling a slight pang of regret that he could not save that child, but he would be safe in their care, he was certain of it.

Instead, he felt Wundull tugging at him, the first of two gods he'd devoted himself to.

The first copy of every single card of the Age of Wonders was created by a follower of Wundull who had witnessed the wonders of the world themselves.

And Corvian Diluvian Medudian Himotonana Farraday the Middling had seen much.

He raised his hand, and within it, six cards manifested from divinity and power.

Chosen of the Weeping Child.

Gnari Family Swordswoman.
Wandering Witch.
Tribeless Survivor.
Traveling Skald.
And finally, the only card that was named.
Dustin the Thrice Blinded.
Corvian smiled as he drew the final card. They Met in a Tavern.

# Remembering

*"Maybe somewhere green . . . somewhere we can run a small shop with all our kids . . ."*

*—Caleb G*

Abe remembered pizza.

Returning home on a hot day, the coolness of the store hitting him. Seeing a perpetually warm smile on his dad's face. Rough, dark hands covered in white flour as they rolled pieces of dough. A few slices of pizza were always available at the end of the day—leftovers, his dad always said. Though it was strange; there was always pepperoni pizza. His favorite for a while, before eating pizza every day got old.

He wasn't old enough to have been drafted at the time. When Europe burned, only other Commonwealth nations would have sent aid. Colonialism left a sore mark on many people, and the last nation that could've feasibly helped was too busy slapping itself in the face to be of any use to anyone.

When the store started struggling, his dad and uncle joined the army. Abe remembered getting diagnosed with anxiety at the time, every day wondering if he'd ever see his dad again.

There were sparse emails, calls, and texts when his dad managed to get out of the EMP-affected areas, but he never talked about fighting. It was always something inane, reassuring teary family members he was okay, asking about how the store was doing with mum taking care of it, complaining about how army food was shit. Even if Dad never talked about anything of import, Abe always looked forward to his calls. Fidgeting for weeks on end when there was no contact.

Then the war abruptly ended.

Abe remembered the day America decided to finally do something. He remembered seeing it in the news—anthrax spores were spread throughout the nation from low Earth orbit, destroying North America's ecosystem and crippling the nation's ability to produce livestock in the span of a few short months.

If the biological attack was indeed perpetrated by Russia as a last resort to keep America out of the war, they could not have done a more foolish thing.

America was a nation that almost entirely subsisted on fast food, meat, and diabetes. The moment someone took away the meat in a cheese-burger—as well as the cheese—and forced them to eat their vegetables, they became a unified and rampant mob.

Abe remembered his aunt laughing as the news came. How the move had done more to unite America than anything the nation itself had done. Bipartisan unity; armed skinheads teaching minorities how to shoot a gun; the US military, known only for its absurd budget, suddenly seeming woe-fully inadequate to deal with the number of people signing up to go to war.

A nation that once cracked in half squabbling like children came together to beat up the bully who took away their lollies.

Of course, they conquered South America first and burned down the Amazon to get that unspoiled farmland, but they eventually got around to Europe.

For a long time, the war was a stalemate, but finally the scales started to tip when hordes of angry Americans began flooding the war.

Where once battlefields were empty save for Russia's mechanized infan-try and drones, they were once again filled with the roar of gunfire. The communists were finally getting pushed back by their ideological enemy.

The Star-Spangled Tide, the White and Blue but Mostly Red Flood, the Horde, the Gun-Toting Vegans—eventually, they were simply called the Greens, after a comedian jokingly said gunfire and artillery bombard-ment was what happened when you forced an American to eat their greens.

The war was finally being won.

Abe's dad no longer had to pretend that things were going well, and Abe didn't have to fake a smile in response, and though the war was ended . . . *abruptly* , no one truly faulted the US for its response. Even if words were said, a few sanctions were made, no hard actions were done. Matching biological warfare with biological warfare, it was simply an eye for an eye.

And when the alternative was a vengeance-driven madman dancing with a button that could set off worldwide nuclear devastation, they really did get the better end of the deal.

Plus the Soviets were all dead, so no one was left to complain.

His dad came home, though alone.

So long ago did it happen that the memory no longer brought tears to his eyes. The black clothes, the day forever darkened by smog. Was it freezing cold or stifling hot that day? Abe no longer remembered.

His dad remained stoic, helping everyone through their grief. Yet as Abe grew older, he couldn't help but wonder a simple question.

Who helped Dad through *his* grief?

The store opened again; the world must go on. Abe grew up, studied at university, and got one of the few jobs not yet automated. Human work slowly became a rarity as the nation advocated and worked toward a world where no one felt hungry or needed to work, freeing up their time to pursue greater things. Unfortunately, they seemed to be the only ones who thought about it that way.

As he neared his thirties, he realized something, something that didn't register because he'd honestly spent so little time with them.

His parents weren't perfect—they had flaws; they were stubborn. His dad, Caleb, held on to that small pizza store for years, and every time he visited, he still annoyingly made pepperoni pizza, even if Abe told him that he hadn't liked it for years.

It was one cool autumn day, and he visited the store once again. Dad already had pizzas out for him and his sister's family. They ate together while Dad kept rolling more in the kitchen, yet . . . as they ate, Abe noticed that the crust had become uneven, lumpy in some places and thin to the point of ripping in others. His nephews got really annoyed at this, since visiting Grandpa Caleb was their highlight of the week. His niece Momo asked why the pizza was bad, too young and innocent to really understand anything.

"Dad?" Abe called out as he moved to the back of the store, toward the kitchen. He called out once, twice, thrice, yet still, there was no answer. Worrying, he hurried until he entered the store kitchen and saw his father, his back stooped and crooked over the benchtop, sleeves rolled back.

His father's hands shook as they tried to push the rolling pin over the dough, trying to flatten it, yet his strength failed to do so, leaving an uneven and broken piece of flat dough.

For the first time in his life, Abe saw his father and thought how *old* he was.

It hurt him to roll that dough flat, yet still, he continued, doing his best despite old age, all for a family who said they didn't like pepperoni.

Abe didn't remember when tears first fell from his face.

The last thing he remembered of that day was simply hugging the frail and old form of the man who raised him.

* * *

He quit his old job.

Now he spent his days in the pizzeria, trying desperately to master the art of pizza making to the amused and smiling face of his dad.

"I'm telling you, Vek'Na is mathematically impossible to beat," a chubby young Asian said to another whose body was half prosthetic.

"There's gotta be a way, a fucking trick to it," the worryingly unwhole child replied as Abe delivered their two meat lovers' pizzas. "Can't we get better stats?"

The chubby child shook his head. "When I said *mathematically* impossible to beat, I mean I used the top raiding builds and then some! The DPS check was still impossible. There is simply not a comp that can both survive to his last phase and kill him during . . ."

Despite the fact both of them pounced on their meal like ravenous wolves, they still talked with fervor about their subject. It was mostly gibberish to Abe, even more so now that their mouths were completely full, yet he liked listening to his two most frequent customers. They always ordered two large pizzas; one and a half always went to the chubby child, and they always seemed to talk about games.

They came about once every other week, sometimes in triumph and celebration, sometimes in deep discussion. It was the part of the week he most looked forward to; every day he only got one or two customers physically in the store if he was *lucky*. Most of the time he spent in the back, baking pizzas for drones to deliver.

The fact he got returning customers at all when everyone just delivered everything probably meant he had gotten really good at pizza making, though Abe admitted that if an actual Italian ever saw his pizzas, they would probably call them a hate crime. Screw them, though—his dad and customers said they tasted great, and that's all he ever needed.

He smiled and waved back as the two kids left for the evening. Abe continued till late at night, when he eventually closed up. Calling his car on his AAD, he let it drive him back home. The house wasn't much; it didn't need to be, since it was just him, Mum, and Dad. His sister had her own family to take care of, something she kept ribbing him about. Abe *was not* a virgin at forty years old, no matter her insistence!

He found his dad by the balcony, dutifully watering a pot of flowers—*natural* flowers, ones not genetically engineered to survive harsh climates, but ones that were completely natural. Those things cost more than cars nowadays, but Abe made sure to save for one and throw away the receipt when he saw his dad look longingly at the few nature reserves and parks that survived.

"Had a good day today," Abe greeted him. "Those kids came again—man, I swear they come so often, they're probably keeping the store afloat on their own!"

And so they chatted throughout the night, Mum usually joining after the sound of their talking drowned out her TV dramas, despite the fact Abe had repeatedly informed her that they had a pair of noise-canceling headphones.

Like this, days and weeks passed by uneventfully, yet he remembered them all fondly, for they were perhaps Abe's happiest years.

Yet somehow, they always came back to this topic.

"You should get an AAD," Abe said, his tone frank. "You're getting old—who knows what's gonna happen in a few years or so? With a somatic implant, everyone can keep track of your health."

His mother shook her head as she looked at the two of them, eyes tired, but she would see this argument through out of a sense of familial duty.

The reply his father gave was always the same: he didn't want one. He lived perfectly fine now. He wouldn't allow someone he didn't know or trust to monitor his every move.

Abe heard these responses, yet they rang hollow against him. For they were relics of an older time when people valued personal freedom above everything else, even their own health and safety.

They knew better now.

And his father's response was just the response of a conservative old man; despite that, Abe usually withdrew, not wanting to damage what they had.


But no matter how good the times were, time always moved on.

In the years that passed, Abe slowly came to notice his father often staring into space, slow in his responses to others, sitting quietly when once he had spoken aloud with bright smiles.

Until one day, when Abe came to meet his father on the balcony, he wasn't recognized. Abe remembered the wrenching feeling in his chest when his dad called him Edison—his dead uncle who was lost in the war.

He didn't remember what happened later. For the memory came back in flashes. Snippets of what his father really spoke about.

That one afternoon soon became two, then three, then four, then five, then six. Always speaking of the same thing to a person he didn't recognize. Repeating to the point where Abe knew what his dad wanted to say every time he saw him. Something about them retiring in a small shop, where they could look after all their children and their children. Somewhere by a park, where it was still green. In a world where his brother was still alive.

He knew the day would come.

Looking back, Abe didn't remember that day from what he saw happen but from what others told him.

His father collapsed in the middle of the day when Abe was working at the shop. He remembered up till the phone call. How in a hurried haze he closed up shop and canceled dozens of orders. How he got in the car without even wiping the flour off his hands. One thing he remembered vividly was that, halfway to the hospital, he received a phone call saying the ambulance carrying his father had gotten in a traffic accident. A *traffic* accident! How did those even happen?

When he finally made it there, he found his father suspended in gel.

"Mr. Green?" a nurse had said. "Your father, Mr. Caleb Green, has suffered a heart attack. We have him in an induced stasis until a doctor becomes free . . ."

Abe didn't hear him. All he heard was the deafening sound of his own thoughts. How this could've been prevented. How if he had been just a bit more stubborn, he could've gotten his father to accept an implant and they could've monitored his body just a bit better.

Abe knew his father's body was failing, yet he'd done nothing.

"Please . . ." he rasped out, his heart broken by possibility, yet he did not cry. "Please save him."

For if they didn't, he would be guilty.

For eight hours he restlessly tapped his foot in front of the still form of his father. When a surgeon finally became available, he stood up and restlessly paced for another three hours. When his sister finally came, he spent an hour reassuring her, or perhaps the words he gave were for himself. Regardless, neither sibling believed Abe's hollow promise of a thing completely outside their control.

Four hours did he wait.

Four hours he bit his nails.

Four hours he paced, restless and worrying.

And four hours later, the verdict came.

Abraham Green was guilty.

*  *  *

The store had been closed for five days.

Abe wondered if this was how his father felt all those years ago for his uncle.

Sadly reassuring everyone around him that his father had lived a good life, staying stoic and helping everyone through their grief.

If this was how his father had felt, then a question was answered.

*No one.*

Back then, no one had helped his dad through his grief; no one had helped him when he cried alone at night, no one, because they were going through their own grief.

He could only lock it away as they carried the casket. For if he didn't, then who would look after everyone else?

There was nothing he could do except help others.

When he looked at the casket, all he remembered were the words never said. During the last conversation they ever had, Abe was still pretending to be his long-dead uncle, Edison. Abe hadn't talked to his father in several years despite the fact he saw him every day.

When the procession was over, he continued looking after everyone. His sister wept; his mother had quietly accepted it.

He simply had to accept it.

Yet he could not.

It was a single moment when he was alone when everything broke. He felt the tears well up in his eyes, yet he wiped them. Even as he wept, he begged the tears to stop, so that he might be fine before someone found him. So that they didn't have to worry about him as well.

Yet someone did find him.

A small hand grabbing onto his shirt. His niece Momo. "Are you sad, Uncle Abe?"

He wiped his tears and gently ruffled her hair. "Yes, I am, but don't tell anyone I cried."

"Mum is crying as well because Grandpa died."

"She is," Abe replied.

"But she also pretends she's not crying sometimes," the child said, eyes staring into Abe's own. "She wants to make sure everyone is fine. She can cry because you're making sure she's fine, but who's making sure you are?"

Sadly, Abe smiled. "No one, Momo. No one is."

"Then I will," the young girl said with conviction.

A notification appeared at the edge of his mind.

* * *

Abe's niece dragged him into a wild and unfamiliar world.

Like a replica of reality, but everything had grown over; the climate was fixed, and nature had reclaimed the land.

His niece was in a dress from a fairy tale; behind them, three small, mushroomlike creatures followed, their caps glowing a beautiful lime.

"I'm sorry, Uncle, but he didn't want everyone to know. He thought it would be too awkward after everything . . ." his niece rambled as she dragged him.

Abe followed her in a daze, not quite listening, not quite there, until they arrived at a store.

She brought him in, and Abe found the place strangely familiar. Though it was a different place, everything was put somewhere he was familiar with. He found he could navigate around the tables with ease as if it was . . . was . . .

Their own store.

Strangers sat by the counter, whom Momo greeted—her friends probably—but it was not them she wanted him to meet, and she dragged him behind, to the back of the store where the kitchen lay.

And he saw someone standing over the kitchen counter, rolling a flat piece of dough. Someone whose body looked unfamiliar, but their movement was one of the first things Abe remembered.

"Are you—" he choked; it felt like there was a golf ball in his throat, yet still he found his voice. "Do you remember me?" he cried toward the stranger.

The man with an Afro of leaves turned; he looked surprised for a moment, before he smiled.

"I remember loving you."

# God Encyclopedia
# (Major Braunad Gods)

*Before we begin, to impress the power of faith to any reader, we will speak first of the anecdote of Fairness before anything else.*

*In ages lost and long passed, remembered only through the Historia, there was a God of Justice. This was not a justice like Bahamut, but a justice of might, of the will of humans over anything else. As such, it was a brutal and subjugating god, teaching its followers to kill and conquer all the races, leading to the slavery of orckind, the humiliation of elves, and the sequestration of dwarves. It was undoubtedly a powerful god, on par with even Light of today.*

*Yet that god does not persist today, for one simple reason: belief. Belief in something utterly insane.*

*When humanity turned north after subjugating the orcs, they met the tall and strange race of goliaths, who believed in fairness above all else. When humans and goliaths fought, the goliaths always matched the number of humans on the battlefield. Even when easily outnumbering them, the goliaths would settle who went to battle through a short game and once again match the number of humans on the field.*

*This honorable conduct was not reciprocated by the humans of the time, and so the goliaths were constantly pushed back deeper into their mountains. Because when the goliaths were outnumbered, they reasoned that they were physically stronger than the humans, thus they fought the humans at severe disadvantages, and when they outnumbered the humans, the goliaths limited the number of them fighting to be equal or fewer than the number of humans in the fight.*

*It was at the final battle when humanity had pushed goliaths to the coldest north, where air freezes before one could breathe it, when the God of Justice summoned, brought to the world through the blood sacrifice of countless goliaths.*

*The goliath army saw the coming of Justice; they saw the mountains shiver with deific power, the world scream in fear. They saw the blood god born from genocide and slaughter, and to even the balance, they added a single goliath to their army to, once again, match the number of competitors on the other side.*

*In the battle that came, it was the goliaths who won.*

*The exact nature of the victory is still not completely known, shrouded in mystery, but this is known: the human empire was broken, Justice was slain that day, and Fairness was made from its corpse.*

*What is best understood about that victory was that it was caused by belief.*

*The goliaths believed that by matching the number of players on both "teams," they would make the match fair. Even when thousands of their kind were slaughtered, even when the ice was made red with their blood and the earth shook as gods came from the sky, they believed it was Fair.*

*And so it was.*

*This is the insane power of faith. The goliath wholeheartedly believes in fair conduct, even to this day. They will endlessly try to pursue it to the point of insanity, and their efforts were rewarded.*

*Know this insanity was not faith in a religion, but in culture. Such a thing is not exclusive to the goliaths. Most obvious are the orcs, who believe that the larger the weapon, the more effective it is. They carry massive and unpractical weapons to the eyes of other races, their simple belief that larger is better making it so.*

*We don't expect such things to have power, because we expect them to be right. That is why such power is often unknown. Perhaps the most recent example of such a cultural faith is the Band of Five, the five brave souls who eventually slew the Revenant King, and the myriad others who battled doom wherever it rises. Why are specifically five people so effective? Simply because people believe it so, because the stories and tales we tell to children tell them of great evils slain by five.*

*This is the power of faith. Of belief. Do not underestimate it.*

*—Introductory page of the* God Encyclopedia.

For the sake of brevity, this list will only include deities with three or more domains or a divine mandate and who originates or whose pantheon also has origins in Braunad. As such, the large majority of gods will not be on this list. The first god of every listed pantheon is its leader, with only a few exceptions.

Some term explanations:

**Divine Symbol:** An object or symbol used to signify a god, usually carried by worshippers to pray and access deific power.

**Domain:** A concept that any of the god's priesthood or worshippers can access and draw power from. Some gods *are* domains but have other additional domains that may relate to them.

**Divine Mandate:** A worldly law, brought into existence and maintained by an extremely powerful god. Unlike domains, anyone can use a divine mandate; similarly, everyone is affected by the divine mandate.

## White Pantheon

A pantheon of gods seeking to protect the world from the forces that be. They mainly hold dominion over goodly aspects.

### Light

> *"The Light is fleeting, but it will return."*

Purity, goodness, things that seem so easily lost. Yet the truth is, no matter what happens, goodness will never be lost. The Light will always be there, watching over you. No matter how you stumble, no matter how you falter, you can rise in the end. Her tenets are simple, her worship far. She is Light, simple as that.

**Titles:** The Lady of Light, The First Purity, The Hope of Man, The Suffering Sorrow, She Who Died to Redeem, and too many to list.

**Divine Symbol:** A white rose

**Domains:** Light, Hope

**Divine Mandate:** The hope undenied: no matter what happens, everyone will always have hope.

### The Great Flame

> *"Do not fear. For it will win."*

In the shadows of great cities lost, where fear runs rampant and hope does not reach, there is a single flame that was burning long before the ascension of Light and will burn long after her fall. It is a testament against the ruin of Shadesmar. Countless souls have been sacrificed to keep the great flame burning, and countless more will be done so that fear may not gain another inch in the world. Those who light their lanterns know themselves beyond fear, for the dark must never win.

To carry a lantern is to consign yourself to eternal war, for when a lantern perishes, their soul is sucked into their lantern and they will burn so long as the lantern is lit, just so the next holder may be slightly stronger, braver, faster, and smarter.

**Title:** The Light in the Dark, The Great Flame, The Gestalt, The Living Fire, Huo, It Which Burns Forever
**Divine Symbol:** A lit lantern
**Domains:** Fire, Light, Courage, Sacrifice, Lanterns, Guidance
**Divine Mandate:** The light in the dark: fire and light will harm and banish the creatures of Shadesmar.

## Bahamut

> *"Man is capable of great things, if only they were also capable of agreeing."*

Bahamut, a name older than the world, older than memory or text. An ancient entity and leader of the metallic dragons, brother to Tiamat, he led humanity from the Age of Upheaval and protected them from great threats. He seeks to raise all mortalkind to a higher and greater purpose. There will be no path for villainy so long as Bahamut has a say.

Bahamut is the leader of the platinum protectorate, a nation-state that seeks to quickly respond to existential threats and is responsible for the mercenary guild system. They possess the largest military force of flight mages across the world and are responsible for delivering contingency contracts.
**Titles:** Platinum Dragon Lord, The White Flame, The Pure Silver, The Platinum Protector, Shepherd of Humanity, He With a White Wing, and too many to list.
**Divine Symbol:** White dragon head regalia
**Domains:** Dragons, Order, Nobility, Wisdom, Protection, Knowledge, Balance, Judgement

## The Silent

> *"The answer to whether or not you are forgiven is Silence."*

Not all who try to do good come from a place that is good. Redemption is a difficult thing, often impossible; many do not even attempt it, and the few who do often die on the way there. Yet for those who try, they are watched by the Court of Silence. They do not judge; they do not tell you you are redeemed. They simply watch; they simply acknowledge. They are not the ones who forgive; they are the ones who do not forget. They are the ones who remember your struggle when no one else does.
**Titles:** The Silent Court, The Watchers, The Carrion Court, They That Watch, They That Remember

**Divine Symbol:** Two scarred hands clasped in prayer
**Domains:** Redemption, Knowledge, Sacrifice, Struggle

## Abram the Unyielding

> *"Pray to the gods but keep a sword in hand."*

The god of stubbornness, he is one who endures, the one who fights with every brave soldier in the dirt and mud of a thousand battlefields. In life, Abram was a paladin errant who found a lesser hell breach in his travels. Fearing that if he left to warn the world, the breach's demons would pass through and wreak havoc, he stayed and defended that location for *eighty years*. Nothing but his sword and shield, his armor, and a ring of sustenance keeping him alive, he fought countless horrors alone, and even the entirety of a hell circle could not move him. If not for the historia, his sacrifice would've been one of countless forever forgotten, yet it was not, and so Abram watches over every man and woman who gives their life to fight horrors, those who hold the line just a moment longer in the dirt and mud.
**Titles:** The Enduring, The Unyielding, The Shield Brother, The Patron Saint of Lost Causes, The Stubborn Old Man (affectionately given by the now-dead demon king of the breach)
**Divine Symbol:** A sword soaked in blood, sweat, and mud
**Domains:** Endurance, Sacrifice, Struggle, Strife, Solidarity

## Rising Pantheon

A pantheon of gods who seek to do good but do not wish to align with the White Pantheon for various reasons.

## Aisha

> *"There is always another enemy, another tyrant, another doom, rising from the shadows even as the last is smothered. Do not let them win."*

The woman Aisha Vashard once partied across the world, a mere mortal snuffing evil wherever it rose, but it was never enough, and so she ascended at the twilight of her life. Fear her, for there are few places where the sun doesn't rise.

Aisha has three chivalric orders, the Sunrise Sabers, the Sunlight Scriptures, and the Sunset Sonata. The Sunrise Sabers are the front lines of her priesthood, battling the tyrannical dictators and a thousand other existential threats with naught but blade and prayer.

The Sunlight Scriptures are present in every court of law, acting as pro bono lawyers assisting the citizenship and tearing apart the legitimacy of any tyrant or corrupt noble with every word said.

The Sunset Sonata works with the population of an oppressed people, hidden within every tavern; their songs are sung in every house, and they inform citizens, educate them, of their state and of the state of the outside world, slowly organizing dissent and revolt.

**Titles:** The Solar Sword, The Regicide, Tyrant Slayer, Mother Necessity, The Dawn, The Noon, The Dusk

**Divine Symbol:** A scimitar and scales with a backdrop of a shining sun

**Domains:** Sun, Strife, law, Sacrifice, Justice

### Fairness

> *"No matter your birth, no matter your condition, a competition deserves to be Fair."*

A city crafted from the corpse of an old god of justice, fairness is the resting place of the souls of people who kept to fair and honorable conduct throughout their entire life, where they compete against each other to the ends of time.

**Titles:** The Warrior's Rest, The Enforced Fairness, Kraag Thetai

**Divine Symbol:** A scale, one weighing a fist, the other weighing a ball

**Domains:** Fairness, Zeal

**Divine Mandate:** The fair referee: in any competition with two or more sides, should all sides agree to a set of rules, they may call fairness to enforce it by summoning a competitor of old, who will act as a referee and punish competitors who break either the spirit or wording of the rules.

### Discovery

> *"The world is an endless horizon; it would be a shame to not see all of it."*

Discovery is an old god who ascended around the same time as the Historian; he is prayed to by all those who seek to discover something, from another landmass to a small coin lost in the house. Recently, his North Star has disappeared and his priesthood weakened. In the Historia, it is said that Discovery is lost. Though this is not the first time a deity has fallen, if his priesthood fails, he may soon be added to the *Encyclopedia of Dead Gods*.

**Titles:** The Joyous Jaunter, The Journeyman, The Deity of Ships and Seas, The Guide of the Lost, The Prelude to Invasion, and too many to list.
**Divine Symbol:** A compass, map or any wayfinding implement
**Domains:** Discovery, Knowledge, Travel, Stars
**Divine Mandate (Former):** The North Star: no matter where you are, you may look to the skies and see a star forever pointing north.

## Tilt

*"Oops! My mistake!"*

A mischievous god of tricksters and pranks. She is a god who delights in small pranks, the timing of which is often very unfortunate for the victim. A proposal may lead to a sudden pantsing or a banana peel placed in the midst of a tavern brawl. Also, do not swear near a follower of Tilt or, gods forgive, Tilt herself, and *especially* not near children. Not unless you want to be pranked for the rest of the month and be cursed to have your swears be forever bleeped. Nonetheless, no one is ever truly harmed in her tricks and pranks.

Her followers are people who never truly lost that childlike wonder, journeying the world, playing small pranks in their god's name, before settling down in a profession helping children, often becoming the "cool" teacher.
**Titles:** I Swear It Was Tilt!, The Prankster, That Tiny Glowing *BLEEP*
**Divine Symbol:** A silver bell
**Domain:** Trickery, Freedom, Loyalty, Children

## Ludal

*"Is anyone going to clean this up?"*

The god of healing for both land and people. He and his followers are the unsung heroes of the world, for when a demon wreaks havoc in the countryside, someone has to fix the corruption left, when the inquisition burns down an entire forest, someone has to replant the trees. When people are haunted by horrors, someone has to be there to comfort them. Ludal works the thankless job of ensuring everything is *fixed* and remains so.
**Titles:** The Janitor, Cleanup Crew, The Aberration Slayer With a Thousand Bloody Mops
**Divine Symbol:** A cleaning rag used so much it is forever dirty
**Domain:** Healing, Peace, Mind, Protection

### Elder Pantheon

Ancient gods, young when the old gods became what they were. They are gods who have survived longer than any else. They represent the old faith, the following of the old rules of honor and hospitality.

Be a good host.

Be a good guest.

Respect nature.

Hunt and gather what you need, but not too much.

Leave the dead to rest.

### Lorn

*"It's not that hard—be a good host and guest!"*

Father of the hearth fire, husband to Gwaina. They teach the lessons of old, to keep to the old laws. He is the god of the household and of work matters. Appeasing him is difficult, but always rewarded.

**Titles:** Father of the Hearth Fire and too many to list.

**Divine Symbol:** A lit hearth

**Domain:** Balance, Hospitality, Home, Hardwork, Teaching

### Gwaina

*"Let up on the kids, will you?"*

Mother of the hearth fire, wife to Lorn. They teach the lessons of old, to keep to the old laws. She is the god of marriage and of domestic matters. Kindhearted, but hard when needed.

**Titles:** Mother of the Hearth Fire and too many to list.

**Divine Symbol:** A lit hearth

**Domain:** Balance, Hospitality, Home, Marriage, Children

### Tasha

*"So much desert, so little time."*

A goddess who travels the world, leaving lush, lively forests in her wake. She is a tough, loud, and hardworking goddess, seeking to heal the world one fistful of dirt at a time. Those that are diligent will feel her kindness, and those that are lazy, her disdain. She is called strict by the new generations, but the old remember that such things matter little to Tasha. A hard day's work is its own reward, after all.

**Titles:** Mother Diligence, The Verdant Lady, and too many to list.
**Divine Symbol:** A seed that will grow with diligence and care
**Domain:** Balance, Nature, Diligence, Endurance

## Qing

> *"Remember the greatest and the lowest of times. Only then can we learn."*

The sole surviving elven god after the humiliation of elves, Qing is a god of wisdom, seeking to help his race learn of the mistakes of the past, so that they may become greater in the future.
**Titles:** Father Knowledge, The Last, and too many to list
**Divine Symbol:** A wooden mask
**Domain:** Balance, Wisdom, Knowledge, Rulership

## Bundriroc

> *"Follow the Path, follow the Stones."*

An immutable god of a thousand forms. It is the god of the wild, the markers that separate the road from the untamed forests. It is a brutal yet loyal god, appearing as one of a thousand different animals. Following it is a difficult and trying ordeal, but Bundriroc rewards commitment and loyalty with the mark of the wild.
**Titles:** The Shapeless One and too many to list.
**Divine Symbol:** A stone or pebble etched with the teeth and claws of wild beasts
**Domain:** Balance, Nature, Wild, Loyalty, Endurance

## Revel

> *"The Day of Feasts has come!"*

A god of wine, parties, and celebrations. He is a god of unchecked revelry and the madness born from such events.
**Titles:** The Mad Drunk and too many to list.
**Divine Symbol:** A wine cup
**Domain:** Balance, Celebration, Wine, Madness

## Knowledge Pantheon

A pantheon of gods who seeks to protect and spread information. A largely neutral pantheon, any God can join and have it overlap with their previous affiliations due to the nature of its head.

### Historian

*"It doesn't matter how many ages passed; I will remember them, even if no one else will."*

The Historian is an old god. Only the old gods are said to be older. He remains neutral, forever updating his Historia with the millions of tiny events that happen every day. In most cases, he is a simple footnote in history, just the person who writes history. But those who dismiss the Historian forget the most important thing, to learn from history. The humbling of Challenge remains a fresh event to the gods, and they know not to provoke the Historian to action.

His historians are present everywhere, discovering and recording all the history they find. They are the ones who search ancient tombs for lost texts; they are the ones who piece together scraps of paper to learn of the diets of ancients. They are the ones who ensure nothing is forgotten.

**Titles:** Deity of History Writ and Recorded, the Lord of Wisdom, He Who Wars Against the Unknown, The One Who Remembers All, and too many to list.

**Divine Symbol:** The Historia or any record or history book

**Domains:** History, Knowledge, Time, Sight

**Divine Mandate:** The Historian's paradox: what is written, that is true, will be remembered by the world.

### Manatheres

*"Magic, or at least the potential for it, should be available to all. We are all made ignorant when we only have our own perspective for reference."*

Manatheres is perhaps the strongest ever high archmagus to have ever lived. During the Age of Wonders, after the death of the Revenant King, the merging and discussion between different schools of magic led to the world-shattering discovery that magic was inherently belief-based and as long as conditions were met, any magic can be cast. From the throwing of sticks on the ground to the most complex equations, they were made all the same with this revelation. During this age, where other mages fought the nihilistic realization that their life's work to understand the universe may have been pointless, Manatheres only saw opportunity. He cast the first Tier-10 spell in existence, creating an energy that any could use to cast magic, named after himself. For this, he underwent apotheosis and became the very concept of mana. But like other conceptual gods, this led to him losing all his humanity, his thought and knowledge, and now he is naught but the energy of mana, used in countless different ways.

**Titles:** The First High Archmagus, Inventor of Tier Magic, Mana, and too many to list.

**Divine Symbol:** An opened spell book

**Domains:** Mana, Knowledge, Arcana

**Divine Mandate:** Mana: mana exists.

**Other Gods who are also part of this pantheon are:**
Discovery
The Morning Herald
Bahamut
Tiamat
Wundull
Qing

### Pantheon Union

A pantheon of gods that have banded together at least in name to become a relevant force.

### Ethelinda the Merchant

*"Hey, twenty gold is twenty gold."*

The mercantile goddess is a recent but powerful addition to the world. Formerly the guild master of (legally not) a multilevel marketing scheme, it is rumored she ascended purely to change her guild to a church, thus avoiding taxes in certain nations. For legal reasons, I must say that these are just unfounded rumors with no basis in reality and that her church sells everything if you have the coin and at very cheap and competitive prices. So you should definitely go to your local M-Church to purchase your daily needs. She currently holds the monopoly for commercial resurrections.

**Titles:** The Prosperous, The First Princess, The Merchant Princess, The Merchant, Green Bastard (given by Travelers, in reference to something of their world)

**Divine Symbol:** A stack of coins held together by a red string

**Domains:** Coin, Business, Order
**Divine Mandate:** Wealth phantasm: so long as a merchant keeps to a non-aggression pact, their wealth will manifest into a guardian spirit when they are attacked. These spirits are stronger the more wealthy the merchant is, but damage to them will also damage their wealth.

### Fortune

> *"I don't control the cards any more than you can control the weather."*

The two-faced god of fortune, appearing as either Miss or Missus Fortune to those that pray to her. She sees the myriad ripples every action takes across the world and divines futures from that. Pray you do not receive Miss Fortune when she divines your fate.

There are twenty-two cards present throughout the world, each representing a card in the Major Arcana. They will appear in the possession of people with the capability of doing great things.
**Titles:** The Soothsayer, Fate, Watcher of the Weave, The Matron, The Two-Faced God of Luck, and too many to list.
**Divine Symbol:** A deck of the Major Arcana
**Domains:** Fate, Arcana, Knowledge

### The Morning Herald

> *"Hurry, hurry! There's news to deliver!"*

The Morning Herald is a god of information and the press. His followers move to gather information from a dozen different places, print them into newspapers, and spread them. Worshipping him is simple: create a shrine to him and leave a small offering, and by the morning a freshly printed newspaper will be there and the offering accepted.
**Titles:** The Reporter, The God of Travels, The Morning News, The Press
**Divine Symbol:** A winged foot
**Domains:** News, Information, Travel

### Jubalon the Oath Kept

> *"Don't waste your life! It is worth so much!"*

For legal reasons, I am to inform you that Jubalon is not an official part of the union and that the Merchant Church vehemently rejects the unethical practices of the devil lord with the strongest possible language. That said, the Soul Market of Abaddon is often a place where merchant priests of Ethelinda are allegedly seen often, selling souls and using Jubalon to guarantee any deal made. Well, better the devil you know.

**Titles:** The Devil Lord of the First Circle, Head of Abaddon, The Merchant Prince

**Divine Symbol:** A contractor's inkwell

**Domains:** Oaths, Balance, Tyranny

## Neutral Gods

Gods with no affiliation to any pantheon who pursue their own agendas.

### Challenge

*"You see impossibility. I see a Challenge."*

The god Challenge is a simple god. She teaches one to always improve themselves, to constantly strive to be better by overcoming that next hill, that next step. So long as you are constantly challenged, you will grow.

Her worshippers range from monster hunters to journeying warriors to chefs. As long as there is a challenge to overcome, she remains.

**Titles:** The Challenger, The One Who Rises, The Humbled

**Divine Symbol:** Two fists punching each other

**Domains:** Challenge, Struggle, Overcoming, Ambition

**Divine Mandate:** Clash: if one faces an opponent of equal or greater skill in a field similar or opposite to theirs, one may declare a Challenge. Should both parties accept, then they may clash with their respective fields. Success may result in becoming greater, but failure may also result in permanently losing something.

### Tiamat

*"Humanity is great. I haven't had this much good food since the Cheese Wars."*

Tiamat, a name older than the world, older than memory or text. An ancient entity and leader of the chromatic dragons, sister to Bahamut, she remains a largely neutral force, terrible when roused but peaceful, if slightly overbearing if approached respectfully. In recent centuries, she has become a massive foodie, seeking to sample every dish conceivable after the Holy Cheese Crusade and the War Over What Gradient Makes Perfectly Toasted Toast, which collectively killed eight million people, whetted her appetite.

**Titles:** The Chromatic Dragon Lord, The Dragon Queen, The Rainbow Flame, She With Many Colors, The Avaricious, and too many to list.
**Divine Symbol:** Regalia of the seven heads of Tiamat forming a circle
**Domain:** Dragons, Chaos, Chromatic, Wisdom, Coin, Knowledge, Balance, Elements

## God Emperor of Dwarves

*"The only earth the weak shall inherit is a grave."*

The tyrannical god of the Grey Dwarves, he is the Emperor of the Deep Imperium, ruling the Duergan Dwarves with an iron fist. It is said he resides in the deepest locations within the earth, where the caverns have their own sky and a black sun burns all. He is the sole forge god for the simple reason that he brutally murdered every other one. His teachings are simple: those who are strong and have conviction are the ones who will inherit the world. The weak should perish if they do not have the capability to survive. Any who say otherwise are fools, covering their ears to the brutal truth of the world.
**Titles:** God Emperor of the Grey Dwarves, The Black Sun, The Enduring Tyrant, The Earth Father, and too many to list.
**Divine Symbol:** A hammer with a head shaped like a fist
**Domain:** Tyranny, War, Forges, Strength, Earth, Will

## Ludwig

*"Some may say that the First Thief Lord is an unfortunate person
to have reached godhood. I say they are foolish nobles who had all
their wealth charitably redistributed."*

The First Thief Lord, an unpredictable god. His actions are clouded, his presence seemingly everywhere. Yet it is known thus: Ludwig seeks to rid the world of those bloated on wealth and power and to share them with the poorest and weakest. Some say he even seeks to bring down the gods . . . His tenet is simple: look out for the weak and do not disdain them, for everyone was once weak. No matter how high you rise, you always struggled on that first step.

Ludwig has a great soft spot for children and is known to help them out best he can. Every winter solstice, followers of Ludwig move out in force, donning bright red cloaks and robbing those unfortunately fortunate, taking toys, food, clothes, and other trinkets, before gifting them to the poorest children. Some may say this method of forced charity is "unethical" and "wrong." Ludwig says they were literally wearing bright-red cloaks! If you wanna stop them, then open your eyes!

**Titles:** The Robbing Hoodlum, The First Thief Lord, The Red Hood, The Should We Really Still be Insulting Him Now That He's a God?, The Sultan of Satire, The Charitable, The Oh, Fuck Check His Titles, Communist Santa (given by Travelers, in reference to one of their own gods)

**Divine Symbol:** A beggar's bowl

**Domains:** Trickery, Charity, Thievery, Freedom, Children


## The Mourner

*"Just here to ensure you are not alone."*


His true name is unknown, as is his true appearance. This god appears in front of dying people who have no hope of recovery, and only if they are alone, with no one else beside them to see their passing, those who have no hope of an afterlife. Appearing as an older man of the dying's race, with mourning attire appropriate for their culture. He simply stays by the side of the dying until the moment they pass. He is known only because of the black roses left behind near the deceased and of infrequent sightings and recordings throughout history. It is thought that he is at least as old as or older than Light.

His worshippers are few but seek to follow this god's Path, mourning those who pass, carrying out burial rites, and mourning those who are alone.

**Titles:** Old Man Death, Thank You, The Silent Watcher, and too many to list.

**Divine Symbol:** A black rose

**Domains:** Death, Mourning, Solidarity


## Tempest

*"When the seas are rough, know you can only pray."*


A fickle goddess of discord and chaos. Unpredictable, but a wild force of freedom and the divine fairness of chaos. She offers no respect to those that cry to her for mercy or power, but the few who cry to her wish to be challenged, to travel in her domain regardless of permission. They are the ones she respects and challenges. Those wanting are stolen away by the depths of the sea.

**Titles:** The Sea Witch

**Divine Symbol:** A whirlpool with an eye at the center

**Domain:** Balance, Chaos, Tempest, Storm

## Wundull

> *"Joy is saying we'll play again tomorrow. Sadness is the day that becomes a lie."*

The god of gnomes and halflings is an oddity among the gods, seeking not great power, influence, or wealth, but to simply create and play games with their fellows until the end of time. His most recent endeavor is the creation of the trading card game Age of Wonders, using cards with inspiration and effects based on real locations, artifacts, and people. What is alarming is the extreme accuracy these cards hold on the abilities of people, leading many to suspect Wundull is not as weak as he appears . . .

**Titles:** The Old Friend, Friend of Death, The Plays Almighty, Current Former World Champion of AoW, and too many to list.

**Divine Symbol:** Anything that could be played as a game—a stack of cards, dice, even dirt used to play house or sticks used to play fight.

**Domains:** Games, Trickery, Loyalty, Travel

## The Chaos Zodiac

> *"Meow!"*

A collection of nine deific cats collectively make up the Chaos Zodiac. Each cat roams the world pursuing its own agenda. They are the constant chaos; so long as there is one, all others of the Zodiac will return. Worshipped by cat lovers, tabaxi, and many more weirdos, they do not seek anything, simply to see the world, and perhaps accidentally cause some mischief on the way.

**Titles:** The Fucked-Up One, The Felinid Chaos, The Cats

**Divine Symbol:** A cat's paw print

**Domains:** Chaos, Trickery, Freedom

## Dark Gods

Gods who seek the end of man, to end the world in a thousand horrific ways. These gods must never gain the power to form a divine mandate. If they do, the world is irreparably damaged.

## Shadesmar

> *"Slam the drums! Ring the bells! Light the Lanterns! Refresh the talismans! The Dark is here!"*

Shadesmar is the reminder that we are not above fear. That no matter how

we advance, how far the light of man is lit, we will fear the dark, and the Dark is worthy of fear.
**Titles:** The First Fear, The Ruined Lands, Hei, The Dark, and too many to list.
**Divine Symbol:** Unknown
**Domains:** Fear, Panic, Dread
**Divine Mandate:** Unknown


## The Weeping Child

*"I am sorry I could not save you."*

There are many stories of good triumphing, of evil failing before good. The black dragon is slain, the good king takes the throne, the orphan leaves their abusive aunt's home and meets their true parents who love them, or grow up to love a child twice as much. This is not the story of the Weeping Child. It is a gestalt crafted by the mad mage Khao from a thousand suffering children in his attempts to reach apotheosis. An amalgamation of suffering born from children kept artificially young and suffering within Khao's labs, a thousand innocent souls stitched together to form this horror. Eventually, it grew too powerful for the mad mage to contain, breaking its bonds, and the Weeping Child entered the world. It is an avatar of despair, the protector of orphans. Sometimes when an orphan or child is abused, the entire region of people will simply . . . disappear, leaving only a child with a doll, capable of seeing and speaking to the dead. Its existence is a tragedy, but the longer it remains, the more of the world will fall into despair and horror. This thing must be slain if only to finally end their suffering.
**Titles:** The Tragedy, The Gestalt, The Tears Wept, The Protector of Orphans, and too many to list.
**Divine Symbol:** A child's doll
**Domains:** Tragedy, Despair, pain, Undeath, Children


## Osshiven'Kai

*"We offer revelations and cookies!"*

The clockwork god of chaos, its motives are as unfathomable as its true form. Summoned to the world by a misaligned attempt to contact the Seventh Hell Circle. Its followers are madmen, nigh unkillable, and seem to follow motives as unknowable as their god. One thing is consistent: they spread anarchy and chaos wherever they go, leaving ruins in their wake, or even worse, more followers.

**Titles:** The Ticking Chaos, The Whispering Clock, The Forbidden Truth, and too many to list.
**Divine Symbol:** A clock that shows the incorrect time and often has a myriad of other random changes
**Domains:** Chaos, Madness, Enlightenment, Life

### The Underdark Gobbler

*"Dig! I said dig, you fool—"*

A massive worm prowling the depths of the Underdark. It is said every tunnel within the Underdark was dug by this entity, which leads to some horrific conclusions when one examines how *old* some of them are. What happens when the Gobbler consumes something is not clear; it is just known that in its wake are left myriad aberrations, each more horrific than the other. This creature is followed by the few sapient aberrations. Their worship of the creature is strange and alien.
**Titles:** The Gobbler, The Unsated, The Worm, The Aberrant Mother, and too many to list.
**Divine Symbol:** Unknown
**Domains:** Madness, Aberrations, Mind

# Character Sheets

**Name: Dustin**
Race: Magic Myconid Level 1
Classes: Fungalmancer Level 4, Keeper of Secrets Level 1

Body:
Strength: 8
Agility: 7
Dexterity: 6
Constitution: 19
Stamina: 10
Vitality: 12

Mind:
Intelligence: 18
Wisdom: 20
Charisma: 6

Soul:
Will: 10
Psyche: 10
Perception: 10
Available SP: 6

Racials:
Manavision, Fungal Body, Sun Sickness, Mana Dependency, Pacifying Spores, Strong Innate Magic, Age-Type Heteromorph

- **Manavision [Passive]:** Your race's innate mastery of mana allows you to perceive everything within a radius equal to your myconid level times five meters. You see in dim light as if it were bright light, and in darkness as if it were dim light. You can't discern colors in darkness, only shades of gray. A dispel or null magic effect will negate this sight. If you have no mana, this sight is automatically deactivated.
- **Fungal Body [Passive]:** You have resistance to poison and bludgeoning damage. You are vulnerable to desiccation damage.
- **Sun Sickness [Passive]:** Being in direct sunlight will drain your stamina; this effect can be mitigated by raising Constitution.
- **Mana Dependency [Passive]:** Taking physical actions with low mana will drain additional stamina.
- **Pacifying Spores [Active]:** Eject spores at a creature within five meters of you; if the target fails a Constitution Save, then it is put to sleep. This skill scales with your Constitution and Vitality.
- **Strong Innate Magic [Passive]:** You gain two Tier-0 spells from the Magic Cap Myconid Spell List, as well as:
  - Choose and gain one of the following options per myconid level:
    - You create one Tier-0 spell and gain it on your spell list.
    - You gain proficiency and knowledge in Arcana.
    - You gain a passive Detect Magic within the range of your Manavision.

Class Skills:
- Fungalmancer:
- Path: Symbiosis
- **Grow Sporage (Visual) [Active]:** You may create a mushroom capable of storing a spore-based spell. These sporages can be activated on visual contact. They glow faintly and last for hours based on your myconid level.
- **Grow Sporage (Proximity) [Active]:** Upgrade to Grow Sporage. You obtain the option to grow sporages with a different activation type. The sporage lets out a thin layer of mycelium around it that acts as a pressure detector. When sufficient weight is applied to any part of the fungus, the sporage will explode. You and targets of Symbiosis do not detonate these sporages.
- **Sporage Wisp Symbiosis [Active]:** Wisps have lived comfortably in your cap and have created a wonderful home there; now, to teach them the wonders of rent. You may create pygmy myconid bodies for

your noncorporeal wisps to inhabit. They are considered tiny creatures and are capable of following simple commands. They possess all the qualities of sporage; however, they can choose to self-detonate.
- **Bracken Polypores [Passive] [Active]:** A species of symbiotic fungus is seeded underneath your skin. They rely on you for food and in return can instantly grow into durable mycelium plates that can cover your entire body. The hardness and weight may vary depending on how much satiety you feed them at any moment. Will gain defensive bonuses if used in conjunction with Bark Skin.

Keeper of Secrets:
Path: Keep
- **Keeper of Secrets [Passive] [Active]:** You know several world-shattering revelations that, if revealed, may change the course of the world. While you hold them secret, you may put one in an active state to gain certain benefits. The less well-known the knowledge, the greater its potential impact on the world and the deeper your own knowledge of it, the greater the benefit you have in keeping it.
- **A Blank Page in History, the Next Voyage of Discovery:** You become difficult to be remembered or perceived; others will not notice your presence without a high stat check or you choosing to reveal yourself, though remains of your passing will stay—e.g. footprints, reflections, recordings, scents. While this is active, you have True Sight.
- **The Balance:** You can see the balance scales of yourself and others.
- **The World Eater of the Seventh Hell:** You may store consumables within your stomach that you may at any time digest. If this ability is deactivated or swapped out, all stored consumables will be digested.
- **The One Order Fenkai and the Clockwork Chaos Osshiven'Kai:** When things are ordered: You are passively aware of the location of the sun and stars, the weather and the cardinal directions. When things are chaotic: You randomly gain two T0 and one T1 spells. These spells cost no mana but can only be cast once each. Upon using all three, you gain another random set of two T0 and one T1 spells.
- **Incomplete Secrets:** More is required to qualify these secrets for keeping.
    - The Maker and Daughter's Madness, The Creation of Indiri,

True Magic, The First Fear's Birth, The Origin of Demons, The Shattered Crown of the Revenant King

- **Et Non-Discent**: This class was not sourced from the system, thus it does not benefit from the system, either.
  - Progress in this class does not rely on Traveler XP, but on your own proficiency.
  - You may not invest levels in this class.
  - This class and its progress will not be displayed on your Traveler character sheet.

Spells:
Magic Myconid Spells:
T0: Sneezing Spores, Acid Spit, Watching Eye

Fungalmancer Spells:
T0: Balm Spores, Light Spores, Shillelagh
T1: Mushroom Meal, Poison Spores, Euphoria Spray
T2: Bark Skin, Fix-Up Fungus, Rot Spores

Available Spell Slots
T0: 1
T1: 1
T2: 1

Languages:
Common
Undercommon

**Name: Noam**
Classes: Skald Level 5

Body
Strength: 12
Agility: 14
Dexterity: 10
Constitution: 9
Stamina: 10
Vitality: 8

<u>Mind</u>
Intelligence: 13
Wisdom: 10
Charisma: 15

<u>Soul</u>
Will: 10
Psyche: 10
Perception: 10
Free SP: 9

<u>Racials:</u>
Darkvision, Hellish Resistance

<u>Class Skills:</u>
Skald:
Path: Spitfire

- **Breathless [Passive] [Active]:** Your body no longer needs to breathe, but you retain maximal efficiency of aerobic respiration. This is at the cellular level, thus your body will never produce lactic acid, and you experience effects similar to oxygen doping. All stats have a +10%.
- **Beatbox [Passive] [Active]:** You gain knowledge of how to beatbox alongside proficiency. You may as a free action, lock up to five seconds of beatboxing in a loop, where it'll continuously emanate from you at the original volume at a negligible mana cost per second.
- **Fire [Passive]:** When verbal-based attacks land a critical hit, the target is set alight by nonmagical flame.
- **Catch These Hands! [Active]:** Once per day, gain bonus stats to AGI, DEX, and CHA for every person around you currently irritated, angered, generally pissed off, and/or who is displaying hostility toward you. Stats disappear when the cooldown has ended or when hostile individuals leave your range or cease being hostile to you.

<u>Martial Arts:</u>
Swift Strike

<u>Spells:</u>
T0: Biting Words, Vicious Mockery

Available Spell Slots:
T0: 2
T1: 2

Proficiencies:
Polearms: Novice
Beatboxing: Novice

Languages:
Common
Infernal


**Name: Utoqa the Tribeless**
Race: Variant Lizardfolk (Oasis Touched Tequalan)
Racials: Variant Lizardfolk Level 1
Classes: Artificer Level 1, Survivalist Level 3

Body:
Strength: 14
Agility: 14
Dexterity: 15
Constitution: 17
Stamina: 16
Vitality: 14

Mind:
Intelligence: 9
Wisdom: 13
Charisma: 4

Soul:
Will: 6
Psyche: 7
Perception: 21

Racials:
- **Natural Armor and Weapons [Passive]:** Utoqa possesses scales as tough as chain mail as well as a bite weapon.
- **Hold Breath [Passive]:** Utoqa can hold his breath for longer than normal, increasing with his Constitution, Stamina, and Vitality.

- **Magic Vision [Passive]:** Utoqa can vaguely sense mana within ten meters. A dispel magic effect negates this.
- **Variant Biology [Passive]:** Utoqa has Poison Resistance and advantage on all Constitution and Vitality saves.

Class Skills:
Artificer:
Path: Scavenge

- **Scavenge:** A trick that allows him to craft magical items out of the corpses of creatures. They are imbued with aspects of the creature's power but tend to be one use only unless the creature was very strong (boss-level mob).

Survivalist:
Path: Survive

- **Survive:** Three charges, at the cost of one charge, Utoqa ignores one instance of lethal damage and is brought back to consciousness. If Utoqa were to die, this automatically activates if he has the appropriate charges. This ability does not heal existing wounds or ailments save for those causing death.

Notable Scavenge Creations:

- **Gift:** An extremely sharp and durable tomahawk made from a bone gifted by the explorer he saved. Can easily cleave through flesh and bone.
- **Finger of Dustin:** One of Dustin's severed fingers, when used will spray Pacifying Spores in a five-meter radius.
- **Goblin Fire Mage Tongue:** Can allow the user to briefly cast the spells of a mage.

Notable Items:

- **Trick Pouches:** Belt pouches that appear normal, however, each contains a small subspace that can store several times their perceived capacity. Items stored inside cannot exceed the size of the opening of the pouch.

Languages:
Tequalan
Draconic
Common (Chanter)

# Boss Sheets



**The Accumulation of White Lies**

Racial:
Aberration of Memories Level 3

Body:
Strength: 8
Agility: 7
Dexterity: 9
Constitution: N/A
Stamina: N/A
Vitality: N/A

Mind:
Intelligence: 9
Wisdom: 4
Charisma: 24

Soul:
Will: 14
Aura: 34
Perception:11

Traits:
- **Bardic Adept:** This creature is a bardic combatant.

- **Ignorance:** This creature may contest knowledge and perception checks targeting it.
- **Devour:** This creature may consume an opponent, keeping it inside its stomach and potentially eating killed opponents for benefits.
- **Ruthless:** This creature will target downed opponents and finish them off when given the chance.

Hidden:
- **Target:** This creature will prioritize specific opponents over others.

Basic Combat:
- **Bite Attack:** The Accumulation may attack with all its heads, dealing puncture and slash damage. Should it succeed in such an attack, it may choose to grapple with the target.
- **Sing:** The Accumulation may stop singing or start a song with an additional head.
- **Wail:** The Accumulation may let out a piercing scream, dealing psychic damage to all creatures that can hear it.
- **Consume:** The Accumulation consumes a creature, placing them inside its stomach. It can have up to three humanoid creatures inside at any time.
- **Digest:** Creatures inside the stomach of the Accumulation will take continuous acid and bludgeoning damage.
- **Immobile:** The Accumulation is a nascent creature. Since it is recently born, it does not yet know how to walk.
- **Grow Head:** Whenever a humanoid creature is digested, the Accumulation will begin growing a new head with fragments of the knowledge and skills of the humanoid creature digested to grow it.
- **Horrific Visage:** Intelligent creatures that see a face that the Accumulation has grown will need to make a mind or soul save or take psychic damage. Damage and severity scale with the familiarity the target had with the face.
- **Conceptual Creature:** The Accumulation is a conceptual entity, thus it is resistant to nonconceptual damage.
- **Aberrant Form:** The Accumulation is a huge aberration, as such, it has the following immunities and resistances:
  - Damage Resistances: Psychic
  - Condition Immunities: Blinded, Charmed, Grappled, Prone, Stunned, Unconscious

Fade:

- **Blind Song (Active):** The Accumulation sings a song of oblivion; all creatures that can hear the song must make a WIS or WIL save against its CHA. Every additional head the Accumulation sings with slightly increases the DC of the save. On a failure, the creature loses all perception of the Accumulation's existence while the song persists. An extremely high Mind or PER check must be met to even notice evidence of the Accumulation's existence while under these effects.
- **Sea of Forgotten Faces (Passive):** Whenever the Accumulation consumes a creature, memories of that creature will be forgotten so long as the creature remains in its stomach. If the creature is digested, the memory erasure becomes permanent.

Hidden:

Special Interactions:

- **Memetic Clash:** Creation seeks balance, as such, the Accumulation must defeat Dustin the Traveler to earn its newfound power. The conditions of a Clash are imposed while both the Accumulation and Dustin are near each other and in conflict. Each of the Clashers may damage or permanently remove abilities from the other at risk of their own. Whoever wins may regain their abilities and will earn their Power.

Weaknesses:

- **Skulker:** The Accumulation is a relatively weak direct combatant.
- **Prioritize:** The Accumulation will attempt to target and kill Dustin the Traveler over all others.
- **Maintenance:** The Accumulation's Blind Song only works when it is being actively sung.
- **Secondhand Source:** The Accumulation's Blind Song does not remove the perception of the Accumulation from secondhand sources such as reflections.
- **Hear No Evil, See No Evil:** The Accumulation's Blind Song works through sound. It does not affect creatures who cannot hear.
- **The Historian's Paradox:** The Accumulation will lose aspects of its antimemetic properties should it be recorded in a medium of a sufficiently powerful level. Should it be remembered by enough people, it'll perish.

# About the Author

Sir Nil is an Australian author who got really bored one afternoon in high school and decided to vomit out a piece of brain-melting word soup he called a "story," dragging the poor netizens of a certain webnovel site through a truly horrific experience. He didn't even compose it on a typewriter, but on a smartphone—the absolute gall! Some say he's gotten better as a writer since then, having started multiple highly rated webnovels, one of which you may be reading as a published series, but he personally denies such allegations.

Sir Nil studies biotechnology, though is not particularly good at it, and his personal writing motto is: "The secret to being original is copying so many people that your detractors give up pointing it out," which he encourages everyone to shamelessly steal without crediting him.

If ever you may face Sir Nil in battle or debate, simply bring up his first webnovel and he will shrivel up like an embarrassed prune, guaranteeing your victory through tried-and-true ad hominem attacks.

Podium
DISCOVER
STORIES UNBOUND
PodiumAudio.com

www.ingramcontent.com/pod-product-compliance
Lightning Source LLC
Chambersburg PA
CBHW020646120726
47906CB00001B/144